Number

BROKEN DOLL

SELENA

Broken Doll

*Willow Heights Preparatory
Academy: The Exile*

Book Four

selena

Broken Doll
Copyright © 2021 Selena
Unabridged First Edition
All rights reserved. No part of this book may be reproduced or transmitted in any form or by any means, electronic or mechanical, including photocopying, recording, or by any information storage and retrieval system, without the express written permission of the publisher, except in cases of a reviewer quoting brief passages in a review.

This book is a work of fiction. Names, characters, places, and incidents are used factiously. Any resemblance to actual persons, living or dead, business establishments, and events are entirely coincidental. Use of any copyrighted, trademarked, or brand names in this work of fiction does not imply endorsement of that brand.

Published in the United States by Selena and Speak Now.

ISBN-13: 978-1-955913-03-4

Cover © Quirah Casey of Temptation Creations

I couldn't forgive him or like him, but I saw that what he had done was, to him, entirely justified.

—F. Scott Fitzgerald

one

Royal Dolce

"I need to book a fight."

"Are you fucking kidding me?"

"Tonight. Now."

"You've got some balls to call and ask me for anything."

"I'm not asking. Make it happen."

"I don't do business with your fucked up family anymore. That includes you, Royal."

"I need a fight."

Dynamo sighs. "You're the one who broke our deal. You almost killed me. Remember?"

"Tell me where your cousin is, and I won't need your help booking a fight."

Dad called us off Preston's family, but fuck him. He had his shot at the Darlings. He needs to stay out of the way while we take our shot. We choose when to make deals. Colt, he had something I wanted, so after he paid his dues, we left him alone. Preston doesn't have shit.

"It's almost midnight on a Sunday," Dynamo says. "No one fights on Sunday. The best I can do is next Saturday."

"Tonight."

"There won't be any money."

"You think I need money?"

"I think you need therapy."

I don't answer for a second. I should laugh at his comment, that he thinks someone could help me when I'm this far gone. But I can't remember how. Not ten minutes ago, the twins dropped me off and went off to do whatever they do to forget a thing like we did tonight. I need to forget, too. I need to hit someone and be hit until there's nothing left of either of us but blood and bones.

"I know where your sister is," I say at last.

Colt doesn't need money, either. I'm asking him for something, and I have to give him something in return. That's how the world works.

He's quiet for another minute. "How?"

"Baron found her. She's in Tennessee, going by a different name."

He pauses only a second. "No one's going to fight you when you're like this."

"Like what?" There's no curiosity in my voice, only challenge, but he answers anyway.

"Desperate."

"Can you get me a fight or not?"

"Do you have an address? A name?"

"I'll text it to you."

He sighs. "Merciless has been trying to get me to set her up with a guy. She'll probably get her sadistic ass out of bed for you."

"No girls," I snap.

I'm done hurting girls. Tonight was the last time I'll fuck with a girl, any girl. I'm done with Dad's clients, with the girls at school, with the Darling girls. There are enough men in that family to exact our revenge. Girls are too dangerous.

"Then all I've got is Colin, and last time I put you up against him, you said you'd kill him if I did it again."

SELENA

Tonight, that's what I want. No rules. No audience. No morality.

Colin Finnegan is the dirtiest fighter there is. He fights like a berserk wolverine who thinks he's trying out for Ultimate Fighting Champion. Last time I fought him, he tried to take off my kneecap, which would have ended my football career, punched me in the nuts, gouged my eyes, and bit me. He's lucky he's still alive.

The smile feels strange and grotesque as it stretches my lips. "Colin would be perfect."

two

Harper Apple

Suddenly, I'm wide awake. The sounds of the swamp are deafening around me, and yet, I find my heart beating in rapid rhythm, a scared rabbit on the run, as I listen for something more. I'm not sure if I was sleeping or passed out from pain. I only know that a sound woke me.

A soft rippling noise skims across the water, and my throat closes with fear. My mouth is so dry around the gag I can't swallow. Pain throbs through me, constant and unbearably intense. Fear is the first thing I've felt in hours besides mind-crushing pain, but it doesn't numb me. It only increases my senses, makes it worse.

I push my feet against the ground at the base of the tree, taking the weight off my numb arms and screaming shoulders. I would cry if I had tears left.

SELENA

"Are you still out here?"

The voice whispers out of the darkness, sliding along the surface of the water, curling around me like a cold snake. My whole body is wracked with a spasm of terror.

They came back.

I don't make a sound. My heart is beating so hard I think it will rupture. There's a soft splash and a curse. Slowly, he sloshes along, plodding through the mud and water, closer with each step. I pray he won't find me. I pray I'll die of fear before he does.

My mind races out of control with my heart. It isn't a cop or a search party. It's too soon for that. They wouldn't bother with the poor girl who attached herself to a powerful family like the Dolces, anyway. After all, they'll say, girls like me run away from home over fights with their boyfriends all the time. No one will be surprised. Everyone knows Royal is all I have going for me.

It won't be like when Royal was kidnapped, when *Local News with Jackie* camped outside the Dolces' house hoping to get a word with the rich new family who moved to town and lost their son. I saw that when I went digging for dirt on the Dolce-Darling feud.

It won't be like when his twin disappeared, and the police organized waves of search parties to look night and day until the Ferrari was dragged from the river and they knew she was gone forever.

For a girl like me, a girl who's already eighteen and has no family to offer rewards, the police will send out a bulletin and be done with it. If they get suspicious, the Dolces will throw a little money at the mayor to make sure no one looks for me.

"Are you alive?"

What if it's one of them coming back to kill me? Duke wouldn't do it alone. Maybe Baron, just for fun. He probably thought he'd give me hope by leaving me alive, and his last cruel joke will be to come back just when I thought I was safe.

Baron would untie me first, lay me on the ground, and take the blindfold off. He'd want to see my eyes, to see the life draining out of me. He'd want to study it. He'd probably get hard from it.

SELENA

Royal would be fast. He'd just stick a knife between my ribs or swipe it across my throat. No mess, no words. Royal is efficient, I have to give him that. He'd throw the knife in the swamp, and no one would ever find it. It would sink into the mud and disappear forever.

"I know you're here. Answer me if you're alive, damn it."

His voice sounds vaguely familiar—or does it? Maybe it's delirium.

"I'm going find a dead body, aren't I?" the guy mutters, as if he's given up talking to me and is talking to himself now. I don't care. I'd welcome Baron back, even if he jerked off while he slit my throat. I don't want to be found, to be woken by a football player with a conscience who came back for me. I want to die.

I sag back against the tree, letting my legs go out from under me again. At some point in the night, my shoulder separated, and now pain drills into it like a bootheel crushing an ant. It's too big to comprehend. A sound escapes me, some desperate plea for it to end. I can't contain it. The last tether to my sanity is fraying.

"Was that you? Fuck. It's creepy as hell out here."

My parched throat cracks with pain from the sound. Suddenly, a spark hits the blindfold. I can only see a glint, but I know whoever is here, he's found me. A high, keening sound rips from me unbidden, and pain slashes across the inside of my throat.

"Holy fuck," the guy says, his voice low with shock.

I want to do something, to hide, to disappear, but I can't remember how to do a single thing, even live.

For a minute, all I can hear is his breathing, his feet dragging through the water when he moves, and the unmistakable whirr of a phone camera. Then the water near my feet ripples, and I can feel his presence so close it's as if he's touching me. I cower away, a sickening mewling sound clogging my throat.

"I'm going to help you." His voice is firm but edged with urgency, bordering on panic. Fumbling fingers pull at the knot of rope behind my head. I almost sob when it loosens, relieving my aching jaw. He carefully draws the gag from my mouth, the rope and the hood along with it. I can feel the wet weight of it come away as he pulls it free, soaked with snot and spit and tears. When he pulls the hood from my head, I can see faint light in the east, through the budding trees, but shadows still shroud the swamp, and I can't see him past the glare of his headlamp.

"Water," I whisper, mouthing the words on a breath.

"Right," he says. He bends and unzips a bag, and a second later, he produces a metal bottle. Some silly, residual warning from my programming shivers through me—*never take an open drink from a stranger.*

It makes me want to laugh. What can anyone do to me that hasn't already been done? What can anyone take from me that hasn't already been taken?

I have nothing left of value, not even my body.

The bottle shakes as he tips cold liquid into my mouth. At first, I can't separate my dried tongue from the bottom of my mouth, but after a second, it pulls free. I drink greedily, swallowing though the water burns my dry throat, my traitorous body performing the act even though my brain knows I don't want this. Water is life.

Royal is right. Death is preferable.

When my rescuer pulls the water back, my body protests, but it doesn't reach my lips. I close my eyes, too exhausted by the small act of swallowing to do more. All I can do is whisper the words that circled my head all night. "They came back for me."

"I know," he says. "But I'm going to get you out of here now."

His fingers work at the knots on my hands next. I bite my lips to keep from crying out. Swallowing the scream of pain that forces itself to my throat, I bite down harder, until I taste blood. He gives up and goes to his bag, and I see his silhouette and the beam of the light fall on a glinting silver blade when he pulls it out.

All at once, my entire body is shaking uncontrollably. My teeth chatter together so loud I can hear them over the sound of the insects and his heavy breathing. He steps toward me, and I shrink away, and then his body presses against mine. He's so hot, so hard, I want to scream, but only a ragged, choked sound escapes my bruised throat. His chest jerks against my shoulder as he makes a swift movement, and I hear a metallic twang, and the relief in my shoulders almost makes me scream again.

SELENA

When my hands come free, I crumple like I'm made of wet paper. With a curse, he drops the knife to catch me as I fall. His warm hand lands on my breast, and my nipple contracts. Neither of us move for a second. A shock goes through me that my body can still feel anything but pain, even if it is an involuntary response.

I'm still alive. My body is alive, even if the rest of me died on that tree.

"They came back," I whisper through chattering teeth, my brain insisting he know something, that he understand. But I can't put into words the horror of what happened to me tonight.

"I brought a blanket," he says. "Can you stand?"

I shake my head, and he pushes me back against the trunk. Instinctual terror rips through me again, and I push away, collapsing in a heap at the foot of the tree. I can't comprehend what's happening. A blanket falls over me. Strong hands grapple to lift me and wrap me. My hands are cocooned inside the fabric, but I don't fight. The last of my fight drained away in the cold hours before dawn.

"Who are you?" I whisper, my voice sounding like someone else's. Or maybe it sounds ordinary, like it always has, but I'm someone else now.

"Don't worry about it," he says.

It doesn't matter. I know as much as I need to know. He's one of the football players, someone who felt bad enough to come back for me, even after he joined in with the others. He did this, and yet, he came back. I don't know if that makes him better or worse.

The sky overhead is partially blotted out by tiny leaves, but the pale light creeping into the swamp from the breaking dawn has increased even since the man found me. All I can see as he kneels beside me putting away his water bottle and zipping his bag is a black beanie and broad shoulders. When he lifts his face, though, I take in what I didn't register when blinded by his headlamp. A silver mask covers the top half of his face.

I should feel something about that, but I don't.

For a moment, in the darkness, I can almost believe it's one of the Dolce brothers.

SELENA

But that's stupid. Of course it isn't one of the Dolces. Most of the guys in the world have broad shoulders and own beanies. And the accent is all wrong. The accent belongs here. The Dolces don't.

Without thought, I pull my good hand free and reach for the mask I can barely make out in the scant light. He grabs my wrist. His grip is hard, punishing the bruised and broken skin.

My mouth opens in a silent cry.

"Don't even think about it," he says. "Or I'll tie you back to that tree and leave you. Understood?"

I nod, pain choking off my words.

"Never, ever touch the mask," he says. "And we have a deal."

I nod again, forcing my throat to swallow. I don't know what he means by a deal, but I don't want it. Deals with the devil are what got me here.

"Deal?" he asks, his grip tightening until I cry out. The piteous sound echoes through the dim, watery swampland around us.

"Deal," I whisper, curling over my arm. Because what does it matter now? What can he take that hasn't already been taken from me?

"Good," he says, releasing my hand and tucking it inside the blanket. "Good girl."

He stoops to gather me into his arms. He takes a second to get his balance with the backpack on his back and me in his arms, and then he steps into the water. Pain lances through me with each step he takes, though he moves slowly, feeling his way through the shallow pools and soft hillocks. He trips on a few roots, but he doesn't drop me. I begin to thaw from the cold, the blanket and his body heat seeping into me as he slogs through murky swamp water, over patches of dry land, slipping on mud.

The rhythm of his steps lulls me, and within minutes, I'm drifting into unconsciousness again. I fight to keep my eyes open, to stay awake, to be aware of where he's taking me. But what's the point? Why bother?

I let myself slip away.

When I wake, he's standing over me, laying me in the back seat of a truck. The sky above is pale morning blue now that we're out of the trees, and by the cabin light, I can make out the features not hidden by the mask. Sharp features, hint of a tan, good lips. Again, I could almost believe he's familiar if I tried hard enough. But I don't because he's not. It doesn't matter who he is. He's not one of my boys, and they aren't my boys any longer. They never were.

It was all a lie.

My lie.

My fault.

I could have stopped it at any time, and it would have been real. But I didn't. Which means it was all for Mr. D.

"Who are you?" I ask again, my voice reedy and rough and without curiosity.

"Don't worry," the man in the mask says. He closes the door and circles the truck to climb in the front seat before speaking again. "You'll be safe with me."

He pulls onto the highway, almost empty this time of day. The whirr of the tires beneath us lulls me again, and I feel my battered body struggling for rest, my mind begging for oblivion. I don't want to think about what happened, about what they did to me. I don't want to remember the look of betrayal on Royal's face, the tiny glimpse I had in the mirror before he stopped the car, before his eyes emptied of all life.

I don't want to remember how he betrayed me, either, the disbelief I felt when he turned away from my pleas and allowed his brothers to take what they've been asking for since the first time he told them I belonged to only him. I sink into the blanket and let myself forget.

I wake in a cold sweat of terror when the truck stops.

"Come on," the masked man says. "Let's get you cleaned up."

I don't move, but he must not expect it. He pulls me out of the back seat, hoisting me into his arms. We enter a building through his garage. There's a set of stairs and another door. He lays me on a leather couch and takes pictures. I think I should protest, but I don't. It doesn't matter.

When he's done, he takes me into a bathroom and gets in the shower with his clothes on, holding me up by the back of my head like a doll as he hoses me off with the showerhead. His hands are gentle but efficient as he washes every inch of me. I don't move, not even when he spreads my legs and washes between with the showerhead. The warm water burns my torn flesh like a torch, and I lose my breath at the pain, blackness swimming over my vision. When he's done, he pulls me out and towels me off, then carries me to a bed and lays me down. He looks at me for a long minute.

"What'd you do to piss off the Dolces?" he asks.

I don't answer. My throat hurts too much.

He covers me with a blanket and leaves the room. Some time later, I wake when I hear voices arguing in the other room. I close my eyes and try to block them out. I just want everything to go away.

A man comes in and tells me he's a doctor. I didn't know they made house calls anymore. He pokes at the torn corners of my mouth, my bruised throat, the burn on my hip. He sets my dislocated shoulder and gives me a sling, puts my hand in a splint. I think how strange it is that before now, losing the use of my right hand would have devastated me. Now, I don't care.

The doctor gives the man in the mask a bottle of pills and leaves. I turn over with my back to him and sleep again.

Later, the masked man comes back. It's dark outside the window. I know I've been here a day or two already. I want to leave, but it's not safe out there.

The stranger gives me juice and pills to swallow and takes pictures of my face. He stands over the bed for a minute, his phone in one hand. Then he pulls off the sheet, rolls me over on my stomach, and pulls me to the edge of the bed so I'm bent over it. I know he's going to fuck me, but I don't fight. What's the point? I won't win.

He puts on a condom and pulls out a bottle of lube from the nightstand, running a line down his cock. Then he lowers it to my entrance and pushes in. It hurts, and I cry, but he's quick. Afterwards, he showers me off again and tucks me into bed. Later, I feel him curl up around me, and I fall back asleep.

SELENA

three

Royal Dolce

The world comes back slow, like water gathering momentum. I hear voices and soft squeaks and a steady, monotonous beeping. It's sickeningly familiar.

It crashes in fast, like a wave that's been building.

I sit up, my heartbeat sending a machine into a frenzy. I start yanking at the tubes and wires in my face, my arm, my chest. So many fucking ties binding me to life.

The squeaks come faster, and a hoard of nurses rushes in, shoving me back when I fight, pinning me to the bed, banging on the button to give me more meds, to sedate me. I don't want to go under. There's something important—

And then it's gone.

BROKEN DOLL

When I wake again, I'm groggy, but I open my eyes this time. My brother is sitting beside me, scrolling on his phone, that damn sucker tucked into his cheek.

"Where is she?" I ask.

His head jerks up, his gaze flying to mine and then to the door, where Dad's standing, his phone held to his ear. Baron takes his sucker out and puts a finger to his lips, turning his back to Dad so only I can see.

"Who?" he asks aloud.

So, he didn't tell Dad.

Dad makes a 'hold on' gesture to us and then steps into the hall.

"What the fuck am I doing here?" I demand.

"You tell me," Baron says. "We dropped you off at home and went out, and the next day when we woke up, we see all these texts from Dad saying you were in the ER with a concussion and a fractured skull. *Again*."

A little more comes back. Calling Dynamo. Meeting Colin alone at the Slaughterpen. Throwing just enough punches to make him think I was trying. How right his fists felt connecting to my face, almost orgasmic.

SELENA

"When?" I ask, pushing up.

I have to get her.

The thought is quick and clear, a blow to the solar plexus.

"A couple days ago," Baron says, shoving the sucker back in his mouth.

"Fuck," I say, yanking the tape off my hand and jerking the IV free. Blood spurts from my vein, and my brain doubles back.

Blood on Duke's mouth.

Blood on Baron's dick.

Blood on her thighs.

"What are you doing?" Baron demands. "Chill the fuck out. You're drugged out of your mind right now. Just go back to sleep."

"Where's Harper?"

He glances at the door and lowers his voice. "Where we left her. She's probably dead by now."

I shake my head. No. She can't be dead.

"I have to get her."

"You wanted her dead," Baron reminds me. "You were going to kill her. I'm the one who told you not to. Remember?"

I don't want to remember that because then I have to remember what she did, the truth Baron showed me on her phone—hundreds of messages laid out over months, revealing the most personal, most shameful details of my life to a stranger on the internet.

No, not a stranger. An enemy.

She is an enemy.

I don't know why my body keeps fighting even when I remember that. But I have to get out, have to find her, have to know the truth, the reason. I yank the tube in my nose, but it hits the back of my sinuses and makes my head swim. Baron slams his chest down on mine, smacking a call button. "What the fuck," he growls. "You're intubated. You can't pull that out. You'll rupture your fucking esophagus or something."

I'm still fighting when the fucking army shows up, the nurses in pale blue scrubs that feature in too many of my nightmares already. I fucking hate hospitals. The drugs that cloud your mind, the helplessness, the way they keep you alive when you don't want any fucking part of it. It's all way too familiar by now.

The way they think they're saving you, but they're destroying you.

The way they keep you from saving her after you destroyed her.

four

Harper Apple

The first few days are hard. I don't get out of bed except to use the bathroom, which is excruciating. So is sex, but I don't say anything when each evening, the stranger comes to the bed, bends me over the side, and fucks me. There's no point in objecting. What I want doesn't matter. It never did. Royal kept telling me, but I didn't understand. Now I do.

The stranger never talks, or kisses me, or touches me, but he doesn't try to hurt me. He uses a lot of lube, and on the fourth or fifth day, it stops hurting. He asks if I'm on birth control, and I tell him I am. He calls me a good girl, but he still uses a condom. He never takes off the mask.

He takes pictures of my face and body each day, sometimes during sex, sometimes not. I don't protest. What's the point? I sleep when he's not asking anything of me. I appreciate, in some detached way, how little he wants, how little he bothers me. Even during sex, he asks for nothing, not even a response. I think if he demanded intimacy of any kind, I'd shatter completely. But he doesn't. He barely touches me.

He wakes me and dresses me and brings me to the table each day. He cooks fancy meals for me, but I don't taste them. I eat, and when I'm done, he carries me to bed, where I curl up under the blankets. The lulling voices on *Local News with Jackie* fill my head as they drone on about the cost of gasoline and someone overdosing on a new street drug. I don't hear anything about a missing girl. I fall asleep praying I won't wake up this time.

It's around the seventh evening, as I'm slumped at the island eating some fancy herbed potatoes with glazed Brussel sprouts and salmon, when my savior and captor lays down his fork.

"I have to go out for a while tomorrow," he says.

I don't answer. I don't care where he goes. I sleep most of the day. Sometimes the apartment is quiet, and sometimes I hear him exercising or clicking away at his keyboard in the big, open loft where he has a standing desk against one wall. I haven't wondered where he goes or what he's doing when he's gone. It doesn't matter.

"Do you need to go home and get your clothes or anything?" he asks.

I shrug.

"I'll buy you some clothes," he says decisively.

I don't answer.

"Where do you live, anyway?"

"Mill Street." My voice sounds creaky and unused. I clear my throat.

"Right." He sips his wine and watches me for a minute. "I'm glad I wore a condom."

I don't say anything. What is there to say?

"Do you live alone?"

"No."

"You have a roommate?"

"My mom."

He swears under his breath. "Shit, that's right. You're in high school."

I don't answer.

SELENA

"Am I about to be arrested?" he asks. "How old are you?"

"Eighteen."

He leans his elbows on the island, closing his eyes. "Thank fuck."

He always sits me on his good side, but I know why he hides under the mask. He's a monster under the mask, disfigured and ugly.

I push a bite of salmon into my mouth. It's flaky and salty, but I don't taste anything. The corners of my mouth have healed, and the angry red tracks across my cheeks from the ropes are gone when I look in the mirror. My body takes in food and water and heals itself. But whatever's broken beneath the surface doesn't change. At least you can tell, looking at him, that he's suffered.

"Your mom," he says after chewing and swallowing slowly. "Will she be looking for you?"

"She won't care."

"Have you talked to her? Told her you're okay?"

"With what?"

"Fuck," he says, raising his hand like he might run it over his face. When he touches the mask, he drops his hand to his lap. "I'll get you a phone tomorrow."

I shrug. I decide I'll call him the Phantom, like the masked man from the opera.

"Why hasn't she called the cops?"

"She won't."

"Oh." He sits back on the barstool, working his tongue around inside his mouth. "She sounds like a peach."

I don't argue.

"I'm going up to water my plants before it gets dark," he says, rising from the island to take his plate to the sink. "Why don't you come? Get some air. It'll be good for you."

He takes my plate and wine glass without asking if I'm done. I sit at the island while he cleans up. Each morning, he dresses like he's going to an office, but every time I wake, I can hear him moving around his apartment, living. His closet is full of different shades of grey slacks and pressed dress shirts in every color. He rolls his sleeves up tan forearms before rinsing the plates and setting them neatly in the stainless-steel dishwasher. Everything here is immaculately clean and organized. I can't imagine him getting his hands dirty.

He opens a door and pulls a small tool bag from a shelf, then gestures for me to follow. I think about staying, but there's no reason to disobey. He pulls down a drop ladder, and we climb up into a tiny attic space with exposed insulation and a door. Opening it, he steps through into the blue evening.

The door opens onto a flat roof that's full of potted plants in different sized containers. Leaving me in the doorway, the Phantom unwinds a hose from a spool, turns on a faucet knob against the wall near the door, and starts spraying water over a rectangular box filled with curly purple and pink flowers. Their perfume lures me out onto the roof. I haven't breathed outdoor air in a week. It's moist and heavy, clinging to my bare arms like algae.

I can hear traffic in the distance, but from the roof, I see only the same field that I can see from the huge windows in the loft below. The grass is tall and brown from winter, but green pokes up in small patches on the ground. I walk to the edge of the roof. I wonder if he'd stop me if I stepped over.

There isn't even a railing. It would be so easy. It would all be over.

I look back at the man who pulled me from the swamp, who went to such lengths to find me and bring me back. He crouches to poke in a big, round pot. His back is to me as he pulls on a pair of gloves from his bag. I could do it. It would be quick.

"I got you an appointment at the women's clinic on Wednesday," he says. "To be tested for STDs. You can take my truck and bring it back when you're done."

I step closer to the edge, until my toes are even with the end of the flat roof. I look down at the parking lot below. Try to remember why being up here is better than down there. I lift one foot, watching it hang suspended in the air, like a diver.

He looks up when I don't answer. His gaze moves to the edge of the roof and back to my face. Our eyes meet, and I know he can tell what I'm about to do. I wait for him to say something, to be angry or afraid. To demand to know what I'm doing, if I want to die.

SELENA

"I'll bring a chair for you next time," he says, unfolding slowly, cautiously, from his crouched position next to some sprouting plants. I watch him move, how comfortable he is in his body, how confident. He's quick but unhurried; tall and slender, painfully elegant. He's built like a dancer, all slim lines and measured grace.

He's at my side before I know what's happening. His strong hands are gentle on my upper arms as they pull me back. "Good girl," he says softly, drawing my shoulder blades flush with his chest.

I know he's thanking me for not jumping, for letting him pull me away, but in truth, I don't have any more desire to die than I have to live. It's not worth the effort.

"You can come up here with me every day," he says when I don't answer. "You could use some sun."

We stare out at the overgrown lot next to his building without speaking. His breath is even, his hands barely holding on. But I can feel his heart thudding rapidly against my back with each heavy beat.

I scared him. The thought registers in some distant way. He wants me to live.

BROKEN DOLL

What I want seems equally irrelevant to both of us. There's no point in telling him, so I don't, and he doesn't ask.

SELENA

five

Royal Dolce

"Where have you been?"

I spin toward the voice, my hands fisting, adrenaline pumping. I don't like being taken by surprise.

"Out," I growl. "What the fuck are you doing sitting in the dark?"

Baron switches on the lamp beside the couch. Duke is sprawled across the loveseat, his eyes glassy, a tumbler of whiskey in one hand.

"You're going to get us caught," Baron says. He picks up a sucker and begins to unwrap it slowly, his elbows resting on his knees and his eyes fixed on me. "This is a small town. It's not New York. It's harder to hide a murder when there are only a couple a year."

"We didn't murder anyone," I snap, hating that he's the reason for that. He reminded me that death is too kind. That we don't kill Darlings.

"That's right," Duke says. "And I'm not afraid of the cops. They're not NYPD. They're hicks. What can they do to us?"

"If we don't get sloppy, nothing," I say. "No one but the three of us know what happened."

The twins glance at each other, that fucking twin telepathy thing that pisses me the fuck off.

"Right?" I grind out.

"Right," Duke says. "We didn't say anything to anyone at school. We're not stupid."

No, not stupid. They've just never done this shit before. Sometimes I forget how little blood is on their hands.

And that's by design.

Protect our brothers.

King would despise me if he knew what we'd done, what I'd let them become. I should have killed her like I wanted, kept them from her, kept myself from having to admit this truth about them—that I knew what they'd do to Harper

SELENA

when I finally let them have her after six months of denying them. It was both their reward for respecting my previous claim and her punishment for betrayal. But I can't remember when they became the kind of people whose attention is a punishment.

The twins look up to King, though, and I'm supposed to fill his shoes. I think of what he'd say, not because I want to be like him, but because it will comfort them. Duke needs that, at least. I'm not sure Baron has whatever it is that makes a person seek comfort.

"We didn't do anything the Darlings wouldn't have done to us," I point out. "We eliminated a threat to the family. That's all. A man has a right to protect his family."

That's not what she was, and we all know it, just like we all know Crystal's blood is on my hands. Harper was no threat to my family. She was a threat to me.

I finally, truly understand what they went through with Mabel. When it happened, I saw it from the outside, and I felt for my brothers, but I didn't get it. I thought they were fuckwits for thinking of her as human at all. I didn't think I was capable of caring about a Darling. But now I know what the Darling girls do to a person when they set their sights on you, when they decide to play. I know how they lie and twist everything until you start to believe that against every odd, even though you know it's impossible, someone could give a fuck.

"Who was she talking to, though?" Duke asks. "Because he might figure it out."

"I don't think we need to worry about him," Baron says, sliding the sucker into his mouth. "She hadn't talked to him in weeks. She cut him off. He won't think anything unless it makes the news."

"So, it's our job to make sure it doesn't," I remind them.

Our eyes meet. He gets it. He may not have blood on his hands, but he's got the stomach for it.

"Exactly," he says. He picks up the bottle of whiskey and pours a finger into a glass, then looks me over, his gaze taking in my wet jeans and shoes. "So, again, where were you? Because we're being careful. But parking beside the road and walking across a huge-ass rice field into the swamp is going to get us caught a hell of a lot faster than anything we might say in the locker room."

SELENA

"I was looking for her phone."

"Fuck," Baron says, leaning back and closing his eyes. "She dropped it when she was fighting us."

I nod. Even a dead phone is easily traceable. It doesn't matter if it at the bottom of the swamp and will never work again. They can still track it.

If the Darlings go looking for her, they'll get the law involved. They don't play by our rules, taking care of their own problems. They have no honor.

Only a person without honor could do what she did, exploiting someone's helplessness for their own gain. For a fucking scholarship of all things. Such a pathetic, pedestrian thing. All along, she was nothing but a gold digger.

We thought she didn't know she was as Darling, but she must have known. Even if she didn't, and she really didn't know who she was talking to, he must have known. And if he gets the cops involved, and they suspect murder, they'll get the FBI involved. And the FBI will find her phone.

So we have to make sure no one else looks for her.

"You didn't find her phone?" Duke asks.

"No," I say, scowling at his drunk ass. "I didn't find it."

"We should tell Dad," Baron says. "He'll know what to do."

"No," I say, holding up a hand. "If we need his help, we'll tell him then."

"Okay," Baron says, looking skeptical. "So, what now?"

"Where'd you put her clothes?"

"Shit," Duke says. "They're in my bag."

"That's the kind of sloppy shit we can't do," I say. That, and letting her drop her phone in the swamp. If they find that, they'll search the swamp, and they'll find her.

At least… I think they will.

They'll have a whole team, dogs and infrared gear and shit that I don't have. I've been in that swamp exactly once before today, and it was night by the time we left, and I was… Not entirely present. I barely remember walking into the swamp. I was in survival mode, like those months after Crystal died that I barely remember, and the ones before that I don't remember at all. I let the monster take care of me, take care of what needed to be done, of what I couldn't. I was weak, and he was strong.

SELENA

Maybe if I put him in control, he can find her. I'll have to go back again. But I have a good reason. I looked today, my first day home from the hospital, searching until after dark, but with only my phone's flashlight and a vague memory of being there before, I couldn't find where we'd left her. I couldn't find her.

"What are you thinking?" Baron asks, sitting up straight and setting his whiskey on the coffee table. "Burn her clothes?"

"Yes," I say, stepping into the living room. "She was a Darling. We need to act like it."

I'll burn everything that ever reminded me of her, all the random shit she left at my house, my notebooks where I wrote poems about her like some pathetic lovesick dog chasing after a bitch in heat. We should burn the whole fucking town to the ground with all the Darlings in it.

"She's one of the disowned Darlings' kids," Duke says. "They don't care about her."

Duke isn't good with the aftermath, the cleanup, the details. He's there for the fun and games, but he forgets that after the games, it's real.

BROKEN DOLL

"One of them cared enough to find her," I say. "Even if the grandfather cut them off, one of them reached out to her."

"Or he did," Duke says.

"Well, she's eighteen, so she's not a runaway kid," Baron says, trading his sucker for the whiskey. "And her mom probably won't call the cops. Right?"

"We need to act like everything's normal," I say.

For a minute, we're frozen in confusion. None of us have the slightest idea how to be normal.

"No skipping practice," Duke says at last.

"Basketball's over, dumbass," Baron says. "No skipping school, though. Now that Royal's back, we have to act like it was just about him."

Irritation flares in me, but he's right. I can't be the one to go off the deep end over this. Not when it means the twins will go down with me.

I should have fucking left them out of it. What was I thinking? I could have done it myself, slit her throat and dropped her in the river.

SELENA

But I didn't want her in the same river where Crystal drowned. That water is sacred. She deserved swamp water.

"I'll talk to her mom."

"What?" Duke asks, sitting up straight. "Are you fucking crazy?"

"No," Baron says, holding up a hand, his eyes on me. "He's right. That's what a normal person would do if his ex disappeared from school. Bring back her shit, ask her mom if she's okay. Act like you think she went back to Faulkner High."

"And in the process, see what she knows," I say.

And see if Harper's there.

I don't add that part aloud. I don't want my brothers to worry.

We left her tied to a tree somewhere in that snake-infested swamp. I barely made it out without being bitten by one of the vipers. She couldn't have gotten away from the ropes, let alone gotten past the snakes and hiked twenty miles back to town without shoes or clothes.

Could she?

If there's one person on earth who's tough and resourceful enough to do that after what we did to her, it's Harper. And she'll be out for revenge.

So, if she's alive, why hasn't she called the cops? And if she's dead, why can't I find her body?

SELENA

six

Harper Apple

I don't count the days. I know there's something wrong with me, that this isn't normal, but I can't muster enough fucks to do anything about it. When the Phantom hands me a box with a brand-new iPhone, the latest model, and tells me to text my mother, I do it. I don't bother telling him I had a third-hand phone that shut itself off for no reason, couldn't hold a charge, and had so many cracks in the screen I could barely read an email. It makes no difference what phone I have, if I have one at all. I don't use it except when he tells me to check in with her.

Days go by, then weeks. I know school is coming to an end, but it doesn't matter anymore. Mr. D will have pulled my scholarship, and I wouldn't be able to face the Dolces and their friends who came back for me that night. School seems trivial and pointless like everything else. It would take effort I can't give, and so, I don't.

One night, when I wake up mewling like some pathetic, drowning kitten, crying that they're coming back for me, the Phantom holds me against his warm chest and tells me he'll keep me safe, that no one will find me here if I don't go outside. He thinks I'm scared, that I'm hiding like he is, but I'm not. I just don't have the fight in me to leave. So, I stay.

He doesn't lock me in or even try to convince me not to go. I'm not a prisoner. I could walk out. I even went to the clinic when he told me, the pharmacy where they sent me. I took the antibiotics he handed me each day. But there's no reason to leave again. I can exist in this neat, orderly space as well as anywhere else. Better. No one demands answers for what's wrong with me. No one asks for things I can't give, for me to make impossible choices. The Phantom asks so little in return for this haven in which I can exist in the bubble he's created, not taking up any space in the world.

Maybe we're both phantoms.

He feeds me, putting my food before me and taking it away when he's done eating, never commenting on how much or little I've eaten. After dinner, we go onto the roof where he trims and waters flowers, sprays plants, and admires his garden. Sprouts have grown into plants, and the older ones come alive as if to show them the way—the saw-like leaves of one produces a stalk with clusters of white flowers that hang like bells; orange blossoms like curling starfish emerge from another.

I don't go to the edge again. I don't care enough to jump. I sit in the chair where he tells me to sit, like the good girl he tells me I am. When it's time to go inside, he brings me back in. He measures me one day, touching my body with possessive thoroughness, detached and entitled, as if I'm a doll and not a human. He runs his thumb over the silky burn scar on my hip, checks my healed hand, sets my birth control pill on the bedside table each morning. I am another plant to him, a fixture, something to tend.

He cuts my fingernails, paints my toenails. He dyes my hair a richer, dark-chocolate brown, irons it straight, and brushes it in front of the only mirror in the house, on the inside of his closet door, while watching a tutorial on how to fix it in different styles. He puts a ring through my bellybutton and buys me makeup and a bag to keep it in. He calls me his good girl. Soon, among his usual deliveries, more clothes for me arrive—a padded bra with heavy gel inserts that make me more evenly proportioned, skirts and dresses that hug and accentuate my curves without looking trashy. I know they must be expensive, and I've never had clothes made for my body, that fit me so well. The style is nothing I'd choose for myself, though. They're rich girl clothes.

But then I realize I don't know what I'd choose anymore. I'm not the girl who liked tiny cut-offs that showed her thigh tattoos, who wore combat boots and hoodies. I don't know who I am. So I try on this girl the Phantom wants me to be, just like I try on the clothes when he tells me to. He watches with arrogant indulgence, picking out the things he doesn't like to send back. I look at the straight-haired girl in the mirror with tits that balance her hips, with a tiny waist and red-soled shoes.

I wonder if she'll ever be me again.

Every morning and evening, he fucks me quickly and efficiently as I lay there not moving, letting him extract his payment.

SELENA

I'm the whore Royal always said I was.

Once, he slides up on the bed next to me when he's done.

"Want me to finish you off?" he asks. "This isn't the kind of relationship where I'll eat you out, but I have a vibrator and a couple clit stimulators."

My stomach clenches with revulsion, almost panic, at a memory I won't let form. I shake my head quickly. I don't want or need pleasure. I'd rather just lie here, my body hollow except for what he puts inside me.

seven

Royal Dolce

She's not fucking here. I stand at the base of what I'm pretty sure is the tree where we left her. It's hard to tell. It's rained since then, and the water is higher, and judging by the rumbles in the distance, it's about to get even higher. I bought a pair of thick waders that make me look like I belong on a whaling ship, and I spend the weekends mucking through a fucking swamp, shooting snakes and being drained dry by mosquitos.

There is no sign of anyone in the swamp but me.

Fuck Harper. She doesn't fucking matter. She doesn't deserve this much attention. I should be at the bridge, where someone important died. I should be mourning Crystal, thinking of Crystal.

Fuck this shit.

SELENA

I wade out of the swamp, tear off the waders, and hurl them in the back of the Range Rover, not caring it if swamp sludge splatters on the back of my seat. I see the blanket there, the one I fucked Harper on so many times. The one I wrapped around her body to keep her warm all through winter. A picture of it hugging her curves rises to my mind, the way it slipped off her thick thighs, showing that fucking tattoo...

I climb into the driver's seat and slam the door, banging my head down on the top of the steering wheel. I'm fucking hard just thinking about her. What the fuck is wrong with me?

I peel out, turn around at the next exit, and drive back toward Faulkner under the bruise-black sky. Harper doesn't deserve a place in my memory. What she did goes so far past betrayal, a cut so deep it could never heal. She found a way, broke the last pieces of my sanity. All along, I thought I was biding my time until I broke her. But she broke me first.

I pull up behind a shitty little sedan in her driveway and glance up at the gathering storm clouds. Her neighbors are outside, the girl with dingy blue hair and the little kid, who's prancing around in a hula hoop, wearing shorts and a bikini top that hangs oddly on her flat chest. The doors to their car stand open, and a song that I can only hope the kid doesn't understand is spilling out from the crackly speakers.

I imagine what my mother would say, and I smile at them as I circle my car to grab the box of Harper's things I brought, as if this were a normal breakup. The blue-haired girl gives me a dirty look, an unlit cigarette drooping from the corner of her mouth.

The little kid stops dancing, the hoop clattering to the cracked walkway at her feet. "She ain't here," she calls. "So you can go on back home!"

The blue-haired girl cuts her eyes at her sister, but she doesn't say anything. She watches me with sullen eyes and fishes a lighter from her pocket to light up. I should have taken a few hits off a joint before I got here. I could use the calm.

I turn away from them and knock on Harper's door. After a minute, the knob turns, and my chest caves like someone punched it. But a woman I've never seen stares out at me, not Harper.

"Help you?" she asks, looking me over.

She's average height, with a barrel chest that she shoves out to make it look like she's got more tits than she does. She's one of those chicks with a boxy frame and no ass, the opposite of Harper's wasp-like figure.

"Is Harper here?" I ask. "I brought by some stuff she left at my place."

"Haven't seen her," the woman says. Her voice is rough, like a life-long smoker's, and there's an edge of belligerence in it. She must be in her thirties, but the layer of makeup caked on makes her look older. Her platinum hair has seen one too many rounds with a bottle of cheap bleach, and an inch of dishwater blonde shows at the roots. Sucking hard on a cigarette, she lets her gaze move over me again, more slowly this time, her black-rimmed eyes keen with interest.

I remind myself I'm here for my brothers. So they don't take the fall for what I let them do. I knew better than to let them loose on Harper, but I wanted her to suffer. They made it happen.

"Come on in," the blonde woman says, pulling the door open further. "Let me get you a drink, look at you for a minute. So this is what's been keeping Harper away so much this year. Can't blame the girl, can you?"

I don't want to go in. My throat is so thick I think I'll choke, and her house looks like a trap, a smoky dungeon of filth and dereliction.

"I just brought her stuff," I say, thrusting the box at the woman.

"Nonsense, come 'ere." She gestures with her cigarette, not taking the box. "I don't bite. Unless you're into that."

I'm used to the way women look at me, but this time, it makes my skin crawl. "Are you Harper's… Sister?" I ask, reluctantly stepping through the door.

"Oh, honey, aren't you a darling?" she says, giving my arm a flirty little push before sashaying down the hall, trying to swing her non-existent ass like an invitation.

My back stiffens at her choice of words, and I only manage a grunt in response.

"Everyone always thinks we're sisters," she says. "Looking at me, you'd never know I had a baby, would you? I think it's 'cause I had a C-section. Kept everything nice and tight, just the way it was."

SELENA

She picks a fleck of tobacco from her tongue and smiles up at me. My stomach clenches, and I look away. If she knew what I'd done to her daughter…

"I ain't seen Harper in weeks," she says. "I work days and have fun most nights. We might not cross paths for days. I'm sure she'll drag her ass home when she's done with whatever trouble she's in this time."

If she only knew…

I try not to look around the place Harper always refused to let me go. The ceiling is low and oppressive, like the roof of a too-small car. The blinds on the tiny windows are closed, and the only light is from the TV. Even in the dim, cave-like room, I can see that the place is a hovel. The coffee table is covered with empty beer cans, fast food wrappers, and ashtrays overflowing with cigarette butts. The carpet isn't even a color, just a dull collection of stains and matted, cheap fibers. The couch looks like the place crackheads go to fuck.

"It's okay," I say. "I just wanted to bring her stuff back. She hasn't been at school."

"Not like she ever bothers to tell me what's going on with her," her mom says, rolling her eyes. "You'd think with all I do for her, she could shoot me a text."

"You'd think," I say, hoping she'll keep talking.

I could write the book on what she's doing, but Harper's the one who summed it up in one sentence when we were done fucking one day and talking about our moms. *The narcissistic mother with a victim complex*, is what she called it. It was funny, how much our moms had in common, though neither would admit it if they met.

But that doesn't matter. I need information. As far as I know, Harper didn't have friends. If she knows we want her dead, who would she hide out with?

That's too fucking easy. She'd go to this asshole she's been feeding information to. I don't know who Mr. D is, but her mom might know.

This is the most fucked up part of all. Even now, she's fucking with my head. I don't want to talk to her mom, to take advantage of her ignorance, if her daughter is dead. But if she's alive, I have to find her. It's pissing me off that I don't know what way to be, to act.

SELENA

"I'll let you know if I hear from her," I tell Mrs. Apple. "I'm sorry she ran off on you."

"I'm sorry she ran around on *you*," Mrs. Apple says. "Some girls don't know a good thing until it bites them in the ass."

The last thing I should care about is who Harper was fucking, but my caveman brain can't think of anything else. "Is that why she said we broke up?" I ask carefully.

"I just figured," she says. "You know, if she's not here, nine times out of ten she's with that boy who does the tattoos. He's been hanging out on the corners with the Crosses lately, probably selling that Alice in Wonderland shit that's been all over the news. They say it makes you go all night, so if he's dipping into his supply, he's got a lady to reap the benefits."

I try not to react. The smell of the place is making me sick. Blood rushes in my head. I don't want to be here, in this death trap. Again, I push the box at Mrs. Apple, or whatever the fuck her name is. I never asked Harper if her mom got married. I just know she didn't marry Harper's dad, the disowned Darling.

"You could always try texting her," she says. "It's a shame you two broke up. If you need to talk to somebody, maybe drink away those troubles…"

"I'm good," I say, backing toward the hallway. Suddenly, I can't be here. Her ghost is breathing down the back of my neck—no, screaming down it.

No wonder Harper never let me come in. Her house is shit. Her mom is shit. Her life is shit. If she worked herself free of those ropes, she probably headed in the opposite direction from Faulkner and never looked back. She's too smart to come back here, especially knowing she's crossed the wrong fucking people.

I ignore Mrs. Apple's attempts to lure me back as I hurry outside, holding back the urge to heave. The low clouds have started spitting rain, and the air is thick and heavy with moisture. The little girl is standing on the roof of the car, dancing in the rain to another song no kid should be listening to.

"Yeah, you go on and go home!" Her high voice cuts through the splattering rain. "You ain't welcome here, on account of you broke Harper's heart."

SELENA

Ignoring her, I hurry to the Range Rover and climb inside, slamming the door to shut out the rain and the girl and the feeling of that house that clings to me like the skin-crawling sensation of dirt and grime and sweat after a football game.

Trash, all of them. Just like Harper.

I try to keep that thought in mind instead of feeling like the piece of shit I am, running from them like a guilty conscience.

I take a few deep breaths, telling myself I'm imagining the stench of her life lingering around me. Then I shift into drive and take off, back toward the side of town where the rottenness makes sense to me.

I don't go home, though. I keep going, toward old man Darling's house, the one where we went after I disowned Crystal but before she died.

I pull off at the bridge. This is where I belong. Honoring the memory of a girl who deserves my remorse. The first girl I killed, two and a half years ago.

Grey drizzle splatters down on the windshield. It's not the kind of rain that fell on the night the river took Crystal.

BROKEN DOLL

It's the kind that was falling the night Harper came to our house the first time, thinking she'd spy. She was good at finding my hiding spots, the places I go to remember, to prove they don't hurt me. I have mastered this place the way I mastered Devlin's balcony.

His house is gone now, and Harper can't haunt his balcony, but she haunts the river. I left her in the swamp, but her ghost is here. It's in the rain on the windshield, the blanket in the trunk. It's under the bridge, where we lay and talked and fucked. It's on the far side of the bridge, where we fought the Darlings, and where I pushed her down and fucked her ass the first time. It's in the back seat of this car, where I plowed into her and made her scream for me while her cunt choked my cock in its grip.

I lean the seat back and slide my hand into my pants. My cock is stiff, my balls ready to dump their contents into her thirsty core. I pull out my phone and thumb it on.

I think of what her mother said. I scroll down to her name and read our last *OnlyWords* messages.

Royal: meet u at ur locker after school
BadApple: c u then

SELENA

It's so normal. So ordinary.

I press the button and shut off my screen. I should delete the whole thread, erase any evidence I ever knew her. Instead, I open the regular texting app that uses our phone numbers, the one we hardly used. It only takes a minute to scroll back all those months, to the first text she sent. It's a picture of her in my letterman jacket, the pic I asked for over Thanksgiving. My dick jerks in my hand, and I close my eyes and take a breath, as if I can coax the smell of her from these leather seats where she lay so many times.

But no. That was a different car. She's only been in this one once—her last night.

When I open my eyes, though, she's still there. She's not showing a lot of skin. She never sent nudes. That only makes me want to see more, to peel open the jacket and see her tight little tits with the caramel nipples poking out at me. She's not wearing anything under it, but only an inch of skin shows between the buttons of the jacket. An inch of flat stomach, the little dip of her bellybutton like a tease. Below the jacket, she's wearing tiny athletic shorts, knee socks, and tennis shoes. Her hair is messy around her shoulders, and she's smiling into the camera, a sassy smirk that tugs at one corner of her lips. But it's her eyes that seduced me then, her eyes that entice me now.

I stroke myself, but it's not enough. I need her, need to crush her little body under mine, to pin it and penetrate her and hear her gasping for mercy. I look at her picture, and I scroll through the others, tugging at my dick until my skin is rubbed raw, but I can't find relief. My balls are so full they ache. I just need one little push, but I can't close the deal. Finally, I throw my phone across the car and slam my head back against the seat.

Fuck. Fuck. Fuck.

I came here as a remembrance of Crystal, not to masturbate to pictures of a girl who used me in her little games, told her sick old man how big my dick was, how I performed, how I licked her cunt until she gushed all over my face, her soft cries a siren song to my ears.

I turn on the car and wrench the wheel around, heading back through the colorless, waterlogged evening. Just when I thought I couldn't sink any lower, I find new ways to

SELENA

surprise myself. Like a fucking serial killer, I just jerked off while looking at pictures of the girl I murdered.

eight

Harper Apple

We're sitting at the island one night when the Phantom reaches for the white wine, pouring himself a second glass. He never does that. It's strange how much I know about him without even trying, without realizing I was learning.

"I need you to go home tomorrow," he says.

"Okay."

"My girlfriend's coming home for the Fourth."

"Okay."

"I'll take you home in the morning."

"Okay."

He watches me take a bite. I don't taste anything. I'm never hungry. I remember when I would have killed to be so well fed, but I don't remember why.

SELENA

"After she goes home, you'll come over every Tuesday and Thursday afternoon."

"Okay."

Talking about going home starts to awaken a tiny part of my brain from its stupor. Though I've lived here for months, I haven't looked around with any curiosity. I've been in his bedroom, in his shower, his closets, his roof. I know every inch of his house, but I've never noticed it. He knows every inch of my body, but I've never seen his face. I've been a snail hiding inside my shell for months. I haven't gone anywhere since the trip to the clinic in April.

Is it really July already?

"I'll pick you up from your house at four," he says. "I won't come in or meet your mother. You'll tell her you're with a friend if she asks."

"She won't."

"You won't tell her anything about me," he says. "You'll stay the night here twice a week. I like you being here when I wake up."

"Okay."

"Finish your wine," he says. "I'm going to shower."

"Okay."

He rests his tattooed hand on top of mine. "Good girl."

I finish my food and wine. He showers, and while he cleans up in the kitchen, I clean myself for him, the way he likes. Shower, shave, brush my teeth. I go to the bed where he's lying waiting, reading a book, his mask still in place.

"Do you ever take that off?" I ask.

"No," he says, laying the book down. "Hands and knees."

I get on all fours, and he stands behind me, taking pictures.

"Good girl," he says at last, setting his phone down before he fucks me. Afterwards, he shuts off the light and holds me while he falls asleep. For the first time in months, I have enough presence of mind to wonder what he looks like and who he is.

He takes me home the next day. I've texted Mom once a week, at his direction, letting her know that I'm fine and that I've moved in with a friend. As soon as I step through the door, she starts grilling me, and I'm surprised at the longing for the familiar, safe white walls of the Phantom's loft apartment. I turn and walk down the hall to my room.

SELENA

I couldn't answer Mom's questions if I tried. So, I don't try. After screeching at me from the door for a while and getting no response, she goes off in a fury and doesn't come home. The house is small and stinks of stale cigarettes and booze. It's both foreign and familiar at once. Everything looks the same, but it feels as if I'm a stranger.

The Tuesday after the Fourth of July, my phone rings at exactly four in the afternoon. I walk out and climb up onto the leather seats of the big, white, jacked-up truck with mud on the tires that sits in front of my house. It's oddly comforting to find him there, behind the tinted windows of the Escalade, hidden behind his mask. Somehow, not seeing his real face makes it easier, this life we've carved out together.

"Did you have a good Fourth?" he asks.

"Yes."

"Did you see anyone from Willow Heights?"

I glance sideways at him. Does he think I went out and partied? That I have a boyfriend somewhere out here?

I turn to the window. "No."

He drives the rest of the way in silence. At his place, I sit on the pale grey sectional while he makes homemade pesto pizza and salad. We each have one glass of wine. We don't talk during dinner. After we shower separately, he comes to the bed and stands over it. I push the blanket off and start to turn over, but he stops me.

"Get on your back and spread your legs. I want to watch you while I fuck you tonight."

I lie down and open my legs. He kneels up between them, stroking himself with one hand and touching me with the other until he's hard and I'm wet. He pushes his cock down, positioning himself at my entrance.

"Condom," I remind him.

"Not tonight," he says. "I want to fuck Royal's bitch raw tonight. When he wants you back, I want him to always know that I've felt your cunt with my bare cock and cum inside you." He pushes into me, no lube, no condom.

He knows Royal.

A chill races through me.

Of course he knows Royal. He knows I was Royal's. Who was the football player who said something on the night that never ended, the one I never think about, when they came back with the twins? Something about being all in for running a train on Royal's plaything. It's got to be the same guy. I think of him as my rescuer, as someone apart from that night, but he's not. I don't have to tell him that when they came back, they brought friends, and they took turns, and they didn't stop until I prayed for death. And then, when that didn't work, I gave up. I gave up everything, even the will to live.

He already knows.

"Dawson?" I ask when he's halfway done. I no longer know if he's familiar because we've been together so long, or if I knew him before.

"What?" he asks, pushing up on his hands to look down at me. His eyes are the same color blue, but one of them is blank and unseeing, like he's blind. Around it, his skin is red inside the eyehole of his mask. I've wondered which of the Dolces' friends would come looking for me in the swamp, someone with enough of a conscience to save me. None of them had scars. Dawson is blond, but he lives with his parents and sisters. This isn't some empty place where he brings girls, or the mistress apartment where a married man comes to fuck on occasion.

It's a home.

Home to a man with scars on his face and letters inked into his knuckles, a swan inked onto his arm, words in Latin scrolled across his skin.

"Who are you?" I ask.

"I can be anyone you want me to be, baby doll," he says, as if he read my mind.

I wish I could really remember what Dawson looked like. I never looked too closely. The Dolce boys drew all the attention. The rest of the guys are paper dolls in my head. With a mask, they could be anyone. I pull my gaze from his strange eyes, focusing on the swan tattoo on the inside of his forearm, an odd reminder of where I came from, while he glides in and out. It seems a lifetime ago that a secret society could mean something to me.

He watches my face while he cums inside me and says it's beautiful. That used to mean something, too, but I can't remember what.

SELENA

He curls around me afterwards, holding me while we fall asleep. In the morning, while he showers off after sex, I look around like it's the first time I've been here. It's everything my old home, my old life, was not—clean, open, bright, and simple. One entire side of the loft apartment is made up of windows, not just the living room but the bedroom, too. The trim is all glass and wood and stainless steel. It's sparsely but tastefully furnished and decorated.

I take in the white brick wall of the kitchen, the island where we eat separating it from the spacious living area with an entire wall of windows overlooking the untended field—an empty lot before a stretch of trees. There's the standing desk where he works and a treadmill where he runs, looking out over the field. He lifts weights on a setup he has next to the treadmill. Looking around, I realize he must be rich.

I go back to the bedroom and sit on the edge of the bed and watch some news story without really seeing it, Jackie going on about someone overdosing on this Lady Alice drug. The Phantom comes out of the bathroom with a towel hung around his neck and one around his hips, his mask in place. I avert my eyes while he dresses.

BROKEN DOLL

He drops me off after breakfast and says he'll be back Thursday. I don't say anything, but I wish I didn't have to leave his apartment. As I watch him drive away, my body grows heavier and heavier with dread. I stand on the sidewalk, rooted in place. Only when I hear Olive's high voice singing out back do I move. I'm seized with a sharp certainty that I don't want to see her or Blue. It's so deep it's almost physical, and I rush into the house and close the door behind me, my heart hammering.

He said he'd keep me safe. But I'm not safe here. So why did he send me home?

SELENA

nine

Royal Dolce

"You doing okay?" King asks quietly, studying me with way too fucking much intensity.

"Fan-fucking-tastic," I say, switching lanes. "Not like I'm stuck in a literal pit of hell. Speaking of, why exactly are you visiting Arkansas in July?"

"I'm not visiting Arkansas," he says. "I'm visiting you."

"No one asked you to come," I mutter.

"You don't have to ask," he says. "I'm your brother."

"Lucky me."

He sighs. "We're still family, Royal. Eliza, too. She can't travel in her third trimester, or she'd be here, too. We can't bring the baby on the plane for a few months, and I don't want to be away from them any more than I have to once the baby comes. I didn't want to wait until Christmas to see you, and you didn't come to New York this summer, so here I am. Whether you like it or not, I'm still a Dolce."

"How the twins doing?"

I'd rather talk about them than myself. When they wanted to spend the summer in New York with Ma, it was a blow, but once they were gone, it's been a relief. They needed to be out of harm's way, and that means out of my way. They need distance from the guilt, or from the crime, if they don't feel remorse. Getting them away from any suspicions that might arise in town was the best way to protect them, even if that meant I couldn't watch over them. So I told them to go, but I couldn't bring myself to leave.

We all needed time apart, anyway. A summer to forget, to put it all behind us, so it's just another shadow lurking in our dark past. Or I hope that's what they're doing, that they're not revisiting the place in their minds like I visit the place north of town, drawn back by some invisible cord tying me to the swamp. I found a dirt road that leads in behind it, so I don't have to park on the side of the highway. No one ever sees me out there, and if they did, they're probably backwoods rednecks who wouldn't think twice about me tromping into the swamp in rubber coveralls that just about bake my balls after ten minutes.

The twins aren't around to ask questions, to demand why I'm going there. They're not around to talk sense into me and tell me not to go. I tell myself it doesn't matter. No one's going to find her now. And if they do, there's nothing linking us to her. We burned her clothes, and I burned all my notebooks. I don't write anymore. I don't want to know what fucked up shit would come out. I still go to the Slaughterpen every Saturday night, but I don't go to the Hockington. I'm a legitimate part of the Dolce empire now, with shares in my name and a spot on the board of directors.

King seems happy to fill the drive from the airport with tales of the twins' exploits, so I let him talk. They're off partying on our old stomping grounds and getting high on this Alice shit, and I'm here with Dad, learning the business I'll someday inherit by day. By night, I wander the streets or haunt the swamps like some fucking forlorn specter of revenge.

It's done. I killed her. So why can't I forget her?

I've been by her mom's a couple times, but I don't want her or anyone else getting suspicious, so I stopped after the second time. I've also asked about her casually when the blue-haired girl who lives next to her was outside. I even tracked down Maverick, the piece of shit she used to fuck before me. She's not anywhere.

"You should come back with me," King says. "It might do you good to get away, too."

My back stiffens, and I glance at him, trying to figure out what he means, what he knows. The twins swore they wouldn't tell him what we did, but they trust him enough that they probably spilled it. Whatever. I'll deal with it. It wasn't doing them any favors to be around me right now. I'd die before I admitted it to anyone, but everything's been shit since Harper. My insides are raw, jagged edges.

From the start, I only meant to destroy her life, not take it. But after what she did, what choice did I have? I did what anyone in my shoes would have done, what everyone expected of me. She fucking deserved to die. She didn't just sell my darkest secrets and deepest shames to my enemy. She sold our relationship to him one dirty detail at a time. It was all fake. And she didn't just play me. She didn't just make me fall for her. She made me believe that someone could do the same in return.

That's the lie I can never forgive.

And it's not that I care if she's fucking dead. It's the fact that she vanished like that, without a trace, just like Crystal…

"Just stay the fuck out of my business, okay?" I say, weaving around traffic and pressing my foot harder on the gas pedal, ready to get home and out of this trap.

My brother sighs. "You didn't have to go to Thorncrown. You could have gone anywhere to play football. Or hell, come back to New York if you're not going to school."

"I am going to school," I growl. "Thorncrown U."

He gives me a cool look. We both know it's a bullshit school. No self-respecting university would be in Faulkner, Arkansas, and yet, the town somehow manages to have two shitty little colleges. I have no artistic talent whatsoever, so the liberal arts school was out. Therefore, Thorncrown it is.

"You could go to any university in the country," King points out. "You're a fucking football star, Royal."

"I could've gone to the CBC," I say, smiling at the thought. Ma would have an aneurism if I went to a Baptist college.

"You could be playing at a division one school."

I shrug. "Just because I'm good at something, that doesn't mean I like it."

"But you do like it."

"You liked it," I remind him. "Are you playing D1 ball?"

He's quiet for a long minute. Then he shakes his head. "I'm doing what I have to do so that you can all go to good schools."

"Because if you didn't work for Al Valenti, I'd have to," I say flatly. I know it's the truth, even if no one else has the *cajones* to come right out and say it. King could have gotten out of working for our great-uncle. Yeah, our parents promised him their first son, but Al's a reasonable guy. He'd have taken me, the best man for the job, if everyone had told him King wasn't the right fit. It wasn't our parents or Al Valenti who insisted on keeping the contract. It was King.

He sighs and runs his hand through his hair. "You have a choice, Royal. That's all I'm saying."

"And I made my choice," I say. "You think you're the only one who can make sacrifices for our family? The twins don't graduate for another year."

I'm not leaving them with Dad. I know what he'll use them for. If it's the only thing I ever protect them from, at least it's more than nothing.

"Our brothers told me about Harper," King says quietly. "Did you tell Dad?"

So, there it is. I knew they couldn't keep their fucking mouths shut. But better to get it all out in New York than to let it slip in this gossipy little town.

"No, I didn't fucking tell Dad," I snap. "She wasn't his mark."

"She's a Darling," he says. "He'd want to know."

"What, you think he's doing business with some trailer park junkie? She's not one of the Darlings he's concerned with."

"And the ones he is concerned with?" he asks. "You're telling him about them?"

"There's nothing to tell," I say, gritting my teeth in irritation. Now that I'm working with Dad, I understand why compromise is necessary. But Preston doesn't make it easy to leave him alone when he's constantly fucking with us, trying to get a reaction. It pisses me the fuck off that there are Darlings walking around this town with impunity.

"Maybe that's a good thing," King says.

He thinks the Darlings paid for Crystal's death already, and maybe he's right. But he's not her twin, and she's not the only one the Darlings killed that winter.

"Until we get the casino running, the Delacroixs are untouchable," I say. "After that... All bets are off."

Once the twins graduate and I get rid of the Darlings, I'll be on the first flight out of Faulkner. The place makes my skin crawl. There are too many ghosts here, too many reasons to look over my shoulder.

The girls who die in this town don't get funerals, don't leave bodies. They simply vanish, as if the town itself swallows them alive.

The boys don't get funerals, either, but they don't disappear. The boys leave bodies—with nothing left inside them.

Our ghosts haunt Faulkner, too.

SELENA

ten

Harper Apple

Every week is the same. I go through the motions, but I'm frozen inside, as if it's not really me there at all. There's a Harper-sized doll in my place, someone I used to be but am no longer. The world has forgotten my existence. Only the Phantom remembers. I wait for him, for the clean smell of his house, the polished hardwood, the curl of his hard body around mine, the detachment I feel when he's inside me that's the closest thing to freedom I can imagine.

When I'm not there, I'm a ghost walking the street at night, waiting for him to come back.

He always does. Two days a week, he takes me home, feeds me, fucks me, sometimes videos me. He fills half his closet with new clothes for me, shoes, jewelry, an expensive purse to carry my phone and keys and wallet. Everything comes to his house in boxes or bags delivered to the door, so he doesn't have to leave the house except to get me and take me home.

He checks the ring he put through my bellybutton to make sure it's healed, puts dark-colored contact lenses in my eyes, touching my eyeballs like they are his own. I think, maybe he'll pluck out my eye and replace his blind one. But I don't move, don't try to stop him when he reaches between my lids and sets the thin lens over mine.

"Good girl," he says, stroking my cheek. "Beautiful."

He opens the closet door and sets me before the mirror. He tells me I'm perfect now, that I'm ready. I stare at the stranger in the mirror with dark eyes and dark lips and brown-black hair, and I think she looks ready, so he must be right. I don't ask him what I'm ready for. It doesn't matter.

That's the first night he wants a blowjob.

When the water gets shut off at home, I don't pay the bill. I ask the Phantom if I can start coming over on Sunday to shower. I got used to the daily showers at his house. He says no to extra time with him, but the next day, the water is back on. Mom says someone paid the rent through the rest of the year, too. I don't say anything. She shakes her head and says wherever I've been sneaking off to, keep on sneaking. Then she laughs and lights a cigarette.

"The rich ones always want a young piece of ass," she says, blowing smoke out the corner of her mouth. "If they're willing to pay for it, all the better."

I wonder again whose whore I've become.

"Better than the last one you had," Mom says. "I mind my own business, but that don't mean I didn't see you come home with bruises more than you should."

I don't tell her it wasn't a guy who gave me those bruises. It was a girl—lots of girls. I know I miss fighting, but I don't really feel it, the ache I used to feel when I was jonesing for a scuffle. I remember how satisfying the fight was, but I can't bring myself to really crave it the way I did. I don't feel much of anything anymore.

A few weeks later, I notice the dark green field outside the Phantom's window turning hay colored as the grasses droop in the late summer heat. Daisies and Black-Eyed Susans and wild asters dot the grass now. The Phantom stands there, looking out with his hands clasped behind his back, like he's looking over an empire and not an overgrown field of weeds.

"Have the Dolces contacted you?" he asks.

I have the same phone number, but no one ever contacts me. Why would they? I haven't contacted them, either. Everyone texted on the *OnlyWords* app, and I didn't download it on my new phone. I didn't have friends, anyway. Only the Dolce boys and their friends got close, and they left me to die. They washed their hands of me, and I have no need to change that.

I give my head a single shake, then realize he won't see it. "No."

He rubs his jaw. I can hear the rasp of stubble. "It's not enough," he mutters.

At dinner, he gives me a little black dress and tells me to put it on and do my hair. The dress is low-cut but not too revealing, and it hugs my curves and falls around me like it must have costs thousands of dollars. I roll on the stockings and garters he left with it. I put in the diamond teardrop earrings he left sitting on the dresser. I put my hair up the way he instructed and dab on some of the makeup he left sitting there for me. The lipstick is too dark, but I smear it over my lips anyway. I'm no longer startled when I see a stranger staring back at me from behind the closet door.

Does it matter who she is?

I know she's a good girl.

The Phantom walks behind me and puts a necklace around my neck. I can feel it resting cold against my chest, and it makes me shiver. I touch the charm, a diamond ballerina. He runs his knuckles up the back of my neck, skims his fingertips along my bare shoulders.

"You look like…" He bows his head, so I can only see his golden hair, not even his eyes or mouth to give away what he's thinking. I've never wondered what he's thinking before. It never mattered.

After dinner, he orders me to the bed without the usual shower. He doesn't undress me, just commands me to lie on my back while he pushes up my dress. Then he picks up his phone, angling it so it gets my whole body.

"No faces," I cry, my voice echoing in the high-end apartment. I throw my hands over my face, surprised I can still react that passionately to anything. He's shot dozens of homemade porn clips of his dick going into me, but he promised me no one would know it was me. Usually he fucks me from behind, anyway. I feel exposed on my back, vulnerable and scared in a way I haven't felt with him before. Suddenly, I'm shaking all over.

"Keep your hands over your face," he says, laying a reassuring hand on my thigh. "No one will know it's you."

He plays with my underwear, rubbing his cock against the outside of them, pulling them between my lips, then down my thighs. I pull a pillow over my face. He tugs it a little higher, setting my necklace straight before going back to work. I try not to feel what he's doing, rubbing his cock between my lips, getting me wet. Finally, he pushes inside me. He lifts my leg and swings it around so I'm lying on my side, so he's filming my hip with the tattoos. Someone could definitely recognize that. Above my hip, there's a D branded into my skin. What if my attackers see it and come back for me?

"Stop," I gasp.

"I'm almost done," he says, moving my leg back where it was, so I'm on my back. He cums quickly, shooting once over my belly before pushing back inside me to finish. He doesn't lower his phone until he's gotten the whole messy scene.

"Good girl," he says. "You were perfect."

Then he steps into the bathroom, and I hear the shower running.

I get up, my limbs shaking, my pulse racing. Something's happening to me. Something awakening, some horrible monster that's rising like a tidal wave inside me, like Godzilla emerging from the ocean. I can't breathe.

I want to race up the ladder onto the roof, to suck in the night and shriek into the sky. I want to sail over the edge, arms and legs wide, and soar to my death below.

Some impulse in me rebels at the expensive silk constricting my waist, the heavy pads of the bra. Suddenly, I'm revolted by the body I'm in, by what I've allowed to happen to it. I yank off the dress, tearing at the strangling fabric, kick off the heels he put me in, rip off the garters and stockings. I throw them aside and pace the floor in my bare feet, naked as an animal. My heart is skittering erratically around my chest. I feel trapped, caged, though he's never once told me I couldn't leave. In fact, he made me leave.

I've been free all along, and yet, I'm not free. He's treated me better than anyone ever has, than anyone should, and yet, I think I'll scream if I see his mask again, if he calls me his good girl one more time.

I pull off the earrings and reach for the box they were in, my fingers shaking. I lay them in the jewelry box. There's a sleek black paper bag with the jeweler's name on the side because he bought them just for me, maybe just today, and had someone deliver them.

There's a little tag stapled to the bag, the kind that comes on flowers. The kind that tells a delivery person where to send them, since the Phantom never leaves his apartment.

There's a name written on the tag. In looping cursive handwriting, the words *Mr. D*.

SELENA

eleven

Royal Dolce

My phone chimes with a notification on the seat beside me. I check the screen. Lo again. I haven't seen her all summer. After I found out what Harper did, I was in a bad place for a while. I don't remember much of the rest of senior year. The monster operated in my place, holding space for me until I was ready to come back.

When school ended, and I had time to think things through, I stopped thinking about what Harper had done and finally looked at the facts behind it. Of course, my mind went straight to the one person who could have told her about the Hockington—Gloria Walton. They'd gotten close, thanks to me, and I fucking paid for it. For letting a Darling into my life, letting her get in with my friends. That's what I get for letting anyone close to *me*.

Still, it's a dick move on my part not to at least give Lo a chance to defend herself. If she wasn't the one who told Harper, I cut her off for nothing. Harper could have bribed someone who worked there, seen me leaving with someone and tracked her down, rooted through my stuff or Dad's when she was at our house and somehow put it together.

It's better this way, though. Better not to have anyone around me who knows shit about my life.

When Lo found out about room 504, it felt safer to keep her close, to give her a reason not to tell anyone. Even if we never talked about it, never talked about our families the way I did with Harper or any real shit, our friendship was real.

But letting people into my life is a mistake. People blackmail and betray. And if it was her, if she told Harper… Well, Preston can fucking have her.

When my phone rings a minute later, I sigh and pick it up. We can talk once. Just to clear some things up. I'm not going to give her a ride anywhere, like I used to when she didn't have gas money. My car smells like a swamp from all the times I've dropped my muddy boots and rubber coveralls in here this summer. Gloria would ask questions, and I'm not about to answer.

"Hey," she says. "I figured you'd ghost me again."

"What's up, Lo?" I ask, my voice sounding weary.

"Do you use the *OnlyPics* app?"

"No," I say flatly, bristling at the insinuation. "Why would I?"

"That's not—I didn't mean you'd put stuff up."

"Why?" I ask. "You don't think people would pay to see my dick?"

"No!" she says quickly. "I mean, they would, if you wanted to put it up. That's not why I was asking, though."

"So, *you* don't want to see my dick? That's not how I remember it."

I'm being an asshole, but she's basically calling me a whore. She knows better than to ask if I use an app that's basically a sex worker platform. I don't get paid for sex, and I don't need to sell pictures of my body for money.

The *OnlyPics* app was supposed to be a companion to *OnlyWords*, which is a texting app with, as its name implies, only words in the messages. Everyone likes *OnlyWords*, but it has no photo sharing capabilities. So the same company made *OnlyPics* but it was basically a knock-off Instagram where you can't use captions and the hashtags are hidden, only used by the algorithms to know who to show them to.

It probably would have died a quick death if it weren't for the sex worker industry, who cashed in on three key features—the ability to add a link to profiles, where they added their payment link; the fifteen-second video limit, which let them put up teases to get people hooked; and the private chat feature, which let them send someone the rest of the video for whatever fee they wanted to negotiate or even video chat for a live show.

I don't use the app because I'm not an amateur porn star, and if I want to watch porn, I can do it for free like everyone else. If I need a live feed, I have a phone full of numbers of chicks who would be happy to put on a show for me, and I can do more than watch and jerk off. I'm not interested in that any more than I am this app.

"Okay, let's try this again," Gloria says. "You remember how Harper dropped out of school and disappeared off the face of the earth when you dumped her?"

SELENA

I stiffen in my seat, yanking the wheel to pull off at the nearest exit at the last second. The car behind me lays on the horn, but I ignore it. The noise is almost drowned by the pounding of blood in my ears. "Yeah, what about it?" I ask Gloria.

"Well, I think I found her."

"On a porn site?" I ask, hoping like hell someone just uploaded the video of her sucking teacher dick from last year. It fucks with my head to think that one year ago today, I didn't even know the name Harper Apple. It was another month before I would see her giving head in the parking lot behind the tampon factory.

"Hey, don't judge me," Gloria says. "Your brothers have been out of town all summer, and you've been ignoring me. I'm having a dry spell."

I could tell her the twins are back, but if she ran her mouth to Harper, I don't want her around my house, running her mouth to my brothers. So I point out the obvious. "There are more than three dicks in this town."

"Once you go Dolce, you never go back," she says lightly. "And anyway, I only saw it because she sent it to Dawson."

I'm glad I pulled over at the exit, because I'd probably run someone off the road right now if I were still driving. I grip the steering wheel with one hand and close my eyes.

My voice comes out so normal you'd think I was just a guy who dumped a girl and didn't give a fuck about what happened to her since. "I'm afraid to ask, but… Does your brother always share porn with you?"

"No, you weirdo," she says. "Someone DM'd him, and I've been obsessing about her all summer, so he showed it to me. He thinks it's funny as shit."

"Why are you obsessing about Harper?" I demand. What the fuck. Maybe I should have kept in touch with Lo. She could find out shit, maybe even the truth.

"I don't know," she says. "Don't you think it's weird that she just… Vanished? I mean, I'm not saying you're not worth going off the deep end over, or that you couldn't eviscerate her heart so completely she could never love again. She liked to play it cool, but she *really* loved you, Royal. Like, the kind of love that eats you alive, and you're never the same again."

SELENA

"Put that shit on a ninety-nine cent Valentines card. You could make real money."

"Keep playing you didn't feel it, too," she says. "But y'all broke a lot of hearts when you broke up, not just your own. Everyone figured you'd get back together after spring break."

"What's your point?" I snap. I don't need a fucking lecture about how much I disappointed everyone. She can add it to my fucking tab for all the times I fucked up and pissed off everyone who matters.

"My point is, even if Harper was devastated beyond repair, she's not the kind of chick who would let a breakup destroy her. She's stronger than that. You may be irreplaceable even to her, but you're still a boy. And it would take more than one boy to break Harper."

Maybe not one boy. But one boy who shared her with two more against her will? A broken hand and a rope she couldn't get free of, a swamp full of snakes more poisonous than her?

Yeah. That could do it.

"Then it obviously had nothing to do with me," I say. "Maybe she got hooked on Lady Alice or Pearl Lady or whatever the fuck they're calling it now, and she's selling herself to pay for it like a regular junkie. Hell, her mom basically said as much."

"It did blow up the scene right around that time…" Gloria muses.

"Maybe she'll tell you for the right price," I say flatly. "That's all she's ever cared about."

"Royal…"

"What?"

"Look, I don't know everything that went down between you, but I know what it's like to walk away from love. Just because you did the breaking up doesn't mean your heart wasn't decimated, too."

My laugh is brittle, like stepping on glass. "You're funny, Lo."

I could ask her, just come right out and be blunt, like King.

Did you tell Harper about the Hockington?

SELENA

But I can't acknowledge that much aloud. The hotel is its own world. When we leave, we don't mention what goes on there. I don't tell the school that Gloria is a scholarship kid. I elevate her, take her to prom, win her crowns. And she never tells anyone that I get a room there every few months.

Would she risk telling someone, knowing she could lose it all?

Even if she hated me, she loves her status too much to risk it.

What would make her turn on me like that? Harper didn't tell that creep where she found out the information. But it has to be Lo. No one else knows.

So, I hang up the phone, letting her think this is about a breakup. That it's not about a murder, not about a girl coming back from the dead, a ghost dragging her broken body from the swamp and crawling back into my brain to fuck with it even more.

I open my email, the one connected to the *OnlyWords* and *OnlyPics* apps by default because it's all made by the same company. I barely remember thumbing away the automatic notifications I got when someone sent me a message this summer. I ignored them all, knowing they were porn spam. My chest is hollow as I open one from my spam folder.

It tells me I have twenty-four new messages on *OnlyPics*. I follow the link and open my direct messages. The first one is a thumbnail of a video, sent this evening. If it's from Harper, she changed her handle from *BadApple*. For a few seconds, all I see is a closeup of part of her tattoo. I take it in, examining it until I realize it's her hip crease, and pressed along the back of her thigh, an expanse of pale skin. It takes me a minute to make sense of what I'm seeing. Whoever she's fucking, he's got her folded in half like her legs are over his shoulders while he nails her into the bed.

There's no caption, and there are no words even on the messenger, so I have to click on the profile to find an explanation.

Apple Cream Pie, $1k/min.

Time seems to skip. Some caveman part of me must take over, because the next thing I know it's five minutes later, and I'm five thousand dollars lighter, and I'm slamming my phone against the top of the steering wheel over and over. I feel it crunch and snap, but I keep pounding it until there's nothing left in my hand, and the pieces of it are scattered across my lap and the floor.

Time skips again. I'm in my driveway at home. Blood is dripping down the steering wheel and into my lap. I open my hand and find pieces of glass jutting from my palm in a dozen places. And all I think about is that day my car was bombed, and Harper tried to pick the glass from my face with her tiny, careful fingers.

I climb out of the car. There's a black Jaguar parked on the gravel, a tall figure leaning against it. I walk up to him. Something in me seems to have been knocked loose, and I think I might fucking kill him, even though it's just Oliver Finnegan, who never goes inside. He doesn't approve of the family business.

"Hullo, Royal," he says, his Irish accent distorting the words. Or maybe it's the ringing in my ears. "Am I in your spot? I can move the car."

"Don't worry about it."

He cocks his head, his weird, pale eyes taking in the blood on my pants, my hand. "You alright, mate?"

I shrug and head for the house. Just as I'm about to step inside, his brother steps out, a black duffle in one hand, probably full of cash or those fucking pearls everyone's on about. Colin Fucking Finnegan. My eyes narrow, my fists clenching until I can feel the glass biting deeper, piercing through my skin and into the muscle and sinew.

"Was it you?" I grind out. Part of me knows it's impossible, but maybe he sent the photo on his way here, or maybe he took it earlier. I need Baron to find the date signature on a video, if it's even possible. For all I know, Harper's dead, and she took those videos herself while we were together. If she'd sell my dignity for a scholarship, why wouldn't she sell videos of herself fucking other guys when she was with me?

"Whatever it was, I bet it was me," Colin says, flashing me a knowing grin that shows off his chipped front tooth. "You still sore about that beating you took last spring?"

"You know what it's about."

"If it's not that, you're pissed you didn't get a cut of this," he says, jiggling the bag.

"Don't fucking push me right now," I warn.

SELENA

His creepy eyes go smug. "Or… You still on about that whore? I figured that's what set you off last spring. Everyone in town knows I fucked her first. Are you just finding out?"

"Where is she?" I demand, grabbing him around the neck and slamming him up against the wall. "Where the fuck do you have her, you cum guzzling, festering wad of infected dick cheese?"

A cocky, defiant grin stretches his lips. "Aww, did you catch something off her?" he asks. "Wasn't me, mate. I popped that cherry when there were barely three hairs on her pussy. Haven't touched her since."

I don't know exactly what happens next. I don't see Colin Finnegan in front of me anymore. All I see is red.

The next thing I know, my brothers and Dad are holding me down on the steps, and Oliver and their uncle are holding Colin back while he curses and struggles and spits. The white gravel is painted red like the day the Darlings vandalized our house, but this time, it's blood.

"Let me up," I growl, shoving off the step and wrenching free of my family. I stalk toward Colin, who writhes like a cat getting a bath. I can feel blood trickling down my face, the jagged edges of a few broken teeth, and the throb of one eye that's already swelling shut. But I don't feel pain. The other thing that lives inside me has swallowed it, and I can't feel a thing.

"Come on," Colin yells, dancing in the grip of his brother. "Let's do it again. I can go all night. Whoo! I feel alive!"

I stop in front of him, ignoring my brothers, who have rushed up behind me to grab me if I lose my shit again. But I'm calm now.

"Enjoy it while it lasts," I say to Colin. My lip is broken and swollen so thick my words come out slurred. "If I find out you're the one who sent those videos, you won't be alive much longer."

I turn and walk inside. I don't know why I care. I watched two guys fuck her. I gave them permission. I made sure to watch, so I knew I could never want her again, never think she was mine. I broke her on purpose, but piece by piece, I'm the one falling to pieces.

SELENA

twelve

Harper Apple

"Are you Mr. D?" I demand, standing in the Phantom's bedroom, my whole body quaking. I hold the tag in between my finger and thumb, waving it at him. He just walked out of the shower, his body all steamy, a towel around his hips, mask over his face.

He shrugs. "What about it?"

Anger seethes through me. "That's how you knew where I was that night. Isn't it?"

He opens his dresser and pulls out his underwear. I know where he keeps them. I know where everything in his apartment is. But I didn't know his name, have never seen his face. I come when he calls, practically live here two days a week, like a goddamn whore. He promised he'd fuck me one day, and now he has.

I don't know why it matters suddenly. I never cared before.

He nods vaguely toward the windows. "I keep an eye on things."

"On me," I say, sinking onto the edge of the bed. "You keep an eye on me."

"I told you, I can be anyone you want me to be," he says with a haughty little smirk. "As long as you're you, *Miss A*."

"As long as I'm Royal's fuck toy," I correct him. "That's why you take those pictures, isn't it? To send to him and show him what you've done to me."

"What I've done to you?" he asks, turning to face me after pulling on a pair of sweats. They hang low on his narrow hips. Above them, the ridges of his abs are carved deep and sharp. His body is a finely chiseled sculpture. I've never noticed, but he's beautiful, even without a face.

"What about what *he* did?" He paces forward, stalking, his voice laced with fury that makes me shrink back on the bed, as if he could hurt me more than I've been hurt. As if he could take something from me that he hasn't been taking all along.

SELENA

"You changed me," I whisper.

"I saved you."

I stare up at him, feeling guilty for feeling anything but gratitude. He works out, takes care of himself, wears exquisite clothes to work at his standing desk with three monitors, an ergonomic keyboard, and a fancy Mac computer. I'm the one who should be ashamed. I don't take care of myself until he tells me to. He tells me to shower, puts me in fancy clothes, makes me look like a girl who could be, in some fairytale in his mind, deserving of him.

And he treats me like I am. He cooks me fancy dinners and buys me everything I need or could want without me having to ask. He even took care of my mother. I don't treat him half as well. I don't cook or offer to help clean up. I don't even talk to him when I come over. While he cooks, I sit curled on his fine leather sofa, sipping his fine wine. The only thing I do for him in return for everything he's done is spread my legs.

If he's made me a whore, I've let him do it. The first day he bought me something, the phone, I could have said no. But I didn't. I let him dress me up like a doll, treat me like property, and fuck me like a whore. If anything, he's shown me he values me more than I value myself. He bought me fucking diamonds. A girl like me, I have no right to even hope for this kind of man, this kind of treatment. I'm lucky to be his whore.

But for the first time in months, I want to speak, to voice my desires.

"You're right," I say. "You've treated me well. But I'm done being your whore."

"You're not—" He breaks off, pressing his lips together and shaking his head. "I didn't mean to make you feel that way. That's not how I see you, Harper."

"How do you see me?"

He stares at me a long moment. "I just wanted to take care of you," he says at last. "I saw what they did to you. You're not the only person…" He shakes his head again. "And yeah, I wanted to fuck you to piss off Royal. I'll admit that. But I never saw you as a whore. I only gave you what you needed."

SELENA

"Like these?" I ask, upturning the jeweler's bag. The box falls out, the lid askew, one of the diamonds dangling out the side like something obscene.

"Fair enough," he says, moving across the room and sitting heavily on the bottom of the bed. "Maybe I had selfish reasons. But I never thought you owed me. I know you won't believe me. I know what I look like. You think I can't get laid unless I buy a girl diamonds. And you're right."

"What about your girlfriend?" I ask, my voice thick.

He scoffs. "I don't have a girlfriend. Look at me."

"So you dressed me up and pretended you did," I say, feeling like some weird blow-up doll. I've acted like one. I haven't been a whole person since before the swamp. I've been a doll, broken into a million pieces, and he's pieced some of them back together—at least on the outside. But he can't fix me inside. He can reach in, but he won't find anything to piece back together. I'm hollow.

"I never pretended to be a good guy," he says. "Don't act shocked that I'm exactly who I was all along."

"But you never told me who you were," I point out.

"You never asked."

"I did."

We sit side by side for a while, neither of us speaking.

"You don't want to know who I am," he says. "Look at me. Look at what I've become."

I could say the same thing.

*

When I tell Mr. D I'm not coming back, he doesn't say anything. But he doesn't get ready to take me home as usual. I ask if he's taking me home, and he says no, but he doesn't stop me when I take his keys. I keep waiting for him to come after me, but he just studies me, his face behind that infuriating blank mask, his one good eye watching me leave.

In the garage, I climb into his truck. I'm sure he's going to come down and stop me. My hands are shaking so hard I can barely get the key in. I open the garage on the bottom level of his building, and I drive out. I keep checking the rearview, sure I'll see him coming after me. But he lets me go.

SELENA

Some sick part of me deflates when I turn into my driveway and he's not there. Not even Mr. D thinks I'm worth hunting down. I climb out of the truck and go inside. Nothing has changed. But everything has.

Without the Tuesday and Thursday excursions, I stop leaving the house. There's no point. I don't even return his truck. It sits like an oversized monster in our driveway, drawing attention from local gang members and Mom's conquests, who stand around it wondering how good my ass must be to warrant such payment. I hide the keys inside a tear in my box spring, knowing that Mom will take off with it in a second if I leave the keys. I sleep with a switchblade in one hand for the men who come in almost every night, as if my fall from grace has given them permission to treat me like her. Or maybe they can smell my brokenness, my weakness, the way I can smell alcohol on their breath.

And even though I was sure I felt nothing all those months, now that I don't see the Phantom, there's an ache left inside me that he once soothed. When I wake myself up croaking feebly, from a dream where I'm gagged, silenced as I try to force sound from my strangled throat, there are only blankets to wrap around me instead of his strong, silent arms.

I stop leaving the house, stop doing anything. I can't remember why it mattered to be clean, to eat, to live. One evening, as I'm lying corpselike in my bed, a tap sounds at my grimy window. I'm so startled I sit up before my brain can kick in and say what it says about everything—it's not worth it. It doesn't matter.

Outside my window, a pale face hovers in the twilight. I squint to see through the dirty window. Blue holds up a pack of cigarettes and points to it with her free hand, mouthing something at me through the glass.

I sigh and drag my ass off the bed and open the window.

"Wanna smoke?" she asks, waving the pack at me.

"Okay."

"Really?" she asks, smiling wide. Her hair has grown out, so only the bottom few inches are a faded blue.

I shrug. "I'll be out in a minute."

I'm already regretting it, my body telling me to crawl back into the warm, welcoming nest of my bed and sink back into the hazy half-sleep oblivion of my life. Annoyance flares inside me. Why is Blue coming to the window? She probably just wants what everyone else wants—gossip.

I trudge outside, where she's standing by the truck. "Can you take me for a ride?" she asks shyly.

I shake my head. "Didn't bring the keys."

"Oh," she says, her face falling. "Well, do you want to go for a walk?"

I shrug. She takes that as a yes and starts walking, and even though I want to go back in the house and fall facedown into my bed, I shuffle along after her, resentment growing with each step. August in Arkansas is hot as the streets of hell, and it's so humid you can't even sweat to cool off. I wish I hadn't come out, that I was in my own bed in the feeble air-conditioning that Mr. D paid for. I'm sure he was the one who put the thousand dollars toward our electric bill, just as he was the one who paid our water. I should be grateful, but I only feel used.

Blue slows to walk beside me, handing me a cigarette. She lights up before passing me the lighter. I light up, too. The bitter taste of tobacco invades my mouth, sharp but still familiar after months without. I inhale long and deep, letting it sink into my lungs. A rush of dizziness races through me, my fingers shaking with the high.

We reach the end of the block and turn right, toward the old white church and cemetery.

"I know I sound like a teacher right now, but, like, are you in some kind of trouble?" Blue asks at last.

"Haven't you heard?" I say flatly. "I'm a whore now."

"I heard a rumor that you were making Pearl, but damn. You got that for fucking someone? I mean, that's a really nice truck, Harper. Most people only get, like, a hundred bucks or something."

"Guess I'm a high-class whore."

She's quiet as we continue to the end of the street, where there's nowhere to go but the church. I'd probably burst into flame if I stepped through a church's doors, so I stop walking. Blue moves through the gravel lot and opens the cemetery gate, leaving it open for me as she steps inside. There are a few cars parked by the fence. Beyond the cemetery, a huge oak sprawls its branches wide, as if embracing the last streaks of orange in the deep blue of the evening sky.

SELENA

I wonder if the Phantom is on his roof, watering his tomatoes.

I sigh and follow Blue, irritated by my thoughts. She stops at a plain headstone with a single bunch of plastic flowers on it, now bleached an indiscriminate color by the sun.

"My dad," she says, ashing her cigarette on the grave.

I nod and drag hard on mine. "At least you know where he is."

A guy at a grave under the oak's branches stands from where he was kneeling and tosses back his shiny blond hair. There's something familiar about him, and for a second, I think it's Colt, but when he turns our way, I see that it's a football player from Faulkner—*the* football player. I remember dropping Lindsey at the bottom of his driveway, and how scared I was to go back and face Royal, knowing he'd see it as a betrayal that I'd helped a Darling. I should have listened to that fear.

Chase jerks his chin at us in a nod as he passes our row of headstones, but he doesn't say anything. He probably doesn't remember me, and Blue isn't the type to draw attention.

"I know you dropped out of school," Blue says after he's gone. "Even I wouldn't do that. You used to be so obsessed with it. You're smart, Harper."

I sigh. "You really do sound like a teacher."

"No, I mean, you're smart enough that I'm sure you know what you're doing," she says, holding up a hand. "If you could get that fancy truck out of it…"

"Then I must be good?" I ask. "What, you want sex tips? Twenty-five hacks to make him cum in under a minute?"

"No." She watches me from the corner of her eye as she drags on her cigarette. "But if your guy has friends…"

"You'd whore yourself out for a truck?"

She shrugs, avoiding my eyes.

I know I'm being a bitch. I've fucked guys for nothing. For less than nothing. I didn't even get a choice out of it, let alone a truck. I said no, and they took it anyway. They didn't care about what I wanted any more than a guy paying cares what his whore likes. Why not take some control over it, sell it like the commodity it is? It's too late for me. They've already taken what they wanted and left me to die. But Blue's not a store that's been ransacked, everything of value stolen, leaving it barren and worthless to looters.

"He didn't give me the truck," I admit, tossing my cigarette butt on her father's grave. "I just borrowed it. And then I didn't return it."

She gives me a slow smile, looking impressed. "You stole it?"

"Kind of," I say. "But I don't think he'll call the cops. And he did give me other stuff. Jewelry and clothes and shit. I don't think he's looking for an escort, but I'll see if he has a friend, okay?"

She nods, tossing her cigarette butt in the withered grass near mine. "Thanks," she says. "And Harper... Can I ask you one more thing?"

I shrug.

"If something happens to me... I mean, I have Olive. If I ever don't come home, can you get her and keep her safe?"

"What about your mom?"

She shakes her head, scuffing her toe in the dirt.

I swallow hard, knowing I can't take care of a kid, not the way she does. But for girls like us, trusted adults are few and far between. They're no more likely to be a help to us than the cops. We make our own way in the world, and we only have ourselves, and sometimes, each other. I know Blue wouldn't ask me if she had anyone else.

I nod and attempt a smile, but it feels more like a grimace. "Okay."

We walk back in silence. By the time we get home, it's mostly dark. I take down the tailgate, and we sit on it and smoke another cigarette in silence. When we finish, we climb down, and Blue wipes her hands on her jeans. "School starts in a week," she says. "Are you coming back?"

I know I should care, but I can't summon the energy. My scholarship is gone. There's no way out. I've given up, accepted the fact that I'll be just like my mother.

"I don't know," I say. "I hadn't really thought about it."

But later, lying in my bed, I think maybe it's time I did.

SELENA

thirteen

Royal Dolce

I open Baron's door and pull up short. Lo is sprawled on her back across the California king, her arms wide and her blonde hair fanned out around her while her legs stretch up the upholstered headboard. Her skirt pools around her hips, exposing long, tan legs.

"What the fuck are you doing here?" I ask.

She sits up, throwing her hair back like a fucking stripper and curling her legs on the bed beside her. "Oh, hey, Royal," she says, like she didn't sell me out to a snake.

"Why are you in my brother's room?" I ask again, my voice hard.

"Unlike you, your brothers didn't kick me to the curb the second prom was over," she says. "So, I'm hanging out. What does it look like?"

"Do you really want me to answer that question?"

She runs her fingers through her blonde strands, bleached from a summer on the beach, and straightens her spine. "In case you've forgotten, I'm still in high school," she says. "While you and Dawson go traipsing off to college, I'm stuck here for another year before Yale notices me."

"And letting two guys take turns with you all year is going to get you noticed? I'm not sure you understand how college admission works."

"Fuck you, Royal. Just because Harper ran off when you dumped her, that doesn't give you a license to make everyone else as miserable as you."

"You sure about that?" I mutter, unable to hold onto my anger when she's looking at me with such unflinching, raw hurt in her eyes.

Baron emerges from the bathroom and nods at me before dropping into his recliner. "What's up?"

"Get her out of here," I say. It's easier to be a dick through him. "She's not welcome here anymore."

Baron raises a brow and reaches for his cup of suckers.

"What did I ever do to you?" Lo demands.

SELENA

I could tell her, but I don't want to do it in front of Baron, so I don't bother. "Go home," I say. "I need to talk to Baron."

"Nobody told me there was a party going on," Duke says, stopping in the doorway. "Where's the beer?" He swings open the glass door of Baron's minifridge and pulls out a handful of bottles.

"That's why I'm here," Lo says, shaking her hair into place and reaching for a beer. "Your parents are so much cooler than mine."

"Forget it," I snap, smacking Duke's hand away when he holds out a beer.

"Hold up," Baron says. "What do you need?"

"To know when a video was shot. I'll come back when you're done running a train on Lo."

"Ooh, is this about Harper's porn site?" Lo asks, swinging her legs off the side of the bed.

I glare at her. This is what I get for letting her in, for letting myself use her to fill a hole another girl left in my life. She's wormed her way into everything, and I can't extricate her from the hundred little places she's cemented herself.

Insults don't work with her. She's oblivious or unperturbed by words.

"What?" Duke howls. "Harper has a porn site?"

"I just need to know when it was filmed," I say, glowering at Baron. "The rest of you can leave."

"Fuck that," Duke says. "I want to see Harper doing porn!"

"Come on," Gloria says, taking his arm. "I have the link. I can show you."

"Show him that shit and see what happens," I growl.

Lo raises a brow and takes a sip of her beer. "So, I can stay?"

I glare back at her. Why am I protecting Harper? She either filmed that before we met, and she's a fucking liar, or when we were together, and she's a liar *and* a cheater.

Or, she filmed it recently, and she's not sitting around thinking about protecting me, that's for damn sure.

"Whatever," I grit out. "Stay, you fucking dyke."

Gloria smirks at me and leans into Duke, who puts an arm around her. "We just want to help," he says, giving me a sloppy grin. "Right, Lo?"

SELENA

"Exactly," she says like some smug bitch who just bested me. At least this way I can control what she sees. I know she can't afford to watch even a minute of the video on her own, but she's not above using Duke to get what she wants.

I pull it up on Baron's computer while he slides to his second monitor to watch.

"Apple cream pie?" Gloria says, crossing her arms and looking over my shoulder. "Clever."

"Damn," Duke says, giving a low whistle. "A grand a minute? She sure thinks highly of that worn out pussy."

"Shut up," I snap, turning to Baron. "Can you tell when it was shot?"

"If she's getting that for the video, you think she's getting more for the sex?" Lo asks.

"Dude, that's not how porn works," Duke says. "That's how it's legal. You don't get paid for sex. You get paid for the performance."

Baron shakes his head and pulls his sucker out of his mouth to talk. "You can't access this. It was a live feed streamed to your messages. All these were. Once the show's over, it's over. He may have recorded them while he was fucking her, but you only got the live stream."

"I can't believe she sent you those," Gloria says. "That's fucking cold. What did you do to the poor girl?"

That's a question I will never answer. I always meant to wreck her, just like we did Mabel. But if I found out Mabel was doing porn, I'd shake my head and maybe laugh, thinking we really ruined her for other guys.

Harper isn't Mabel, though.

"It could be someone else," Duke says, but there's no conviction in his voice. We all know it's her. Even if someone got the exact same tattoos as Harper, she wouldn't have a body like that.

"Yeah," Lo says. "That's not her *OnlyWords* handle. Maybe someone else sent it. Which of your enemies would send you something like that to fuck with you? Colt?"

That's not a question we're going to answer when she's in the room.

Baron scrolls up through a dozen thumbnails she sent me this summer, none of which I watched. "Here's a recorded clip."

SELENA

He pays up, pops the sucker in his mouth, and starts the video. He goes to work, doing his magic to dissect whatever coding is behind the video, not even watching the screen. I can't watch, either. When I see the dick come out of the guy's pants, I think I'm going to fucking lose my sanity.

"Turn it off," I snap.

The minute runs out before there's a dick in her, but it's no better. I already saw five minutes that I can never forget. I can feel myself slipping away, under the surface where it's calm. Baron watches me for a second, like he's waiting to see if I'll lose it like I did when I saw that sadistic fuck Colin coming out of our house. But I'm in control, just like he is. Duke's too busy feeling up Gloria and dumping beer down his throat to think right now, but Baron's sharp. He knows what this means.

"What can you tell?"

"It was filmed this summer," he says quietly. For a minute, none of us speak. Even Duke's finally gotten serious, his face sober as his gazes meet ours.

She's alive.

I don't know what I expected, something welling up inside, rage or relief, but nothing comes. I knew she was alive. Some part of me always knew. I didn't go wander the swamp thinking I'd find her bones. I didn't sit under the tree where we left her to mourn her each evening. Maybe some fucked up part of me was waiting for her to return, to tell me I had it all wrong or at least explain herself.

It wasn't something rational. Of course she's not going to go back to the place we tried to kill her. She's not me. But some unconscious part of my mind must have been waiting for that. An explanation as to how she could do that. How she could have fooled me so hard. Something to convince me she wasn't like all the other Darlings.

But she is. She played me, she took her punishment, and she moved on with some other guy. And now, she's trying to destroy me for what I did to her. She knows me so well that she knows even after what I did, I can't let her go. She knows she still has claws in me, and she's going to make me pay until she drives me over the edge. I tried to kill her, but she's the one who will succeed. She'll keep going until I'm dead. Then she'll be satisfied.

"If it makes you feel any better, I don't think she filmed that," Gloria says, looking at me with something way too fucking close to pity.

"That's obvious. The guy is holding the phone," Duke says, gesturing to the thumbnail left once Baron rejects the prompt to put in another thousand to keep watching.

"I meant, that's a dude's homemade porn," Lo says. "Not a girl's."

I narrow my eyes at her. "What, you make porn now? Since when are you the expert?"

"No," she says slowly. "Stop being a dick and I might tell you."

I cross my arms and glare down at her. "Explain."

"I'm just saying, a dude's going to get all up close and personal with the act of penetration. Like that." She gestures to the screen. "If it was Harper trying to make you eat your heart out, she'd give you something less crude than a closeup shot of her lady business. She'd give you her face, some inviting smiles or come-hither looks. She'd drive you crazy, make you wonder if she'd go through with it before she got to the killing blow. She'd want you to see her face when he put it in."

"Dude, you're evil," Duke says, pushing her away.

Gloria grins like he just gave her the highest compliment and takes a swig of beer.

"There's plenty of tease in the live video," I say. "He's rubbing his dick all over her. And she'd never show her face. She's more obsessed with college than you are."

"I stand by my reasoning," she says. "Even if she wasn't showing her face, she'd still tease. She'd undress for the camera, touch herself, let you see her climbing on the dude. This is just fucking."

"That's the good stuff," Duke points out.

"See?" Gloria gestures to him, widening her eyes at me. "I rest my case."

"Or maybe she's not making porn for you, Lo," Baron argues. "Maybe she's a pro and knows what guys like."

"Hm, I doubt it," Gloria says. "I mean, I suppose it's possible. But I'm willing to bet a guy is behind that screen name."

"You need to leave," I say.

SELENA

She's probably right, but I need to talk to my brothers now, figure out a game plan. I know what they'll say already, though. The problem was taken care of. She didn't die, but she kept her mouth shut. It doesn't matter where she is or what happened to her as long as she didn't go to the cops or make trouble for our family. It's fine. She disappeared just like Mabel. She's gone. That's what we wanted, after all.

"Walk me home," Lo says. "And I'll go quietly."

I grit my teeth, but she just sips her beer and waits. I yank the bottle out of her hand and shove it at Duke. "Let's go."

I grab her by the back of the neck and haul her out of there. I'd let her walk her ass home on her own if I trusted her not to lurk and snoop. She's worse than Harper when she gets something in her head. When we step out into the baking August heat, I give her a little shove toward her house.

"This is the last time I'm walking you home," I snap.

"Fine," she says. "I knew it would be."

For a minute, we stalk along beside each other, neither of us speaking.

"You told her, didn't you?" I ask at last.

"Told who what?"

"Don't fucking bullshit me, Lo," I say. "She knew, and there's only one person who could have told her."

Gloria's eyes widen, and she visibly gulps. "I…"

"Don't," I snap. "I don't want any excuse. I just want to hear you say it."

"I'm sorry," she blurts.

We stop at the end of her driveway. She stares up at me with her big blue eyes shiny with crocodile tears. Fuck her. She doesn't get to cry about fucking betraying me, trying to make me feel bad. I have to ball my hands into fists so I don't reach out and choke the shit out of her.

"Say it."

"I didn't mean to," she wails, a tear spilling down her cheek.

I hold up a hand. "I don't want to hear a single word out of your mouth except a confession," I say. "So until you have that, don't speak to me. Don't text or call. And don't let me see you in my fucking house. My brothers are too good for your conniving, low-class, fake-ass family."

SELENA

I hit her where it hurts—her family's financial situation. She's not the only one who knows secrets. I know they're all on scholarship because they can't afford Willow Heights. Hell, Dad sponsored their scholarships last year. I know that everything about them is as fake as the manicured lawn and custom landscaping outside the house they inherited from an uncle because they were destitute.

Gloria swallows and wipes her tears away, squaring her shoulders and facing me like the tough chick she is and not the sniveling little bitch she plays to get sympathy.

"I told her," she says. Her voice is weak, barely above a whisper. But I respect her for having the decency to say it to my face.

"I know," I say. "And now you can be dead to me, too."

fourteen

Harper Apple

I look back over my shoulder at the prestigious façade of Willow Heights one last time before climbing into Mr. D's truck. It feels surreal in a different way from when I'd walk in Royal's world. Now, it just seems unreal altogether, like coming back for a ten-year reunion, a different girl in a different decade than the one I was when I went here.

No other kids were here, since school hasn't started. I just had to talk to the admin, who are here getting ready for everyone to return. Even though public school starts in August, Willow Heights' students don't return until the first of September, so there was no chance of running into anyone I know. I think about Blue as I drive home, about inviting her to go for a ride in the truck today. I try to remember what it was like to be a girl who thought a ride in a Cadillac was exciting, but I'm not sure if I was ever a girl like that. I don't remember what kind of girl I used to be.

But I know that Blue shook some sense into me, even if she did it in her quiet, unassuming way. I'm too smart to give up without a fight, too smart to drop out of school. Maybe I'll never get into an Ivy League school or even the University of Arkansas, but a community college is within reach. I got the runaround at school, but the counselor said I could probably make up most of the work I missed and not be held back, since I'm already older than most people in my grade. I'll have to pull double duty, making up work from junior year at WHPA while going to Faulkner, but at least I'll graduate.

Or hell, maybe I'll leverage my connection with Mr. D to get me and Blue jobs as high class hookers and live the high life, spreading our legs for our keep. It's not like I have any special skills, anyway. Lying on my back is a pretty leisurely way to make a living.

I pull up onto the side of the road in front of our house, since Mom's car is in the driveway. She's halfway out the front door, struggling to haul a mountain of grocery bags inside with both hands, a cigarette tucked in the corner of her lips. I hop down and go to help her drag the haul inside.

"What's the occasion?" I ask. "You having a party or win the lottery?"

She stands up and flicks her hair out of her eyes, leaning a palm on the edge of the counter and surveying me. "I didn't buy all this shit," she says. "I figured you got paid."

She cackles as I shrug and start putting away groceries. If Mr. D wants to feed me even though I didn't return his truck, I'm not about to complain. The bags are full of stuff we never buy—instead of discount hamburger, there's steak; instead of instant rice, it's quinoa; instead of canned green beans there are bags of fresh vegetables I never ate before living with Mr. D and sure as fuck don't know how to cook. What do people even do with artichokes?

When I'm done putting stuff up, I head back out to grab the packet of stuff the counselor gave me to look over and fill out. I'm not motivated the way I used to be, when I wanted to leave Faulkner, but it's as if I'm coming out of shock. My brain is still moving slow, processing things in a disjointed way. Which explains why I'm three steps out the

SELENA

front door before I see what's waiting for me. My heart stops in my chest.

Royal Dolce is standing by the Escalade.

My brain balks for a second, as if it can't comprehend this vision out of my worst nightmare and fit it into reality. Instinct tells me to turn and run back into my house, to slam and lock the door, to crawl back into the bed that I never should have left. He's here. Everything I did was for nothing. Mr. D was never going to risk showing his face to the world to expose the Dolces. He just sat there in his apartment with me all summer, doing nothing.

I should have known Royal was untouchable.

I should have known the Darlings had already lost.

I should have known I was the only loser left in the game.

But here's the thing about someone taking everything you own—your body, your soul—and destroying even the darkest, most hidden parts of it.

There's nothing left for them to break.

So I don't run back in the house. Because fuck Royal Dolce. Fuck them all. I'll drive over him if he tries to stop me.

I march straight up to the truck, the muddy splatters on the sides somehow endearing instead of sloppy. Royal just stands there watching me approach, his expression almost wary, like I'm some demon risen from the dead after he watched the life drain out of me with his own eyes.

I suppose I am.

"What's the matter, never seen a girl in a truck before?" I ask as I unlock the door with the fob. "Or do you think I'm a ghost?"

"Why the fuck are you in that truck?" he asks.

"Maybe it's mine," I say. "A whore needs her wheels."

"That's not your truck," he says, glaring at me from hollowed out eyes with shadows under them, like he hasn't slept in days.

"What, you know every vehicle in Faulkner?"

"I know every Darling's vehicle," he counters. "And why are you dressed like… That?" His gaze travels down my body, and I have to fight the urge to cover myself, though there's nothing sexual in his look. It's an examination, as detached as Baron's assessing gaze.

SELENA

I was just going to get something from the back seat, but I know I won't be able to walk back inside and act normal. Not when he's here, when he can find me so easily, come back for me. I might act tough, but inside… The screams I can't force out in my nightmares are playing on repeat, the time loop I never visit spinning at breakneck speed.

I need to feel bigger, more in control, to have something solid to hold onto. I climb up into the high seat, so I'm taller and surrounded by steel, and I turn to face him. "What's this about, Royal? You're afraid that since I lived after you tried to kill me, again, that there's a witness to what you did? Don't worry, even if I went to the cops, I'm sure your whole football team would back you up and say they didn't rape me that night."

"What are you talking about?" Royal demands, stepping toward the open door of the truck.

My entire being recoils, and my heart beats once, so hard I have to press my fist to my chest to keep from crying out.

He stops, watching me with that dark, brooding gaze.

I force myself to speak like I'm not smothering on the air itself. "Even if I filed a report, and could afford a lawyer, who do you think a jury would believe?" I ask quietly. "One whore from the bad side of town, or the entire football team full of golden boys from Willow Heights?"

His jaw clenches, and he rests a hand on the open door. It's not a threatening pose, but all I can think is that I can't close the door now. I'm trapped. My body is screaming at me to scramble across the seat, jump out the far door, and run until my heart explodes. But I won't give him the satisfaction of seeing my fear.

"It wasn't the whole football team," he says, his voice low, a stitch between his brows like he's genuinely confused. "You know that. You rode in the car with us. It was just the twins."

"Until you left," I whisper, wishing I'd never engaged, that I'd turned and run the other way when I saw him waiting at the truck. We stare at each other for a long moment, and the rest of the world seems to fall away—the buzz of crickets, the stifling afternoon heat, the smell of exhaust and baked asphalt.

"Harper…" Royal says at last. His eyes, his voice, are so full of the pain that always got to me. I thought it made us kindred spirits, that we were both battling some inner darkness. Now I know the truth. Nothing can help him. His evil knows no bounds. I'm not the demon. He's the demon, the one who possessed me and stole my soul, leaving nothing behind. I'm the empty shell of a girl, all that's left after the demon gets what it wants and moves on to the next victim.

"No," I hiss, turning to kick his arm off the door. I put all the force I can behind it, and he actually winces, rubbing his arm as I reach for the door handle. "Don't you dare apologize. You're a sick, broken man, and now I'm broken, too. I will never recover from what you did to me. You don't get to make yourself feel better about it now."

I slam the door in his face and fumble the keys into the ignition, my heart racing and my hands shaking so hard it takes three tries to get the truck started. I don't look to see if he's clear of the vehicle. I slam on the gas, and it lurches forward, powerful and dangerous. It's not enough, though. I'm like Royal in his big, bulked up body with his little shattered soul hiding inside. I still feel small and helpless inside the huge monster. I'll never feel safe again.

BROKEN DOLL

When I get to Mr. D's, I sit in the garage and punch the steering wheel until my knuckles bleed, and for the first time since it happened, I let myself cry.

SELENA

fifteen

Harper Apple

My head is pounding. I blink into the long rays of warm summer sun and sit up, grabbing onto the chaise lounge when a wave of dizziness hits. It takes me a second to get my bearings, to take in the red jalapeños dangling from their plants and the towering sunflowers overhead. I wince at the incessant noise of cicada song, sawing into my brain instead of soothing me with its familiarity, and the constant, hot wind that blows steadily from the south. My heart races erratically, and I stumble to my feet, gasping for breath past the ache inside me.

I want to—need to—step off the edge, to make it happen this time.

Last time, the thought felt like a question, something to ponder absently, the consequences being equal either way. This time, it feels like an answer, the only possible solution.

It only takes a moment to cross the roof. I'm almost at the edge when Mr. D grabs my arm and spins me around. He's not gentle this time. His lips are set in a tight line, and he keeps his grip on my arm and marches me back to the chair. He pushes me down into it, the plush outdoor furniture he bought for me to sit on that probably cost more than the furniture in my house. My head throbs when my ass hits the cushion.

He sits beside my knees and just looks at me, his good eye piercing into me until I have to look away.

"What happened?" I ask.

"You led Royal here," he says flatly.

My voice comes out as barely more than a breath, almost stolen by the wind. "What?"

He rakes his hand through his blonde hair, which he's cut since I saw him last, when I left him. "I just… Why here, Harper?"

SELENA

I close my eyes. My fingers shake, and I have to ball them into fists to steady myself. "I was bringing back your truck," I whisper.

"And you don't have a garage."

His words are uninflected. It's not a question.

I don't argue. I remember coming back, parking the truck, closing the garage to put one more wall between me and Royal. But he found me, anyway. And now he found Mr. D, and I'm not safe here, either. There's nowhere safe.

Even worse, I exposed Mr. D. Will he have to give up his beautiful home? His plants? His life?

"I'm sorry," I whisper, tears brimming in my eyes.

Words aren't enough to fix what I've done.

"Maybe I should have gotten you help," he says with a weary sigh. "Instead of thinking you'd heal here if I gave it time."

"No," I say, sitting up and pulling my knees up to my chest. "It's not your fault."

He turns to me, swallowing and searching my eyes. "Do you need to be under surveillance? I can't change what I did, but I can take you now, if you need it."

I shake my head. "I don't need that."

He takes my hand between both of his, slowly threading his tattooed fingers through mine. "What do you need, Harper?"

I remember all the times he told me he needed more, that my information wasn't good enough. Maybe it wasn't enough because he couldn't ask for what he really needed. He seemed so cold, so heartless. But he's not the same in person. He's just as broken as the rest of us.

I remember how it felt to be needed by Royal, how much I needed that. Maybe that's all Mr. D ever needed, too, even if he didn't know it. Maybe that's all any of us need, at least once in our lives. I don't know what I need anymore, but I still remember how to give. So I swallow past the ache in my throat and give him the answer he deserves.

"You," I whisper. "I need you, Mr. D."

*

Later, I sit at the island where I sat so many days. I fill out the paperwork from school while Mr. D cooks and *Local*

SELENA

News with Jackie puts up a map showing the hotspots where the new designer drug has popped up. I look up every now and then, checking the TV or thinking how strange it is that I never took the time to admire Mr. D the way he admires me. I was always an object to him, something to dress and decorate and compliment, something to consume the way he consumes his fancy meals, drink in with his eyes the way he drinks his one glass of fine wine with dinner each night.

And he was the opposite to me, an idea with no substance. I was happy to let him hide behind his mask, to call him the Phantom, to ask no questions. I rarely admired the beautiful, long lines of his trim physique, the impeccable wardrobe, the skill it takes to sear pork chops and roast green beans and frizzle leeks at the same time.

"Where did you learn to cook like that?" I ask.

He glances back at me from where he's arranging the plates, sprinkling crispy leeks in a neat line over a heap of real mashed potatoes, not the powdered kind from the box. "I'm a recluse," he says. "With energy to burn and even more time to kill."

BROKEN DOLL

"You taught yourself to make all this?" I ask as he slides a plate in front of me, everything on it looking both appetizing and visually appealing, like it could be served in the finest restaurant in a big city, not a bachelor pad in Faulkner, Arkansas.

"I take no credit," he says. "It was all TV and the internet."

"TV and the internet didn't cook this dinner," I say, accepting a glass of wine.

I feel strange, like a stranger in his house, the same way I felt when I went home after being here for months. Nothing quite fits right anymore. Maybe it never did. You'd think we'd be perfect together, two lost people with no place, no purpose in the world anymore.

Maybe it could have worked before, if he'd agreed to meet instead of being too scared to show his face. Now I'm too broken, too fragmented to ever fit together with anyone. And though he's broken, too, our pieces don't match up. They grind against each other as we try to force them together in a desperate attempt to make something bearable from our lives.

SELENA

Mr. D sits beside me, and we eat in silence for a few minutes.

"I'm going back to school," I say at last.

He pauses, then finishes chewing before answering. "Because you missed the last few months? You should be able to work something out if you're that close to graduating."

"I was only a junior," I remind him.

"You said you were eighteen."

I shrug. "My mom forgot to enroll me in school when I was five."

He nods. "Royal graduated. You won't have to see him."

"He knows your truck," I say.

There's a beat of silence, heavy with the words I left unspoken. He knows more than Mr. D's truck. He knows his house.

"You're sure he followed me here?" I ask at last. "That he knows where you live?"

"I'm sure."

My stomach lurches, and I can't swallow the food in my mouth. I have to spit it into a napkin and suck in a loud, ugly breath before I can speak. "Are we safe? Is he outside right now?"

He snorts. "Now you're worried about your safety? We both know what you were doing today, Harper. What you were trying to do."

"I wasn't…"

Was I? I don't remember. I remember sobbing so hard I thought my chest would implode. When I woke up on that roof, though, I knew what I wanted, the first time I've truly wanted anything since the morning Mr. D pulled me off that tree.

"You left the truck running," he says quietly, spearing a green bean. "And closed the garage."

I take a sip of wine to get my throat working again. I was so out of it after I saw Royal, I don't even remember driving here. I should have been terrified, watching for him in the mirrors. Instead of being paranoid, I forgot the games he plays.

"I can't protect you when I'm not with you," Mr. D says. "If he makes you do that again…"

SELENA

"He followed me here," I repeat, as if just realizing it, as if saying it again will make it untrue, make him contradict me. Panic rises in my voice. My head swims, and I have to grab the edge of the counter so I don't fall off the barstool. He could have run me off the road and killed me right there. He could come after me again. He will, too. He won't stop until I'm dead. He knows where my mom lives, and now he knows my hiding place.

Mr. D frowns at his plate. "You should have protection for when you're not with me," he says at last. "I can't give you a gun, not after what you pulled today. But I'll have you fitted for brass knuckles, and if you know any other weapons you can't turn around on yourself…"

"I won't," I say.

He fixes me with his unflinching, turquoise gaze. "Until you see him again."

I don't answer. I don't know what I'll do. I don't know myself anymore, the person I am now. I didn't know I'd be able to face Royal, to talk to him and even to snark back at him like nothing changed. I didn't know it would be the thing that finally pushed me to the edge.

BROKEN DOLL

I finish dinner with Mr. D and slide into his bed. I'm ready for him, but he doesn't use me the way he used to. When he returns from the shower, he climbs in beside me and pulls me into his arms, and we go to sleep.

For the next few weeks, that's how it continues. I don't leave again. I don't want to risk running into Royal. I dive deep into the makeup work my teachers sent for the last two months I missed at WHPA, so I can turn in everything and start senior year at Faulkner. It helps to focus on something and get out of my head. Day by day, I feel myself emerge, not the girl I used to be or the one Mr. D made but someone else, someone whose raw edges are sealed over with scar tissue, whose broken pieces at least resemble a human.

SELENA

sixteen

Harper Apple

The last week in August feels like a countdown, the days ticking down to when it's over between Mr. D and me. We both know everything shifted when I left, and maybe it did again when I came back. I'm more awake now, too awake to be his doll. I try to still my hammering heart when I think about going back to school, but I hold onto the determination, one of the only feelings I can manage.

The day before I plan to return to Faulkner, Mr. D is quiet all through dinner and our visit to the garden. He cuts a huge sunflower blossom and lays it on my chest where I'm reclined on the chaise lounge. Then he sits down beside my legs, his back to me. Crickets chirp in the golden field below. The air is heavy and dense, that late August heat that lays thick on the day like a weighted blanket, threatening to smother you even after the sun has sluggishly drifted below the horizon.

I pick up the flower, stroking the soft petals between my finger and thumb.

"Thank you," I say. "Is this a sun to brighten my first day of school tomorrow?"

"You know why they're called that?"

"Because they look like suns?"

"Because they follow the sun," he says, pointing up at the half dozen tall stalks towering over us. They're all facing west, where the sun just disappeared.

"Every day?"

"Every day."

"What if it's cloudy?"

"Even when it's cloudy, when they can't see what matters, they never waver in their path."

Is he talking about the Dolces, about revenge?

He turns to me, pulling his knee up beside me, and watches my face like he expects a response. "Maybe they should," I say, because I know what revenge does to a family, what it costs those who seek it and those in their path. "Things change."

"At night, at their darkest point, when the sun is furthest from them, they turn back to the east," he says. "They wait for the sun to come back. They know it will."

I swallow hard, my chest tightening as I search his eyes. He's not talking about revenge. He's talking about living again.

"Are you my sunflower?" I ask, my words barely more than a whisper. "Or am I yours?"

He takes my free hand in his, lacing his elegant fingers through mine. "You're a sunflower, but you're not mine," he says. "I'm not anyone's sun anymore."

"You could be," I say, my throat tight.

He shakes his head, the corners of his mouth pulling down. "No, Harper. You don't belong here. You never did. We both know that."

My eyes blur over, and I have to blink a few times. I don't want to let go of his hand, to leave this cocoon with only brass knuckles for protection. I crave the oblivion, the weightlessness of life in his pristine world. "I can't thank you enough for… Everything."

"You don't have to thank me," he says. "Just promise me one thing."

I tense, ready for the demands. I know what he wants, but I don't want to be part of that world anymore. I have no fight left, not even for the boys who destroyed me. "I can't."

He squeezes my hand. "Find your sun, Harper. That's all I want for you."

A tear spills down my cheek, and I reach for his face, my fingers faltering before I make contact. "Can I?"

He stiffens, but he doesn't move. I carefully untie the silk ribbons that hold the silver mask in place and lift it off.

My breath catches, but I force myself not to drop my gaze, not to look away. His skin is tight, red, and angry, over half his forehead and down one side of his face, the side with the unseeing eye. His eyebrow and lashes are gone, his eye slightly skewed and smaller than the other. My fingers shake as I reach up and touch the edge of the mark.

"Some people like playing with fire," I whisper, remembering Colt's words.

SELENA

He doesn't look at me, but I know it's over. He wouldn't have shown me if he thought I'd come back. I should say something, tell him it's not so bad, but I don't want to lie to him.

"Maybe we all do," he says quietly.

"I'm no use to you anymore," I whisper. "Royal doesn't care about me. I'm dead to him."

"Do you think you could stay one more night?" he asks, the ache of his vulnerability making my chest contract painfully. "Just let me hold you one more time."

I nod, my eyes burning. He slides onto the chaise with me, fitting his body along mine. He doesn't put the mask back on, and he faces me, but he closes his eyes, as if he can't bear to see my face now that I've seen his. I turn toward him in the chair. I run my fingertips over his unmarked cheek and then his scarred one. Finally I lean in and brush my lips over each eyelid. The contrast brings tears back to my lashes.

"Thank you for saving my life," I whisper.

The corner of his mouth tugs up the slightest bit. "Ditto."

I let out a quiet laugh through the tears. "I didn't do anything."

"You never know."

Sometimes you do, though.

*

For months, Mr. D woke me up to fuck every morning. Since returning to him, he hasn't touched me. Not that way. On the first day I planned to return to Faulkner High, the first day of classes at Willow Heights, I wake to the sun streaming in the wall of windows. We came down after dark last night, and he lay me in bed between his high thread count sheets. He didn't take pictures. We didn't talk. He just turned off the light without replacing his mask.

This morning, he's still asleep, his terrible, scarred face even more heartbreaking in the light of day. I get up and shower, since I didn't get a chance last night. When I come out of the bathroom, he's sitting up in bed, his mask over his face again.

"One more time, for old time's sake?" he asks, patting the bed beside him and giving me a tentative smile. It's different, though. We're real people now, not marionettes. He hasn't fucked me in weeks, since I told him I wouldn't be his whore.

"Can I get my scholarship back?" I ask.

It's too late for me anyway. I'm already a whore.

"I have no idea what you're talking about," he says with a little smile, like he's thinking about the same thing, like he wants to assure me it's not a trade for sex.

I've been considering this since I started making up the work, debating whether I'm strong enough. I've finally decided.

I'm not *strong* enough.

I'm *broken* enough.

If I could bear the brutality of the Dolce twins and their friends for one night when I was whole, I can bear to see them every day now that nothing matters. I might have freaked out when I saw Royal, but that's because I loved him once. He won't be at Willow Heights, though. If I do this, I will never have to see any of them again in my life when it's over.

If this is what I have to do to leave this place and never look back, start over somewhere far away, where no one knows my name or my body, I will. I once felt a kinship with Mabel Darling, but now I truly understand. Now I know what would make a person change their name and disappear like a ghost, cutting ties with even their family. Some rottenness is too severe to fix, and the only way to live is to cut it all away, like a gangrenous limb.

And I'm just numb enough to cut away mine.

I climb onto the bed and sit back on my feet. "Take off the mask," I tell Mr. D.

He hesitates, and I watch his Adam's apple bob as he swallows. Then he reaches back and unties it, dropping it onto the nightstand before reaching for me. He pulls me into his lap, then grabs the lube in his top drawer. I catch his wrist.

"Do it right," I say, sliding off him and pulling him back down on the bed.

SELENA

He draws the covers over us and scoots close, until our bare bodies are pressed together. I try not to think about all the things we said to each other in those messages, so many months of messages. It doesn't seem real, that he can be the same person. He's not what I pictured at all. But maybe no one is.

He presses his lips to mine for the first and last time, cupping my cheek in his hand, saying goodbye. The ache in each slow kiss twists tight inside my chest until I'm sure my ribs will crack. He slides his other hand between my thighs and touches me, and when I'm ready, he rolls onto me and pushes inside me.

"Good girl," he says, his lips skimming mine. "So fucking good."

I close my eyes. "Mr. D," I whisper, as if to make it more real.

He lets out a little laugh of breath. "You don't have to call me that when I'm inside you," he says. "It makes me imagine you're picturing my dad."

I nod, and he moves slowly on top of me, sliding in and out, watching me like he's waiting for something. I felt nothing for him all these months, but now I can't help it. Since seeing Royal shook me awake, made me feel something again, I've been coming back to life despite myself. I wanted to stay numb forever, but every day my mangled soul twitches a bit more than the day before.

I look up at Mr. D, and I try to remember what I should feel when a man is inside me, but I can't. I don't love him. I know that. All I feel is sadness. Tears slide down my cheeks, wetting my hair.

"Is it my face?" he murmurs. "I can put the mask back on."

I shake my head, trying to stop the tears, to stop my lip from trembling and my throat from squeezing so painfully tight it brings more tears.

"Do you want me to stop?" he asks.

I shake my head again. I wrap my arms around his neck, and I hold him close and give him what he wants, not sex but closeness, however empty it is. I wish I could fix all the broken in him, that he could fix me, and that we could be that for each other. But we're just not.

SELENA

When he's done, he showers, and I go to the kitchen and make eggs and toast. Everything in his kitchen is clean and shiny and expensive. No chipped plates or mismatched knives. I think about how angry my mother will be when I tell her I've walked away from this. She'll tell me it's every girl's fantasy—every girl like me. That I'll never do better. And maybe she's right.

Mr. D comes out wearing his mask, charcoal grey dress pants, and a blue button-up shirt that matches his mismatched eyes. We eat in silence, but it's different, the air heavy instead of relaxed.

"I want to go back to Willow Heights," I say. "Not Faulkner High."

He makes a noncommittal sound and forks through his eggs. "Thanks for cooking."

"How old are you?" I ask, pulling back to study him—his sharp chin freshly shaven, his lips that never touched me until today. It's hard to tell with the mask, but I know he's younger than I pictured. He's the furthest thing from a gross old guy jerking off in his trailer and offering me the moon.

Or even a gross old rich guy jerking off at his computer while I told him about sucking dick.

"Nineteen."

Damn. He's only been out of high school for a year. He seems so much older, at least in his mid-twenties.

"I've caught up on everything I missed last year," I say, trying to keep the nerves from taking me over at the thought of setting foot in the same school as the football team. "Maybe you can go in and talk to them about my scholarship?"

"That again." He shakes his head and takes the plates to the sink.

"I think I've earned it."

"You know I never leave this place," he says without looking at me, turning on the water to rinse the plates.

"You left to get me every time I came over this summer," I point out, crossing my arms, some little seed of stubbornness sprouting inside me, sinking its roots into the ground. "And when I lived here, I heard you leave at least a dozen times in the evenings."

"I don't get out of my truck."

"I'd rather have that than all the clothes and shoes and jewelry."

He doesn't say anything. I want to be angry, but I can't summon that much emotion. So I turn and go to his room. While he washes up, I get the designer bag he bought to keep my new phone and keys in, and I put on the red-soled shoes he slid on my feet one day. He's spent so much, I feel guilty asking for more. But that's the only gift I've ever wanted. I didn't ask for fancy things.

I return to the island that separates the kitchen and main room of the loft. "I'm leaving the things you bought me here. I'll bring back the shoes and clothes I'm wearing."

"I don't need them," he says, coming around the end of the island. "I have a phone. I'm not into women's clothes, and even if I were, I couldn't wear your size."

"I don't feel right taking them. You've done so much."

"Then let me do this," he says, his familiar, entitled hands falling to my hips. "Let me at least pretend I did something good for you these last five months."

"Okay," I say, swallowing hard. I search his eyes, my gaze moving from his blind, unseeing eye to the one that's so sharp and alive, but just as guarded as the mask makes him. Is it unfair to ask for my scholarship back, to ask him to go to the school and fight for me? He's done more than buy me things. Things I can never repay him for. But all he'll remember is that I accused him of treating me like a whore after accepting every gift he gave.

I can't ask for more.

He runs his finger down the chain of the necklace, looping it through the bottom, where the ballerina charm hangs. "Don't take this off, okay? I like knowing that wherever you are, you're wearing it. That I'm with you."

"I should get to school."

He hands me his truck keys and steps back, his lips tightening. "I'll be down in a minute."

I watch him disappear into the bedroom, and heaviness settles in my belly. He wouldn't even fight the Dolces after what they did to him and his family, even when I gave him all the ammunition he needed to take them down. There's no chance he's going to fight for me.

I'm going to have to remember how to fight for myself.

SELENA

So, I take the keys, ready to face the admin at Willow Heights on my own. Taking a deep breath, I pull open the door.

Colt Darling is standing on the other side.

seventeen

Harper Apple

"Colt?" I say, as if making sure this is real, that he's the same person he was before.

"Harper?" He looks me up and down the same way. I guess I'm not the same girl he knew, either. My body has changed in ways he can see, but he doesn't know the rest of me has changed, too. At least, I don't think he does.

"What are you doing here?" I ask, glancing back over my shoulder.

"What are *you* doing here?" Colt asks, his voice sharp. "Why are you dressed like that?"

I recover from my surprise quickly. Mr. D is a Darling, and Colt is a Darling, so it's hardly a shock. Colt, however, seems a bit more shaken. His eyes narrow, and I take in his face. I haven't seen him since last year, when the Dolces beat him almost to death. He looks nearly the same, but everything is just a bit off, which is all the more disconcerting. It's like looking at a life-sized doll version of Colt. His nose is just a little straighter, his jaw a little squarer, his teeth a little whiter.

I'm not sure how to answer him, and before I can even try, he grabs me and drags me back into the apartment.

"Preston!" he bellows, his voice booming through the sleek loft.

Preston Darling.

"Preston," I whisper to myself, saying his name for the first time, trying it on. It fits. I'm less surprised than I was to find Colt here. I've had no indication that they're still close, the way they were when they ran this town. For all I know, Colt's the one on the receiving end of the videos, though. In truth, I don't know much about Mr. D beyond what I can see.

I've never really tried to figure out who my rescuer is. It didn't matter. Maybe I always knew, I just didn't think about it. Or maybe I only knew this morning, when he told me he was nineteen, but I hadn't had a chance to think about it.

I try to fit the name and what I know about it into my conception of Mr. D. I guess I don't have to call him that anymore, just as he stopped being the Phantom when he became Mr. D. He was who I needed him to be each step of the way, until I needed something else. He's no longer a man behind a mask or a shadow behind a keyboard. Now he's more real than ever, a man with a scarred face and a name and wounds that aren't for me to know.

The Phantom—Mr. D—Preston—steps out of the bedroom.

"*This* is your girlfriend?" Colt demands, fury snapping his words through the space between them. "*This* is who you're moving on with? Are you fucking suicidal?"

Preston shrugs and strolls over to lean on the island, seemingly unaffected by Colt's fury. "Could you really blame me, *cuz*?"

I glance from one of them to the other, sensing the rage shimmering in the air between them like a mirage. For the first time in months, my curiosity is piqued. I stopped trying to figure people out, stopped even caring. Nothing mattered.

SELENA

I don't know if this matters. But I'm interested, if only in a detached way, in where it leads.

Colt stands there breathing hard, glaring at his cousin. "I don't blame you, I blame *them*," he says. "I blame them for everything, and you should, too. When are you going to stop—*this?* Whatever this is. Self-destruction, suicidal tendencies, punishing yourself?"

When I said he saved me, he said *ditto*. But I didn't save him. I endangered him.

Preston smirks, stretching out his arm and beginning to slowly roll up one sleeve. I'm captivated by his every movement, his every word. This man came inside me every Tuesday and Thursday night, every Wednesday and Friday morning, for months, and I never gave a single fuck. Now, it's as if my brain is going into overdrive to compensate. He's not the same man who sat on the barstools beside me and served me steak and asparagus, the one who dressed and undressed me like a ritual, the one who never took off his mask and was therefore a blank cutout of a person to me.

He's the Phantom, a man with a mask and a safe place for my body to rest while my soul was gone.

He's Mr. D, a man with a keyboard and a sick mind, digging for secrets and hoarding them like a dragon.

He's Preston Darling, a man whose house I destroyed, whose bed I destroyed when Royal made me cum so hard I drenched the mattress, whose leather jacket I stole.

He's alive and utterly fascinating. He has a family. A name. A face. He smirks and rages. Maybe, he even laughs. I want to devour his soul, to dissect his brain, to study it under a microscope.

"Trust me when I say that fucking Harper is the furthest thing from a punishment," he says when he's finished rolling his sleeve with painstaking care.

"You know Royal claimed her," Colt says, his voice low and fierce.

Preston's tone hardens. "He threw her away."

For a minute, there's no sound, nothing but the inaudible crackle of tension in the air.

"It doesn't matter," Colt says. "When they claim someone, it's forever. There's no way out."

"He said I was dead to him," I say.

SELENA

I want to believe Royal's done, that he'll never speak to me again, that he'll look right through me like I'm a ghost. But after he saw me outside my house, I'm not sure I believe that, no matter how hard I try. He followed me here, which means he wants something. If the torture isn't over, what then? I'm not a Darling, a girl who can afford to check herself into a swanky resort-style mental facility to hide or blow out of town and legally change her name. There's nowhere to hide for a girl like me.

"You think I don't know how they operate?" Preston asks, ignoring me.

Colt glares. "He'll take more than your eye if he finds out you messed with her."

His eye that never sees. It clicks into place then. It's not blind. It's prosthetic.

"I didn't *mess with* her," Preston says, jerking his other sleeve straight. "I fucked her. Four times a week for months, and every day before that. I came inside her every delicious little hole, and I fucking loved it. What have you done this summer?"

"You know what I did," Colt growls, his hands balling into fists.

Preston starts rolling that sleeve, his movements jerky and sharp now. "You gave them exactly what they wanted. You bent over. You play nice, but for what? They'll kill us all, anyway."

"Not if you play along."

Preston scoffs. "How many nights did you spend in the hospital, getting how many surgeries, because of those assholes? How much time did you lose? Maybe it would've been worth it if you'd been lying there knowing what their girl's cunt feels like from the inside, with nothing between you but cum. That they could never undo what you got to do to her."

"You're going to get yourself killed," Colt says quietly. "I can't watch you do this shit anymore."

"And what would you have me do?" Preston asks. "Get on my knees and suck their dicks like you? I'd rather fucking die."

"Those aren't the only options."

SELENA

"Aren't they?" Preston finishes his sleeve and measures that they both stop at the thickest part of his forearm, golden tan with golden hairs glistening on them.

"You could leave," Colt says.

"No fucking way," Preston says, yanking the mask off his face and throwing it down on the counter. "This is *our* town, not theirs. Enough people in this family have run like dogs."

Colt sighs. "How long are you going to hold onto that delusion? Devlin didn't run, and he's not coming back to save us all. If he was coming back, he would have done it by now. He's fucking dead. Accept it."

"Bullshit," Preston snaps. "No one takes millions of dollars from their trust fund right before they commit suicide."

I perk up automatically because this is something I didn't know.

"He didn't commit suicide," Colt says, rubbing his forehead with his thumb, like this conversation gives him a headache. From the weariness in his voice, I get the feeling they've had this fight before, so many times they both know all their lines. "It was an accident. A tragic, shitty accident with bad timing. That doesn't mean it didn't happen, no matter how many guys you pay off to keep quiet. You're not letting them live a happy life. You're wasting our money."

"*I* didn't pay them off," Preston says evenly. "I'm not the only one who thinks they're alive."

"You control the money," Colt says. "And enough with the conspiracy theories already. Yeah, out of the hundreds of people in our family, three of you think he's alive. That doesn't make it true. That makes y'all delusional."

"He said goodbye to us," Preston says, looking incredulously at his cousin. "Dolly saw him, goddamn it. How can you honestly believe he's dead?"

"Because it doesn't fucking matter," Colt says, throwing up his hands. "Whether he's dead or not, it doesn't change anything. He's not here. We're here."

"And I'm not leaving," Preston says. "They may have beaten us, but we're not dead yet. We can still fight, if you'd stop being such a pussy."

"And you're planning to fight them… How? By putting trackers on their cars and following them around? Fucking their girlfriends in secret? Or do you have some new plan you think is brilliant, but in the end, will amount to nothing more than a spiteful little prank?"

Preston works his jaw back and forth. "I would have fucked their sister, but Devlin took off with her. So that leaves their girlfriends. Isn't that what they did to us? It's called revenge, cousin. Look it up sometime."

"Which of the things you've done is going to bring our family back?"

They glare at each other for a second before Colt answers his own question. "None of them, that's what. They're not playing the same game we did, and they never were. It's over, Preston. Accept that before it costs you your life."

Preston straightens, staring down his cousin until I stand from where I sank onto the arm of the grey sectional. "As enlightening as this has been," I say. "I have to get to school."

They both ignore me.

"If petty-ass revenges are all I get, I'll fucking take 'em," Preston says. "I'll take everything I can from them at every opportunity, whether they know it or not. I'll know. And I'll never stop."

I picture him sitting up here on his fancy computer, reading my salacious tales, collecting them into a file he will never use. He has so much on the Dolces, but he can't do anything with it. He can't go to the cops because they're in the Dolces' pockets. He won't show his face in town, so he can't get anyone else to follow or join him. He was never going to help me. He just has to feel like he hasn't given up. I can respect that. The man's got his pride, if nothing else.

"I really do need to go," I say again.

"Take my truck," Preston says, barely glancing at me. "Bring it back this time. And don't leave it running in the garage."

I take the keys and head for the door. Somehow, it still surprises me when he does shit like this, like it's nothing to let me borrow his fancy truck or pay my rent for six months.

The last thing I hear before closing the door is Colt answering something Preston said with, "Fuck you. You don't get to bring my sister into this. Your sister is still here."

So, I guess it wasn't all for nothing. I saved Lindsey last spring, even if I couldn't save myself.

SELENA

eighteen

Harper Apple

It takes a week of runaround from the office staff at Willow Heights before I can get an appointment to see the headmaster, but I'm not too worried about it. I know not much goes on the first week, even at a prep school. I can make up the assignments. I just need to get in.

I text Preston before I go in for my appointment—we don't use the app anymore, since he put his number into my new phone the day he gave it to me—but he just says he can't show his face around town, especially there. In another lifetime, the Dolce boys said something about that, about him threatening Gloria and escaping to hide like a cockroach. Funny, that's what they called me, too. I guess these two cockroaches found each other, though I can't imagine any comparison that would be less apt to describe Preston Darling, with his impeccable house and wardrobe.

I go into school in the afternoon, when everyone else is in class. I decided too late that I was going to Willow Heights, but now that my mind is set, a little red tape won't stop me. I've survived so much to get here. I'm not walking away with nothing. I'm done with the Dolces, done with the Darlings. I want no part of any of it. The only way out was through, and now I'm through. I didn't realize it at the time, but that's what Mr. D was doing. He was the other piece of the puzzle, the Darling side that had to use up whatever was left when the Dolces were done. He finished me off, and now I'm so empty there's nothing left but a perfectly polished shell.

That shell is hard, though, hammered into the fiercest, steely determination, the only thing left when everything else has been smashed into bits so small they can't be broken again. They've all gotten what they want. They've all fucked me and used me until I have no value to any of them.

My mother would lose her shit and tell me I was beyond fucking stupid for letting them take everything from me and then toss me away. Both the Darlings and the Dolces might think I'm useless now. But I know the truth. I'm not worthless now that they've used me up, scraped every last trace of potential from inside my body.

I'm free.

And I'm going to use that freedom to fly right the fuck out of this town.

I'm not going to do it as a teenage runaway with no high school diploma, though. So, I steel myself with the hard, cold shell that hides my scars the way Mr. D's mask hides his, and I march inside. Unlike Preston's, my scars are invisible to the naked eye, but I can feel them, and beneath them, the hollowed out place where Harper herself used to sit. My identity is gone, my soul, my heart, half my mind. But some instinct for self-preservation remains, a dogged will to live that's hardened inside me since the day I almost died, and with it, a poison seed of the most wretched of all torments—hope.

It's not the shining kind that poets wax on about, but something ugly and deformed, a dark and twisted thing. This golem doesn't tell me life will get better, that I'll start over and everything will be fine. But it whispers that a future of nightmares is still a future, that though my heart and body have been decimated in ways there's no going back from, even those missing a soul can keep breathing. Even a mutilated, broken thing can find the sun.

Preston told me that.

I sit in the office and wait until the headmaster can see me, and I don't pay attention to the whispers and furtive glances from the office staff. When my heart starts to beat erratically, I remind myself Royal is not here. And when it's time to talk to the headmaster, I walk in on steady legs.

"Your scholarship is not the problem," he says after I lay it all out. "You didn't enroll in this school. Every application goes before the enrollment committee, and you didn't put yours in for consideration. You are no longer a student here."

"Then make me a student," I say.

He folds his hands on the desk in front of him. "I'm afraid it's not that easy, Miss Apple."

"One more thing," I say. "I want my schedule arranged so I'm not in any classes with any of the Dolce boys, or Cotton Montgomery, DeShaun Rose, and Dawson Walton."

SELENA

"Several of those boys are no longer students here," he says, adjusting his glasses on his peaky little turtle nose.

"Right," I say. "That should make it easy."

"I don't know if your request would possible, anyway," he says. "We don't arrange student schedules that way."

"Make it possible," I say, leaning across the desk and resting the intricate design of the faux rings covering my brass knuckles on the surface. "Or I let your dirty little secret leak."

"Threats are not going to work here, Ms. Apple," he says, stiffening. "There are no secrets at Willow Heights."

My eyes blaze at the little worm of a man. "I bet the town would think differently when they find out you allow your school's secret society to have a rape room under the library."

His face freezes, and I know I have him. "That's preposterous," he splutters. "We disbanded any such organizations several years ago, and before that, I can assure you no such activities took place."

"Isn't that convenient." My voice is flat, not asking.

"Ms. Apple," he says, his lips tight. "As I've explained, you are no longer a student here, and even if you had completed the admissions process, we have filled all the scholarship spots."

"I'll expect my thug-free schedule on Monday," I say, standing and heading for the door. The school day is almost over, and I want to be out before anyone sees me. I know it doesn't make sense. They'll see me when I come back. But that will be on my terms.

As soon as I step around the last row of cars and the Escalade comes into view, my heart sinks. A fucking Range Rover is parked beside it. Again.

I don't want to see him. I never want to see him again. But the only thing I want to see less is the twins, so I keep walking. Royal climbs out of his car into the paralyzing heat and waits for me to approach. "Harper," he says. "Don't drive off. I won't touch you."

He holds up both hands, like it matters to me that he's unarmed.

He doesn't need weapons. He is a weapon.

SELENA

"What do you want, Royal?" I ask, noticing the weariness in my voice, my blood. I'm not scared the way I was last time. I just want to get it over with.

"I... Wanted to see you," he says quietly.

"Why?" I ask, stopping in front of him. "What could you possibly want from me that I haven't already given? No, actually, that you haven't already *taken*. There's nothing left, Royal. *I'm* nothing, just like you always said."

"I never said that."

I cock my head. "Didn't you, though?"

He rakes a rough hand through his hair. "Harper, listen," he says. "Can we just—can we talk?"

A laugh escapes me, but it's more of a bitter snort. I don't think I'm capable of laughter anymore. "Fine," I say. "Whatever you want, whatever you think I still have left to take, take it. I don't care. I'll give you anything you want if you'll just leave me alone for the rest of my fucking life."

"I don't want anything," he says, having the nerve to look offended, like he's never asked me for a thing.

"Then why are you here?" I ask.

"Are you—no," he says, shaking his head. "Of course you're not fucking okay."

"Now that we've established that, can I go?"

His dark eyes search mine, as if trying to find something real behind my snarky attitude. But that's locked up tight now, where he can't reach it. I'd like to say he'll never touch me again, not anything below the surface. But I've made a hundred promises of *never* when it comes to Royal, and he turned every one of them to *always*.

"Were you really trying to end your life?" he asks after he doesn't find whatever he's looking for in my eyes.

"No," I say. "Of course not. My life is even more glamorous now than it was before I was gang raped and left for dead in a swamp. I mean, what could possibly make a girl like me want to end it?"

"I don't know," he says slowly, a frown creasing his brow. "I wouldn't know what could make a person try that. I never did."

"And see, that's the thing. You and I are nothing alike. We never were. So stop thinking I'll react the way you do, or take something the way you want me to. I won't."

SELENA

"Just seeing me made you do that?" he asks, like it fucking matters why.

"I have to go," I say. "I really don't want to see the rest of the football team today." I turn to the truck, but his voice stops me, the quiet rumble of it raw with concern.

"You're not fighting anymore."

"You kinda broke my hand." I lift my fist, and the silver rings glint in the sun. For a moment, neither of us speak. Royal stares at my knuckles, swallowing so hard I can see his Adam's apple bob.

The word *DOLL* is spelled out over my knuckles, just like Preston's tats spell the word over his fingers. He had the weapon custom made to fit my hand exactly, and because he'd spare no expense, he had them set a diamond into the center of the *O*. To a normal person, they just look like gaudy rings, but a thug like Royal probably knows what they really are. I'm okay with that. With him knowing I'm armed, but that I won't fight him.

"He's the one who sent those videos, isn't he?" Royal asks at last, his gaze rising to meet mine. There's something so raw in his eyes it makes my dead heart throb once inside me, like it might come back to life.

I don't want that part of me to live again. At some point, I caught on to what Preston was doing with those videos, or at least suspected. I don't remember when. But seeing Royal in the flesh and knowing he's watched them is different than some abstract, detached theory in the back of my mind. I should feel shame, but the ability to feel that emotion hasn't returned. All I feel is belligerent spite. I'm glad he sent them to Royal. I hope they made him sick.

"Look, whatever you want, just take it," I say again. "You want to talk, talk. You want to fuck me, I'll lay down on the back seat and you can fuck me in the ass or whatever sick thing you want to do that you think can still hurt me. It won't. Don't you get that? It doesn't matter, Royal. Whatever you do to me, I don't care. If you want to kill me, here are my wrists. Fucking slit them. I won't fight. I don't care."

Royal takes a quick step forward, and I instinctively cringe, my body betraying me, though my mind flatlined that night in the swamp and there have only been a few blips since.

"I want you to fucking fight," Royal growls.

"Why, is that what gets you off?" I ask. "Oh, wait, never mind. Nothing gets you off now that I'm not around, right? Is that why you're here?"

"No," he snaps, frustration etched into his every beautiful feature. "What the fuck, Harper. I'm not here to fuck you."

"You can see where a girl could be confused," I say. "Seeing as how all of last year, you told me that was my sole purpose in life."

Even if I'm willing to give him everything, my body is on high alert, ready for him to make a move. I see his fingers twitch, but instead of reaching to hurt me, he rakes them roughly through his hair again.

"Would you—" He stops and takes a ragged breath. "I just wanted to see you."

"Why?" I ask incredulously. "To gloat? There's no need for that. You won. A resounding victory, in fact. There's no doubt in anyone's mind. You annihilated the competition. Gloating is small even for you, Royal."

The bell chimes, and my body stiffens.

"Be at the Slaughterpen on Sunday night," he says. "I have something for you."

I just stare at him in disbelief. "How fucking stupid do you think I am?"

"Just be there."

"Why?" I demand, crossing my arms and glaring at him.

"It's just for a fight," he says. "I promise."

I can hardly keep myself from hysterical laughter. "There are no fights on Sundays," I point out. "And a promise from you means less than nothing to me."

"It should."

I snort. "Oh, and also, I don't answer to you anymore, Royal."

His jaw tightens, and he glances at the students starting to meander out of the building. When he turns back, his eyes are no longer filled with pleading and vulnerability, the real Royal. They've hardened into resolve.

"Then get used to seeing me around," he says.

Before I can answer, he turns and strides to the Rover and climbs inside, swinging it around the Escalade and toward the front of the lot. The realization that he must be picking up his brothers slams into my chest, and my heart lurches into my throat. I scramble up into truck, not wanting to see them. I know I will as soon as I'm admitted back to school, but I'm not ready. Maybe I'll never be ready. Maybe this was a huge mistake.

I roar out of the lot, not looking back, not wanting to catch a glimpse of them or for them to catch one of me. My hands are shaking. This time, I watch the mirrors constantly, my heart ricocheting around my ribcage every time I glance back and am sure that I'll see the Rover looming.

But this time, he doesn't follow.

nineteen

Harper Apple

When I get home, I sit in the truck, afraid to get out, afraid he'll come up and park behind it like he did before. I sit there in the bubble of cold AC until the bus pulls up at the corner. Blue and Olive climb down and start along the block toward me. When they get to their drive, Olive waves and jogs over, her little backpack bouncing, her gangly legs making the run even more awkward. She hops up on the running board and makes a face at me through the window.

I roll it down even though she's right there in my face, too close.

"Can you take us for a ride?" she asks.

Blue lingers on the other side of the street, in front of her house, watching.

"Sure," I say, managing a small smile.

SELENA

"Yay!" Olive throws her arms up, and I'm sure she's going to topple onto her back on the road. She loses her balance but hops down, landing on her feet despite the clumsy execution. I remember what it was like to have that much confidence in my body, to know it would take care of me, and my chest aches. Sooner or later, we all realize the false sense of security that lends us, when someone bigger and stronger and better comes along and strips it all away.

I look down at my brass knuckles, reading the word over and over as Blue climbs into the back seat and Olive climbs in front.

"Wow," the little girl says, running her hands over the supple leather seats. "White leather! Are these custom?"

"I don't know," I say, shifting into drive.

"Where are we going?" Olive asks, standing to look over the dash. "Can we go to the movies? Or Boehner's Burgers? A bunch of kids were going after school, and if they see me in this…"

"Put on your seatbelt," Blue says from behind us.

"Sure," I say to Olive. I have nowhere better in mind. I just want to get away from my house, and I can't go to

Preston's, because Royal knows where that is, too. If I can make a kid look cool in front of her friends, I've done something good in the world today.

We swing through the drive-through because I don't want to go inside. Boehner's is a hangout for high school kids, too, and I don't want to run into anyone I know. Olive sees a couple kids she knows at a picnic table and rolls down the window, hanging halfway out and waving to them. When we have our food, I suddenly realize Preston wouldn't want us eating inside his car.

"Let's go somewhere to sit," I say, swinging back onto the road. I take the highway out of town, heading north. I stare straight ahead like my life depends on it as we pass the rice paddies with the swamp beyond, just like I do every time I take this road to and from Preston's house. Only when I reach the exit do I relax.

"Can I eat?" Olive whines. "I'm hungry."

"Fine," I say. "Don't spill anything."

We pull up at the quarry, and I park the truck but leave it running so we're not all baked alive in the Arkansas heat. But

SELENA

Blue opens the door and hops down. "We can eat on the tailgate."

I join her while Olive stays inside to play with the radio and finish her food.

"I thought you disappeared again," Blue says as we spread our food on the tailgate. "I haven't seen you around."

"I'm going back to Willow Heights."

"You living with this rich guy?" She turns to check on Olive, who's fiddling with the radio stations.

Suddenly, this whole thing is too big for me to carry. Even if she's never had anything like that happen, she'll understand. I feel myself crumbling, and it terrifies me. I need a friend, even if it's one I don't know well. The depth of that need scares me, but I don't know where else to turn.

"Remember when I disappeared last spring?" I ask, my throat tight.

She nods and opens a ketchup packet with her teeth.

"I… I was gang raped," I blurt out.

Her flat blue eyes rise to mine. "Shit," she says quietly.

I nod, swallowing past the lump forming, trying to choke off my words. Even if Blue can't help, even if this doesn't help, I can't hold onto it anymore. There's no purpose, no motive in telling. It's just spilling out like the water from the swimming hole when it rains and the banks can't contain it all anymore.

"That guy I was seeing, with the Range Rover," I say. "It was his friends."

"Does he know?"

I let out a little breath and pick up a fry. "Yeah. He was there. And now he's trying to talk to me, and I just... I don't care what he wants. I just want him to leave me alone."

"He wants to get back with you?" she asks, watching me as she bites into her burger.

"I don't think so." I shake my head, remembering Royal's drawling voice saying he was bored that night. "No," I say, more emphatically this time. "Definitely not. But he's still fucking with me. I just want to survive until I can get out of this town, and then I want to forget everything that ever happened before I left. Most of all, him. But he's not letting me."

"Do you know how you'd go?" Blue asks.

"What?"

SELENA

She nods toward the cab, where the bass is thumping from some music her sister found. "You could always dump the truck somewhere once you get out."

I realize she thinks I'm leaving now. I could. I don't even think Preston would call the cops. I could just blow right the fuck away, like Mabel Darling. But then I'd be a high school dropout, maybe one with a criminal record if I underestimated Preston's reluctance to involve anyone else.

"He saved me," I say quietly. "At least, I thought he did. But I'm not so sure anymore."

"What do you mean?"

"He's not a hero."

"But he's taking care of you," she says, biting into her burger. "And all you have to do is fuck him? I mean…"

"Yeah," I say. "For girls like us, that's as good as it gets."

"No," she says. "That's better than most girls get."

"But now I need protection from Royal," I say. "And he can't give it to me. He won't."

We eat in silence for a while. When we're done with the burgers and fries, Blue turns to make sure Olive is okay before scooting back into the bed of the truck, resting against the wheel well while I match her position on the other side. She sets her soda beside her and takes out her cigarettes.

I stare at our shoes—her scuffed Vans that probably cost ten bucks at a second-hand store, and my new leather Doc Martens that cost over ten times that much—and guilt swells inside me. It's not that I don't appreciate what Preston's done. I do. And I don't want more from him. He doesn't owe me anything, not even what he's done already. I have no right to expect him to protect me, especially since I know what it'll cost him. Colt already paid that price.

My phone chimes, and I glance at the screen to see an email notifying me that I have one new message and 27 unread messages on the *OnlyWords* app. I haven't used it since I cut off Mr. D, but he probably wants his car back. I'm about to close it when another email comes through. Blue gives me a mildly curious look and hands me a cigarette.

I take it with a sigh and hit the button to download the app, though it makes a clammy, cold sensation crawl up my back despite the sweltering blanket of summer spread over

SELENA

us. I set down my phone and light up, take a drink of my Dr. Pepper, and wipe my hands on the floral dress Preston bought me sometime this summer. It's funny how much of the past few months feel like a dream.

I pick up my phone and open the app. My soda catches in my throat, and I choke, dropping my phone on the tailgate. It clatters across the surface, and Blue gives me a funny look as I try to suck in a breath. I pick up the phone, my fingers trembling. I don't know why I'm surprised.

Royal: What r u doing?

I drag hard on the cigarette, remembering how Royal almost never texted first. He made me come to him every time. Even then, half the time he ignored my texts, probably just to prove he could. Now he wants to know what I'm up to, and it's so far past too late that I can't even comprehend that he thinks it's okay to text me.

I'm tempted to say something smartass, but I remind myself that I did that for six months, and it got me nowhere. I've given up. I won't fight him anymore. I type in all the information he could want, so I won't have to see his name on the screen again and feel that sickening lurch in my stomach.

BadApple: Eating w friends at the quarry. Plz don't text me.
Royal: doesn't seem like a good place 4 someone who wants 2 die.
BadApple: seems like a good place 2 me
Royal: Don't make me come find u.
BadApple: I'm fine. I wont jump.

I set my phone down and wave to Olive, whose greasy fingers are pressed to the glass as she makes faces at us out the back window. Blue flicks her cigarette butt over the edge of the truck bed. "If you need protection, you should talk to Mav," she says. "He's running with the Crossbones now."

I think on it for a second before shaking my head. There's no way to defeat the Dolces. I've already tried. I lost, and everyone I involve will lose, too. I needed to tell someone, but some tiny tendril of self-preservation has sprung to life inside me. That's why I told Blue, who won't do anything more than Preston will. I could have told the cops, or someone who would go to the cops or pressure me to. But I didn't. I told Blue because I needed someone safe, someone who won't be hurt by my secret because she will never whisper a word of it, and no one will ever know that she knows.

Colt had it right all along.

Speaking up, fighting back, will only make things worse for me. For the longest time, I fought back tooth and nail, refusing to accept what was right in front of me. I thought if I knew the rules, I could play their game, maybe even win.

I understand how it works now, and I accept the truth.

Winning was never a possibility.

It doesn't matter what cards I play. I could play the perfect hand, but I'd still lose it all. It was rigged from the moment I sat down at the table.

But I sat down, and now I'm caught in a nightmare that never ends. I will lose over and over and over again, but I can never leave the game.

Again, it's like Colt said.

I thought I was free, but now I know. Royal will keep showing up. There's no way out. Once they claim you, it's forever.

I'm trapped, a fly in their poison amber. I can see their secrets, but I'm frozen inside them, and I can't do anything about it. I can fight, but I can't win. I will always belong to them. Duke branded me, just like ranchers brand cattle so they can prove it's theirs if anyone fucks with it and so if one happens to find a way out and escape, anyone who finds it will return it to captivity. I am the same to the Dolces—a piece of property, branded with a scar on my hip that tells the world I will never be free.

The thought fills my body with dread. My blood is sluggish and heavy, like mercury on a cold day, pulling me down until I think I'll sink into the ground and disappear. Suddenly, all I want to do is get in the truck and shift into gear, close my eyes, and press the pedal to the floor. Royal threw a guy over the edge once, into the quarry, because he was fucking with me. If he really wanted to protect me, he should have pushed me over instead.

But I can't take Blue and Olive with me, and I couldn't make them watch it, either. They don't need that trauma, and I don't need an audience or attention. That's a spectacular death, a blaze of glory. I'd end up on *Local New with Jackie*, like a rich girl.

I'd rather go quietly, without fanfare, a single line buried on a random page in the back of the paper.

Body Found Near Tracks.

Local Teen Dead of Overdose.

There would be no candlelight vigil, no fake tears. That's the last thing I'd want.

When I pull into the driveway later, Blue climbs down and then turns to me. "You could always come back to Faulkner," she offers.

"I might," I say. I can't remember where I got the fight to go up against the headmaster at Willow Heights, but I think I used it all up. If he's going to keep fighting, he'll win. I don't care enough to keep going, knowing defeat is inevitable. If the Dolces want me gone, no amount of threats from a girl like me will sway the headmaster. I don't pay his salary.

Blue hesitates. "I know if I could change schools and not have to see the guys who did that to me… I wouldn't have to think about it."

I go inside and lie on the bed and stare at the ceiling, replaying her words. Then I replay the conversation I had with Royal. Suddenly, my skin goes cold even though the window units can't begin to cool the house in August.

He asked if I tried to end my life.

He followed me to Preston's, but I closed the garage. He couldn't have seen me. He couldn't have seen me on the roof, either. So how the fuck does he know that?

Is he checking up on me?

And why would Preston tell him that? Why would he tell him anything? I remember last spring, the day it all went to shit when Preston bombed Royal's car. One of the Dolce boys mentioned that Preston's family was off limits, that their dad was in with them. Has Preston been feeding Royal information all along? Did Royal actually ask for those videos?

My stomach lurches, and I stumble to the bathroom and fall to my knees, my head spinning. I try to puke, but nothing comes. I tear through the cabinets, searching for something to take, some pills, anything to get me back to the numb state I spent the summer in. But that's the thing about living with a junkie. There are never drugs around when you need them.

All I can find is a packet of razors, and they only slice the skin. It's nowhere near deep enough, but after a minute, the frustration turns to relief. Somehow, watching the blood well up in little lines numbs me, brings me a moment of singular focus. In the back of my mind, I'm aware that I'm too old for this shit, that all the other girls went through their cutting phase in middle school and junior high. I remember thinking how silly it was for girls to hurt themselves voluntarily when there were so many other things in the world determined to hurt us already.

But now I understand. It's like walking on coals. It's not about the pain, not exactly. It needs to hurt to work, but that's not the end goal. The end goal is living completely in this exact moment, the willpower it takes to override instinct not just once, at the edge of the roof, but over and over again, with each step forward over the coals, each red line on my smooth skin.

My focus is sharper than the razor blade. Nothing else matters. I make my way up my arm, each stroke one of pure, potent life. For one moment and then a hundred, I can barely breathe with the rawness of this edge I've found, a barely perceptible line between reality and illusion, between life and death, pain and bliss. I hold onto it, feeling my way along, tiptoeing along the tightrope toward some ending I can't see and that doesn't matter.

This matters.

For the first time in months, something matters. For these sacred minutes, as I kneel on the faded linoleum of a stuffy, windowless bathroom on the wrong side of Faulkner, I have unwavering control of my mind in this world where nothing is under my control, and I live again.

SELENA

twenty

Harper Apple

When I call Willow Heights on Monday, they give me the same runaround about not having a scholarship. If I had money, they'd make it happen, but I don't. Then again, if I had money, I wouldn't need a scholarship. The next two days, my hope fades when it's more of the same. I may have only missed a few weeks at Willow Heights, but I've missed a month at Faulkner, and I'm just getting further behind by postponing it. So, I don't bother calling on Thursday. I walk to the corner, ignoring the handful of gangbangers sitting on an old red El Camino across the street.

"Hey, baby," calls a familiar voice. I turn to see Maverick sitting on the hood of the car, gesturing for me to come to him like the lazy asshole he's always been. I cross over because I have nothing else to do, and there's no use fighting.

"I hear you been selling your ass to some rich guy," he says, looking me up and down with slow appreciation. "That true?"

"So what if it is?"

A couple of his buddies crack indulgent smiles as they look me over in their too-cool way, watching with lazy disinterest, their feet dangling against the side of the car.

"What's he got that I don't?" Maverick asks, a little challenge in his voice.

"Money."

"Bet he doesn't give you what I did."

"Nobody gives as good dick as you, Maverick," I say, batting my eyes. It's what he wants to hear. I've always liked watching people, but lately, when I can watch with complete detachment, I've learned not just to watch, but to deliver. That's what whores do, after all.

Mav's friends slug his tatted shoulders, giving him props. He puffs up a little, and I'm glad I made him feel good. I have nothing else to give, nothing to offer, but I can do something kind for someone else when it costs me nothing.

"So why haven't you come around?" Maverick asks, reaching for me.

I pretend I don't care when he slides his hand down my wrist and takes my hand. Maybe, if Preston hadn't fucked me from the start, I'd have some weird aversion to touch. But he didn't give me time to get frigid, to get weird about sex. I've been having it since the day after the assault. I'm not scared of sex, of touch, of anything. I am an undisturbed pond—still, shallow, reflective. I show him what he wants to see.

Only Royal can make ripples in the serene surface of my nothingness.

"Since when have you been hanging with the Crossbones?" I ask, jerking my chin toward his friends. "I heard you're selling. I thought we were about more than this. We were going to get out of here."

"No, *you* were going to get out," he says. "You and Zeph. You're not about that small town life. Y'all can get out, do something bigger."

"So can you."

He grins. "I'm not like you, baby. Faulkner's in my blood. This is my town. I was born here, and I'll die here."

"If that's what you want," I say with a shrug.

"It might be," he says, licking his lips and looking me up and down.

"That's not how I remember it, but whatever."

Maybe he was just saying what I wanted to hear to get in my pants, or maybe we're all growing up, cutting away our childhood fantasies, and facing reality. And who am I to judge? Girls like me do what we have to do to survive, and so do boys like him. His brother's been running with the Crosses for years. It was only a matter of time before Mav got sucked in, too.

He's not stupid. He knows his chances. And hell, if I had a whole gang to have my back when I needed them, I wouldn't be where I am.

Blue and Olive approach on their side of the street, Olive hopping over the cracks in the sidewalk, singing "Gangsta's Paradise."

"Sing it, sister," calls one of the Crosses.

"You going to school?" I ask Maverick.

"Nah," he says. "Want a ride?"

"I'm okay."

"If you'd rather, I can give you a little blue pearl, and you can ride me all day."

I think about it for a second, about how life would be if I joined. I know how girls get in. Ironically, that gangbang would protect me. But I'd be stuck here, and I'm not ready to give up that one last seed of hope, the only thing that's regrown inside me.

I tell Maverick I'll think about it, and I turn to walk over to the bus stop. Blue gives the guys a shy wave.

"You too?" I ask.

"Oh, I could never join," she says. "I'm not tough like those girls."

We climb onto the bus, and I spend the day at Faulkner High, going to the classes I want and sitting there like I belong. This isn't WHPA. The teachers are too frazzled to fight with me for more than a minute. I just tell them I'm new, so I'm not on their rosters, and they give up. Who would come to a place like this voluntarily? Ninety percent of the kids don't want to be here. They're not going to kick out someone who does.

After school, I head through the choking blanket of diesel exhaust toward the buses. I'm halfway there when I hear squeals of excitement from a group of girls I've never seen, either freshman or sophomores who started last year, when I wasn't a student here. They're shrieking and clutching each other, gaping at something behind me. My stomach clenches with dread, but I turn to look.

Royal Dolce is standing there, surrounded by fangirls and fans. He has that expression on his face that I've seen at parties, halfway between irritation and indulgence, like he's trained himself to grin and bear it, but he fucking hates it. His gaze locks on mine, but I tear my eyes away and turn, hurrying to the bus.

"Harper," he calls behind me.

I ignore him and plow up the steps of the bus and down the aisle. I drop into a seat and try to get a breath.

What the fuck is he doing here?

I mean, I'm not stupid. I know he's here for me. But why? Why can't he leave me the fuck alone? I have nothing, absolutely nothing, he could possibly want, because I have nothing left. He took everything, even my voice, my ability to submit, my ability to fight. I want to scream with frustration that after all that, somehow, it still wasn't enough to satisfy him.

I slouch down in my seat, my heart hammering. I hate that I only feel this way for him, that I only feel anything when he makes me.

But no. I also felt something when I cut my arm.

I slide my thumb under the cuff of my long-sleeve T, finding one of the cuts, now scabbed over. Closing my eyes, I run the pad of my thumb over it, searching for calm. My heart does a little flip as I dig my thumbnail in, breaking the scab.

"Hey," the bus driver protests. "You can't be on here."

"It'll only take a minute," Royal's voice responds. I can feel him moving closer, the bus sinking under his heavy footsteps, the hair on my arms rising as if to greet him. I press my thumbnail deeper into the cut, into the pain.

"Harper," he says.

I open my eyes. My heart doesn't even race when I see him.

"Why are you running away from me?" he asks.

"Gee, I wonder," I say, rolling my eyes.

Normal. I sound normal.

It's everyone else on the bus who isn't. It's usually deafening, but today, it's dead silent. Like one boy has that much power over them. It's sick. They're all sick. Why can't they see it?

I inch my thumb up to the next cut and scratch the scab open. I'm sick, too, just in a different way.

Royal crouches between the seats, his big body barely squeezing into the space, so he's on my eye level, a little lower. "Talk to me, Harper."

"Or what?" I ask, jabbing viciously at the cut with my nail. "You're going to toss me over your shoulder like a caveman and carry me out of here kicking and screaming?"

"You know what happens when I don't get what I want," he says with a little smirk, like I'm supposed to find that funny.

"And you know someone will call the cops if you do that."

"I don't think so."

"I wouldn't be so sure," I say. "This isn't Willow Heights. Everyone here may know you, but they're not employed by your family."

"No one here knows me," he says quietly, sliding onto the seat next to me. "Except you."

For a moment, my gaze is caught by that black hole inside him, and I have to swallow hard and force my eyes away so I don't get sucked in. I watch the crowd that bottlenecked behind him stream to their seats, everyone craning around to see him, to see us, to see what the unpredictable, untouchable Royal Dolce will do next.

I remember how much he hated that.

"And what would you tell the cops when they showed up?" he asks, leaning an elbow on the seat in front of us and turning to me, so we're blocked from some of the prying eyes. I'm also boxed in. I try to steady my heartbeat. It's fine. I'm fine. He can't take more from me. I have to remind myself of that every time.

"You're afraid I'd rat you out?" I ask. "I already told you I wouldn't. So if that's what you're so concerned about, you can rest easy. You got away with it. Y'all all did. Now can you leave me alone?"

"Then what would you tell them?" Royal asks, cocking his head and watching me with curiosity.

"Get off the bus or you're riding the route," the driver calls back. One girl who trailed her friends on leans down to kiss her girlfriend, then hurries off the bus. Royal doesn't move.

"You're going to ride a public school bus?" I ask, quirking a brow.

"I guess so," Royal says, not moving a muscle to get off the bus.

I sigh. "Seriously, Royal. Why won't you leave me alone?"

"Why won't you answer the question?"

"I don't know, maybe I'd get a restraining order," I say. "Since you keep stalking me."

"Then I better stay on the bus," he says. "If this is my only chance to talk to you."

SELENA

The bus driver mutters and closes the door, shifting into gear. I'm glad for the noise of the bus, which drowns out the silence. A few seats around us are quiet, but everyone else starts talking, and I relax a little.

"How did you even know I'd be here today?" I ask. It's my first day at Faulkner. Has he been skulking around there all week like a perv, since he knows I'm not at Willow Heights?

"Are you going to come on Sunday this time?" he asks. "You wasted last weekend's chance."

"Do I have a choice?"

He takes my hand gently, and I quickly hide my other hand under my thigh, not wanting him to see my bloody thumb. I let my left hand go completely limp in his, so he knows I won't fight and make this fun for him. He turns my hand over, flattening it and stroking my palm with his thumb. His touch—god, his fucking touch nearly kills me. I can feel the familiar warmth blooming along my skin, taking my breath, sending prickles through my blood. I close my eyes, trying not to react. It's all a deception. His fucking touch is a lie.

"You're bleeding," he says quietly.

My eyes fly open, but before I can think what to do, he pushes up the sleeve on my wrist. My gaze locks on him, but he's staring down at my arm, pushing the sleeve higher. He swallows so hard I can hear it. I look down, feeling sick at the sight of the first two cuts, which were just thin lines of scab, now torn open and ragged from my thumbnail. The next five or six lines are still small and neatly sealed over.

Royal pulls my sleeve back down and raises his gaze to mine at last. "You need to get some help, Harper."

"Like you did?"

"You helped me," he says quietly.

"And look where it got me," I say. "Fucked up people do fucked up things and make more fucked up people. So here we are. I'm as fucked up as you, and my pussy can't be your therapy anymore. Are you going to get real help? Or just give me shit for the way I'm coping? At least I'm not hurting anyone but myself."

"You're wrong," he says, stroking the back of my hand with his thumb, his long lashes casting shadows over his cheeks as he watches our linked hands.

SELENA

"What's your excuse?" I ask. "Don't tell me you can't afford a psychiatrist. What are you afraid of—that they'll tell you you're a psychopath?"

I know I'm being a bitch, but I don't owe him anything. He took everything already, left me hollowed out and scraped clean, empty of all meaning. I want to hurt him back, even if it's only in some petty little way that makes me even smaller than I already feel. This must be how Preston feels. Bitter and resentful and smart enough to know he's beaten, but too stubborn to give up the last inch.

"I can't be fixed," Royal says, his dark gaze rising to mine.

I wonder if he's stating a fact, or if he's telling me that's what he's afraid of. I hate the way my throat tightens when our eyes meet, the way I can still feel him, the darkness that always called to mine. I should be immune now, and I want to scream and rage at the whole world because I'm not, and it's not fucking fair. I endured things no one should endure. I walked through hell, and I made it back, if not quite alive. If there's a merciful god, I should get to feel nothing when I look into the devil's eyes. I fucking earned it.

"I can't, either," I say, my throat tight. "You made sure of that."

I turn to the window and swallow past the agonizing ache. I will not cry.

twenty-one

Harper Apple

We don't speak until the bus stops at the corner. Then we climb off and start down the block.

"Is Preston at your house?" Royal asks, glowering at the truck. "Or did he give you the Escalade?"

"Does it matter?" I ask.

"It matters," Royal grits out.

I sigh and force myself to give him what he wants, still clinging to the hope that he'll get bored if I submit to his every demand without resistance. "He let me borrow it," I say. "He takes care of me—of us. Mom, too. He pays our rent, and our bills, and buys us groceries."

"Why?" Royal asks, his voice guarded, careful.

"Because I'm his whore, okay?" I say, throwing my hands up.

Royal visibly flinches. "You're fucking him?"

I let out a huff of disbelief. "Is that what you want to hear? Yes, he fucks me. You know that. You've seen it."

"I don't know what his dick looks like," he snaps. "I knew he sent the videos to fuck with me, but I hoped it was someone else in them."

"Nope, just me and your worst enemy. But really, Royal, why does it matter? You'd never have let your brothers fuck me if you were going to do it again, so it's really none of your business who or how many I add to my body count. My pussy is no longer your concern."

"I get it," he snaps.

"How do you think I got all these new clothes, this new look?" I ask, knowing I'm poking the beast but unable to stop myself. "Why else would a man do anything for a woman, right? You should know that. Buy a girl a steak dinner, you get to fuck her in the ass, whether she agrees or not. Except here's the difference. Preston doesn't make me beg for scraps. I didn't ask for any of that. He just did it. Because he's a good person, Royal. And no matter what you do to me for daring to sympathize with a Darling, you won't convince me otherwise. You'll only convince me that you're not."

I storm ahead of him down the block, fighting back tears. Part of me wants to turn back, to make sure he's not going after Blue, who got off behind us. But I'm barely keeping it together when all I have to worry about is myself. I can't protect even one more person. Sometimes I wish I was like her, that I had an Olive to love and care for, someone who came first and who loved me just as much. But right now, I'm glad I don't have to be responsible for anyone else.

I stop at the truck and take a few deep breaths until I'm under control. I hate that Royal has this effect on me, that he can make me feel anything at all. I liked being numb. What I said about Preston is true—he did do all those things for me. But the kindest thing he did was let me be numb, not force me to face all this ugliness that I can't deal with right now. It's too much. It's all too much. I've never felt so frustrated, so helpless. I just want it all to go away, and he made a safe space for me to do that. Out here, there's no way out.

"Get in the car," I say when Royal reaches me. "I'll give you a ride back to school."

"I can walk," he says.

"In this heat? Don't be stupid."

"I have practice in this heat every day."

"Then why aren't you there?"

"Because I'm here," he says, like it's that simple.

I don't have an answer. I'm too tired to argue. I just climb in the truck and start the engine. Preston texted today asking me to bring it back, anyway, and if I go to Faulkner, I can ride the bus. I don't need it anymore.

"I should return this before you wreck it out of spite," I say. "Do you want a ride or not?"

Royal looks like the last thing in the entire world he wants is to climb in the vehicle with me. He's glaring at the truck like the very sight of it makes him sick. "Let me drive," he says at last.

"Whatever." I sigh and climb over the console into the passenger seat. It doesn't matter. Nothing matters. I repeat the words over and over, my new mantra. If Royal wants to wreck the truck, I don't care. If he takes me outside town and ties me up in the swamp again to die, it doesn't matter.

SELENA

He lifts himself up into the driver's seat and closes the door. For a minute, we just sit there in silence, the air conditioner blasting. Then Royal pulls out onto the road and drives back to FHS. Neither of us say a word. He parks next to the Rover in the mostly empty parking lot, his eyes fixed straight ahead.

Finally, he breaks the silence. "What do you want me to say?"

"Nothing," I say truthfully. "There's nothing to say. Just go."

He turns to me, those dark, hypnotic eyes threaded with so much emotion it makes me recoil. "You said you didn't want an apology."

I let out an incredulous laugh. "You think words are going to fix this?"

"Then what do you want?" he asks, sounding like he's this close to losing it with frustration, like I've given him any indication that I want anything at all from him.

"I want you to leave me alone," I say flatly.

He turns to face forward again, his jaw working as he stares out the windshield. "I can't do that," he says quietly. "I'm sorry. That's the one thing I can't give you."

"Why?" I demand. "Why are you still torturing me?"

"Torturing you?" Royal asks, grabbing my arm and shoving my sleeve up. "I'm not the one torturing you."

"Don't fucking touch me," I bark, yanking my arm away.

We stare at each other a long moment, and I curse myself for giving him what he wants, for fighting back. He's asking me for the one thing I'm unwilling to give, too—a response. It's the one thing Preston never asked for, the only reason I could give him what he wanted.

"Look, Royal, I don't know what you want. I'm the one who should be asking you that. You won. You broke me. I will never be unbroken. Isn't that enough?"

"What about what you did?" he asks, his voice quiet, his eyes searching mine. "I read the messages you sent that creep. You were playing me all along."

"I wasn't," I whisper, swallowing past the quivering, sick feeling in my throat.

"Bullshit," Royal says, turning to face forward again. "You wanted to destroy my family."

I take a deep breath. "You're right."

We sit in silence for a minute.

"Are you even sorry?" Royal asks.

"Of course I'm fucking sorry," I snap. "Look at me."

"But are you sorry for what you did? Or just sorry you got caught?"

"Nothing happened to you," I remind him. "It never came out."

"It could. You don't know who he is."

I swallow hard.

Royal catches my hesitation and swings his head toward me. His eyes narrow. "Do you?"

"It's Preston," I whisper.

He flinches, then turns to face forward, his fingers gripping the wheel so hard his knuckles whiten. "Preston knows," he says flatly. "I knew it. They all know, don't they?"

I press a fist to my chest, trying to breathe. It's like I can feel his pain, the pain of my betrayal. I didn't just lose. I lost *him*. I didn't just try to take down his family. I hurt this beautiful, terrible boy.

But he did worse than hurt me. I can feel bad about what I did, can even hurt for him, but I can't forgive him. Not even if I deserve what I got.

"He won't tell anyone," I say.

"I trusted you, Harper," he says to the windshield.

I shake my head. "My turn to call bullshit. You didn't tell me your secrets. I found out on my own."

"And if I had?" He turns to me, searching my face, as if the answers will be written there.

I don't answer. I don't know. It doesn't matter.

"You'd still have spilled them."

I swallow hard. He's probably right.

"Why do you do it?" I ask at last, horrified that some sick part of me still wants to understand this broken boy who broke me so completely I didn't think I'd ever want to understand anyone again. I didn't think I'd ever want anything, period.

He closes his eyes, resting his head back on the headrest. "I don't."

SELENA

"The no-questions rule doesn't really work when the person doesn't want anything from you. So, if we're done talking, it's time for you to go."

He's quiet a minute, and then he speaks, his voice so low I have to lean in just to hear him. "It's Dad's thing," he says. "We're all pawns to him."

"That's… Illegal." I don't know what to say, and that stupid thing is what comes out.

A tiny, ironic smile twitches at the corner of his lips. "We didn't take money. It's part of closing a business deal. It's not illegal, and even if it were…"

"Right," I say when he stops speaking. "Your family doesn't care."

He doesn't answer, just stares ahead at a group of guys coming from around the back of the school and climbing in their cars, probably football players leaving practice. Faulkner High's team doesn't scare me, though.

"I still don't understand why," I say at last. "I mean, Baron told me he used to threaten your sister to get you to do his bidding, but after she was gone…"

"I still have two little brothers."

I close my eyes and take a shaky breath. I didn't consider that. The twins don't seem younger than Royal—less fucked up, maybe, but even more psychotic. I never would have guessed he was protecting them. In truth, they probably should be the ones protecting him. They were adamant that nothing sexual happened when he was kidnapped, and if they're right, he's plenty screwed up from his dad using him as some kind of escort service for his business clients.

But I get it. Even though I don't have an Olive to protect, I understand people who do.

"I'm sorry," I say after a minute. "I'm sorry your dad does that, and that you feel like you have to do it to protect them from it. And I'm sorry I told Preston, and I'll talk to him and make sure he's never going to use it against you. I never wanted to hurt you, even when I wanted to stop you."

His jaw tenses, and he gives me a scathing look. "Don't fucking talk to Preston about me. Just knowing he knows that about me, and everything else you told him, makes me want to rip his intestines out and hang him with them."

"And you think it's so easy for me to know all those guys know what I look like and feel like? You want to know why

I'm here? Because Willow Heights wouldn't give me back my scholarship, and the thought of fighting that hard just to go to school with your brothers and all their friends…"

"That's why you're here?" he asks, staring at me.

I shrug. "Part of it. I don't want to see them. Not enough to keep fighting for it."

"It wasn't all their friends," he says.

I want to laugh, but my throat is too tight and my eyes ache with the pressure building behind them. "It doesn't matter who it was," I say. "The truth is, I don't want to know who did it and who didn't. I know what they did. And I know you know. You know the most shameful thing that's ever happened to me."

"It's not shameful," Royal says, reaching for me.

I lean away from him, not wanting his lying hands on me. Tears force themselves past my eyes, and I blink hard, trying to hold them back, but one slips out, trickling down my cheek. "You watched," I say, my voice quiet but fierce. "I can't look at your face without knowing you witnessed the worst thing that's ever happened to me. You watched them break me, and you could have stopped it, and you didn't. You ordered it."

He swallows so hard I hear it, but he doesn't drop his eyes. "I made a mistake."

"Yeah," I say, swiping the tears off my cheeks. "So please make it right, if you ever cared about me even a little, and go away. I don't want to see you, Royal. I can't. I can't be around you. That's going to be the thing that finally kills me. So unless that's what you're still trying to do, just leave."

He sits there a few seconds, and then he climbs out of the truck and closes the door quietly behind him. I fold over on myself, wrapping my arms around my knees and sobbing so hard I can feel something inside me tearing open like a black hole swallowing everything left of me. And then my door opens, and Royal climbs up in the seat, pulling me into his lap.

"No," he says, pressing his face into my hair. "I'm not leaving, Harper. Not again. Not ever."

He wraps his arms tight around me and holds me like he can hold my broken pieces together, like he's not the reason I'm broken, like he's not the reason I'm falling to pieces.

SELENA

I think he means his words as a promise, but they bring no comfort. They're a curse I can't escape, no matter how well I hide. *He's* a curse. I brought it upon myself. I made him need me, fed his darkness with my own, let him consume me day by day until he couldn't live without. I loved the way he needed me. I thought it would kill me when he stopped. I should have known. I had it all wrong. It's his need that will kill me.

Because now I'm empty, but he still needs more. He's still here, demanding more, and I have nothing to give him but tears. I'm as hollow and soulless as he is. I can't fight his claim, but I can't accept it, either. I can only sob out my anguish and fury and regret, knowing I will never be free as long as his venomous heart craves mine, as long as the void of his soul seeks mine, calling for it in the empty cavern inside me where only echoes live now.

twenty-two

Harper Apple

I get a call from Willow Heights the next day saying the admission committee will hear me out if I want to present my case on Monday. I thought they'd given me a hard no, and I'd started to accept that I wouldn't be going back, but I'm not going to miss the chance if they're giving me one. I hope to hell it's a coincidence and Royal isn't behind this, because the last thing I want is to owe him.

Either way, I stay home from school on Friday and work on what I'm going to say. I'm so wrung out from the encounter with Royal that it's hard to focus, though. He insisted on following me home before he'd leave yesterday. The irony is not lost on me. What does he think can happen to a girl that's worse than what he already let happen? What he caused?

SELENA

I don't bring the truck back, though. I like having a vehicle that Mom can't sell. I like having a way out, an escape. It makes me feel safe. I text Preston and tell him he can come get it, but I know he won't show his face. I tell him why I need it through Monday and explain the admission board hearing. He doesn't respond. Once, maybe I would have been upset that he was pissed. But that's the thing about not caring. It's freeing.

On Saturday evening, I'm still in bed when Mom comes stomping in.

"Get your ass up," she yells, dragging the dusty blinds up.

I throw my arm over my eyes. "What do you need?"

"I need my daughter to get her ass up and come to my retirement party," she says. "Get some of them fancy clothes on and come out and help. I got friends on their way now."

"Retirement party?" I ask, sitting up.

"Yeah," she says with a grin. "It's your party, too, baby. You made it happen."

I just gape at her until she laughs and perches her ass on the windowsill like she's settling in to chat. She takes out a pack of smokes from her back pocket and lights up, blowing a cloud of tobacco fumes toward my bed.

"Can you not?" I ask, waving it away. I hate when she smokes in my room. It makes my clothes stink.

"See, your sugar daddy paid all our rent and our bills for the year, and since the electric company wouldn't give the money back, and the landlord's a piece of shit and would probably take it for himself if I tried to get it back, I figured hey, instead of spending the money, why not just… Retire?"

"Because you're thirty-five?" I offer.

"The bills are *paid*," she crows. "That's the reason I bust my ass all day and night, trying to find something that'll keep the hot water on. But I ain't gotta do that anymore. We're set for the whole year!"

I don't bother pointing out all the fucked up logic in her comments. I definitely don't bring up the fact that she parties more than she busts her ass, and that's why she keeps losing her jobs, or that the hot water was only on half the time before Preston came along. She's the parent who stayed. I can't exactly be picky.

"And what happens next year?" I ask. "It's September. That's only three months away."

"Don't you dare lose that man," she warns, jabbing her cigarette at me like an accusatory finger. "Only took eighteen years, but having a baby's finally paying off."

"Glad I could be of service," I mutter.

"I mean it, Harp," she says. "Don't fuck this up for us. Girls like us, we get one chance. It won't come along again."

"I'll try not to fuck it up," I agree with a sigh.

"He won't want you forever," she says. "The thing you gotta do is, when he starts to get tired of you—and you'll know it, a woman can always tell, can't she?—you gotta look around at his friends. Those rich men, they don't mind passing around a little thing like you for a while. Get everything you can from him, do anything he wants, even the weird shit, and then move on to the next one."

I throw off the sheet and swing my legs off the bed, rubbing my eyes. "Are you seriously telling me to do kinky sex stuff with old men right now?"

"They ain't all old," she argues, waving my comment away with some smoke. "They're all married, sure, but they see their wives different. Once they give them kids, they can't be pulling their hair and choking them and shit. They respect them and shit. That's where girls like us can help, give them what they've been missing."

"That's not what this is," I say stiffly. "He's not married, and he's not into any of that. He respects me."

My mother cackles with laughter.

I get up and go to the closet, looking at all the designer clothes Preston put me in. My last words echo back in my head, doubt gnawing at the edges of my mind. Preston cares about me, but it's going a little far to say he respects me. He treated me well, but he used me. I was his whore, exactly as Mom is describing, minus the wife and kinky stuff.

The hair pulling kind of relationship is what I had with Royal, but he doesn't respect me, either, and I didn't get any of the things Mom wants from him. He didn't take care of me. He did the opposite.

Mom finishes her fit of laughter and taps the ash from her cigarette onto my carpet. "Those rich guys, they're used to women throwing themselves at them," she explains. "They got their wives for regular maintenance, but they can get a side piece any time, too. You gotta set yourself apart. You're the… Spice. Oh, and tell them you're still seventeen. They like that."

"Mom, no. Just no."

"The key is not to let your heart get involved. That's when you lose your head and it all goes to shit, and next thing you know, you got a snot-nosed brat, and you're wondering how you're going to make the rent for a trailer, let alone catch the eye of a rich guy." She sucks hard on her filter, trying to get the last of the tobacco from the cigarette butt.

"Wait a minute," I say, turning from the closet. My heart does this weird thing in my chest that it does when I have to remember anything about the Dolce boys. "Are you talking about John Darling?"

"Yeah," she says. "How'd you know about that?"

"So it's true," I marvel. "You dated some trailer park junkie who's actually a Darling."

"Oh, you talking about JT?" she asks.

"Who are you talking about?"

We stare at each other for a minute, and then a loud knock interrupts us. My heart drops like a stone, and for one breathless half a moment, it's the last day of spring break, and Duke's pounding on the door. My head swims, and I have to grab the closet door to keep from buckling.

"Get cleaned up and come on out," Mom says, heading for the door. "You made all this happen, I figure you're old enough to party with us."

Sure, now she's fucking proud of me. I shake my head and turn back to the closet. I have nothing better to do, so I put on a dress and heels and go out to meet Mom's friends. A couple of the guys try eye-fucking me, but Mom smacks one of them across the back of the head and tells him I'm too expensive for him. I sit in the cloud of smoke in the living room, taking an occasional sip of my drink and watching my mother get progressively more and more wasted.

She keeps trying to get me to smoke, but I saw them sprinkle some crystal in with a joint, so I don't even want to smoke that, despite her aggressive insistence. It's like she has to prove to herself that I really am like her, or maybe under her pride, she's still pissed at me for ruining her life, and she wants to bring me down with her. Either way, I pass on the joints and just watch the party unfold.

One of the reasons I've never truly hated my mother is that I understand her. Studying her made me want to get in people's heads, see what makes them tick. Seeing into someone else's life let me be someone else for a moment, see everything from their point of view. It taught me to sympathize with every single person, no matter what they've done, because if you go deep enough, they have a reason. There's always a reason. You just have to be willing to see it, even when it's terrible, or being inside their head makes you sick.

I leave the party early, returning to my room, but I sleep with my brass knuckles on and my knife in one hand. I've almost forgotten Royal's request the next day until the texts start.

Royal: Slaughterpen 10 pm. Dont ghost again.
BadApple: not in the mood
Royal: I'll pick u up

BROKEN DOLL

BadApple: No
Royal: wear something comfortable
BadApple: I'll drive

I don't know why I still care if he comes here. But I don't want to be in his car. Even when he drove the truck, I didn't feel like I was at his mercy. Not completely.

Despite my decision to drive, at quarter to ten, my mom yells back that I have a visitor. Shit. I start to be ashamed of my house, but then I remember I have no reason to care what Royal thinks. I toss my phone and my keys in my purse, slide my feet into the steel-toed combat boots Preston got me, and head out of my room. My stomach clenches when I see Royal Dolce standing in the middle of the living room, inside my ramshackle house, with party detritus still scattered over every surface.

My mom is standing too close, hanging on Royal's arm in that flirty way she does where she constantly touches the man she's hitting on. I feel a little sick. I try to tell myself it doesn't matter. He already knows I'm trash. Why do I care what he thinks?

SELENA

"Look who it is," Mom says to me, still clinging to Royal's bicep. "You know they say he could have played college ball anywhere, but he chose to stay right here in Faulkner."

I almost snort out loud. My mother cares about sportsball exactly as much as I do.

"Is that so?" I ask, giving them a tight smile. "I said I was driving."

"It's on my way," Royal says, the lie slipping off his tongue so easily you'd never know it wasn't true if you didn't know where he lives. "Besides, it's nice to catch up with your mom."

Mom giggles sickeningly.

"Catch up?" I grind out.

"Oh yeah," Mom says, batting his abs. "We're old friends now. He came around a few times this summer, when you were too busy for your lonely mom. Kept me company."

I want to vomit. She'd never turn down dick that good. And Royal likes older women. If he fucked my mother—

It doesn't matter.

I remind myself that yet again. It's the kind of thing he'd do out of spite, but I don't care. It doesn't matter if he fucked my mom, if he wants to drive. It doesn't matter where he's taking me. It doesn't matter if he kills me. Nothing matters.

"Cool," I say, turning my indifferent gaze on Royal. "Ready when you are."

"See you soon, Mrs. Apple," Royal says, detaching himself from her clutches.

"It's Ms., silly," Mom says, batting his arm this time. "I'm not married."

"Right," Royal says. "See you, Ms. Apple."

I'm already out the door. He hurries to catch up. He parked right behind my truck in the driveway, blocking me in. He probably thought I'd fight it, that I would insist on driving, and he could win again by blocking my truck and not letting me leave, making me get in his car instead. I don't give him the satisfaction. I climb in the front seat of the Range Rover, almost spiteful in my apathy.

I haven't been in his car since the day he kidnapped me and dragged me to the swamp, and I swear I can still smell it here, the rich, oily scent of rotting plants and murky water. I close my eyes and swallow the thick feeling in my throat.

We drive for a minute in silence. "What are you so pissed about?" Royal asks at last.

"Nothing," I say. "I'm not pissed about anything."

"Is it because I talked to your mom?" he guesses.

"Nope."

"Come on, Harper," he says. "I know you. I know you're pissed. Just tell me why."

"Does it matter?"

"It matters to me."

"Why?"

He shrugs. "I don't know. It just does."

"Fine," I say. "First off, you don't know me. You *knew* me. You knew the girl who wouldn't want you to see the hovel she lives in while you prance around your fancy mansion with your butlers and maids and shit. You knew the girl who would care that you talked to her mom behind her back, that you probably fucked her because she's your type, right? And she'll fuck anyone who can keep it up long enough for her to climb on. You knew the girl who might not want to get in a car with a guy who kidnapped her and took her to the middle of nowhere to have her gang-banged and left for dead."

"What the fuck, Harper," he says quietly. "I didn't fuck your mom." He looks at me, his gaze so wounded I almost believe he's capable of hurt. But I know better than to buy into that game.

I take a deep breath and go on, though, because I'm not done. "You'd think the girl you attacked wouldn't get in a car and go anywhere without knowing what she was getting into after that little incident. But that's because you think I'm still that girl, that I'm the same Harper Apple you knew. But I'm not. I'm no one. And no one doesn't care if you saw her house and know you were right all along, that she's trash. She hopes you fucked her mom and got all her diseases, too. And it's not that she's stupid for getting in your car, it's that she simply doesn't care."

"I didn't say you were stupid."

"I don't care," I say. "I don't care if you take me right back to the swamp. I don't care if you have a whole fucking parade come by and fuck me before you kill me this time. I don't care what you do to me, Royal, because *I'm already dead.*"

Royal pulls up in front of the Slaughterpen and parks. He turns to me, and after a second, he reaches over, swiping his thumb across my cheek. I didn't even know I was crying until he wipes the tears away. "I think you're wrong," he says. "I think you care."

"I don't."

He leans in, sliding his hand over my cheek and under my ear, cradling my head and pulling me forward. Before I realize what's happening, he presses his lips to mine.

I shove him so hard I break out of his grip and fly back against the door, my head slamming against the window. My breaths comes quick as I stare at him, my eyes wide with shock.

"See?" he says with a little grin. "You do care."

He opens his door and climbs out, closing his door before I can say a word. I sit there, my heart ricocheting crazily around my ribcage. What the fuck just happened?

Royal opens my door and holds out a hand, that little smirk still on his lips, and all I want to do is bash every one of his teeth out of his stupid head with my brass knuckles.

"Don't fucking touch me," I say, leaning away from him.

"I didn't fuck your mother," he says. "And I give less than zero fucks about your house. Your house isn't you. And you're not trash."

"Since when?" I demand.

"Trust me," he says. "I wouldn't give trash more than an hour of my time. And you, Appleteeny, have taken an entire year of my life. I wouldn't be here right now if you weren't worth it."

"Well, *I'm* here right now because you said if I didn't go, you'd keep showing up. So here I am. Let's get this over with, and then I never want to see you again."

"Would it be that easy for you?" he asks, cocking his head to one side, like he really has to ask.

"You're psychotic," I say, slapping his hand away and climbing out of the Range Rover. "Of course it would be easy. You spent our entire relationship telling me I was nothing, a worthless whore, and then you destroyed me until

I really was nothing. And now that I proved you right about everything you ever said, you're going to try to convince me otherwise? Is this just another part of your sick game? See if you can build me up and break me down all over again?"

"It's not a game."

"Good," I say, starting toward the building, ready to get this over with and get away from him. I slip my phone out of my purse and into my pocket. I don't want to get separated from it. "Because it won't work. You can't fix what you did. You can't fix me. And you don't have to pretend to care now that you don't have me. You don't have to put on some fake show of remorse to get me back. If you want me, just take me. You can have me. Do whatever sick things you have to do to me before you get bored and toss me. I don't care."

"Is that what you want?" he asks.

"It doesn't matter what I want," I say. "You taught me that from the moment we met until the moment you had your brothers gag me so I couldn't withhold my consent while you shared me with them as punishment. I've finally learned my lesson. I don't matter, so it doesn't matter what happens to me."

We reach the tall chain-link fence around the front of the building, and I stop and stand there, staring straight ahead. I've been here so many times over the past few years, and yet, no nostalgia rises in me when I look at the plain warehouse building bathed in the orangey glow of security lights. I don't miss Dynamo standing there manning the gate with his four-fingered hand and his tattooed neck and hollow smile. I don't miss the stink of blood and sweat, the weight of a fat roll of bills in my pocket. I feel nothing.

Royal comes up behind me and takes my elbow, turning me around. "You matter, Harper." His eyes burn with that dark intensity that's more dangerous than the fury or the emptiness. "You matter to me."

A ghost of a smile tugs at my lips. "The old Harper would have liked to know that."

"Not you?" he asks, his gaze searching mine, like it can find something that's no longer there. He hooks his fingers into the links on either side of me, watching me while I stand looking up at him, unafraid though my back is to the fence and he's caging me in.

SELENA

"No," I say. "I don't care about her, or you, or if you're lying through your teeth. I could matter to you, or the whole town, or no one, and it wouldn't make a difference. I don't matter to *me*."

twenty-three

Harper Apple

Royal stands there searching my eyes for a long time, like he's waiting for the other side of me to bubble up and burst out like it did in the truck last week. But that's the thing about my bombed out interior. Even I don't know when he'll step on a grenade. I can't predict my reactions, can't control my hollowness like he can. I don't know when I'll be totally numb and calm, and when I'll burst into uncontrollable rage or sobs.

I just know that when I'm still, when no one is walking around the craters inside my soul, there are less explosions. When Royal lets himself in with the key he stole, walks around and touches the fragments of my soul like they belong to him, they're likely to blow up, shaking whatever's left of my foundation. I should know he's a masochist, that this is what he does, another sore spot he can poke, like when he goes to the bridge or the basement. But now he's not just hurting himself. He's hurting me, too.

"What if I could change that?" he asks at last.

I shrug. "You can't."

He hesitates a moment, then takes my hand and pulls me to the gate. "Come on," he says, leading me inside.

I don't bother fighting. I won't win, not even here, at the Slaughterpen, where I almost always won. I never win against Royal.

We enter through the heavy industrial door. Inside, instead of the usual—an abandoned chair or two, a haphazard pile of tumbled boxes, wisps of insulation drifting across the floor from the abandoned piles at the edges—it looks like a functional warehouse. Stacks of boxes sit in neat rows, like they've just been unloaded from a forklift.

"What the hell?" I mutter.

"Don't worry," Royal says. "They left the pit alone."

"Why?"

He cracks a small, ironic smile. "You think the owners of this place don't get a cut?"

The owners. He pretty much told me his family owned the Slaughterpen. So that's what he meant.

"So… This is for the casino?" I ask, gesturing around at the boxes.

He puts a finger to his lips. "Not everyone knows."

A little chill goes through me. Who is he hiding it from?

Before I can ask, we come out the end of the aisle of boxes he led me down, and he pulls me to the back corner, where the pit remains, as promised.

The pit is exactly what it sounds like—a dirt hole in the ground where the slab was broken at some point, and some genius decided to drag the concrete off and dig about six feet down. It's small, maybe eight by ten feet, with uneven edges that are a bitch to climb up and down over. Some chunks of the concrete foundation used to line the edges for people to sit on, but they're gone now, leaving just the jagged hole.

This isn't a place MMA hopefuls are going to get discovered by scouts and go pro, like the back of a rec hall somewhere that puts down mats or opens a real ring at night. This is literally underground, bareknuckle boxing. The goal isn't skill and finesse that people can see, though it takes plenty of both to do what has to be done here. The goal is to keep a fight going for as many rounds as you can, draw more blood than your opponent, and walk away with money and no broken bones. A KO on the first round will get you booed out of the place, spit on, and sometimes worse.

Tonight, there is no crowd, no women like my mother lounging on the cement blocks pretending they're not trying to look sexy. No men stand around with tepid beer in plastic cups. There are no betting slips. The usual chatter and edgy, bloodthirsty excitement is gone. There are only three people, sitting in three chairs at the far end of the pit. In the dim security lights of the warehouse, I can barely make out that they're all wearing hoods pulled down over their faces, like something out of a hostage video.

I turn to Royal, my heart giving one hard thud and then skipping the next beat. "What the fuck?"

"You're welcome," he says.

"Again, what the fuck, Royal?"

"They're all yours," he says. "Go talk to them. I think you'll find they have some interesting things to say."

I swallow hard, balling my hands into fists to keep them from shaking. "Why are you doing this?" I whisper.

His eyes turn earnest. "I'm trying to make it right."

I stare at him incredulously. "You can't make this right, Royal."

"Can you just let me try?"

We stand there another minute, our wills battling as we gaze into each other the way only we can. The fucked up part is, I still understand him, even after what he did. I worked on it for so long, and it didn't just go away. I can't unknow what I know about him. He really thinks this is what I want.

"No," I say, pushing past him, toward the door. He thinks he still understands me, because we used to be the only ones who understood each other. But he can't understand me now, after what I've been through. No one except maybe Mabel Darling can understand that.

Royal grabs my elbow from behind and spins me around.

"Go deal with them, or I will," he says quietly. His gaze is stormy, intense. There's no question in this look. He's giving an order and telling me the consequences of disobeying, just

SELENA

like he did when I climbed over the gate into his neighborhood. I should have listened then, but I didn't, and he did exactly what he said he would. I have no doubt he'll follow through on his promise this time, too.

A shiver runs through me when I remember what he did to Colt. I know how he deals with people. It's what they deserve, and yet...

When our gazes meet, I can see so much in his eyes, so much rage and pain, that it shocks my own system, like my heart has stopped and he has enough energy to shock it back to beating. "I don't want to see them," I admit.

"You're going to see them, anyway," he says. "You can't hide away forever."

"Why not?" I ask. "They'd be happy to pretend I died that night. Tell them I'm a ghost, that they can't talk to me at school. If you say I don't exist, they'll make it true."

"I don't go to your school anymore, Harper."

"So?" I demand. "You still have power in this town."

"That's not going to help you."

"I didn't ask for your help."

We stare at each other another long moment. "You have no fucking idea how hard it was to bring them here without bashing their skulls together until there was nothing left but bloody stumps on their necks," he says. "If that's what you want to do, do it. If you want to cut their dicks off, stuff them up their own asses, and watch them bleed to death, do it. But stop running, and fucking take care of it."

"So, I'm supposed to thank you?" I ask. "This is some kind of gift that's supposed to make up for what happened to me?"

He gives me that hooded look, staring me down. "If that's what you want it to be."

"Sorry, I'm not a sadist," I say. "I don't get off on hurting people. I just want to be dead to you and all of them, like you said."

He swallows hard. "You're not dead to me, Harper. You know that. Obviously, you're not."

"Obviously," I snap. "Since you're still here torturing me."

"I'm torturing you by letting you get revenge however you want?"

"Seeing you is torture," I say. "Why can't you understand that?"

His eyes harden. "Talk to them, Harper."

"I'm not a masochist, either."

He gives a little snort. "Don't kid yourself. You can fight here without being a masochist—once. You keep coming back as many times as you did, you're just like the rest of us."

I swallow hard. He's right. I fucking loved taking a good hit, the sting of it. It made me feel alive, mortal and invincible at once. I loved when he fucked me so rough I couldn't tell where pleasure ended and pain started or the other way around. It made me forget why one was supposed to be better than the other. And I lived for the sweet ache of loving him, even knowing it made me a dumb bitch to keep going when I already knew he would eviscerate my heart and soul if I even made it out alive.

"Fine," I say, pulling away from Royal. "I'll face them. I've already faced you, and you're the worst of them. I'm not going to kill them, though. Just like I wouldn't kill you. But don't take that as kindness or weakness on my part. I could do it. I'm not taking mercy on you because you deserve it, either. You don't. I choose not to have that on me. That's the only reason I won't fight back the way you deserve."

I turn around and march over to the pit, crouching to brace my hand on the edge and jump down in, like I've done a million times before. My feet hit the dirt, my knees unlocked, before I pop up to my full height. My heart beats fast, but it's not because I'm pumped for a fight. I tell myself to breathe, tell my feet to move. I feel disjointed and uncoordinated as I stride across the pit and yank off the first guy's hood.

Duke blinks at me with confusion. "Hey, Harper," he says at last, offering me a hopeful smile. "You look like—different. Your hair and…" His eyes fall on my necklace, and he stops speaking.

I yank off Baron's hood without answering, then hesitate at the last guy. The first guy I don't know, the first one of the football team I'll face besides the Dolces. Suddenly, my palms feel clammy, and my heart is stutter-stepping at a sickening, lurching pace. But fuck this guy. Fuck all these guys. They don't get to have power over me anymore. I have the power here. Even if they weren't tied, I have something none of them ever will. I have integrity, if only a little, and I have the bulletproof armor of not giving a fuck.

And I'm missing something they'd all die to protect—their reputations, their names, their secrets. I have nothing to lose, nothing for them to take. Which means they have nothing to use against me, no weapons in their arsenal. They can't touch me. They've done their worst, so what can they do now?

I yank off the last guy's hood.

Dawson Walton blinks back at me in the dim light, and my gorge rises to my throat. I knew he was a football player, but I didn't know the depth of disgust I'd feel for him when I see his face. I can't remember a single time he even spoke to me, but now I'll always remember that he saw my naked body, touched me while I was helpless to stop him, pushed his bare cock into me with no condom, came inside me.

Something in my head thuds heavy and solid, and I feel a shift inside me, like an earthquake, the plates slipping and making the whole world stagger. I sway on my feet, and my fist connects with the side of his head so hard his whole chair tips backwards. He hits the floor and topples sideways, and my breath comes a little quicker. My heart is racing, but it's found the correct rhythm at last, after months of being just a little bit out of sync. I didn't know I was going to hit him until I did it, but fuck, that felt good.

I wouldn't mind punching out the entire football team after all.

I glance over my shoulder. Royal's sitting at the edge of the pit only a few feet away, his legs dangling in, my bag resting in his lap. I catch his eye, and I have to turn back quick so he doesn't see me smiling. It's just adrenaline. It's not because I feel alive.

At least, I won't let him know it. Fuck him. He doesn't deserve credit for this.

I raise my fists and look from one of the twins to the other.

"Can you take your rings off first?" Duke asks. "I'm not saying we don't deserve our lights knocked out, but those look like they'll hurt like a bitch. You don't want to mess up this pretty face, do you?"

SELENA

"We didn't fuck up your face," Baron adds. He hasn't said a word, but he's watching me with that unnerving intensity that makes me want to look away.

I don't.

"Really?" I ask. "Is that what we're going with?"

I take out my phone and send a quick text. When I look up, the twins are sharing some look that carries meaning I don't understand.

"Coach will bench us if we look like we've been fighting," Duke says quickly. "And hey, you broke one of my teeth and my nose already."

I remember my knee connecting with his face. The crunch when my elbow hit his mouth that night, as I fought to free myself. It's such a small, insignificant thing compared to what they did.

"And that's equivalent to tying me up and letting your whole football team rape me?"

They exchange another look.

"Tell her," Royal grits out behind me.

"It wasn't the whole team," Baron says, nodding his head toward Dawson. "It was just the three of us."

BROKEN DOLL

I stare at Baron, trying to swallow. Trying to fit this information into what I know about that night that never ended, that nightmare that never did. I don't want to have to piece the puzzle together, to think about it that hard, to look at it that closely. I can't.

"Bullshit," I say, glaring at him.

"It really was," Duke says. "I swear. We just wanted to fuck with you a little."

A text comes through on my phone, and I pull it out again and open it. A sick flash yanks tight behind my navel, making me lightheaded. I grip my phone and turn the screen toward them.

"Does that look like you fucked with me *a little?*" I ask, shoving the phone in Duke's face. I've never looked at Preston's pictures. I wish I hadn't. But I want them to see when they're not in their fever of perversion like they were that night. "Does that look like three guys fucked me?"

Duke turns his face away, struggling against the binding that holds his hands behind his back, against the chair. "Okay, okay, maybe we got carried away," he says. "Put that up, and we'll tell you what happened."

SELENA

"I fucking know what happened," I growl, scrolling to the picture of my face and pushing it in front of him. "And how's this for not messing up my face? I look like the fucking Joker. I looked like that for a week. So, you want to tell me why I shouldn't make what your brother did to Colt look like mercy?"

"I'm sorry," Duke says, squeezing his eyes closed. "It was just a game."

I swallow hard, my stomach sour and shaking. "To you," I say quietly, tucking my phone back in my pocket. "Everyone else's life is a game to you. But it's not a game to them. It wasn't a game to me."

"I'm sorry," he says again, and I think the psycho is actually going to cry. "Please, just knock me out."

"Like you knocked me out?" I ask. "Oh, wait. That would have been too merciful. You wanted me to suffer. That's more fun, isn't it?"

Duke's mouth opens and then closes, and he stares up at me with such pleading eyes I almost fall for it. But I know better.

"You like humiliation, right?" I say, leaning down and resting my hands on his knees. His legs aren't tied to the chair, but I know he won't kick me. He's a sad little boy, a coward like all bullies. He knows I could singlehandedly kick his ass, that the only reason he overpowered me before was because there were three of them and only one of me. Royal won't save him this time.

"Then you should love this," I say. "Call it a freebie. You can throw it back in my face any time."

"What are you talking about?" he asks.

"Get this," I say. "I actually thought you were my friend. How's that for humiliating? I bought into your little game, and I cared about you. Not like all your Dolce girls who just want a fuck boy, or someone to buy them a necklace, or to be seen on your arm. I genuinely cared about you, Duke, as difficult as you made that. You were like… The obnoxious little brother I never had."

He swallows, his nostrils flaring. "We *were* friends," he says. "We still could be."

"No," I say sharply, straightening to stand over him. "You don't get to tell that lie, even to yourself. Because here's what's even more humiliating. I was so excited to have a friend, so fucking *desperate,* I actually believed the feeling was mutual. You didn't have to pretend I liked it when you raped me, Duke. You could have just thrown our fake friendship in my face. That's more humiliating than a biological response I had no control over. I should have had control over my mind. I should have known you could never genuinely care about anyone. After all, your love drove a girl to suicide, didn't it? It must be scary to think about truly caring for someone again after that."

"Harper," Baron says. "You're being a bitch."

I let out an incredulous laugh and cross my arms. "I think I've earned the right to be a bitch. I think I've earned the right to crush your testicles until they rupture if that's what I want to do. And you... You've earned the right to remain silent unless you're kissing my feet and telling me how fucking sorry you are."

"I am fucking sorry," Duke says.

I lean down until our noses are almost touching. "I. Don't. Accept. Your. Apology."

I growl out my words one by one, and Duke flinches.

Baron's right. I'm being worse than a bitch. I'm being a monster. But they woke this monster inside me, and it has something to say.

"He wasn't the only one there," Baron says.

I smile and turn to him. "Don't worry. Your turn's coming too, Baron."

He just watches me from behind his glasses, and unlike Duke, I can't read anything in his expression. He doesn't look sorry, and I know if I get an apology out of him, it won't be real. He's not sorry for what he did. If he starts to regret it now, it'll be what Royal accused me of—only being sorry for being caught. Baron might come to regret what he did to me, but he won't be sorry for hurting me. He did it intentionally, and he liked it. He liked that he made me bleed. He's the sadistic fuck in the family.

I look from one of them to the other, and then shake my head. "You know, I don't know which is worse. Destroying someone's life because you believe you have the right, and you actually want to do it and enjoy it, or doing it even though you know it's wrong."

Dawson groans from his spot on the floor beside Baron.

SELENA

"What about him?" Duke asks. "How come you're not tearing him a new one?"

"I have nothing to say to him that can't be said with fists," I say. "I don't even know him."

"Lucky bastard," Duke mutters, yanking at the ties on his hands.

"Let's get this over with," Baron says. "What do you have for me, Jailbird? Hit me with your best shot."

"You don't get to call me nicknames anymore. We're not friends, and we never were. And I don't have much to say to you, either, besides that you're a worthless piece of garbage that your mother probably prayed she'd miscarry into the toilet every time she went to the bathroom. I think you're the one who needs to do the talking now."

He glances at Royal, a frown darkening his brow, before returning his gaze to me. "It was just us," he says, nodding to either side. "The three of us. After we dropped Royal off, we picked up Dawson, and then we went back for you."

"That's not possible," I say, shaking my head, trying to fit this with the reality of what I experienced, the nightmare of the night that never ended.

"It is," Duke says, giving me a small smile, the ghost of his awe-shucks grin. "We wanted to fuck with you, make you think it was all different guys. See, I like to drink, and Baron likes to tag team, so he'd been working on this little… Chemistry project to cure whiskey dick."

"And that's how a little cocktail that you might know as Alice in Wonderland was born," Baron says, looking so fucking proud of himself I want to castrate his ass. "Or maybe you've heard it called Lady Alice, or the Pearl Lady, or Blue Pearls."

"We convinced Dawson to go with us, and we all took a few pearls so we could go all night, and then we went back to Wonderland to find our Alice," Duke says.

I widen my stance, pressing my boots into the packed dirt, trying not to sway on my feet. I can't seem to get enough oxygen, and I think I might faint if I get more lightheaded. I shake my head slowly back and forth, hoping that if I keep moving, the dizziness will pass and I won't black out.

"Pretty clever, right?" Duke says, grinning up at me hopefully. "We put on some body spray and different stuff, and moved around and made noise, so you'd think it was everyone."

I stare at him, trying to swallow but unable. I think I'm going to puke in his face.

"Wow," I say at last, slowly beginning to clap. The noise sounds far away and small in the huge warehouse. "You didn't bring your buddies to gang rape a girl. You only made her *think* you did. You're an excellent human being, Duke Dolce. Give yourself a fucking gold star."

He looks up at Royal behind me, confusion written across his face. "I mean, that's good, right? It was just us."

"You know, you'd think I'd care," I say.

The truth is, I want to be relieved, and I think I should, but there's only rage inside me. It's too late. The damage was fucking done. I can't undo it just because I know the truth. I can't undo months of nightmares, not knowing how many of them fucked me, stepping up to take their turn in a silent procession, stripping away my dignity and humanity. I can't undo the memory of it, the horror of feeling them closing in on me, not knowing who they were or what they'd do, strangers touching me and pushing inside me one by one, taking everything from me until there was nothing left, not even my soul.

I can only know that these boys intentionally made me think that just to psychologically torture me more than they already had. What kind of person even thinks up something so horrific? I like to understand people, to see things as they might, but this is beyond my ability to comprehend.

"So, what are you going to do?" Baron asks. "Because we've been here a while, and my shoulders are cramping."

I just stare at them, and it feels so hollow. Royal brought me a fucking prize, but I can't enjoy it. I'm not like them. I'm not that sadistic. Hurting them won't undo the hurt they caused me. They'll never understand what they did. They can't. I'm not sure they're capable of real remorse, anyway.

"Fine," I say. "I'll do what your brother wanted and knock you out."

I step behind Duke and see that they're zip tied. I look up at Royal, who tosses me down a knife. I catch it, and my eyes meet Baron's, and some understanding passes between us. I could cut him. I remember when he cut off my clothes, and he told me he wasn't going to cut me. Like that was the worst thing he could do. And now Baron knows that I could cut him. I could carve him up, and Royal wouldn't stop me. He'd sit there and watch the same way he watched them punish me.

And for some reason, that's the moment it clicks for me—what a momentous gift he's giving me. Not in that I suddenly value it more, since it means next to nothing to me, but in that I understand how much it means to Royal. In his twisted mind, this is a huge sacrifice, a public show of his respect for me. He's not bowing down to me—Royal doesn't do that—but he's lifting me up, showing his boys that I am not to be fucked with, that I am a boss, too, maybe even his equal.

He could have kicked their asses to avenge me, but he didn't. He deferred to me. I know how much he must have wanted to mete out this punishment himself, how hard he's holding himself back to let me get the revenge *I* want instead of going ballistic and doing it for me, getting the revenge he thinks I deserve. And though he didn't bring an audience because that would expose what was done to me to people outside the group who did it, he's making a point. The three of them are witnesses, and they'll make the rest of the school falls in line. Royal's making a statement, and they'll spread it like gospel: I'm not only under his protection, but I have his blessing to do whatever I want on my own, and he'll support me.

Suddenly, I don't just feel strong. I feel invincible. For the first time in my life, I have power. Not just protection, like I had as Royal's girlfriend, but something that's all mine, even if it's derived by my association with him. I feel it swelling inside me with the realization that I can do anything I want right now. These boys are too scared of Royal to stop me, and he owes me too much to stop me. As tempting as it is to gorge myself until I'm drunk on this new sensation, wreaking havoc and raining down fire on those who have wronged me, I pull back. I could paint the pit with their blood, but I won't.

I'm smarter than that, smart enough to take this currency and leverage it into something more than one night of revenge. I'm not impulsive. Sometimes I let myself pretend I was with Royal, but it was just for fun. It's not the way I want to live my life. It's like winning ten thousand dollars in the lottery. My mom would quit her job, go balls to the wall with partying, and blow it on a week or a month of debauchery. I'd pay the rent, apply for the best schools, buy some nice clothes for an interview with the admissions board, and fly out to visit the best schools. Maybe her way is more fun, but after the party, she'd be right back where she started, and I'd be out of here forever.

I remember Colt saying I attacked everything with brute force. Maybe he was right at the time, but I've learned a thing or two since then. I'm not that girl anymore. I don't attack every challenge with a sledgehammer. A wrecking ball is not the only way to demolish a condemned house.

I cut Duke's zip ties and stand back, watching him rub his hands together and roll his shoulders. "You want me to fight you?" he asks, nodding to the pit behind me. "Because I don't hit girls."

I could laugh at the irony, but I don't. I'm focused now. Power comes with responsibility, after all. I won't be a glutton and use it all at once like some novice who's never tasted the sweet uncertainty in someone's eyes when they look at you like you're someone who could hurt them. I may have no experience with it, but I have a brain. This power has to be used carefully if I want it to last.

"Are you the one who burned me?" I ask, thinking of the D that's branded into the back of my hip, the ugly scar that makes me unable to look over my shoulder into the mirror without reliving that night. It's small, not even an inch tall, but it's all I see.

"Burned you?" he asks, standing and smirking down at me. "No, baby, I didn't burn you. I just left my mark so I know where I've been."

I swing, and he ducks. My blow glances off his jaw. He's still rubbing it when I come in with a left hook. I don't have a weapon on that hand, but I still bring him to his knees.

"Give me your lighter," say, standing over him and holding out a hand.

"What?" His gaze jerks up to mine. "No way. You're fucking crazy."

"Your point?" I say, gesturing again.

He looks up and to my left, where Royal is sitting. I don't turn to see what Royal will say. In some sick way, I have complete confidence in him right now. I know Royal. His brothers may not be able to believe he's going to sit here and let me do whatever I want, but I know.

He brought them here for me, and he must have decided before I got here that he wasn't going to stop me, no matter what I did. He was prepared to watch me kill his own brothers if that's what I wanted to do.

But he knows me, too. He knows I wouldn't do that.

They might not know it, though. They only know he put me first, and I can't help but think what this will do to his already irreparably broken family.

That won't stop me from doing what I need to do for me, though.

Duke reluctantly hands over the lighter, grumbling as he does so. I slip off the brass knuckles on my right hand and turn them over, heating them the way he heated his ring. I know what he used to brand me. I've noticed his chunky D ring before. Seeing it on his finger tonight just made the realization click into place that it matches the D on the back of my right hip.

"Whoa, no way," Duke says, scrambling to his feet and backing away. "You're not branding me with the word *Doll*."

"I'm not sure you have a say in it," I say. "I didn't ask to be branded with your initial, either."

"Dude, *please,*" he says, looking truly freaked. "You don't know what that word means around here."

I hesitate at that. He's right. I didn't know it had deeper meaning. I never asked Preston why he had the letters put on the rings that hide the brass knuckles, what the significance was, even though he has the same letters tattooed on his own hand. If I'd thought about it, I would have dismissed it as having to do with the way he thinks of me, the way he treats me. I am his doll to dress and groom and tend, his property, the same way I was Royal's plaything. I've become a pawn between these powerful families, inextricably linked to both, tangled in the webs they continue to weave around me even as I struggle to break free.

"What does it mean?" I ask, cocking my head at Duke and letting the flame die when the lighter gets so hot it starts to burn my thumb.

"It means… I belong to the Darlings," he says quietly, his eyes full of some resignation I don't understand. "Just like that necklace you're wearing."

SELENA

His hands drop to his sides, and he just stands there, waiting for me to do it. There's no fear in his expression, no bitterness. He understands this is punishment, and he accepts it because he knows he fucked up. He knows he deserves whatever justice I serve.

I'm not sure I can dole it out, though. For a second, I think about it. About how much their family hates the Darlings, how much he'll hate having their claim permanently etched into his skin. And then I think about how little thought he gave to making me live my worst nightmare. How little he hesitated. How much worse he made me think it was, reveling in his sick game.

I heat the rest of the letters, step forward, and tell him to lift his shirt. When I press the thick rings to his skin, I have to bite my lip because the heat of the metal sears into my hand, too. Duke sucks in a breath and looks away, up at the ceiling, his jaw clenched and his nostrils flaring. But he doesn't fight. He's accepted his punishment.

When I pull away, his skin is angry and red, blisters already forming. I turn to Baron. I think about burning him, too. Or I could fight him—he'd hit back, I'm sure. He likes pain. It might even turn him on.

A shudder goes through me, and I have to school my face into a neutral expression and force my rational mind to keep the reins. This is no time to freak out. I need to find the thing Baron values most.

After a minute, I hold out my hand. "I want the key."

A stitch pulls between his brows. "What key?"

"The master key to the school."

He swallows and glances at Royal, and though he's always hard to read, I can see the flash of surprise in his eyes, maybe even panic.

"You don't even go to Willow Heights," he says, returning his gaze to me.

"I will."

"I can't just give you the key," he says. "I'm sworn to protect it."

"I'm sure you are," I say. "I know how it works. The top dog gets the key. It was Royal's last year, and now it's yours. And I want it."

His eyes narrow. "What for?"

"You'll see."

He hesitates a long moment. "I can't give it to you," he says at last.

"I thought you might say that," I admit, stepping behind him and cutting the ties on his wrists. "So let's fight for it, fair and square."

Royal tenses, his hands gripping the edge of the pit beside his hips, like he might jump down and intercept. I step around the chair and turn away from him to face his brother.

Baron rubs his wrists together and works out the kinks in his shoulders for a minute before stepping away from the chairs, into the dirt ring. "Rules?" he asks.

"No rules," I say. "Fight 'til knockout."

He nods and raises his fists. I raise mine, and a spark flickers to life in my belly. I love the focus, the adrenaline, the clarity of a fight. I didn't know how much I fucking missed this. When I land the first blow, the spark burns brighter, growing into a burning ember as I duck Baron's first swing. It's too hard, and I use the power against him, darting in to sink a knee into his stomach while he's trying to correct himself. He curses but spins to face me instead of dropping to his knees. He's breathing hard, his eyes alive behind his glasses.

I remember him saying we were alike, and maybe in a way we are, because I'm alive in this moment, too. We trade blows, and this time, he gets my jaw. But he pulls his punch, overcompensating for the last one. He's learning fast, though. This fucker should be in the ring every Saturday night with Royal. I need to take him out fast if I want a chance.

I knock his chin with an uppercut, and he steps back, spitting blood onto the dirt floor. Then he swings, but when I block, he pulls back from it and spins to land a kick to my lower back. His foot hits me so hard I go flying, slamming into the dirt wall and bouncing off, hitting the floor hard enough to take what's left of my breath. Unlike Merciless and some of the other girls I used to fight, I'm not a mixed martial artist. I'm a boxer. But Baron doesn't fight here, so he doesn't know the rules, and I told him no rules. Which means tonight, anything goes.

He comes over to me and reaches down like he's going to grab my hair and knock me out while I'm down.

SELENA

Fuck that.

If we're fighting dirty, I have a few moves in my back pocket for when I fought dirty bitches in the pit before. Bracing my hands on the floor, I swing my body around, scissoring my legs around his and sweeping his feet from under him. It's one of my only moves from the ground, but he hasn't seen me fight long enough to know that. His knees land on the floor, and I roll away, jump to my feet, and deliver a kidney shot with my boot. Tit for fucking tat.

He falls forward onto his hands and knees, and I jump around, grab his hair, and pull his head up. I want to see his face when I deliver the KO. He swipes at me, sinking a fist into my ribs. Pain explodes through my side, and my torso folds that way, but I don't let go. I use the momentum to slam my fist into the side of his head as hard as I can, and he crumples to the floor.

twenty-four

Harper Apple

I drop to my knees, breathing hard. For a minute, I can't hear anything but the ringing in my ears from the pain. My kidney, my back, my side, and my jaw throb with fierce stabs of agony. I forgot how much it hurt to take a blow, and Baron's stronger than anyone I've ever faced in the ring. I climb to my feet, roll him over, and pull out his keys. After tossing them to Royal, I step over to the chairs. I kick Dawson's chair around so he's lying on his side, and I press one foot down on the side of his neck.

"I don't know you, but I know your sister," I say. "I know how bad you want everyone to believe you have it all, but you don't. It's all a lie. You're a fake, just like everyone in your family. You're probably going to tell me you were faking this, too, that you're a nice guy under it all. That you were just doing what you had to do so you could stay with the in crowd, following orders. But there comes a point when being a spineless little coward doesn't make you pathetic, it makes you evil."

I step back and deliver one swift kick to his nuts. It must be a good one, because he instantly vomits.

"Just because I didn't report you, that doesn't mean I can't," I say. "I may have looked like an easy target when your buddies pointed you in my direction, but I have buddies now, too, you little worm. One of them has a name even bigger than yours, bottomless pockets, pictures of that night, and a blanket he wrapped me in. I'm guessing it's covered in your DNA, and from the comments you made that night, I'm guessing you know the implications of that."

It feels like cheating to bring up someone else in a fight, to threaten him with power that belongs to the Darlings and not me. But it's no different than using Royal's name. And here's the thing—I've been alone all my life. I've done things on my own, and this is where I ended up.

Rich people don't get there on their own unless they win the lottery. I saw it with my own eyes the night Royal took me to Cliff's. The Rose family and the Dolce family are woven together. They help each other instead of clinging to some stubborn individualism. All the rich families in town do each other favors, and they all benefit. If I'm going to be stuck in the webs of both feuding families, if they're not going to let me go, then I'm damn sure going to get something out of it, even if it's only power by association. They both used me. Now it's my turn.

I bend down and look into Dawson's deceptively pretty face, now blanched white. "I'm going to make a deal with you, Dawson Walton. I'm going to hold onto that evidence just like I held onto the secret about you being on scholarship. I'm not sure your whole family deserves the shame you'll bring them. Since you already graduated, I'm assuming you're going off to school somewhere, and I'll never see you again. Make sure that happens. Understood?"

He nods, squeezing his eyes closed while he lies there in a puddle of his own vomit. "Got it."

"Good," I say. "You might think girls like me don't go to the cops because your sisters didn't. Your family might've swept it under the rug to keep your reputations intact, but I have nothing to gain by keeping quiet."

He nods, his eyes still squeezed closed. I lean down over him. "You think guys around here get away with anything. You have the Dolces on your side, after all, and I'm an easy target. A girl like me has nothing. But I'm smart, and I have allies. Unlike you, I've lived here all my life. I know which cop believes girls from the trailer park because he's from there, too. I know which one will fight for me to be heard. Remember that when you come back here. Every time you set foot in this town, you're in *my* territory. Tread carefully."

I turn and walk away, over to the edge of the pit where Royal sits. He hands me a key and tosses the others onto Baron, who's lying in the dirt. Only Duke remains standing, just staring at us with this lost little boy expression that makes my heart ache. I can't help but feel for him, even after all he did. But that doesn't mean I have to forgive him.

I reach out a hand, and Royal takes it and pulls me up before giving back my purse and the key. We don't say a word as we pass through the aisles of boxes, walking side by side. When we step out into the sultry night and the door closes behind us, he turns to me. "That's all you have for Dawson?"

I take note of the fact that he didn't say anything while anyone could overhear us. Even though he obviously doesn't agree with my decision, he didn't question me in front of anyone else. He showed them that I had his full support in whatever I wanted to do or not do. Only when we're alone will he voice his disagreement. His gift wasn't just delivering my revenge, and tonight wasn't just about kicking someone's ass for what they did. It's so much more than that. It's about what he's sacrificing for me, what he's giving me to build me up after they all tore me down.

I shrug. "I know you think what he did is worse, but that's only because he did it without your permission. You understand and love your brothers. You know why they are the way they are. I'm sure Dawson has his reasons, and he has a family that loves him, too."

Royal scoffs. "He's weak."

"You're right," I say. "And that's part of it. He might have participated, but he did it out of some sick sense of bonding with your brothers, and I'm sure they promised him immunity for it. But it wasn't personal. What your brothers did..."

I can't even begin to say those words to Royal. I want to die when I think that he already knows. I take a deep breath and stop at his car, squeezing my hands into fists and pressing my nails into my palms so I won't tear open the scabs on my arms again. Royal opens the door, and I climb in and wait for him to get in the driver's seat before speaking again.

"I don't expect you to understand," I say. "I have my reasons for doing what I did. Sure, Dawson's shit, but he doesn't even live here. I'm guessing he's only back in town because you brought him back for me. But I don't need revenge."

Royal starts the car but just sits there, staring straight ahead. "If I were you, I'd have killed them all."

Again, the thought of how much power he's given me threatens to intoxicate me. He would have let me kill his own brothers, and that means... Everything. Family comes first with Royal. If he'd choose me over his own blood...

I don't even want to think what that means.

"And you?" I ask, turning to him. "Are you blameless in all this?"

"You know I don't think that."

"Good," I say. "Because it's the environment you created that lets a guy like Dawson think he has immunity from consequences. That he can get away with anything."

"You just let him," Royal points out. He shifts into gear, and we turn onto the road, heading through the deserted streets of Faulkner.

"What's your punishment?" I ask.

"What do you want it to be?" he asks.

I shrug. "I got what I got. The twins and Dawson got what they got. What do you get?"

"I get you."

A snort escapes me. "I'm your punishment?"

"Aren't you?"

I turn to the window. Maybe I am. Seeing me is his penance. It's torture for me, but I didn't think that it might be torture for him, too. Letting me take what I wanted from those three boys is penance for him, too. I know how much he'd like to hurt them. But I have my own ways of doing things, ways that are even more cruel. Taking away what they value most will hurt them more than a beating. I don't know what Dawson values except his reputation, and he's already out of Willow Heights, so I can't take that. It's enough to never see him again, even if Royal's right, it's an insufficient punishment.

Maybe I don't need more than for him to know I could still end him if I wanted. What I did to the twins, though, that was satisfying. It helped me more than Royal beating anyone for me. More than it would have helped *me* to beat them up. I realize as we turn onto Mill Street that I feel... Empty. But it's in a good way, like I'd feel after a long, hard fight where I came out on top. Something inside me has clicked back into place, like a dislocated shoulder that's been set. It's still tender, still sore, but it feels right again.

I fucking hate it. I hate that Royal knew what I needed when I didn't. That he gave it to me, and now he's part of it. The glory isn't all mine. He's a piece of that, coloring it the way he colors everything in my life, as if he's part of me now and there's no way to get free. His touch has tainted everything, my body and soul, my destruction, and now, my redemption. He was part of my fall, and now he'll always be a part of my rise from it. It makes me want to scream. Why can't I be free of him?

I hate him. I hate that he forced me to do what I needed instead of what I wanted, the way Preston has. That he forced me to face things instead of avoiding them, and that it worked. I hate that he makes me care again—not for him, but for anyone, for anything, for *life*. I hate that he knows me so well, even now, when I pretend I'm so changed that he doesn't know me at all. I hate that he's the one who made this happen, this good feeling inside me, the peace, the satisfaction and hope that I might live again.

He fanned the ember into a flame of life inside me, reminding me that there is a reason to keep breathing. I hate that he helped me after everything he's done to ruin me. He doesn't deserve credit for putting two pieces back together after he shattered me into a thousand. And most of all, I hate that when I gave in and stopped fighting and did whatever he wanted, he didn't lose interest. He didn't try to finish me off and walk away. He tried to heal me. And maybe, in some small way, he did.

SELENA

twenty-five

Royal Dolce

"Where are we going?" Duke asks.

We're back in the car. After I dropped Harper at her place, I returned for them, but I haven't spoken to them.

"How long have you known?" Baron asks quietly from the back seat.

"Long enough," I say.

"You told us we could have her," Duke argues. "You said you were done, and we could do anything we wanted to her. You were going to kill her!"

"You didn't kill her."

"You said she was dead to you."

"I said that to Crystal, too," I say quietly.

Silence falls over the car. We don't say her name. For almost two years, no one has spoken it aloud. Not to us, and not among us.

But I got used to talking about her to Harper. At first, it hurt in the way that makes you want to say it again just to see if you can, to see if it'll hurt as much the second time. After a while, though, it became almost normal. Like something I could drop into a conversation, and it wouldn't shut my brothers up for five minutes straight.

"What are you saying?" Baron asks at last.

"Now you're not done with her?" Duke asks.

"Did it seem like I was done with her all summer?"

"I thought you were just worried about her body being found," Duke says. "Or that she'd go to the police."

"I found the link to the *OnlyPics* videos," Dawson pipes up. "I sent it to you so you'd know she was alive."

"You mean, you sent it to your sister?" I ask. I would feel angry if I could. But tonight's not the time for anger.

"I knew Lo would go to you," Dawson says. "That's why I showed it to her. If it weren't for me, you wouldn't even know she was alive."

SELENA

He has a point. I'd stopped going by her house. If he hadn't shown us the video, I wouldn't have been driving by the day I saw Preston's truck parked across the street from her house.

I wouldn't have followed her to his house. And she wouldn't have tried to fucking kill herself. Rage swells inside me when I have to come to the realization all over again that she'd be better off if I didn't know she was alive. But it's too late now. I do know, and I'm going to make it right. Somehow, I will.

Baron sighs. "It doesn't matter if she's alive as long as she didn't go to the cops. She disappeared, just like Mabel. She was taken care of. Why are you digging this shit up?"

"That's all we ever want from the Darlings, right?" Duke asks. "To chase them out of town. You even said that once they're gone, we don't follow them. You said that after Mabel left."

"And when you were done with Mabel, did I fucking bring my friends to have some fun with her?" I ask. "Or did I pull her out of the river so she couldn't die on you, because I knew you *weren't* done with her."

"But we were," Baron says. "We didn't go after her."

"You didn't drop out of school and chase her to another state," I clarify. "But you know where she is. And *I* know you're just biding your time. Don't try to fuck with me like I don't know you, Baron. I'm not one of your experiments."

"If you know me, then you know the world is my experiment," he says.

I glare at him in the rearview as we pull through the gate, but the asshole looks cool and collected as always. It's fucking impossible to ruffle my brother. I was born with a temper and a burning urge to destroy that's closer to Duke's urge to destroy by burning than Baron's level-headed, analytical way of making sense of this bullshit called life.

"So we were supposed to know you weren't done with Harper?" Duke asks. "How? You told us to take her and do whatever we wanted. You saw what we did. You were the one who wanted to watch, to make sure we knew she was really ours."

SELENA

"She isn't like Mabel," Baron says quietly. "Mabel didn't do shit to us. Harper would have ruined our family if we hadn't stopped her."

I pull up in front of the Walton's house. I can't even look at it. They're all snakes, as bad as Darlings. "Go get your car," I say to Dawson. "We'll follow you."

"Where are we going?" he asks. He doesn't move to get out. He sounds scared, like a pussy. But I know he'll obey, because he's not even as strong as a pussy. Cats have claws. Dawson is a sheep. He has no mind of his own, no edge, not even an instinct for survival. He's stupid and soft and weak, the kind of person you can't help but want to crush from existence.

The only reason he ever had anything at our school was because we let him. We allowed it because we'd wronged his sisters, and enduring his friendship was our penance. Because he played football and could fit into our crowd. We let him be one of us, sit at our side like he'd have our backs. We let him on the team so he could get the girls we didn't want. And in return, he fucking touched the girl I did want—the only girl I ever wanted.

He will pay for that.

A few minutes later, we're back on the road, following Dawson. I knew he'd come back. He's not even going to try to run. The dumb fuck doesn't even know we're not his friends anymore. He didn't have my back. He touched my girl. All ties were cut the moment he made that choice, and no amount of showing us she's alive can erase what he's done.

He's fucked my girl.

He should know he won't walk away from that mistake.

We stop at the bridge, where I told him to go, and I grab a bag from the back seat. Dawson climbs out of his car like an obedient little dog when I tell him to. I can see him sweating in the warm night, can smell the stink of his fear.

"What's going on?" he asks, his voice high with alarm. I gesture for him to follow, and I walk to the center of the bridge. He's not going to fight. He's the type to think if he keeps following orders, if he keeps obeying, it'll make it better for him. He should know. Nothing can change the outcome of this night, the consequences of his actions. Nothing can make it better.

SELENA

"You're paying for what you did," I say simply.

"I did," he says, his gaze flying from one of us to the next, like my brothers can help him. "I just did, man. Look, I'm sorry I ever touched Harper—trust me, I'd never have done it if I knew you were still into her. They said you were done, that you didn't care. They promised."

I look at my brothers.

"That's what you said," Duke points out.

I speak slowly. "I pulled her out of the river for you when you were done with her."

He swallows and looks away. He knows.

This isn't just Dawson's punishment.

It's theirs, too.

They won't fight, either. Not for the same reasons—my brothers aren't weak. They know how payment works, though. Baron knows most of all, even better than I do. In his mind, everything is a transaction. That's how his brain measures the appropriate response in the absence of a moral compass. They won't interfere now any more than I interfered with them and Mabel.

"I thought you were letting Harper settle the score," Dawson says, backing away from us. "That's what you said when I came home. That I had to face Harper. Not you."

"She settled her score," I say. "This isn't for her. This is for me."

Dawson looks around, like he might run now, when it's too fucking late. I didn't expect it to take so long for him to figure out he's never walking off this bridge. He's even dumber than I thought.

"What do you want me to do?" he asks.

"Get out your phone," I say. "You're going to write a little post before you jump."

His eyes widen, and he glances over his shoulder.

Baron steps past him, then turns to face me. We stare at each other across the center of the bridge. Even Dawson knows better than to think Baron's taking his side, having his back. He's there to make sure the asshole doesn't try to run like a scared rabbit.

"But… The water's shallow," Dawson says, having the balls to show disbelief.

SELENA

"Don't worry," I say, pulling a package of rope from my bag. "You won't be hitting the water."

"No," he says, shaking his head. "No, man. You can't do this. I didn't mean to do anything! I was just going along with your brothers. They told me to, that they'd make things bad for my sisters again if I didn't go. That's the only reason. I'd never have touched Harper otherwise."

"Why not?" I ask, tossing the rope to Duke. "Are you saying you didn't want to fuck Harper?"

"What? No, of course not."

"You don't think my girl's hot?"

"No!" he blurts. "I mean, yeah, but—"

"Well, which is it?" I ask, pacing forward. "You think she's hot, and you wanted to fuck her, but you didn't before that because she was mine? Or you don't think she's hot, and you only did it because my brothers told you to?"

"Both," he says. "I mean, what does it matter if I think she's hot?"

"It doesn't," I say. "You touched her, and she was mine, and this is my revenge. She had hers. She wanted to knock you around a little for touching her. But you didn't just take something from her. You took something from me. This is your punishment for touching something that's mine."

"It's tied," Duke says, holding out the other end of the rope. He looks at me, and I can see the question in his eyes, but he won't ask if I'm sure about this any more than I'd ask Harper if she was sure that's all she wanted to do when they were right there to hear it.

"You know what to do with that," I say, nodding to the rope.

He stares at the end of it hanging in his hands. I went easy on them before. I've always gone easy on them. I took every one of Dad's clients out when he asked so my brothers wouldn't have to. After King was gone, I stepped up and took care of the rest of the Darling men with Dad, so the twins wouldn't have blood on their hands. I was going to kill Harper myself, too. If they hadn't reminded me how many times I'd promised they could have her when I was done, I would have. But they wanted to play, and I had to convince myself that I was done with her.

Watching them with her should have made it impossible to want her.

SELENA

Somehow, it failed.

Even after all that, her noose is still around my neck.

This noose isn't my job to place, though. My brothers have done worse than killing a man who participated in their debauchery. It's time I stopped protecting them and admit they're just as fucked up as I am, just as capable of getting their hands dirty. Out of guilt, I've given them too much leeway. I told myself I was letting them be who they are, accepting them even when I don't understand their version of fucked up. It was my job to protect them and their job to back me up.

But the truth is, it hasn't been that way for a long time.

Not since we moved here. That's when it all went to shit. For a while, King held us together. He was a pro at keeping up appearances. After I killed Crystal, he made it look like we were still a united front, like it was all the Darlings' fault. They hurt me, they took Crystal, and we had to stick together and fight back. The bastard was so good he even had us halfway convinced.

Gloria Walton herself would've been impressed if she was around then.

We're as fake as she is. When King moved away, we kept pretending nothing had changed, to the world and maybe ourselves. But in truth, the twins are as far from me as King. I cut him out when he left Faulkner, but I'd already cut them out long before that. I told myself they didn't need to know, that I was protecting them just like I protect them from Dad, like I always protected Crystal.

Until I didn't.

I already face that shit every time I catch them looking at me, and some unspoken weight settles between us, and I know we're all thinking the same thing—that I'm to blame for all of it. For her dying, for us falling apart. Maybe they wouldn't say it, just like no one said it when King hammered into our heads that the Darlings were to blame, but we all know.

So, when they wasted Mabel, I saved her fucking life for them. That was penance.

One girl in the river.

One girl out.

They should have done the same.

An eye for an eye. A life for a life.

SELENA

But the difference is, they don't owe me. I was paying back a debt, if only some small part of it. I have no right to ask for them to do the same for me, even if I would have done it for them. I can't despise them for keeping the truth from me all summer. They owe me nothing. The lies between us started with me, after all. For that, I have only myself to blame. Not even the Darlings can take the blame for that. It's my burden alone.

"I'll do it," Baron says after a long silence when we all stand frozen on the bridge, lost in our own internal wars.

"No," Dawson says again. He turns and tries to run, but Baron steps in front of him and shoves him back. "I was just doing what you said! I was following *your* orders."

"Then follow them now," Baron says coldly. He takes the rope and makes the slip knot in the loose end. Then he hands it to Dawson. We wait for him to put it around his neck.

"Now kneel," I say. "And get out your phone."

Dawson sinks unsteadily to his knees.

"Don't worry," I say when he gets his phone out. "We'll tell you what to say."

I start, and Duke and Baron jump in after a minute. I think they're actually having fun with it. At least, Duke is. I consider telling him to stop clowning, we're at a fucking funeral. If he's having fun, he won't have to think about the consequences. But I decide the punishment is enough, considering the confused asshole's crime was justified.

Baron's enjoyment is something different than fun, but I don't stop him, either. We're all dealing with it in the ways we know how.

When the note is done, I order Dawson to post it.

"I was just protecting my sisters," he says, his shoulders heaving with a sob. "You would have done the same."

"I did protect your sister," I say. "Better than you ever could."

"You did the same to them," he says, hanging his head. "They told me what you did to them our first year. I didn't want it to happen again when I wasn't around to put an end to it."

I know he's not talking about protecting them anymore. He's talking about the fact that his three best friends have all banged his sisters, and instead of putting a no-touch policy in effect on them, he let my brothers keep doing it. Now he's going to pretend he's the heroic big brother when he didn't do shit for them. I'm a better brother to Lo than he ever was.

"Don't kid yourself," I snap. "You never protected them from us. You didn't put an end to anything. I did."

"Yeah," Duke says. "If they hated it so much, why are they still coming around begging for a nice deep dicking every time they get thirsty?"

"Keep telling yourself we're the bad guys," Baron chimes in. "You want to believe your sisters are sweet and innocent, and I get that. But everyone on this bridge knows you're full of shit. They're whores like all the other girls we fuck. They've been throwing themselves at us since the minute they walked into Willow Heights, and there's nothing we could ask them to do that they wouldn't do willingly—and then some."

"You just don't want to admit in front of Royal that you couldn't resist a chance to bang his plaything."

"You did it to my sisters!" Dawson screams, raising his face. It's tear-streaked and bruised from Harper's knuckles.

"And you should have done this to us," I say. "That, I could respect. But you're less than a pussy, and you didn't do shit. This is how a real man takes care of someone who touched his woman without his permission. Now step to the edge."

When he's through the railing, standing on the ledge, he starts sobbing again. Baron steps forward, but I shake my head.

"Don't push him."

He wasn't always an enemy. He's not a Darling. He deserves to die with dignity. We stand on the bridge for a long time while he comes to terms with his mortality, with his mistake, with his defeat… And my brothers come to terms with theirs.

They may not owe me, but they should have fucking known what would happen.

I'm a patient man, even a forgiving one. I let them all make up for the mistake they made by making the right choice this time. I let them take their time with it. I let Dawson beg and blubber, and Duke question me while Dawson's crying too loud to overhear. I let Baron silently obey, though I know he's dying to see how it feels to take a life, to be a god.

Finally, everyone accepts the inevitable. We watch in silence as Dawson disappears over the edge. We even observe a moment of silence for him before we turn to go.

twenty-six

Harper Apple

I stand at the small mirror in our bathroom on Monday morning, staring at myself through the film of smoke on the glass. I wish Royal hadn't delivered my revenge right before my hearing with the admissions board, as much as I might have needed it. I feel disconcertingly raw, as if every nerve ending is exposed and the single touch of a feather could make me scream.

I don't want to walk into a panel of rich school board members and cry.

I wash my face and return to my bedroom. I need something, a shell of armor to cover the painful vulnerability. I text Preston and then lay my phone on the dresser. I can't count on him to protect me. While I cake on a layer of makeup to hide the bruise from where Baron hit my jaw, my gaze falls on the case for the colored contact lenses Preston put in my eyes. I open it and put them in one at a time, covering the exposed blueness of my eyes with a veil of darkness. The relief is small but instant, and I feel my chest loosening, as if I can breathe a little easier.

I know what to do now.

I go to the closet and take out a dress he bought me. I lay it on the bed next to a pair of black pumps with red soles. I find the belt that goes with the dress, the necklace he buckled around my neck, and the earrings and thick bra. I take out the straightener and do my hair the way he liked, then put on the jewelry, then the clothes. Each piece of the puzzle that I fit into place is another part of my armor, another layer of cool on top of the molten lava in my soul. When I'm done with my clothes and makeup, I step into the heels and stand back from my mirror.

I look like the girl he made me, a girl worthy of a Willow Heights scholarship, one with a 24-karat pussy who's frigid and collected at all times. Not one who took the football team.

I step outside. The truck is gone, but in its place sits a shiny, new Escalade SUV with a giant bow on the hood. I smile and pull the bow off the sleek surface. A key is taped underneath. The paint is so beautiful I can't help but run my fingers along it—it almost looks black, but up close it's actually a deep, dark, shimmering red color, like blood mixed with liquid obsidian. I climb inside. The car smells like new leather. There's an oversized envelope on the floorboards. I peek inside and find the title in my name, the manual, and assorted paperwork along with two fobs.

I start the car and drive to school. I hold the calm, detached feeling like a treasure as I walk into school.

Maybe Royal gave me what I needed, but Preston gives me what I want.

When I step into the office, the reception desk sits empty. At the desk where student office aids wait to show new students around and print tardy slips, Dixie Powell sits arranging papers. She stands when I walk in, circling the end of the desk and holding out a hand before she stops in her tracks, her eyes going wide. She looks like she's seen a ghost.

"Oh my god," she says, her hand going to her mouth. "Harper?"

I guess I did drop out of school and disappear after spring break.

I give her a tight smile. "Just me."

"Whoa," she whispers.

"I'm here to talk to the admissions board," I say, feeling weird about the way she's staring. I discretely run my hands over my hips. I'm wearing a red dress, but it's not like, sexy. The pencil skirt of it hits just at the knee, and it's belted and has a modest neckline. The heels are a little high, but not slutty. The lipstick is a little dark, but again, not scandalous. My hair is straightened and tied in a low pony, draped forward over one shoulder. Nothing to warrant the way she's gaping.

So, it's not my clothes. It's me.

Suddenly, my pulse quickens. Did the twins spread rumors about what happened?

"Why are you disguised as Crystal Dolce?" Dixie asks at last.

"What?"

"I mean, if you want to fuck with the D boys, that'll do it," she says, shaking her head. "But damn, that's cold."

"I'm not," I say stiffly, my heart hammering in my chest. Is that what Preston was going for? It makes my skin crawl in the weirdest way.

"Unless Royal dressed you up like that…"

"No one dressed me up," I snap.

"Oh, then that's a relief," she says with a breathy little laugh. "I mean, I know Royal's fucked up, but that would be, like, next level weirdness."

Before things can get any more awkward, the receptionist emerges from the little hallway behind the desk and tells me they're ready for me. I check my phone before turning to follow her, but Preston hasn't answered my last request for help.

I remember what I said to Blue at the quarry. He's not a hero. He's not untouchable. He's just one more person the Dolces ruined, one more screwed up guy in Faulkner. He doesn't owe me anything. He's already given me a thousand times more than I have a right to ask for. It's not like he loves me. He has no reason to fight for me.

SELENA

Only I have a reason to fight.

I stand tall and stride into the conference room. I am not a victim of this town, of these families. I'm a survivor of them. And if I'm not quite intact or unscathed, that doesn't mean I'm weak. It means I'm human. But human or not, I don't need a hero.

I can be my own damn hero.

I took everything they threw at me, and though it broke me, I picked up the shards of my shattered life, and piece by piece, I am fitting them back together. Not the way they were, as no one could go through what I have and remain unchanged. But I'm forming them into something new, an armor to protect my life, even if it couldn't protect me. I will pick up the weapons they threw at me and use them to build an armory of my own. As I lay out my case, I draw strength from the steely coldness of my armor that a Darling boy gave me and power from the untouchable status that a Dolce boy gave me.

The only thing I don't have is money, which is exactly what I need. Still, I make my plea for enrollment, my eyes moving over the men and women on the panel, knowing each of them has the chance to take my future into their hands. They're from the founding families, though the only person I recognize is Lindsey's mother. It gives me a little shock when our eyes meet, though she doesn't recognize me. She didn't see me that night, the night she lost her house. She doesn't know I was there, that I helped destroy it—or that I saved her daughter. She doesn't know that her son has already given me so much, or all the shameful things I've done in return.

I tear my gaze from her and focus on the others. Any one of them could write a check that will get me through another semester or my entire senior year at Willow Heights. I just have to be good enough for one of them, the one who needs one more charitable tax write-off.

When I step out of the room, I know I did good. I'm just not sure how good I have to be to get a scholarship that doesn't exist, to have them make an exception and add one more. I pull the door closed behind me just in time to see the receptionist take a stumbling step backwards, her hand flying to her chest.

"Mr. Darling!" she exclaims.

SELENA

My heart does a funny little twisting thing in my chest, and I hurry past the corner to see who she's talking to. My eyes drink him in like finding a tall glass of water in the desert—long, slim lines of pure elegance and poise, so unlike the thuggish Dolce boys; tailored, silver-grey dress pants with a crease still ironed up the front of the thighs; a dress shirt rolled up a few times at the cuffs, a few buttons undone at the neck, in a deep, royal blue color; a silver mask covering half his face.

"Preston," I cry, rushing forward and throwing myself into his arms so hard he stumbles backwards a step, a surprised little laugh escaping him as I crush him in my tightest embrace. I didn't realize how much I wanted him here until this moment, until I feel his familiar body against mine, inhale the sharp, clean scent of him.

"You came," I say, my voice catching, my eyes aching with tears even as I pull back, laughing a little. I touch his scratchy chin, not quite believing it. "You never go anywhere."

"You said you needed a scholarship."

"Thank you," I say, hugging him hard again. "And for the car, oh my god, I didn't even say thank you. I'm sorry I didn't bring back your truck sooner. I don't deserve you."

"I didn't do anything," he says dismissively, like just the fact that he showed his face for me means nothing, not to mention all the money he's spent.

"Shut up and let me thank you," I mutter into his chest.

"Come on," he says. "Let's get out of here, and you can tell me what happened in that meeting, since I missed it."

He holds open the door for me, and I step under his arm and into the foyer of the school. My spine stiffens and my blood turns to ice water. Baron Dolce is heading for the office, not ten paces away, his usual sucker back in place. Preston lets the office door fall closed before he catches a glimpse of his enemy moving in. He slides a protective arm around my shoulders, his body tensed as if to spring at the first sign of aggression.

"What the fuck are you doing here?" Baron asks, glowering at us. The enormity and darkness of the bruise on the side of his face makes me downright giddy with pride.

"Didn't you figure that out when I took the key?" I ask. "I go here."

"I wasn't talking to you," he says coldly.

"Well, you'd better get used to seeing him if you're going to see me," I say. "We're together now."

Baron snorts. "You're joking."

"Nope," I say, sliding an arm around Preston's back to secure him to me. The pressure of his body against mine makes my ribs throb where Baron punched me, but I grit my teeth and keep my face from showing it.

"You don't care that he's the reason for everything that happened to you?" Baron asks, cocking his head and watching my reaction.

I swallow hard. I told Royal who Mr. D was, and he must have told Baron. And even though I've known for a while, I never thought of it that way. If I hadn't been spying, if he hadn't demanded all that information, I would never have ended up in that swamp.

"No," I say at last, fighting to keep my voice steady. "*You're* the reason. You and your brothers. Don't you dare blame him for what you did. Maybe what I told him pissed you off, but you're the ones who did it. Preston's the one who saved me. He gave me a scholarship, a car, and took care of me. Don't even think about talking shit about him or any of the Darlings to me."

"You're with them now, huh?" Baron asks, crossing his arms and smirking down at me, the sucker stem tugging at the corner of his mouth.

"Who I'm with is none of your fucking concern," I say. "Look the other way if it bothers you. You had your chance, and you chose to destroy me. Preston chose to build me back up. He's ten times the man you and your brothers are or could ever hope to be."

I'm breathing hard, anger pulsing through my veins by the time I get done speaking.

"He's your cousin," Baron says flatly.

Preston tenses, his arm retreating from around me.

I don't pull back my arm from around his hips, though. I stare up at Baron, a laugh bubbling up in my chest and forcing its way out. "You can't be serious. I lived in a trailer park for most of my life. I'm the furthest from blonde you can get. Do I look like a fucking Darling to you?"

"No, you look like a Dolce, which is real fucking creepy, no matter which one of you thought up that twisted little game."

"See?" I say. "Not a Darling."

"Then tell me, little girl," he says, leaning in, his eyes lit with viciousness. "Who's your daddy?"

I swallow hard, my heart doing a little flip in my chest. All I can think about is what my mother said the other day.

I shove the thought away, hard. He's fucking with my head. There's no way my father is from one of the richest and most influential families in town. That my cousin is little Lindsey Darling, who floated through the halls of Faulkner like a princess on her dainty feet. That I have this huge family right here in Faulkner who could have taken care of me all these years but let me live in a roach infested rat trap instead.

No. I know who I am, and it's not a Darling. I'm the daughter of a junkie and one of her revolving door boyfriends, some other junkie who was there for a good time for a few nights or months, if he was a good one. Someone so shitty she doesn't even want to talk about him to her own daughter, even when I asked. Eventually, I stopped asking.

"You've got the wrong girl," I say. "It's not me."

"You were never special," Baron says, the gleam of cruelty still in his eyes. "You were just a name to cross off our list."

"You're wrong," I say again, though my voice lacks conviction.

"Have fun fucking your cousin," Baron says, pushing past us to the office door. "Gotta love Arkansas."

The moment he disappears inside, Preston steps away from me, breaking my hold on him. I rub my hand on my skirt, as if I can wipe away the icky sensation of Baron's words. I'm scared to even look at Preston, but I force my gaze to his.

"It's not possible," I say. "Right?"

"No," he says, his lips tight. "No. Of course not."

We stand there for a moment in awkward silence, something that's never happened between us. Preston's looking at me with way too much calculation in his good eye, though. I edge away from him another step.

SELENA

"He's lying," I say, forcing a small laugh. "Obviously he's lying. They're just pissed that a Darling went through their trash and valued something they didn't. Now they want me back, not because they think I'm worth anything, but because *you* think I am."

"Exactly," Preston says, sounding relieved by my explanation. "So, let's go talk about that meeting. What happened?"

I follow him out of Willow Heights, but I notice he doesn't touch me with his usual possessive entitlement as we walk out and climb in his truck. In fact, he doesn't touch me at all. He's careful to step away instead of linking his fingers with mine or resting a hand on my back to help me into the Escalade after opening the door for me. He waits until I'm situated before closing the door and coming around the driver's side. Without a word, we take off.

Preston drives to the north end of town, but instead of turning onto the highway and leaving Faulkner to go to his apartment, he turns onto a road that leads toward the Dolce neighborhood. I tense, but he keeps going, winding along a two-lane road that's just as familiar and filled with even more unwelcome memories.

At last, when we make a final turn, I can't hold back.

"Why are we going here?" I ask, gripping the door handle, my fingers cold and numb.

"You know this place?" Preston asks, turning to me. I can't read his expression behind the mask, but I think he sounds surprised.

I squeeze my eyes closed, trying not to remember the hundred times Royal took me here—the first time, after his race, when he kissed me like I was everything he'd been missing but stopped me when I tried to go further; the second time, when I pushed him off the bridge and he almost drowned; the time he brought me here after we'd hooked up and he'd ignored me all week and then he got the test results back. That was the day I always thought of as the day we really got together. We were both clean, and the agreement to stay that way meant we were going to keep seeing each other.

My chest aches so deep I can't breathe as Preston's truck lumbers up onto the bridge. I press my fist to my sternum, as if it might fracture and let my heart free if I don't hold it back. The flood of memories continues, assaulting me with the beautiful and terrible pictures we made together. There was the time we went under the bridge and a sudden downpour hit, and we huddled in the scant shelter, laughing and fucking and talking until it stopped; the time I ran from him and he threw me down and fucked me in the ass and then forced me to cum for him; the times we dreamed of traveling together and compared stories about our mothers, so similar in constitution yet so different in circumstances. And then there were all the times we didn't even make it out of the car because we wanted each other more than any of that, so much that nothing else mattered.

I feel the tires leave the wooden planks and land on the asphalt beyond the bridge, but I don't open my eyes until a minute later, when it sinks in that we're still driving. I suck in a loud, ugly breath. Preston glances sideways at me but doesn't speak. We continue another mile before turning onto a narrow, unlined, blacktop driveway. It winds up a gentle slope with white horse fences on either side. At last, we arrive at a tall, wrought iron fence with a fancy gate. Preston puts in a code at an electronic screen, then has to put in a fingerprint and take off his mask to show his face to a camera, which snaps a picture. Finally, the gate swings open.

By now I've gotten my wits about me, and I turn to him and arch a brow. "That's a lot of security," I say. "Is this your secret superhero lair?"

A tiny smile tugs the corner of his handsome mouth. "You've seen my secret lair."

"Then what's this?"

"This," he says, pulling up at the front of a sprawling mansion that makes the ostentatious house we dismantled look homely, "Is the Darling estate."

SELENA

twenty-seven

Harper Apple

Preston pulls the Escalade around one side of the sprawling mansion to where a row of six garage doors wait. He hits a button on his visor and maneuvers the vehicle in beside a Ford Raptor.

"What are we doing here?" I ask, climbing down from my side before he can come around to open my door. A light came on above us, but the rest of the garage is dim, and I can't make out all the cars. I just know there's a lot—more than any one family needs.

"There aren't many safe places for Darlings in this town," Preston says. "We can talk here without risk of being overheard."

He leads me out of the garage and around the back. Calling the place a house doesn't do it justice. There are several buildings, and behind them, a maze of manicured landscaping and water. The "pool" isn't a blue rectangle, but a stone-rimmed, curving thing with a lazy river flowing from one end and a fountain at the other. It leads down to an elevated area with a hot tub that overflows in trickling waterfalls into the pool. We make our way along a raised path beside the water and past it through the gardens to a gazebo. Beyond that is a long, oval pond that's shallow enough that I can see the bottom. Dragonflies skim over the mirrored surface in the late morning sun, which has just risen over a grove of trees in the expansive lawn beyond the pond. I spot a flag a little way off in the grass.

"Is that... A golf course?" I ask in disbelief. I've seen Royal's Confederate mansion, have been in Preston's modern three-story mansion with a pool. But this... This is something else entirely.

"Nah," Preston says. "It's only nine holes."

"Only nine holes," I whisper, shaking my head. My brain refuses to comprehend this level of luxury.

Preston sits down in the gazebo and pats the seat beside him. I sit but leave a healthy amount of space between us because I'm still unnerved by Baron's words.

SELENA

For a minute, neither of us speak. I stare out over the green water of the pond, so different from the clear flowing trickles in the pool area.

"What's this for?" I ask. "Don't tell me you have cows who come to drink here."

Preston laughs. "It's a catfish pond."

He put the mask back on after the photo op, but he removes it now and sets it on the bench beside him, closing his eyes and letting the sultry breeze ruffle his short blond hair.

"I did okay in the interview," I say. "If you paid for my scholarship, I'm in, right?"

He opens his eyes. "He had to be lying," he says. "But if he wasn't... I mean, in other countries, it's totally normal. And no one else knows."

"The Dolces know," I say quietly. "Right?"

I haven't asked him outright about the videos, and after last night, I cringe to think of them having that ammunition. I need all the leverage I can get, not for them to know something shameful about me that I don't want anyone to ever know. It's one thing to spitefully hope Royal had to suffer the torture of seeing me with another guy, knowing what a jealous asshole he is.

Kinda kills things if he thinks I'm disgusting, not desirable.

I swallow and nod. His lack of an answer is an answer.

"Is there any way… I mean, could it be true?" I ask.

"No," Preston says firmly.

"I didn't think so."

We sit in silence for a while.

"Is your mom Mexican or something?" Preston asks.

I laugh and pull out my phone, thumbing back to a selfie of Mom and me that she made me take the other night at her retirement party. I show it to Preston, who visibly relaxes. He takes out his phone and scrolls for a minute, then turns it to me.

"This is our last family reunion before the Dolces."

I take the phone and look at the picture for a minute. "Wow," I say at last. "Looks like Hitler's wet dream."

Preston laughs quietly and reaches for his phone. I point to a single brunette head in a sea of blond. "Her mom married in," he says. "She's blonde now."

SELENA

"Then I'm surprised you didn't bleach my hair," I say, running my fingers through the end of my ponytail.

I wait for Preston to make excuses or explain why he made me into their sister, but he doesn't say anything. I watch the dragonflies skim over the still water of the catfish pond.

"We could get a DNA test," he says after a long pause. "Just to be sure."

"I'm sure," I say. "He was just fucking with us. My dad's not even white. At least, the guy my mom thinks was my dad."

I break off, remembering our conversation before her party again.

"If there's any chance, though," Preston says, gesturing to the golf course surrounded by old growth oaks. "This is the Darling estate, Harper. You'd be cut in."

I laugh at that. "I seriously doubt your grandpa is going to claim some illegitimate lovechild of one of his disowned sons."

"Then I'd cut you in," Preston says. "When I graduated, he made me treasurer of the entire Darling estate. I'm good at it. I like numbers more than family drama. If he objects, you can have half my share."

"Why are you so nice to me?" I ask, searching his eyes for answers that make no sense. "Is it guilt? Do you really think what they did to me is your fault?"

He lays an arm along the railing of the gazebo and turns to the water again, his jaw tight. The silence stretches until I think he's not going to answer. Finally, he speaks. "They said to me once that everything we did to them, they'd do tenfold to us. That everything we tried to do but failed, they'd do to us and succeed."

"Yeah, Baron told me something like that, too."

"They think I tried to do that to their sister," he says. "I always thought they were coming for Lindsey, that they'd do the same to her. But they went after you instead. Maybe that's why. Maybe they really think you're a Darling."

It hits me then, what I didn't even consider. I thought Baron was fucking with us, trying to make us think we'd fucked our cousin or keep us from teaming up because they don't want the Darlings to have friends, and they don't want me out of their sights. That he'd tell his brothers and they'd

SELENA

laugh about it later, replaying how we jumped apart when he said it. But what if they really believe it?

It explains so much.

I close my eyes, my breath shaky as I try to calm my spinning thoughts. As soon as Mr. D gave me the scholarship last year, they must have known it was donated by a Darling. They came after me hard, too hard to warrant the little rebellions I managed. They weren't targeting me just because I was new, or poor, or defiant. They targeted me because they thought I was part of the family they were destroying, and I had to face the same sentence as the rest of them.

Or maybe they didn't know it just yet, and they were just doing the usual hazing—making me bow and kiss their feet, tossing me in the dumpster when I put myself in their way. When did they find out? When did the hazing become something more serious, more sinister?

And how much did Royal suffer, thinking he'd fallen for the enemy? He accused me of plotting against him all along, but he's the one who was plotting. He knew all along that he'd kill me at the end. He wasn't even going to tell me why.

They didn't care that I don't want to be a Darling, that I didn't even know I was. They just picked a Darling at random to incur their wrath, the next punishment on their list of retaliations.

How long had they been planning to have the team rape me?

A chill races up my spine, and I grip the wooden bench seat under me so I don't pitch off it.

"You tried to do that to their sister?" I ask, steering the conversation to something I can comprehend better than my own experience.

Preston shakes his head. "No. I'd never have gone that far. I was pissed that she was coming between us, so I did something to force Devlin's hand, to make him admit he was putting her before family. That he cared about her, and she wasn't just a piece of ass or the enemy. I'd never have done it if I didn't already know what would happen, that he'd protect her."

I swallow hard, remembering that night in the woods, when Royal didn't protect me.

SELENA

Is that what Preston did? Make Devlin—and the Dolces—think that the team was going to rape her if he didn't step in?

But Devlin saved her, just like Preston knew he would.

Royal didn't save me. He's not the hero in this situation. He's not Devlin, the boy Dixie said was the good one, the golden boy, stepping in to take the fall for his girl, admitting he loved the enemy even if it meant his family would cast him out.

He's Preston, the one she said was evil. The one who set her up.

"And what if he hadn't?" I ask quietly, remembering Royal turning away while I begged for forgiveness. "What if he'd let it happen?"

Preston shakes his head. "I knew my cousin well enough to know what he'd do. I already knew he cared. I just wanted him to admit it. But even if I'd been wrong, I'd never have let anyone else touch her."

I nod. Royal didn't just set me up and wait to see if someone would defend me. He took me somewhere that he knew I couldn't get help, and he brought the weapons of my destruction.

Preston shifts on the bench and glances sideways at me. "I might have, though," he admits quietly. "If he didn't want her."

"So, that's what this is all about," I say, running my hand down the sleek pony pulled over one shoulder. "You wanted to fuck your cousin's girlfriend."

He doesn't say anything. When Dixie said that shit this morning, I figured Preston had given me this makeover to fuck with the Dolces. Maybe in part he did, and that's the only part they'll see. But I know him better than they do. I know that it's never that simple with him. He might have dressed me up like a Crystal Dolce doll to fuck with them, but also because he wanted to fuck me when I looked like her, and also as penance for what he did. With him, it could be any of those things, or more likely, all of them.

"Is that what they did to Mabel?" I ask.

Preston shifts on the bench again. "No," he says. "They don't do the same thing twice."

SELENA

"Well, that's a relief, then," I say. "At least this won't happen to some other girl."

He looks at me strangely. "It happened to you, though."

I shrug. "I'm stronger than most girls."

"What happened?" he asks, still watching me with narrowed eyes. "You're different."

"Maybe I am," I say, turning away. I don't want to admit that what Royal did jarred me back to reality, brought back more of my old self than I want to give him credit for. "So, about this cousin thing... There's no chance, right? It's impossible."

"Pretty impossible," he agrees with a thoughtful nod.

An idea hits me, and I shiver. "None of the Darling dads could be mine? Especially not yours?"

"My father, for all his faults, would never cheat," he says, his back stiffening. "Not after the mess Grampa Darling made with his dick."

"Sorry," I say. "I wasn't trying to offend you."

"You didn't," he says flatly. "Dev's dad would never cheat, either. Colt's... Maybe. He has a weakness for women, just like Grandpa Darling. But eighteen years ago, probably not. He was already busy having an affair with Devlin's mom. That leaves the twins."

"And the two who were disowned."

Preston glances at the house and then back to me before nodding. "Right."

"Baron said John Jr. lived in the trailer park where we lived when I was born."

"I'll get a DNA test," Preston says. "It's a long shot, and you're not going to be in Grandpa's will, but you have legal rights. And some of us would give you a cut, not just me. Who do you think pays for JT's stints in rehab? We might have to do it under the table without our grandfather knowing, but we're not all his puppets. Not anymore."

I shake my head. "I don't want to be anyone's puppet, either."

"You'd be set, Harper. No more worrying about scholarships or anything."

I think about it for a long minute. About being set for life because of a name that I didn't choose, that I don't want. About how hard Mabel worked to escape that name and all that goes with it in this town. I think about being a Darling, putting myself back in the Dolces' path, putting a target on my back and advertising that I'm the enemy. I think about how hard I've worked all my life, and how little the Darlings cared then. How little they did for my mother, and how hard she worked when she was able. They never paid for her to go to rehab. They let her suffer. She didn't want me, and neither did they.

I replay her asking if I was talking about JT, which must be her nickname for John Jr. So, she knew he was a Darling, even if he was disowned and had a different name. If there was anything she could have gotten from him, she would have. She would have told him I was his child and tried to get something from it even if I wasn't. Which means she knows there's no chance I am.

At last, I shake my head. "I'm not a Darling," I say. "I'm an Apple. I don't need a DNA test to prove it."

Preston looks like he might argue, but at last, he nods instead. "If you change your mind, let me know. We can send away for it, make sure it's not some local quack the Dolces put in place to do their bidding."

I raise a brow, but I don't tell him he's being ridiculous. I know what they've done to his family. If they'd done the same to mine, I'd be paranoid, too.

"If you want one just to put your mind at ease, I'll do it," I say. "But I don't need that. I don't need anything more from your family. As long as I have my scholarship, I can get out of here on my own."

He nods. "I get it. But I'd also like the chance to defend my family."

"Fair enough."

"We would have taken care of you," he says. "I would have. And there are others with the same mindset. Family is family. If you have Darling blood, you're a Darling. In my eyes, it's that simple."

I shiver despite the damp heat, remembering Baron saying something similar when we were in the Midnight Swans' basement. Now it all makes sense, why they did what they did to me, why they targeted me at all, why they went to such lengths. But understanding the mind of a psychopath doesn't change the crime he commits. It doesn't matter if they had a reason for ruining my life or Mabel's, or Preston's, or Colt's. They did it. That's what matters.

Still, some part of me is reassured by the fact that they did it all for a reason, that they thought I was the enemy. It feels less personal, what Royal did to me. Why he turned his back on me. I didn't just feed information to his enemy. I was one of them. I'm surprised he let me in at all, that he told me all those things under the bridge, that he spent any time with me at all. Part of me wants to question whether it was a lie, whether he made me fall for him on purpose just to break me worse. But even if that was the goal, if we were both lying and using each other, each plotting against each other... What we felt was real. That part can't be faked.

"The last thing I need is one more powerful man trying to control me," I say to Preston after a pause. "No offense."

He runs a hand over his face, freezing when his fingers meet his burned skin, as if he'd forgotten for a moment that he isn't just Preston Darling, heir to this grand estate. He's not just a rich benefactor offering to take care of me. He's a victim, a phantom hiding away from the world because he's hunted like prey and hideous to look at. At least, he thinks he is. To me, the scars remind me that he's a survivor, too.

"He doesn't control everything," Preston says. "Not the way he used to, when my dad was here to help him. Now, there are plenty of us who are moving the family in a different direction. It doesn't matter to me if your mom was married to a Darling any more than it matters when one of our women gets married and takes her husband's name. Blood matters. Not all of us agree with what our grandfather did, disowning his own kin."

"But it's okay for him and, from what I've heard, several others to knock up women all over town and take no responsibility for that?"

Preston's lips tighten. "You know I don't agree with that, either."

"You're right," I concede.

After all, he made sure I was on birth control before he stopped using condoms. He laid out my pill every morning like clockwork, as if to make extra sure it was effective. Now I shudder at the thought of what would have happened if I got pregnant, and if I really am related to him.

"We didn't know you were out there," he says. "It's not really fair to act like we didn't take care of you on purpose."

I nod again, laying a hand on his arm. It's the first time we've touched since Baron told me I was a Darling. "I know that," I say. "You've taken care of me since the moment we met—hell, even before that. And you had no idea I might be a Darling. It just pisses me off that your family does that. I may not know what it's like for a man to be all in for the sex and then want nothing to do with the consequences, but I know what it's like to *be* the consequence of a man like that."

"You have every right to be pissed about that." He shifts subtly so his arm moves out from under my hand. I realize then that he still thinks it might be true. He's handling it with way more poise than I would if I believed it. "And if you want nothing to do with this family, I get that, too. You've already suffered plenty for us just because the Dolces *think* you're a Darling. I'm going to look into it, though."

"If it'll put your mind at ease, get the DNA test," I say again. "And I'll ask my mom about the Darling she dated. She mentioned a JT. I'm assuming that's John Jr?"

Preston nods. "I thought we'd wait until our granddad passed before we went looking for illegitimate Darlings, but if the Dolces are going after people who don't even carry our name and those who never did…"

"Will he cut you out of the will if you do that?" I ask.

"Probably," Preston admits. "But what choice do I have? I can't let anyone else be targeted without warning like you were."

"I don't think it would have helped me to know they thought I was a Darling."

Preston shrugs. "Maybe not. But it might have. You could have come to us, and we'd have at least tried to protect you. We got Sullivan out of town."

My mind quickly runs over Baron's recounting on the Darling family that night in the Swans' lair. "Magnolia's brother?" I guess.

"Yeah," Preston says. "They'll probably start going after the people who left once they've made every Darling in Faulkner pay. They'll probably find Devlin then, too."

"You really think he's alive?"

SELENA

"I know it," Preston says with complete confidence. "If they find them, though…"

I rub the goosebumps on my arms. "They'll make him pay," I say, halfway to myself.

"We've all paid," Preston says. "They'll *kill* him."

"You don't think they'd have found him by now if they could?"

"I think their thirst for revenge goes deeper than their ability to love," Preston says.

I nod, watching the dragonflies in the lazy morning sun as we sit in companionable silence. He doesn't know those boys like I do. I owe them no loyalty, but I know how much they loved their sister. So much that it destroyed them, all of them, in a way.

And maybe all of Faulkner, too.

twenty-eight

Harper Apple

"Mom, can we talk?" I ask that evening. I stand in her bedroom doorway as she hunts through her closet.

"Not now," she says. "I've got a party to get to. Retirement suits me, don't you think?"

She holds up a skimpy dress that will make her look as wide as a billboard. It's not like we can afford clothes that flatter us. If she could fit into the ones Preston got me, she'd do it, but even if she could, they'd look just as bad on her as the cheap ones, since we're not the same shape.

I shrug. "It'll just take a minute."

"Well, go on, then," she says, peeling off the black V-neck with *Baby* written in curling, rhinestone letters on the front. "You can tell me while I get dressed."

SELENA

"The other day, you said something about JT Darling," I remind her. "But then you acted like you were talking about somebody else."

"Yeah, what about it?"

"Who were you talking about?"

"What's that matter?" she asks, peeling off her jeans and tossing them onto the bed.

I know I won't get anywhere without giving her something, and even though I know she's a greedy bitch, if there's one thing she'll respond to, it's a name drop.

"I just… The guy I've been seeing for the past six months is a Darling, and I just wanted to know your exact history with them. For obvious reasons."

She turns to me, trying to hold back a laugh that bursts out in mean little volleys. Finally, she throws back her head and laughs out loud, reaching to brace her hand on the wobbly bureau. "You think you might be a Darling?" she asks at last, wiping her eyes. "Girl, don't you think I would have gotten something better than a baby I didn't want out of that deal?"

I give her a tight smile. "That's what I thought."

"Hand me a cigarette, will you?" she asks, shimmying into the tight black dress.

I sigh and hand her the pack from the table near her bed. "Would you tell me what happened, anyway?"

"Not much to tell," she says, smoothing her hands over her body as she turns sideways to the mirror and sucks her stomach in. "I had a chance with them, maybe, but you came along and fucked all that up."

"Of course," I mutter. "Story of my life."

"Story of *my* life," she says, stopping to light a cigarette.

"So tell me," I say. "Tell me the story of your life so I can be sorry for ruining it."

"Don't get smart with me."

"Sorry," I say. "Please, Mom, can you tell me about the Darlings and who my dad really is, so I don't have to be worried I slept with my cousin."

She cackles and sets her cigarette down, reaching up her dress to pull her underwear off. "You got one thing right," she says, digging through her drawer for a new pair. "Everything changed when JT moved in the trailer park. He wasn't like the other boys down there. You could tell he didn't belong from the start. And the way he looked... whoo-boy, he was a hottie."

"I believe it," I mutter.

"Course I was still living with your nana and papa back then," she says, working her way into a thong before pulling her dress back down. "Daddy didn't like him much, but he charmed the pants off Mama and all the rest of the women down there."

"I hope you don't mean that literally."

She waves a dismissive hand and picks up her cigarettes, lighting up before speaking through a mouthful of smoke. "Nah, he made his way around the girls his age, though."

"His age?" I ask, narrowing my eyes.

"Yeah, he must've been about... Twenty-five, thirty. Just had a falling out with his family. His daddy came down sometimes, trying to patch things up, I guess. That man... He had money. Drove a Mercedes and everything. He was a looker, too, and liked to stop by and flirt if I was outside. We got to talking one day, and he offered me a job the summer I turned sixteen. I wasn't about to pass that up. Made a hell of a lot more than I could babysitting, and no more drunk ass creeps coming home and making a pass at me while their wives were checking that I'd put the kids down right."

"Just one creep, from what I hear."

"Oh, well, I wasn't babysitting for John. I was working at his law firm, but after hours is when the fun happened."

She gives me a wink and trades her cigarette for a tube of mascara.

"So that's the rich guy you had an affair with," I say. "That's what you were telling me to leverage."

"Hell, yeah," she says. "If I could have gotten in with his friends, I'd have been set. But I had to go and get stupid and fall in love. He didn't want some clingy teenager coming around, tipping off his wife. So he dumped my ass. That's when I met your daddy."

I sit up straight on the bed. "Who was he?"

"Some other asshole," she says with a wave of her hand, batting cigarette smoke out of her face. "He was playing poker with Daddy one night, and I was feeling rejected, and he paid me the good kind of attention, if you know what I mean. We snuck around a few months, but I was still hung up on John Darling. Ain't nobody as good at sweet talking a woman as a Darling, that's for damn sure. And he'd buy me shit, just like yours does. Your daddy couldn't compare to that."

"So you dumped him?"

"We had our fun, but it wasn't anything that'd last."

"But you know who he is. What's his name? How old is he? Where is he now?"

"Course I know who he is," she snaps. "What do you take me for, some kind of slut?"

"It never crossed your mind that I might want to meet him?" I ask, measuring my tone because I want her to keep talking, but I can't help being irritated. She always avoided questions when I asked, and eventually, I got the picture. It didn't matter who he was. He wasn't here, and we were.

"It's too late for that," she says. "Got hauled off to jail about ten years ago. I heard he got stabbed his first night there. Serves him right, if you ask me. Worthless son of a bitch never lifted a finger to help me out, not even when I came up pregnant and Daddy kicked me out. Straight up denied you were his when I told him, probably just so he didn't get booted from Daddy's poker game. Guess that shows how important you were to him. At least I kept you."

"Thanks, Mom," I say, because what else can I say? She's right. She could have given me up for adoption. Who knows, maybe I would have been better off. But there's no way to know that now. Even if she hasn't been the best mom, she gave up a lot for me.

"Yeah," she says grudgingly. "So don't go talking shit like I should have taken you to meet him. He didn't want nothing to do with your ass."

"Okay," I say. "You're right. It doesn't matter. I just wanted to know who he was."

"I always told you he was a worthless piece of shit," she says. "Guess that ain't enough."

"It's enough."

She smooths on her lipstick and drops it back onto her dresser, picking up her cigarette, which burned out while she was talking. She relights it and looks over herself in the mirror. "You know, I did try to give us a better life. I wasn't looking for a baby, but I thought maybe I could still make something good for us. I tried talking to John, but he wouldn't have nothing to do with me. So I tried with JT, since I wasn't showing yet. He took me in after my daddy kicked me out. But I think we were both just trying to get a rise out of John. And then you came along, and everybody could tell you weren't JT's, what with your coloring."

"He kicked you out?"

"Yeah," she says, crushing out her cigarette. "He thought I'd cheated on him, couldn't be convinced otherwise. And a man's got his pride, especially a rich man. Even when he's lost his money and ain't rich no more. You weren't his problem, and he wasn't going to support some other asshole's kid, especially if it came from his girlfriend cheating on him."

I'm horrified by this story that I never knew, in part because I can see so much of my own self in it, so many mistakes that any girl could make. One forgotten condom and you're a homeless teen mom begging for places to stay. If Royal didn't have money, or hadn't taken me to the clinic that day, this could be my life. No wonder she hates me.

"Mom... I'm sorry."

She shrugs. "I lived with the Gunn family for a while, a couple years at least."

I think of all the times Officer Gunn picked me up back in the graffiti days, how he always asked after my mom and went easy on me. For some reason, it makes me feel weird as hell.

Mom keeps talking as she adds more blush to her cheeks. "Then your papa got his arm caught up in a propeller while he was out on a friend's fishing boat, and he didn't make it. Your nana married some asshole from Beebe and moved up there. I got the trailer, and you know the rest of that story."

"I'm sorry, Mom. I'm sorry it was so hard for you, and that my existence ruined your life. I really, truly feel for you. I know you think it's my fault, but it's not like I asked to be born."

"I know you didn't, baby," she says, sitting down beside me on the bed. "And I know I wasn't always the best mama to you. But you're doing real good for yourself, and I want you to know I'm proud of that."

SELENA

She reaches out to hug me, and I let her pull me in, squeezing her solid body to mine and inhaling the scent of tobacco and cheap perfume.

"Thanks," I say, my throat suddenly tight. Compliments from my mother are as rare as jewels, and I'm not going to fuck it up by asking for more. Even though I'm relieved that she confirmed my suspicions, I'm still glad I gave Preston a Q-tip with my saliva when he asked. Just in case. After all, she was with two Darlings around the time I was conceived. Which means I couldn't only be Preston's cousin, but his aunt, which is somehow even more disturbing. I know I'm not, but still. A DNA test will put both our minds at ease.

twenty-nine

Harper Apple

I get the call on Thursday. Not only did the admission board accept my application, but I've been given a full scholarship for both semesters. I'm so happy that, after closing the blinds, I jump up and down and scream like a preteen girl who just won tickets to see her favorite boyband. And that's not the kind of thing I do. But just this once, I let myself. I didn't just win a contest on the radio for one night of fun, after all. I won a whole fucking year at a top school, one that can launch me to a top college.

After the excitement wears off, I send a text thanking Preston and then sink onto my bed, shaking with nerves.

I'm officially returning to Willow Heights.

It's the longest weekend of my life, but on Monday, my first day of school rolls around at last. I've missed a month

SELENA

already, but it's still too soon. I'm nervous as hell. I don't know how I'm going to be strong enough to do this. At least Dawson and Royal won't be there, so I only have to face the twins every day. After the night at the Slaughterpen, though, I know I'll survive it. Another fucking thing I have Royal to thank for. I might never have been ready to see them if not for him, and I'm beyond grateful that my first time seeing them won't be at school, where I might freak out publicly.

I get up early and put on my armor piece by piece, fixing myself until I look like one of the Dolce girls, perfectly made up and in designer clothes. Then I'm ready. This year, I don't have a fancy bike. I have something better. I climb into the Escalade, feeling like a badass bitch as I roll up on campus. My stomach falls when I see a black Range Rover parked in the spot next to the one I was assigned. I sigh and climb out of my car—just saying *my car* makes me feel giddy enough that he can't ruin my mood.

"Why are you here?" I ask when Royal steps out of his car.

"It's your first day."

"And?" I ask. "I did what you wanted. I went to Slaughterpen. You were right. It helped. I admit it. Now you can gloat."

"I'm not here to gloat," he says, frowning down at me. I can see other students from the corner of my eye, lingering and watching us.

"Fine," I say. "Then know that you made things right. I'm letting you off the hook. Now, can you please stop following me around and just let me live my life?"

"I already told you the answer to that," he says, his voice a low rumble as he steps toward me, almost like he's going to put his hands on my hips the way he used to, pull me in…

My fucking heart flutters at the thought, and I slam the door closed on that stupid bitch real quick. I take a deep breath, drawing on my patience, before addressing him again. "Shouldn't you be off at college by now? Can't your daddy buy your way into Yale or some other top school in the country? Or did you drop out to stalk me full time?"

"Someone should be watching you full time."

SELENA

I sigh. "I'm not going to kill myself, Royal. And trust me when I say having you around isn't making things better. It's making them worse."

"Let me walk you in today," he says, a challenge in his eyes. "If it makes things worse, I won't show up tomorrow."

We stand there for a minute, facing off. We both know he's right. Royal showing up here for me will only make things better for me this year. He may have graduated, but he was the fucking king of this place for the past few years. No one's going to mess with his girl.

But I'm not his girl, and I don't want to pretend that I am.

Still, I'm not stupid enough to throw away what he's giving me just to prove I can do it on my own. I learned the hard way that I'm not enough. On my own, I won't survive this place. Dixie told me as much last year, on my very first day. I spent the whole of last year trying to prove her wrong, only to prove her right in the end. I need allies. And Royal isn't just any ally. He's Willow Heights *royalty*.

Sure, I could be a brat and make a big point of flouncing off and leaving Royal Dolce in the dust. Some petty part of me wants to, just to hurt his pride. But the stubbornly rooted part of me that survived, the instinct for self-preservation, is stronger than any silly notion of pride. This is a gift, just like he delivered my revenge to me as a gift. That time, he was showing his brothers that I am not to be trifled with. Now, he's offering to show the whole school.

"Okay," I say, pressing my nails into my palms until I know it'll leave marks. "I'll let you walk me in today, but only if you don't show up every morning."

"Fine."

"And that doesn't mean you can skip one day," I say, glaring at him. "Make your point now, and that's it."

"Every other day."

"Once a week."

We stare at each other a long moment. "I'm not bound to that," he grits out. "If something happens…"

"Then you can put on your hero cape and come save the day."

He scowls at me but holds out a hand. I want to tell him there's no way in hell I'm holding his hand, but that would defeat the purpose of him walking me in. So I slip my hand into his, remembering when I was the one who wanted this, when I bargained for it with a blowjob. The memory swallows me as his hand swallows mine, and I'm glad his grip is firm, because I think I might buckle if he wasn't holding onto me, steadying me. The force of the memory hits me right in the chest, like the memories hit me at the bridge.

Despite everything, despite us both playing a game all along, both seeing how far the other could go before we broke, we were happy.

The realization is shocking and absurd and tragically, terribly real. We may have been toxic as fuck together, but for those brief months when we were together, we were happy. I can't remember ever feeling better than I did when I was in his arms, or on my knees in front of him, or just lying under the bridge with him, my head pillowed on his arm, talking. For a girl like me, that's as close to happy as I will ever come, and I didn't even realize it at the time.

Or maybe I did. Maybe that's why I reveled in it with such abandon, soaking up every drop of bliss I could. Because some part of me always knew that one day, it would be over, and all I'd have left were memories. I just didn't anticipate how much they'd hurt.

It's not some bittersweet ache. It's raw and immediate, a piercing pain that's worse than I thought possible, drilling right through my sternum. Royal has torn me open, cut away the scar tissue and forced me to feel again, even when I'd rather stay numb and sealed up in the safety of the shelter Preston helped me build around my heart. Royal doesn't give a fuck what I'd rather do. He forces me to face the harsh reality the way he does, never shying away from the places that hurt the most.

By the time I've caught my breath and stopped my head from spinning, we're at my locker. I pull my hand from his, glad I was too stunned with pain to notice how good his hand felt around mine, how big and warm and protective, like it would never hurt me.

His touch is a lie.

I know that. I remind myself as I put in my combination and open my empty locker.

Royal leans against the locker next to mine, bracing his elbow over my head and leaning down.

SELENA

"Please don't," I say, resting a hand on his chest to maintain distance between us. Maybe it looks like a romantic scene to everyone gawking, but they can't see my lip trembling, can't see that I'm not laying a hand on Royal's heart but stopping him from coming closer. I can't handle this today. I need to get away from him before I lose my shit completely, but he won't let me breathe, won't give me a break. He's in my face, everywhere I look, never letting me forget.

"Why not?" he asks, using his free hand to wind a strand of hair behind my ear. His dark eyes are drawing me in, warm with… Desire. A shiver runs through me, and I feel the answering pull inside me, and suddenly, I'm looking at his mouth, remembering his warm lips on mine, the way his kiss was a blitzkrieg that I grew to crave.

Fuck my stupid memories.

I swallow hard and force my words out, keeping them low so the crowd watching us won't hear. "I don't want to kiss you."

"I want to kiss you," he says, resting his forehead to mine. "I want to kiss you until you're so wet I can smell it. I want to taste your black cherry tongue and hear you moan."

"Don't," I whisper, my eyes dropping closed. I can't afford to feel that way again, the way he threatens to make me feel. I'm shaking all over, and I don't know if I want to devour him or destroy him for thinking he can still say those things to me.

"I want to kiss you here." He brushes his knuckles down the side of my neck. "And here." His fingertips skim over my collarbone before his hand drops to my hip.

"Stop," I whisper.

"And here."

"Royal…"

He runs his thumb along the inside of my hipbone, in my ticklish spot. "I want to kiss you right here until you lose patience like you always do and push my head between your legs like a greedy bitch. I want to lick your cunt until you gush in my mouth the way you used to. I want to lick up every drop and start all over from here."

SELENA

He lifts his hand from my hip and runs his thumb across my lower lip, smashing it while he grips my chin between his fingers. His eyes are hot, so hot it makes my thighs quake, but I don't know if it's desire or fear or some Molotov cocktail of both. I just know I hate it with every fiber of my being.

"Royal." I grab his wrist in both my hands, my gaze flying to his. "No."

He blinks at me a few times, the fog of lust clearing from his eyes. "I think we've made our point, don't you?" he asks, giving the slightest tip of his head toward the hall.

I swallow hard, trying to clear my own careening thoughts, jealous of how quickly he can pull himself together. He's had years of practice putting on a fake face, though. I've always been myself, and fuck everyone who didn't like it. Now, I'm learning his way.

"Well, look what we have here." Gloria's slow, Georgia drawl cuts through the tense silence in the hall. "If it isn't Faulkner's favorite couple, together again."

She stops beside us, and I notice even more people staring. The hallway has fallen dead silent, and no one is even pretending not to stare. There's a full crowd standing around watching now, leaning on the walls and the lockers, like they're waiting for a showdown. Suddenly, my heart is pounding. I don't love attention unless I'm in the pit, and even then, I don't fight for the audience. I might give them what they want—a long and bloody fight—but it's only so I can fight again. It was never about them.

And here, where I don't fit, I've always hated attention. Even now, when I look the part, I have zero interest in being in the spotlight. I can't help but feel, yet again, like I'm the last to know something. What exactly happened after I dropped out of school last year? Are Royal and Gloria official, and they think we're going to fight for him? Or are they just staring at me because I disappeared and now I'm back, and I'm with Royal?

Except I'm not with Royal, and Gloria deserves to know that. She stands there looking as perfect as ever, but there's a spark of defiance in her eyes. Is she waiting for us to contradict her?

Even in clothes that fit me as if they're tailored to my every proportion, I feel suddenly out of place, as if I'm playing dress up. Yeah, the rich clothes fit my body, but they don't fit *me*. The little freshmen girls swooning over Royal might not know it, but Gloria sure as hell does. And though she's on scholarship, too, somehow she looks every inch the polished, perfect southern belle, her long blonde hair flat-ironed and hanging down her back and topped with a gold headband, a schoolgirl skirt with her freshly pressed shirt, and perfect makeup.

I realize I don't know her life at all anymore, not even in the superficial way I used to. I open my mouth to say we're not together, but Royal gives me a warning look, like he's reading my mind and knows exactly what I'm about to do. I shut up and smile at Gloria, wondering if my betrayal got back to her, if she's an enemy now.

I won't underestimate her again. She may look sweet as pie on the surface, but she's savage underneath—and stronger than me. She's been where I was. She didn't break. She used that shit to propel her to the top, to become a queen.

"Move along, Lo," Royal says, his voice bland as he straightens and faces her.

She cocks a brow, but her knuckles whiten as she clutches her books harder to her chest. "Shouldn't you be off at college instead of chasing jailbait in high school?"

"I'm less than a year older than Harper," he points out.

"It's fine," I say, sliding my arms around him from behind. It's for show, but I don't miss the way he tenses in my arms or the way my stupid heart swells until it aches at the familiarity of his body against mine, the casually intimate gesture I used to do as a matter of course instead of faking it for status. "I'm fine. Go."

"I was just leaving." He turns in my arms, squeezing me against him so hard I can't breathe for a second, and I wonder if he's feeling the same ache I am, the ache of missing what we had. We might be right in front of each other, but we're not each other's anymore. Faking a touch, an embrace, almost makes it worse than not doing it at all. It only reminds me that it's all been destroyed.

"For the record, I don't approve of this," Royal says, stepping away from me and gesturing between me and Gloria. I search his face, his eyes, for something real, some hint of longing for what just passed between us, but I can't find even a trace. I'm not surprised. Royal shows the world what he wants them to see, and he wants them to see that I'm still his, that I carry his mark of approval, and that I'm off limits.

I don't fight it. There's no point. Like Colt said, his claim is forever. I can't escape it. All I can do is use it for whatever the currency of his status is worth here.

It must still be worth something, because a crowd of preppy freshman girls giggle behind their hands and cover their hearts and roll their eyes back in their heads like they're about to swoon when Royal walks away. Irrational irritation rises inside me, the urge to knock their heads together and tell them to find a boy their own damn age. I'm far too aware of Royal's complete and utter dismissal of them, the way he doesn't even spare them a glance, and of the idiotic satisfaction it brings me.

"Oh my god, it's *him*," squeals a doe-eyed, dewy-skinned girl with blonde ringlets and pouty pink lips.

"I can't believe we got to see him," says her friend, a short, full-figured brunette with flat-ironed hair and what looks like her first attempt at winged liner. "He doesn't even go here anymore."

"I feel like I just saw Brody Villines," agrees another friend, one who obviously hasn't gotten through her awkward, pimply adolescent phase, though she's wearing a pound of makeup to try to hide her pimples. "I heard he broke, like, every football record at this school last year."

"I heard he's running his own company now," says the blonde. "Dolce Sweets. That's him!"

I turn back to Gloria just in time to see the girl at the next locker rolling her eyes before closing the wooden door and hefting her backpack over her shoulder. I don't recognize her from last year, and it's a small enough school that I'm pretty sure I would remember a tall brunette who wears flannels that are definitely bending the dress code's 'collared shirts' policy.

"Who's that?" I ask.

Gloria wrinkles her nose as she watches the girl clomp off down the hall in her Doc Martens. "That's Josie," she says. "Transfer student. Obvs on scholarship. Might be pretty if

SELENA

she bothered to try. Did she even comb her hair this morning?"

I cock a brow and give her a meaningful look. "Judge much?"

"Speaking of trolls," she says, scrunching her face up like she smells something bad and looking someone up and down as they approach behind me.

I turn, and my heart nearly stops beating. "Colt," I choke out.

"Hey, Appleteeny," he says with a slow smile, the one that might look casual, but if you know him, you can see the guardedness in his eyes. "Or should I say… Hey, Darling?"

"For the love of all that's holy, please don't."

Didn't take Preston long to spread that around. Guess that answers the question of whether or not they're close.

"Considering I hear we had our own little afternoon delight last year, I think I'd rather forget it was ever mentioned, too," he says.

"You guys hooked up?" Gloria asks, looking at me like it's a personal affront to her that I'd dare to hook up with someone she considers beneath her. I guess if I want to be her friend, I have to keep up appearances like she does.

"No," I say firmly. "We just hung out once."

"Yeah," Colt says with a smirk. "That's what happened."

"Why are you talking to us?" Gloria asks in her bitchiest voice. "Go crawl back into your creepy little cave like the goblin you are."

I sometimes forget that she wasn't just my friend last year. She was the bitch queen of the school. Now that she's a senior, her reign will be supreme. It's hard to imagine anyone could rival her even without Royal on her arm, but if I know Gloria, she'll secure one of the other top dogs just to make sure.

Colt gives her a slow once-over. "I wasn't talking to you, sweetheart," he says. "But since you're the goblin queen, I guess you'd know a thing or two about frosty little holes."

"I said *creepy caves*," she corrects, looking scandalized by his words. "Now get lost, loser."

He opens his mouth as if to answer, then clamps his jaw shut and just fixes her with his haughty asshole look instead.

SELENA

"Colt's my friend," I interrupt, turning to Lo. "And Royal's not here anymore. You don't have to enforce his stupid rules."

"Aww, look at that, she's defending me," Colt says, draping an arm over my shoulder. "I missed you, too, Teeny."

"Why are you here?" I ask. "Didn't you graduate?"

"Oh, didn't our cousin tell you? Since I had to drop out of school after Halloween last year, I get to repeat senior year with all you lovely ladies. Lucky me."

"I didn't know," I say quietly, guilt twisting inside me. "Dixie said were taking classes online."

"Yeah, it's a little hard to get shit done when your head's wrapped like a mummy and you can't see for three months. Plus, y'know. I lost a bunch of memories and retaining shit's a little harder than it used to be."

"So, you're brain damaged," Gloria says with a snort. "Too bad they don't have a short bus at this school. Maybe you should try Faulkner High. I hear they have more… special services."

"Gloria, shut up," I say, swallowing hard. "And Colt, I'm so sorry."

Even more sorry because during those three months, I was happily fucking Royal.

"It's okay, baby," he says. "I like playing with fire, too, when it looks like you."

"Can you just not flirt with me until the DNA test comes back?" I ask, scooting out from under his arm.

"Whatever you say, Teeny," he drawls, giving Gloria a lazy, two-finger salute before sauntering off down the hall.

I pray like hell she won't ask what DNA test I'm talking about, because the last thing I want is to be known as the whore who fucked her own cousin.

SELENA

thirty

Harper Apple

"Oh my god," squeals a high, sweet voice from behind us. I've never been so relieved to see Dixie, but I'm also terrified Gloria's going to ask about the DNA test in front of the nosiest, gossipiest bitch in school.

"Oh great," Gloria mutters.

Dixie bustles up, her eyes rounded with surprise. "You're back!"

I give her a little frown before I realize she's not looking at me. She takes Gloria's hand and gives it a squeeze, her smile full of sympathy. "I'm so sorry about your brother. Are you okay?"

"I'm fine, Dixie," Gloria says, glancing around at the whispering crowd and squaring her shoulders. She holds her head high, but when I look at her closer, I notice the dark circles under her eyes, maybe even a little puffiness.

"If you need to talk," Dixie says. "On or off the record. You know you can talk to me."

"I have to get to my locker," Gloria says, prying her hand away from Dixie's and starting down the hall without bothering to say goodbye to me.

"Are your sisters back?" Dixie asks, scurrying after her.

I look around, overwhelmed by all the people staring and whispering, the confusion of the morning, the sensation of having half of every story. I shoulder past the ogling freshmen girls, relieved that at least no one is gaping at my clothes this year. Still, paranoia nags at me.

Were people staring at me, or Royal, or Gloria? Last spring, did the Dolce twins and Dawson tell everyone they ran a train on me, or that the football team did? I mean, it's a relief to know that the twins are the only ones at this school who really fucked me, since Dawson's already graduated. I don't have to walk around wondering which of the football team has been inside me. But what did the rumors say?

SELENA

Most people wouldn't even blink if they found out I'd been with the twins. That's old news. They've thought that happened since the first time Royal dragged me to the basement to give him head. The twins fuck everyone, anyway. I'm hardly special. But a rumor that I took the whole team…

I've dealt with rumors about my sexual prowess before, and though it seems too cruel to have to endure it twice before I'm out of high school, it's whatever. It didn't kill me when Colin Finnegan told everyone at Faulkner that I was a slut freshman year, and it won't kill me now. If it's not about that, were there rumors of my death? Or is it just because Royal walked me in this morning?

Beyond my own little drama, what happened with the Waltons? I punched Dawson out and kicked him in the nuts, but I didn't beat him up that badly. And I didn't even see the Walton girls, so why have they been out?

I can't tell if people are staring at me as I walk to my first class. My head is crammed with all the new information, but there's obviously more that I don't have. I missed the last two months of junior year and the first month of senior year, and I have no idea what happened while I was gone. But knowing Willow Heights, I missed a shitload of drama. Now, it's like starting over from scratch, trying to figure it out all over again.

I sit in first period, trying to pay attention, but my mind keeps returning to what Colt said. He didn't seem pissed at me, though he has every reason to be. In fact, he didn't seem pissed at Preston's either—not at me, anyway. That day, he was irate at Preston for sleeping with me, and today he seemed more interested in needling the queen bee than anything.

Even if he doesn't blame me, I feel guilty as fuck. But the blame for that situation doesn't fall entirely on me. He invited me to his house knowing what he was risking, even if I didn't. He gave me Mabel's clothes and told me what happened to her, conveniently leaving out the part about how the twins are still obsessed with her. Maybe everything would have been the same if he hadn't done that, but maybe not. After all, if Royal hadn't seen me with Colt, he might have never gone apeshit with jealousy. That was the day he claimed me as his plaything, said I belonged to him.

SELENA

The day I wore Mabel's clothes, the twins freaked out. Royal made me change and then took me to the basement to fool around for the first time. After that, he ordered me to go to his game. We hooked up. And everything went from there. If Colt hadn't invited me over that day, would any of that have happened the way it did?

There's no use wondering, since he did invite me over. But him holding it against me is like me holding it against him that Royal claimed me. And the truth is, I like Colt, and I could use his friendship, but I won't risk it if he's going to be hurt again. I have to feel out the new order, figure out how things have changed now that Royal's not on the throne.

I walk into second period and see an empty seat next to Josie, the girl in flannel, who's sitting slouched in her seat with her earbuds in, fiddling with her laptop. I head her way, but a deep voice calls my name, interrupting my progress. The girl looks up, taking me in with a single glance, and then goes back to her computer.

"Yo, Harper," DeShaun calls again, kicking out a chair for me. "Come sit with us."

I sigh and relent, joining him at a table with Cotton Montgomery and some Dolce girl whose name I don't remember. Suddenly, all I remember is that she and another girl giggled as they told me that Duke would give me a "more permanent" mark than a necklace. I think of that ring that he wears, and I shudder. He told me it was to know where he'd been, and he used it on me. Do all the Dolce girls have that same scar?

We really are branded like his cattle.

I feel bile rise to my throat, and I'm not sure I can sit through this class with a girl who thinks that's cute and a guy who's known by his own friends as someone to watch out for because he might slip something in your drink. I start to rise, turning to see if the spot next to Josie is open, but just then, Colt drops into it. Of course he's friends with the cool chick. Of fucking course.

Class starts, and I sit there trying to remember why I fought so hard to be in this group last year. It's obvious I chose the wrong crowd. I'm haunted by the look this girl I don't even know gave me when I walked in and was going to sit with her. Josie looked me over and dismissed me in a single glance. She doesn't know me, doesn't know I spent all of last year wishing I had designer clothes like everyone else, that I could fit in.

Now I do, and the first person who looks cool and interesting took one look at me and decided I was like every other rich bitch. She saw me with Gloria this morning, after all. She probably thinks I'm one of the mean girls, that I belong with these people. She didn't know I was heading for her table, that I singled her out because I wanted to be with someone who looks more like... me.

Except the truth is, I don't look like her anymore. I don't know where I belong this year. Maybe I don't belong with girls like Josie or Blue, girls who look like opposite ends of the spectrum of FHS kids. After all, I wear thousand-dollar shoes and drive an Escalade. From the outside, I'm just like Gloria. But under it all, I'm still a girl from the trailer park, no matter how much Preston tries to change me by putting me in fancy clothes and draping me with diamonds.

Maybe, for a few months last year, I did belong in this group. I was Royal's plaything, and though we never made it official, everyone knew I was his girlfriend. But I only belonged because he said I did. I got invited to their parties, but not their spring break trips. None of that has changed. Just because I have expensive clothes now, Preston's not going to fund my trips with his enemies and their friends. They'll call me over in class, sit with me because Royal says I'm good enough, pretend for my sake that they don't know where I came from and who I really am. But they'll always know I'm not one of them, and I'll always know they're faking it.

I make it through class without freaking out, but I'm only halfway down the hall toward the next one when I see Duke for the first time. Adrenaline spikes through me, and all I want to do is run. Luckily, he's busy flirting with the pretty blonde freshman from this morning, and he doesn't even see me.

I hurry past, so busy looking back over my shoulder that I miss what's right in front of me until I step on something soft. Jerking to a stop, I whip around, barely noticing a few dirty looks cast my way. Under my foot is a smashed carnation, one of hundreds piled on the floor against the

SELENA

lockers. Cards, teddy bears, and handmade signs float in the sea of flowers.

Suddenly, my head swims, and I brace my hand against the locker, fighting for breath as Dixie's words come back to me.

I'm so sorry about your brother.

I'm here if you need to talk.

I think I'll be sick. I push off the locker and rush down the hall to the bathroom, slamming my shoulder into the door so hard it flies open. Even though it's a passing period, the bathroom is strangely deserted, like it was waiting for me. I grip the edges of a sink, closing my eyes and sucking in deep breaths. I'm glad I didn't eat breakfast, so I have nothing to puke up. My legs are shaking like jelly.

Suddenly, I'm aware of the unyielding rigidity of the brass knuckles binding my fingers, and I yank them off and drop them into the sink and jump back like they might bite me.

Did I kill Dawson?

I've heard of someone being hit on the head and dying of an aneurism they didn't know they had. But isn't that instantaneous? Or can it happen later, after he falls asleep?

Or is that a concussion? Did I hit him hard enough to cause a concussion?

"You better be some idiot freshman who doesn't know who I am," says a voice from one of the stalls. The door flies open, and Gloria Walton stands there, looking pissed.

"Gloria," I say, swallowing hard.

"Oh," she says, giving me a cool once-over. "It's you."

We stand there staring each other down for a minute. This girl was my friend, but as the seconds tick by, I count the ways I've wronged her. I didn't just hurt her brother. I told someone Royal's secret after swearing to her that I wouldn't. I betrayed her, and judging by the way Royal talked to her this morning, there were consequences.

Disgusted with myself, I snatch up the rings from the sink and push them back on before turning to face her. There's no use in putting it off, in hiding from the truth.

"What happened to Dawson?" I ask flatly.

"Suicide," she says, her voice equally devoid of emotion.

My fists clench involuntarily as I remember standing on the edge of that roof, Preston's hands on my arms, holding me back. Nausea roils in my stomach. Did I contribute to what Dawson did? When I confronted him, did his guilt become too much?

"Can we... Go somewhere and talk?" I ask, feeling incredibly, uncomfortably vulnerable in addition to unsteady on my feet.

"Why?" Gloria demands, bowing up. "You want to know all the grisly details? How he did it, who found him, what the suicide note said?"

She turns to the mirror and leans in, blinking as she watches her own dry eyes. Sometime between last Sunday and this one, she lost her brother, but looking at her, you wouldn't know she'd cried a tear. Only the undereye circles that makeup can't quite hide give it away.

"I'm sorry," I say.

"For what?" she asks, turning from the mirror. "For my loss, or for having the nerve to think you can ask me about it? If you were a friend, I'd already have told you."

"That's fair," I say, my lips numb.

"You're not a friend, though, and you never were," she goes on, anger lacing her words. "You just wanted to get close to Royal, and when you couldn't get there yourself, you found another way in. You think you're the first thirsty bitch to use me as a steppingstone? Please. You're basic."

The door swings open, and Gloria barks an order for them to leave, and the girls stumble against each other in a rush to obey. When the door settles closed, she turns to the mirror and snaps open her purse.

I swallow hard, glad for the distraction so I had a moment to let the sting of her words sink in. "You're right," I say. "I was a terrible friend."

She snorts. "Don't even bother, Harper. You weren't a friend at all. I was a means to an end. The embarrassing part is that I thought you were different. Guess it's my own damn fault for assuming. I know better than anyone that appearances are deceiving. I'm the last person who should have been fooled."

I remember saying something similar to Duke in the pit the other day, how I was so desperate for a friend that I'd believed he could be one. Why would Gloria need a friend so badly? She's popular, always surrounded by twenty people everywhere she goes—her sisters, the other Dolce girls, the cheer squad, the dance team, the Dolce boys, her brother and his friends…

But whatever the reason, she believed we were friends, and I hurt her by betraying that friendship.

"I'm sorry," I say again, crossing my arms and leaning my hip against the sink. I don't know how many more times she can cut me down before I'll be on the floor. The worst of it is, every word she's spoken is the truth. I genuinely cared about Gloria, but I did use her. I was so single-minded in my focus on getting in with the Dolces that when I saw a way in, and I took it. I climbed over anyone in my way to get what I wanted, just like they do.

The bell signaling the start of third period chimes, and Gloria sighs and drops her lipstick into her bag after reapplying. "Stop with the fake sympathy and go read Dixie's blog for gossip like everyone else. I know better than to say a goddamn word to you."

"You're right," I say again. "You're right about everything, Gloria. But I really, truly am sorry."

She crosses her arms and turns to me, mirroring my posture. "Go on, then. I'd like to hear your excuses so I can know how full of shit you really are."

I'd rather eat dirt than be vulnerable to a person who already has the upper hand, but I force the words out. "I was obsessed with getting close to Royal at the expense of everything else," I say. "I treated you like a disposable friend because I knew your loyalties were always to him first, and some part of me knew that he and I wouldn't last, so you and I couldn't, either. And the truth is, as pathetic as it sounds, I didn't even really know I was doing it. I've never had a close friend, and I'm not sure I know how. When we were hanging out, I was being genuine. I liked hanging out with you. I like you. You're cool as shit and the strongest girl at this school."

She smirks. "Stronger than you?"

I can't help but snort at that. "Uh, yeah. Way stronger. Unless we're talking about fighting, in which case, can we please do that instead of talking? I'd rather spill my blood than spill my guts to you."

"Why'd you tell him?"

SELENA

I don't have to ask what she's talking about. We both know.

"When I was trying to get in with them, it wasn't because I liked Royal. At least not at first. It was because... I needed information."

She narrows her eyes. "Information?"

"This is going to sound insane, but this anonymous guy contacted me online, and he gave me a scholarship here on the condition that I get him dirt on the Dolces."

"Oh my god," she says, her eyes widening. "You're, like, a spy?"

I shrug. "Kind of. But it wasn't glamorous. It was gross. I just... I really wanted to get out of this town. You know how much a diploma from Willow Heights is worth. And it wasn't just about the scholarship, either. When I found out more about the Dolces, I kind of wanted to take them down. They're not good people, Gloria."

"You think I don't know that?" she asks. "I've known them longer than you have, and I guarantee you I know them better. Those boys are all complete psychos, their mom is a worthless waste of space, and their dad is a total creeper who'll try to convince you that you owe him a blowjob for driving you a block home in the rain."

"Well, those are all my excuses," I say, feeling relieved to have it out there and also kind of drained, like carrying the burden of that secret has worn me down. "If you want me to go all into my daddy issues and fucked-upness, I was probably also afraid of having a real friend, someone who could walk away, so I didn't let anyone become a real friend."

"So even when I told you all my secrets, you kept yours."

"Yep," I say. "And now that I say all that out loud, I feel about as big as a worm in dogshit. If it makes you feel any better, I didn't tell anyone else what you told me. Just Mr. D—the scholarship donor. And then Royal found out, and you can guess how things went from there."

Her eyes widen. "Oh, shit," she says. "That's why you broke up, isn't it? I mean, he figured out who told you and dumped my ass this summer, but that was way after you disappeared. I didn't realize when it happened. So if you think about it, I kinda broke you up by telling you, and then you broke me and Royal up by telling someone else."

SELENA

"Sure," I say, giving her a look. "But not really."

"He would have dumped you when he found out you knew, even if you didn't tell anyone. He's so ashamed."

"Yeah, probably," I admit.

"So, who'd you tell?" she asks. "Who's the mystery donor?"

I shrug. "One of the Darlings."

She narrows her eyes. "Which one?"

"Preston," I say, realizing she knows him. They were both students here the year before I started. "But I didn't know who I was telling at the time. I couldn't figure out who he was until he told me."

"Wait, you had all that going on last year?" she asks. "You were starting at this crazy-ass new school, trying to get information to feed to some psycho you didn't even know, while trying to figure out who he was and also take down the most powerful family in town, who just happened to be the family of the dangerous psycho you were dating?"

"Yep," I say, rocking back on my heels. "That about sums up junior year. Hopefully, senior year will be a little less exciting."

"And you were doing all that on your own?"

"Pretty much."

"I just have one question."

"Shoot."

"How the hell is Royal still talking to you?"

"I wish he'd stop," I say, squeezing my arms tighter around my middle. All this spilling of guts is giving me a stomachache. "You have a lot of experience with him. Know how to get him to permanently ghost you?"

"You could try telling his girlfriend that he's basically a hooker," she says with a little smile.

"That would require him to actually have a girlfriend," I say. The thought makes more than my stomach ache. As many times as I've told him to leave, and as much as I meant it each time, the thought of him with someone else is a sucker punch to the heart.

Gloria shakes her head and pulls her purse strap onto her shoulder. "We just thought you were some poor, slutty scholarship chick who came along and made good by strapping herself to the richest guys in school, but all along, you were actually playing all of us like a fucking pro. Damn,

SELENA

Harper. I'm honestly not sure if I'm more pissed or impressed."

"It wasn't like that," I mutter.

"Sure it wasn't," she says, rolling her eyes. "God, I'd kill for a cigarette while I digest all this."

"I might know somewhere we can sneak out to and smoke," I say. "And someone who has cigarettes. But you have to be openminded, okay? Can you put aside the bitch act for a cigarette?"

"I'll sure do my best," she says, smiling sweetly.

"After you," I say, pushing open the door and sweeping a hand out for her to go ahead.

"I'm still mad at you," she reminds me as she steps out into the empty hallway. We're halfway through third period, which means I'm starting off my first day even further behind. But whatever. I can do homework at home. This can't wait.

"I know," I say. "I deserve that."

In truth, I want to believe we're friends, that we can be again. She may act like an evil bitch to maintain her image and keep her reign, but she's a fucking queen through and through. I admire and respect her, and I want her friendship. I know I have to work for this forgiveness, though. No more lies and sneaking around this year. I need real friends to get through this, and if I want the best, I need to be the best for her, too.

SELENA

thirty-one

Harper Apple

Colt's not outside, so we sit on the hot metal bleachers, trying not to burn our legs, and talk for a while longer. I don't tell Gloria the full truth in the words I used with Blue, but I don't think I need to. She knows Royal. She knows what he's capable of.

"I just don't get why you left school," she says. "I mean, you could have at least told your friends where you went. No one knew what happened to you. I even checked Faulkner High and Cedar Crest, in case you went cray-cray when Royal dumped you, but you weren't anywhere. I thought you were dead, Harper."

I never expected anyone to look for me, and I find myself feeling even more guilty. She really was a friend, one I didn't even know I had. But she doesn't know the extent of what I went through.

"Not everyone is as tough as you, Gloria," I say. "I was scared and… And fucking traumatized, okay? I couldn't have come back to school and held my head high and pretended nothing was wrong like you do. I'm not that good at being fake."

"I guess I deserve that," she says with a shrug.

"Look, I know I made a mess of things last year," I admit. "But I was literally doing the best I could to survive. You might know what it's like to have the Dolce boys fuck with you, but you haven't been their enemy."

"No, but I might have been able to help," she says. "You didn't give anyone a chance to be on your side."

I can't help but scoff at that. "Oh, you want me to bare my soul and be all honest, but you're going to tell me you wouldn't have stuck by Royal?"

"Fine, you're right," she says. "I would have."

"Everyone in this school would have," I remind her. "It was bad enough that just those three hated me. I'd be dead right now if I'd tried to come back here."

SELENA

At the time, there was no way. I was barely able to function, let alone try to learn anything. Not to mention, I'd have had to see the football players every day, thinking they'd all fucked me out there in the swamp. And then there's the matter of the Dolce boys. Maybe a couple of them even feel remorse now, but it took almost six months. Back then, there's no way they would have let me come back to Willow Heights like nothing happened. Royal was too pissed about my betrayal. If I'd come back, he would have tried to kill me again.

And who the fuck knows what the twins would have done.

There's one other person who knew what happened, why I disappeared. And of course he wasn't going to tell Gloria why I never came back after spring break.

Now he's dead, so I can't exactly blame him. I will never tell Gloria that he knew, though. No matter what kind of person he was, she deserves to remember her brother the way she wants. It has nothing to do with her, and now, it never will. She hasn't said anything to indicate that he mentioned me or what happened. She hasn't said the cops are investigating his busted up face because it might have been murder.

So, I don't bring up Dawson, even though I want to know what happened. Gloria made it clear that is a privilege reserved for friends. So, until I earn her friendship, it's not my place to ask. If she wants to come back to school a week after her brother died and act like nothing happened, that's her business. Maybe she's scared someone will take her place, or maybe she doesn't want to think about it, and being at home makes that impossible. All I know is that I'm not entitled to ask her, and that I don't want to think about it right now, either. Later, I'll dissect it and pull it apart and figure out how guilty I need to feel about it.

The lunch bell chimes, and a few minutes later, I hear footsteps on the grass behind the bleachers. We hop down to see Colt heading our way.

"I can't smoke in front of him," Gloria hisses. "I can't even be seen with him!"

"No one will see you but us," I point out. "I seriously doubt he's going to spread rumors about you smoking."

SELENA

"It could get back to someone," she growls through clenched teeth. "Or they could see me coming in and guess I've been with him."

"Who?" I ask.

"The Dolce boys, for starters," she says. "Their girls, the squad, Rylan… Anyone!"

"Hey, darlin," Colt drawls, strolling across the grass to join us. "Skipping school on your first day, Teeny? I thought you were a nerd."

"I skipped school on your last day," I point out.

"Ah," he says, reaching into his pocket and pulling out his cigarettes. "Dad did tell me that."

"Your dad?" I ask, arching a brow.

"Yeah," he says, tapping out a cigarette and tucking it between his lips. "I had to piece together a lot of the last few months before that from texts and Dixie's blog. She and my family tried to fill in the rest. I don't remember."

"Shit," I say, accepting a cigarette from him. "Your family must really hate me."

He lights up and drags on his cigarette, tipping his head back to exhale a series of smoke rings before looking back at me. "So, did we fuck or what?"

"Um, no," I say, lighting up as well. "Definitely not."

"Cool," he says, nodding and stuffing his left hand in his pocket the way he does, so his missing finger is hidden. "My dad said you were over there, and then we kinda figured out what happened from there, but I wasn't sure what happened while you were at my house."

"So, not to interrupt this little trip down memory lane, but can I bum one of those?" Gloria asks, her voice all prim and formal, like she's awkwardly asking a stranger for a tampon in the bathroom.

"You smoke?" Colt asks, giving her a skeptical look.

She glares at me.

"Yes, she smokes, but it's a big secret, so don't tell anyone," I say.

Colt just shakes his head and pulls out his cigarettes again, passing the pack to her.

"So, like, do you think it'll ever come back?" she asks. "Your memory?"

SELENA

He shrugs. "Probably not."

"I mean, I wouldn't mind forgetting a few things from my past," she says. "But I'd want to choose what months I forgot."

"Wouldn't that be handy?" he drawls.

"You forgot you broke up with Dixie, so you got back together," she says. "Isn't that a good thing? Or did she not tell you that? Oops."

He makes a silent little snort of breath. "She told me."

"You're back with Dixie?" I ask. "What else did I miss?"

"Let's see," Gloria says, worrying her lip between her fingers and squinting up at the sun leaking through the gaps in the bleachers. "Last year there was spring break, and then of course you disappearing. That was the talk of the school for at least a week, until everyone found out Royal had dumped you. I already knew, of course. He told us on the ski trip. But everyone figured it made sense that you disappeared after he dumped you, so most people forgot about it. Then we had prom, which I won, of course. A bunch of people took that new Alice drug after prom, and some people went to the hospital, but no one died so it wasn't that big a deal.

And there were finals and graduation, so that was pretty boring."

"If you want more details, I'm sure Dixie's blog has a full account," Colt adds, tossing his cigarette butt and opening the pack again. He takes out a joint and grins at Gloria. "You smoke this, too, Queen Bee?"

"Oh my god, no," she shrieks, stepping back like it might get her high before it's even lit. "I'm going in. If you get caught smoking that, you could lose your scholarship, Harper."

She gives me a meaningful look, and I know it's not my scholarship she's worried about.

Colt chuckles at her scandalized expression and lights up.

"I'm not too worried about my scholarship anymore," I say with a grin.

"Well, good for you," Gloria snaps. "I'm going in. Rylan will be pissed if I don't show up for lunch, anyway."

"Then you better run and make your man a sandwich," Colt says. "Gloria Walton, bringing feminism back to 1950."

"Shut up, troll," she says. "Or I'll tell Dixie what you said about her after you dumped her ass on Bye Week last year."

SELENA

He takes a slow drag on the joint, his eyes hooded as he stares her down before answering. "Go right ahead," he says. "I have no memory of that night, but whatever I said can't be worse than what I did to her freshman year, and she's still dick whipped, so…"

Gloria rolls her eyes. "Colt Darling, bringing chauvinism back to, what was it? 1950?" She smiles sweetly up at him, bats her lashes, and then turns and flounces away.

I've been ignoring their little squabble while marvel over my own words—that I'm not worried about my scholarship this year. Even though I don't have money of my own, I'm basically a kept woman, and I'm starting to see what it would be like if I wasn't desperate every day of my life. It feels good to have security, to know I'll be okay even if I screw up sometimes. It's about so much more than having nice clothes and fitting in.

It's about feeling safe.

Money is safety, security, and basic necessities all rolled into one. I don't worry that I won't have a hot shower anymore. If Mom's boyfriends get handsy, I can take my car and get the hell out. Missing lunch, even after skipping breakfast, doesn't mean I won't eat for twenty-four hours.

I don't even have to fight at Slaughterpen to make sure I'm fed. I have someone who steps in when I need it. I have someone who will defend my scholarship. For the first time in my life, someone has my back. Maybe he can't protect me or take down the Dolces, and he's not a hero, but he's my fucking hero.

"Now that she's gone," Colt says, his gaze still fixed on Gloria's retreating figure. "Did we really fuck?"

I laugh and shove his shoulder. "No, asshole. We just kissed, thank god."

"Hm," he says, raising a brow and sucking on the joint. "Are you sure? Because it seems like we would have fucked."

"Well, we didn't," I say. "Which is a good thing, because that would be even more weird."

"Because you fucked Preston?"

"Because Baron said we're related."

He snorts. "Yeah, I believe Baron Dolce about as much as I believe that Elvis is alive. He's probably partying it up with Marilyn Monroe and my cousin right now."

SELENA

"So, what's your situation this year?" I ask, accepting the joint from him and leaning on one of the supports. "Is it dangerous for you to be out here with me?"

"I don't know," he says slowly, speaking through a mouthful of smoke. "Is it?"

I think of Royal showing up everywhere I go. I wouldn't put it past him to have spies at this school, and not just his brothers. It could get back to him.

And yet...

Things are different now. I have power now, too.

"You know, they don't have to have absolute power," I say. "I know I didn't take them down, and you're not in a hurry to go up against them, which I totally understand. But there are only two of them at this school now. They've lost their god. The twins are mortal."

"You sure about that?" he asks, giving me some side eye as he takes the joint back. "Because I think demons are immortal, unless you disembowel them, dip them in acid, and boil their entrails in a vat of goat oil for a half century."

I can't help but laugh. It feels strange and rickety coming out of me, like whatever's inside a person that produces that sound is broken in me. I guess it is. I can't remember the last time I've genuinely laughed.

Colt grins, watching me with a strange expression that lets me know the laugh didn't sound normal to him, either.

"I'm not saying we need to mess with them," I say. "But maybe you could have a friend. If they think we're related, they have no reason to be jealous when we hang out."

"Probably why they told you that," Colt agrees. "To keep you from being all up on my dick again this year."

I roll my eyes, but I can't help but wonder if he's right. Is that the whole reason they said that? To keep me from fucking one of the Darlings again? After finding out what lengths the twins will go to just to mess with someone's head, I wouldn't put anything past them. They might have just told me to watch me freak out.

"Well, my mom says there's no way it's true, and I believe her. She may not win awards for mom of the year, but she has no reason to lie about it."

"Of course it's not true," Colt agrees.

"I'll work something out with the demon twins," I say. "So you'll be protected."

SELENA

Colt just gives a little snort and shakes his head, but he doesn't argue. He doesn't think I can do it, but that's okay. I'm used to being underestimated, and today I'd rather lie low and catch up on what I missed. When I'm ready to show my cards, he'll know exactly how much power I have at this school.

thirty-two

Harper Apple

Relief swells inside me when I walk out of school that afternoon and see that no one is waiting by my car. Royal stayed true to his word. I ignore the irritating flicker of disappointment that pops up. What the fuck is wrong with me? He's giving me what I wanted, what I asked for.

But the truth is, seeing him so much has made it less painful each time. At first, it was shocking and terrifying and soul shattering. Now, some dumb bitch part of me misses his big broody presence, misses him being here to show me that he's still sorry, even if he doesn't say it, and that he still owes me, even if I told him I didn't want anything from him except to be left alone.

I try not to think about what he said to me this morning, but I can't help it. Now that I'm not on high alert just trying

SELENA

to make it through the minefield of Willow Heights social scene without getting myself blown up, his dirty words come back to me. I shiver and press my knees together. He could always get me going with his filthy mouth, but I shouldn't be so basic now. I shouldn't be affected. In fact, I should punch him in the nuts for thinking he could say those things to me.

By the time I get home and see the Range Rover parked on the other side of the street, I'm pissed. Mom's car is not here, so she must be out with her friends enjoying her retirement. I park in our driveway and march over to the Rover, ready to give him a piece of my mind, but he's not in the car. Disconcerted, I check all the seats, like he might be hiding in the trunk or something. The car is empty. I shake my head, trying to clear it of the crazy-town thoughts that invade when he gets under my skin. He's not here. I have no clue why he left his car—maybe a warning that he's not done with me even if he didn't break our agreement? That's none of my concern right now, though. I have makeup assignments. That's my concern.

I grab my backpack and head inside.

BROKEN DOLL

Royal is sitting on our couch—no, not our couch. Our couch is a camouflage print of stains left from liquor and beer and piss and semen. Even I don't sit there without putting down a blanket.

"Hey, Cherry Pie," Royal says with a smug grin. "How was your first day of school?"

"Why the fuck are you in my house?" I ask. "Did Mom let you in?"

"Your locks are shockingly easy to pick," he says. "Living in this neighborhood, you really should invest in some better ones."

"Again, why are you here?"

"Just visiting," he says, lounging back and lying his arm along the back of the couch like this is his fucking house. "I said I wouldn't show up at school. You didn't say I couldn't come here."

"Get out of my house," I snap.

"And while I was dropping off more food, I realized there's no good place to sit while I wait for you," he says, looking so fucking proud of himself I want to knock his teeth out.

SELENA

"You know my mom's just going to sell it the second she runs out of drug money."

He shrugs, still looking amused.

I glare back at him. My heart is banging around my chest like a bouncy ball, because apparently sometimes I get to be totally cool when he's around, and sometimes I'm on the edge of a nervous breakdown. And the fun part is, I never know which I'll get. Just when I think I'm immune to his effect, this shit happens.

"Get the fuck out of my house, Royal," I say quietly.

"Okay," he says, lumbering up from the couch. God, his body is so fucking massive. In my tiny living room, his head nearly touches the ceiling, and between him and the big, new, fancy sectional, there's barely room to breathe.

"Wait," I say, my eyes narrowing. "What do you mean, you were dropping off *more* food?"

"Preston said he'd paid all your bills," Royal says. "I'll be damned if someone else is going to take care of you while I sit on my ass and don't lift a finger to help. So, food and furniture it is."

I just gape at him for a second, trying to comprehend what he's saying. I thought Preston sent that food. I hate knowing it was Royal, that he did something nice for us.

"Since when do you talk to Preston?" I grit out.

He shrugs. "It came up."

"When?" I demand.

"When I pulled you out of the car," he says with a shrug, like it's nothing.

We just stare at each other for a long minute.

"You pulled me out of what car?" I ask, narrowing my eyes at him.

"Preston's truck," he says. "When you left it running. I kicked in the garage door, broke the truck's window, and pulled you out. How'd you think you got out?"

I swallow hard, blood rushing in my ears. It's not true. Preston pulled me out. He told me he did.

Didn't he?

Or did he just accept my thanks?

And if Royal is lying, how would he know those details? I try to remember the days after that. Preston did go out a few times. He must have had his truck window replaced. And the

SELENA

garage door—someone would've come to fix that, probably while I was upstairs in my daze of numbness. All that time, he never told me. He let me think he'd pulled me out. He didn't tell me Royal had touched me while I was unconscious. That he'd probably been alone with me. He could have taken me—

I stumble back against the TV stand, gripping it to keep myself upright.

Royal's lying. He has to be.

He would have taken me. He hates Preston, and for whatever reason, he can't seem to leave me alone. He still thinks I belong to him. He'd never have handed me over to Preston. Not when he had me at his mercy, completely helpless.

I know what Royal does when I'm helpless.

Suddenly, I'm cold all over. Preston must have caught him. That's the only explanation. He heard him breaking into the garage and came down. They didn't fight—I would have seen marks on Preston that night. He must have stopped him, probably held a gun on him and demanded he give me back.

But Royal's not afraid to die. He would have just walked away with me, daring Preston to shoot.

"You saved my life?" I ask at last.

Royal nods. He's just standing there watching me, like he's waiting for something.

"Why?" I ask. "Why would you do that?"

"He didn't know you were there. You would have died."

I struggle to keep my breathing under control. I can't get enough oxygen, and I'm starting to hyperventilate. "I'd rather have died," I say. "I didn't want you to save me."

"Yeah," he says. "I got that."

I want to scream. I didn't want him to save my life. I don't want to owe him, to feel anything for him, not even obligation. But I do. I feel way too fucking much. Hatred is not a big enough word to describe it. I want to obliterate his soul, to rip him to shreds until there's nothing left of him but molecules too small for the human eye to see.

"Then why did you?" I demand. "You left me to die in that swamp, Royal. You told the twins to kill me."

"I went back for you," he says quietly.

SELENA

His choice of words sends ice water down my spine. He didn't come back for me that night. Only the twins came back. I listened for him, when the others came, but he wasn't there. I'd been his plaything, and when he was sure I was broken, he got bored, tossed me in the trash, and walked away.

"You said I was dead to you."

"I looked for you all summer."

"I wish I was dead to you," I choke out. "I wish we both were. I will never look at your face without picturing the moment you're dead and I can finally breathe again."

He steps toward me, but he stops, his fingers curling, as if he's holding back from reaching for me. "Then let me breathe for you until you remember how. Because I'm not going anywhere, Harper."

"Why?" I whisper. "Why did you come back? Why do you keep coming back?"

"I didn't want you to die."

I stare at him, and I know this is the closest thing to an apology I'll ever get.

This is Royal admitting remorse.

That's the best he can do. But it's not enough.

Maybe once, it would have been, but not anymore.

I deserve more.

"You looked for me," I say slowly. "And then you found me. You found me at my house, and you followed me to Preston's. You must have known then that's where I'd been hiding all that time."

He nods, letting me put it all together without interrupting with his side of the story.

"But you didn't take me when you could have. Why? What bargain did you make with him, Royal? I deserve to know."

"No bargain."

"Then what?"

"I didn't want you to die," he says again.

"Why'd you let me stay with your enemy, though?" I ask. "Preston's the one you hate worst, the one who dares to fight back, even if it's just a little. He's the only one who refuses to bow and accept defeat. And you finally found him—and me. Why didn't you just kill him and take me with you?"

"I told you why."

"Because you knew that I'd die if I woke up and saw you."

It hurts something deep in my chest to know I'm right, to see him just standing there, not denying it. He knows he's so toxic that it would kill me to be with him. He didn't just save me by pulling me out of that car. He saved me by giving me to someone who could take care of me, knowing he couldn't. He gave up control.

I know how hard that is for Royal. I know that must have been a sacrifice even bigger than bringing me revenge. That time, he set it all up before he gave over control. He didn't set things up when he followed me. He truly believes I belong to him, and it would have been his right to take me home. But he knew that I wouldn't survive it, so he ceded control—not just to anyone, but to his worst enemy.

And he didn't even take credit. He didn't do it to get a thank you. He did it to protect me, honestly and truly, without even needing me to know.

I want to cry, but I'm too furious. I'm furious that I still understand him so well, that I ache for the sacrifice he made, that I see how selfless it was and I can't go back in time five minutes and erase that knowledge from my head and make it simple to hate him again. Why couldn't it have been Preston who pulled me out, like I thought?

I want to hate Royal. I do hate him. I hate him for not letting me hate him completely. I can't bear another minute of the fucking turmoil rolling through me. Something inside my head cracks. I don't see red. I see white. All the confusion and overwhelm of the day, the guilt and fury and pain and fear, erupts.

"And you expect me to thank you?" I ask incredulously, prowling toward Royal. "You think I owe you because you saved my life once after you tried to take it? Because you saved my life when you're the reason *I* tried to take it?"

"No," he says, a frown creasing his brow. "You don't owe me anything, Harper."

"You're damn right I don't," I snap. "Because if you think for one minute that buying groceries is going to make this okay, you're even more psychotic than I thought. You have no right to pretend you care, Royal. No right to say that shit about taking care of me now or tell me you pulled me out of that car. You didn't take care of me, Royal. You didn't protect me. You ordered my execution, and you have no right to even speak to me again, let alone say the things you said to me this morning. You have no right to make me feel anything for you ever again."

I stop, my breathing ragged, and gulp in air. My eyes are burning, my hands shaking, and my chest aches with a clenching tension. My temple throbs, like my anger is driving a bolt slowly through my skull.

Royal glares back at me, his eyes an icy, inky black. "That implies you ever felt something to begin with."

I just stare at him, trying to get my breath, but he's taking all the air in the room for his huge, oversized body and huge, oversized presence. "I did," I say. "I fucking loved you, Royal. Is that what you want to hear? You want me to lay my heart out for you to decimate that, too? I told you, I won't fight. I already laid it out, and you smashed every bit of it under your bootheel until there's nothing left to feel anymore. You may not believe me, because you don't think anyone could love you, but you're wrong. Someone could have. Someone did."

"Bullshit." His word is quiet, his eyes intense and so fucking full I want to drown in them, just give myself to that darkness inside him and let it devour me until I disappear forever and I don't have to hurt anymore.

"You have no right," I grit out again. "You don't get to tell me what I felt wasn't real. You've taken every single part of me and destroyed it. I can't feel anything anymore. You don't get to erase what I felt before you, too."

"You were faking it the whole time," Royal says, his voice hollow, hopeless.

"You don't fucking know how I felt," I snap. "You may not think you're worthy of love, and maybe you're not, but that doesn't mean someone can't love you anyway. That doesn't mean I couldn't choose to love you despite it, whether you deserved it or not. That was my choice, and I paid for it. But I don't love you anymore, Royal. You're not worthy of even my shitty trailer park love anymore. That was your choice. You have no right to keep coming around here, stalking me like it's some cute game between us. It's not a game, Royal. I fucking hate you. I hate your face, I hate your stupid couch, I hate that I can't go to Preston's without putting him in danger. I hate that you're in my house, so I can't even maintain the illusion of safety in the shithole I call home."

I'm crying now, and Royal steps forward like he might hold me again, like he still has that right. I dead-arm him with my brass knuckles when he tries to touch me, though. I'm so fucking beyond done with this shit. I don't want to have to feel something new every time he comes around, to be reminded of what he did and how thoroughly it annihilated my soul.

"I'm trying," he says quietly. "I'm trying to make it right."

"You can't fucking make it right," I explode. I don't care if I'm an ugly mess. I want him to see all the ugly inside me, all the ugly he created. I want him to quake before the power of my hatred, but he never will, and it infuriates me beyond all rational thought. "You have no right to even try. You have no idea what you're asking. You think I can fucking forgive you? You have no idea what I've been through. You have no idea what it's like to be tied up, completely helpless, while someone takes every part of you until there's nothing left, not even your soul."

"You're wrong."

I'm crying so hard I don't know how I'm still speaking, but I can't stop. "You have no idea what it's like to have no choice in how your body responds, and to have it mocked and used against you. You don't know the shame of hearing them fucking reveling in it. You have no idea what it's like to be completely vulnerable and have someone command your deepest fears be realized while they turn the other cheek when you beg for mercy."

"You're wrong," he says again, his voice quiet and emotionless.

"You have no idea what it's like to be left in the dark, never knowing when they'll come back. You don't know what it's like to have people touch you without your permission, to not even know who's been inside you and done the most intimate act possible to you, how many of them, who they are, who has violated you in a way that you will never come back from, even if you find out it was just three of them instead of ten. It doesn't fucking matter, Royal. Don't you get that? It's too late. Knowing the truth doesn't change what I experienced that night."

SELENA

"I know."

"You do?" I demand. And then I see the look in his eyes, and all the fight drains from me. They're so dark and full of a hurt so deep it aches in my bones, my core, my soul. And I know we're not just talking about him knowing that the trauma doesn't change because I found out it was just the twins and Dawson.

"You do," I whisper, swallowing down the rawness of tears in my throat.

He doesn't say anything. I take a step forward and wrap my arms around him, squeezing him hard. He should be the one falling apart after a confession like that, but I'm the one who does. The anger that kept me going has deserted me, and I just hold onto him and sob because everything else is gone. After a minute, his arms slowly rise and wrap around me. He scoops me up, cradling my body as he sinks onto the couch. Then he just holds me while I soak his shirt, unable to stop the shuddering sobs that wrack my body. I don't think about how right it feels to be engulfed in his arms, to have his body wrapped around mine, cradling me to his chest like a baby. I just cry like one, until there's nothing left inside me.

When the last tears are spent, I pull back and wipe my face, letting myself slide off his lap even though the false sense of protection he provides feels so real when I'm in it. At last, I look up at Royal. His face is stony and expressionless, but his eyes are not empty.

I take his face between my hands.

"I'm so sorry that happened to you," I say. I lean forward and brush my lips against his, and my heart tears in two with longing for him, for more than I'm willing to give it.

"But that doesn't justify doing it to someone else," I say, pulling away even though it hurts so much I can barely breathe.

Royal nods, his jaw still set, his face hard. "I know."

"Then how can you ask me to forgive you?"

He searches my eyes. "What?"

I don't answer. I don't have to. I watch the realization grind slowly into place. What they did to him, he did to me. When they hurt him, he destroyed their family, killed and mutilated people, burned them, destroyed their lives one by one. He knows he would never forgive them. So how can he expect me to forgive him when he did the same to me?

His face may have been set in stone while I cried, but for a moment, his eyes were more vulnerable than I've ever seen them. Now, though, the depth and pain in them fades, hardening like lava after the volcano erupts. I want to tell him to stop closing himself to me again, that he has to stay open to me. It's what I wanted so much for so long, I can't turn off that longing. But that's not fair. So I swallow the knot of spiked iron in my throat and let him wall himself up in the hell inside his head, where no one can reach him.

I have a chance, and I know I might never get it again. But I can't go there again. Last time I climbed over his walls, it nearly killed me.

When his eyes are as flat and solid as a prison wall, he nods. "You're right," he says, standing. "I won't bother you again."

Our eyes meet for one moment, and then he turns and walks away. My body feels as if it's floating, out of touch with reality.

This is it. The end.

I feel it in a way I haven't before, not when he dumped me or even when he said I was dead to him. When I was at Preston's and I hadn't seen him in months, I still felt him somewhere, as if I knew we weren't finished. He wasn't finished with me.

Now, he is.

I should be relieved. It's what I wanted. He's letting me go at last. He finally understands the severity of what he did, what it did to me. I finally found the way out of the maze, found the weapon that could cut me free of the net he snared me in. But there's no relief, no feeling of freedom or lightness. I bite down on my fist as the tears start again, my chest folding in on itself as I watch him go. Some stupid, infuriating part of me waits for him to come and comfort me, to hold me like he has when I cried before—in his bathroom after our first time, in the truck after he said he'd never leave me alone.

But this time was the last time.

He doesn't come and wrap me in his arms again. He steps out of my house, and he closes the door behind him. Maybe

SELENA

he thinks it's a test. He's proving himself. Giving me what I said I wanted. Leaving me alone.

Or maybe it means he's really done, that he knows he has no right to comfort me when he's the one who always makes me cry. This time, he's not here to hold me. I listen to his engine start. I hear his car drive away. When it's quiet outside, I wrap my arms around myself, and I cry alone because it's finally over. He's really gone.

thirty-three

Harper Apple

I hate myself for watching my mirrors for Royal the next morning. I hate that some sick part of me hurts that he's not behind me, that he's not in the spot next to mine at school when I arrive. Everything I felt for him was real, and it didn't just disappear when he hurt me. It's still there, all twisted around the pain like a malformed tree and even more fucked up than ever.

It's hatred, but it's still love, too, some perverted form of it. It's sympathy for what he went through, something that breaks my fucking heart, but it's also a bone deep inner resistance to forgiveness. Even if I wanted to forgive, I can't. When I think about it, something rebels inside me, like a steel trap snapping shut, keeping even me at bay. If I had control of my heart, I'd never have fallen for him to begin with.

Before I know it, I'm back at Willow Heights, where I have to pretend. I wonder if this is how Gloria feels, faking every second of her life. Here, I have to be on alert, to watch for snakes in the grass and hawks circling in the sky. Everyone has the potential to be an enemy, to swoop in or strike and snatch away the treasure I'm guarding so closely. No one knows I have it yet, but if I wait too long, it will lose its power.

Royal's word is still golden, but his influence will ebb as the new order is set in stone. I'm not too late, though. The balance has been upset, and everyone hasn't quite found their places in the new regime. I have to strike fast, but I can't be reckless. If I time my reveal just right, leverage Royal's status and whatever sway conveys to the holder of the key, I can make an impact. I have to do it before the twins find a way to undermine me, and Royal's social currency loses its value or his brothers tell everyone he's no longer involved with me.

I head inside and track down the girl with her finger on the pulse of the school—Dixie. I need to know what cards the twins are holding that I haven't seen, which means I need to know everything I missed so far this year, when the twins have been ruling the halls of Willow Heights.

After striking out in the halls, I open *OnlyWords* and shoot her a message, wondering if she's under the bleachers with Colt. But a second later, I get a text that she's in the café, so I join her for breakfast. Only about half the lunch crowd eats breakfast, and half of those people are groggy and barely awake, so the café is sparsely populated and pretty quiet at eight in the morning. I grab a bagel and slide in next to Dixie and Josie.

"Tea, please?" I ask without bothering to do the whole small talk thing.

"Okay," Dixie says. "Though usually I'm the one asking for tea."

"Gloria caught me up on last year," I say. "What'd I miss so far this year?"

"Colt's back," Dixie says.

SELENA

"I know," I say. "Are you two back together officially? Like, openly? Is he allowed to have a girlfriend? Or are they still ostracizing him?"

She shrugs. "I really don't know, Harper. You were the one in with the Dolces. Maybe you should ask them."

"I will," I say, wondering if I'm about to get raked over the coals by yet another person who's pissed at me. "And I'm happy for you."

"Thanks," Dixie says, seeming to soften. "It wasn't the first time he dumped me, or the first time they fucked him up, but it was the worst time for both. I mean, when he broke up with me on Bye Week last year, he sounded like he was done for good. But I knew we'd get back together. It's fate. We're meant to be together. It was only a matter of time."

"Pretty shitty way to get back together, though," I say, spreading cream cheese on my bagel. I try not to feel weird about her words. When it comes to happiness, we all take what we can get and make the most of it. If Colt doesn't mind that she used his attack to her advantage, it's not my business. They have years of history I know nothing about, but I already know he hasn't always been good to her. If she can forgive him, good for her for going after what she wants.

"Well, I was there for him, like I always am," she says. "Through all of it, even when he first woke up and hardly remembered anything. He still doesn't remember breaking up with me, but of course I told him. I'm not going to lie to him. He had to go through months of texts to try to remember what happened. Thank goodness for my blog, so he could get caught up on the social scene after missing last year."

"Right," I say, shaking my head and trying to focus on my own problem instead of sticking my nose in hers. "So, he came back at the start of this year, right?"

"Yeah," she says. "With Royal gone, things are definitely more relaxed, but also kind of uneasy. It's like when a dictator falls, and there's this power vacuum, right? The government is still unstable."

"Thank fuck," I say, sitting back in my chair.

Dixie raises a brow. "Something I should know?"

"Nothing on the record," I say. "But let's just say I have some moves up my sleeve."

SELENA

"Are you planning revenge on the Dolces?" she asks with an eager smile, leaning in and lowering her voice. "Because I know people."

Josies shakes her head. "Are you going to smash the patriarchy and reinstate democracy, too, or are you more of one-issue voter?"

"I like to focus on one cause, yes," I say before turning to Dixie. "Hit me up in a few days?"

"Just remember where it got you last year," Dixie says. "And Colt."

"Noted," I say. "I'm not bringing anyone into this who doesn't want to be. I'm not risking anyone but myself. But be ready."

Josie gives me a curious look. "Aren't you Royal's girlfriend?" she asks. "Y'all made that big scene yesterday morning."

"Oh my god, I didn't even properly introduce y'all," Dixie says, straightening in her seat. "Josie, Harper, meet. Harper went here most of last year. She started out here at our table before becoming a Dolce girl, and yes, she dated Royal Dolce before she went missing over spring break."

"Rumors of my death have been greatly exaggerated," I say, rolling my eyes.

"I always suspected Royal," Dixie says, leaning in and lowering her voice. "But then, I wasn't his biggest fan, and you weren't the first girl close to him to disappear. What ever happened between you, anyway? You hated him, and then you loved him, and then you disappeared. I figured you were locked in his basement or something. Want to tell me what happened?"

"For the blog? Nah, I'll pass," I say. "And you can't seriously blame Royal for his sister's death."

"I blame their whole family," she says. "Not just Royal."

"Fair enough," I say. There's no use arguing. She and Royal took opposite sides in the Darling-Dolce feud, and there's no crossing that line. She doesn't want to hear how much Royal loved his sister and worships her memory even now. She wants someone to blame for the loss of her best friend.

"Josie's a transfer from Hellstern," she goes on, gesturing at her friend.

SELENA

"Recent refugee from Hell High," Josie agrees, tossing a piece of bagel in the air and catching it in her mouth. Gloria's wrong. She may be lacking curves and a flatiron, but she's pretty even without fixing herself up. Her thick, dark hair hangs to her elbows, and her striking, pale jade green eyes are framed by long, full lashes and heavy brows.

Dixie gestures to her. "Josie's a senior like us. I'm trying to convince her to join the dance team, but so far, no luck."

Josie shrugs. "Shaking your ass for a bunch of dudes who run around bashing each other for the town's entertainment… I don't know, it's kinda gross, right?"

"But it's an extracurricular," Dixie says. "It'll look good on college applications. That's the only reason to move here for senior year. So your diploma shows you graduated from Willow Heights."

"I'm on debate and student council and the tutoring team," Josie says. "Besides, the whole football scene just perpetuates and reinforces the culture of toxic masculinity."

"Oh boy," Dixie says. "Don't let anyone at this school here you say that."

"I think we're going to get along just fine," I say, grinning at Josie.

"I seriously doubt that," she says, popping a piece of bagel into her mouth and giving my outfit a meaningful glance. I remember her dismissive once-over yesterday, and I'm not sure how to respond. I'm used to being the chick who doesn't give a fuck what people think. I'm used to people judging me for being poor white trash. Now, I'm someone whose survival depends on having allies and friends, and that necessitates caring what people think. Now, I'm being judged for looking rich, even though I'm not.

"Don't take everything at face value," I say, a little less enthusiastic about finding a boss bitch to hang out with. "You don't know my life."

"And you don't know mine," she says blandly, stuffing the last of her bagel into her cheek.

I shrug. "You're right. I'm just here for information, not to make enemies."

"And yet, you're friends with Gloria Walton," she says, pushing back from the table. "See you in class, Dixie." With that, she turns and walks off.

SELENA

"Wow," I say. "Guess I misjudged that one."

"You know I like everyone," Dixie says. "But Lo's been on X-Games mode this year."

"Her brother just died," I point out.

"Yeah," Dixie says. "He *just* died. We're a month into school."

"Maybe something's been going on with him before that," I say.

I don't like being forced to choose sides. I like both these girls. I don't know Josie from the next bitch, though. Obviously I need to take my own advice and not judge a book by it's cover. She may look cool, but that doesn't mean shit. But I know Gloria, and she's good people.

"Well, Royal ditched her before school started," Dixie says. "It must have been just between them, though, because the twins are letting her keep her spot for now. But she's got this new boyfriend she dragged into their crowd, and I'm not sure they're all happy about it."

"Ah, right," I say. "Rylan?"

Dixie nods. "Have you met him?"

"No," I say with a shrug. "But I'm sure I will. Anything else I should know?"

"Okay, new kids," she says, glancing around before counting off on her fingers. "There's Josie, Rylan and his sister Amber, and of course Colt. And the freshmen. I can tell you about them, but I'm probably the only senior who cares about their gossip, since it goes in the blog."

"Magnolia Darling," I say. "Anything going on there?"

"She's one of the populars in their grade," Dixie says. "I've known her for a few years. She's a sweet girl, but she's been sheltered, and she's a little immature. I mean, she's fourteen, so..."

The warning bell chimes for our day to start, and we both stand. "Thanks," I say. "Anything else I should know real quick? Ones to watch?"

"Definitely Rylan," she says, then fills me in on the populars as we walk out. "Cotton's back and creepy as ever. His dad married Rylan's mom, so that's why they're at this school, and according to my parents, that's the big gossip with the ladies who lunch. They're from... Georgia, I think. DeShaun's dating Eleanor Walton. Everleigh's been talking to Gideon Delacroix, who's a sophomore and the only new guy in the Dolces' inner circle this year. The twins are still manwhores, of course… And I think that's it."

"You're a lifesaver," I say. "Thank you so much."

"Any time," she says. "You made last year's blog a big hit, so I can't exactly hold your Dolce dissention against you."

"I didn't dissent," I say, waving as we split off to our different classes, hurrying past Duke and the blonde freshman girl I keep seeing him with.

I can't help but feel like a bit of a traitor when I talk to Dixie. I should want to destroy the Dolces for what they did, but I can't quite find it in me to despise them. I know them, and it's hard to hate someone you know. In truth, I don't want to put myself in their path again, but I don't want them to get away with doing that shit to anyone else, either.

I'm not a Darling, though. I'm not on their side any more than I was ever on the Dolces'.

I don't want to choose a side.

Yes, the Dolces did terrible things to me. But they never pretended to be nice guys, and I can't pretend I ever thought they were. I knew there would be consequences to getting in with them, and I didn't just gain their secrets. I betrayed Royal.

I willingly revealed his deepest shame to his enemy. I knew what I was doing. I can't pretend now that I was innocent just because the consequences were worse than I anticipated.

And the Darlings… Well, it would be easy to say they're the innocent victims in all this, but I know it's not so simple. They're trickier, sneakier, and they play dirtier. Preston saved me, but he didn't do it out of the kindness of his heart. He saved me to use me against Royal. He sold my shame on the internet to hurt Royal. He dressed me up as their sister, unbeknownst to me, and rubbed it in their faces, trying to use me as a weapon. He let me believe he saved my life that day in the garage. When I thanked him, he didn't say a word to stop me.

Colt's done something similar, if far less sinister. He told me his side of the story, the one that makes his family look good. Then he used me to hurt the twins, giving me Mabel's clothes and letting me parade around in front of them.

SELENA

They're all obsessed with destroying each other, and it's destroying all of them. I've already been destroyed. I'm not looking for more.

At lunch, I contemplate my next move as I walk in alone. I hear a few murmurs as I make my way through the café, but not like when I walk in the halls with Gloria. Apparently the fuss is about Dawson, which makes sense. Even though he graduated last spring, a suicide is way more dramatic than a girl who *isn't* dead. The flowers around the locker he used last year are proof enough, as are the only three girls still in the food line, who are sighing about how sad it is.

"It's just such a tragedy when someone loses a life," says the hot blonde freshman. "Especially when it could have been prevented."

"You read that on a poster outside the counselor's office?" I mutter, rolling my eyes.

She looks over her shoulder at me and scoffs. She's wearing some kind of pink tulle skirt that reaches midcalf, like an overly long tutu, and a pair of baby pink Doc Martens with daisies on them. The infantilized style is a far cry from

Gloria's *Mean Girls* squad, and I'm reminded again how very young the freshman class is.

She lowers her voice to her friend. "I never met him, but I saw him play every Friday, and I feel like I knew him."

"I know," gushes her pimply friend, casting a nervous glance at me and moving forward along the line to put distance between us. "He was a hero. I hope they put up a statue of him outside the school."

"It's too soon," says the blonde with a little sniffle. "It would be too painful to see him every day and know he's never coming back."

I stifle a snort. Nothing like a rich kid dying to have everyone else acting like their world is fucking ending, even if they'd never met the guy. I was in sixth grade when the first kid in one of my classes died by suicide, and it's hardly rare at FHS. I know the histrionics it brings out in the drama queens, who want to act like they knew the person even if they were total assholes to the victim while they were alive. I wonder if some fake-ass bitches did that shit when I disappeared last year, and it makes my skin crawl.

SELENA

"I just feel so bad for his sisters," the bigger friend whispers as they exit the line. "Do you think they found him?"

"Can you imagine finding him there, just... *Hanging*?" the blonde asks, her eyes round.

Suddenly, I don't feel like eating.

"I can't believe Gloria's back at school," says the acne prone one.

"Yeah," says the blonde. "When Sully was in trouble, I stayed home with him for, like, two weeks to make sure he was okay. And he wasn't...*unalive*."

They walk away talking, and it takes me a minute to remember where I've heard that name. Then my stomach sinks. Fuck. The too-pretty-for-her-own-good blonde freshman is little Magnolia Darling.

I shouldn't care. It has nothing to do with me. And yet, I feel some weird connection with the Darlings now, even if I don't want to be part of their drama. I keep telling myself I'm not related, but I feel a kinship, anyway.

Even before Preston, I was tied to them. From the moment I engaged with the Dolces, I was pulled into their family. Hell, even before that, when Mr. D contacted me. Despite their families being enemies, they're two opposing threads, inextricably twisted around each other, passing through the eye of one needle. The deeper I got with the Dolces, the deeper I was woven into the Darling story, too, whether or not I knew it.

I took the scholarship from Mr. D. I already knew Colt as Dynamo from the fight scene, so I became friends with him. I pulled Lindsey out of her house and got her to safety. I fucked Royal on Preston's bed and helped destroy his house, never knowing he was my benefactor. I got my ass dumped by the mighty Royal Dolce for putting my foot down when they threatened to go after Magnolia.

And it's a good fucking thing I did, or the Dolces would have succeeded in killing me that night in the swamp. If Preston hadn't been tracking their cars and come out there and found me…

I shake the thought away, trying to clear my head to get through this lunch without spiraling back into my nightmare. Coming here is the best thing I could have done. I can already tell. I was aimless, lost in some dark swamp of nightmares for the past six months, unable to leave even when my body was pulled free and carried out. My soul never really left that night, though.

I'm not sure it ever will. But being back in this world sets everything in front of me in an immediate way. Physically, I'm here instead of home, where I can too easily sink into bed and wallow in despair. Everything is crucial, keeping me from going back into my shell, locking myself in my head. There are other people with their own traumas and dramas, people I have to interact with. Every moment I have to be sharp, to make decisions based on new information I only gained the second before.

As I step off the line and turn to face the café full of the new and the familiar, I have another decision to make. There's Dixie's table of gossip girls, where I see her, Quinn, Susanna, and Josie. Those are the student council girls, the career path girls. I should sit there. That's what I want—to get out of this town, to go to college. Maybe I wasn't the 'stay home and bake on a Friday night' kind of girl last year, but maybe now I am. Maybe I'm done with all drama, Dolce and Darling both.

But then a whistle cuts through the noise in the café, and I look up and see DeShaun Rose mid-wave. Before he can summon me, though, Duke elbows him in the arm and shakes his head. Duke Dolce, who sang "Folsom Prison" while he waded through the swamp toward me after telling me he was coming back with friends. Duke Dolce, who told me the other night that we could still be friends. Duke Dolce, who I saw talking to Magnolia Darling just this morning.

My blood runs cold, and I grip my plate. I may not be gathering information for Mr. D anymore, but my work here is not done.

SELENA

thirty-four

Harper Apple

Each table in the café fits eight chairs. Last year, the Dolce boys sat at one table with their closest friends and Lo. Another table was pushed over against it for the overflow of "lesser" friends and Dolce girls. Royal had the middle seat, with his back to the wall near the door, so he could look out over the café like it was his kingdom. The spot across from him was always empty, so no one would block his view.

This year, Duke and Baron sit at the center. DeShaun and Cotton sit to their left. To their right, I spot a vaguely familiar boy from last year's "lesser" table who must be Gideon, because Everleigh is busy swooning over him. Gloria and Eleanor round out the table. There's no empty seat. At the one pushed up to theirs, where the tables meet, a sullen, dark-haired boy sits next to Gloria. I peg him as

Rylan, her boyfriend. The rest of the table is filled with pretty girls I assume are this year's Dolce girls.

There are no empty seats, but I'm not going to let that stop me. They can squeeze in one more. They never pack the tables with extra chairs like the rest of the students. Keeping the tables to eight makes their company all the more coveted and elite.

As I approach, I take in the group, but my gaze lasers in on the Dolce boys. Duke watches me with a wary expression while Baron just stares in his intense, unnerving way. I circle the table so I'm standing behind the reigning kings.

"Get me a chair," I say.

Duke glances at Baron. Baron doesn't move.

I tap my toe and wait.

"You're going to sit with us this year?" Duke asks at last. "Because I thought since Royal wasn't here…"

"That I'd disappear?" I ask. "Wouldn't that be convenient?"

"Kinda," he mutters.

"I'm sure sorry I can't make things easier for you," I say. "But I'll be sitting at the head of the table this year, so be a doll and pull up a chair for me, would you? Right between you two."

"But… That's where Royal sat."

"And Royal was the king," I say. "Since he's gone, that leaves me on the throne all by myself, doesn't it?"

"We're the kings," Baron says quietly. Everyone is watching. The café is silent as a cemetery, even though probably only the adjoining table can hear us.

"Are you, though?" I ask.

I hear an audible intake of breath from around the table. No one has challenged their kings for years. And here I am, a girl who started out getting thrown in dumpsters, demanding the best seat in the room. I stand straight, my chin up, but inside, my stomach is in knots and my pulse is trembling. This is all a gamble that depends on too many variables I don't know, things that happened between Royal and the twins before and after he brought me to the Slaughterpen. That may have been the main event, but there were days of planning that went into that, fights that happened off stage between the Dolce brothers to get them into those chairs.

Duke shares a look with his brother, and some unspoken knowledge passes between them. And then Duke pushes out his seat. I fight to keep from closing my eyes and sighing in relief or whooping with joy. Instead, I consciously focus on keeping my face unchanged, like there was never any doubt in my mind that the twins would obey my command. But inside, I'm silently thanking Royal like he's a fucking god.

I want to throw my arms around him and kiss him for this, because Duke has sauntered over to a nearby table and snagged an empty chair. I remind myself this is only the barest edge of the beginning. But it could have all come to a screeching halt or blown up in my face. They could have laughed at me or worse. Instead, I gambled on Royal Dolce. And just like he always wins, I win when I bet on him.

"Your majesty," Duke says, spinning the chair around with a flourish and a mock bow. "Your throne."

I set my plate down, and Baron scoots over a few inches. It's not much, but it feels like the sweetest triumph. Duke pulls his chair over and drops into it, but I'm not done.

"Thank you," I say. "Now, do you remember what you had me do the first time I came to your table?"

SELENA

"What?" Duke asks, glancing at Baron, his eyes widening in alarm.

"Don't look at him," I say, taking his chin in my hand and tugging it toward me. "I'm talking to you."

Duke swallows and raises his gaze to mine. I see him, the real boy behind all the jokes and laughter, the easygoing, dirty-mouthed asshole. He's scared. He loves his position of power, but he knows it isn't guaranteed. He knows his time is limited, and he's just met his match.

"No," he says quietly. "I don't remember."

"Oh, come on, Duke," I say with a smile. "You don't get wasted and forget your evil deeds until after school. What did you make me do when you called me to your table?"

He darts a glance at Baron again, but I nudge his chin back to me, forcing his gaze to mine.

"Bow," he grits out.

"That's right," I say as if I've just remembered. "You made me bow and kiss your feet like your loyal subjects. I think it's time for you to return the favor."

"Are you fucking kidding?" Baron asks from behind me.

"Not even a little."

"No way," he snaps.

I quirk a brow at his words, but I'm still facing Duke. "Are you saying you don't owe me this much?"

"Okay," Duke says, a grin spreading across his face. "But if you're into some dominatrix shit like making me bow down, surely I should kiss something a lot more exciting than your feet."

He reaches out and slides his hands around the back of my thighs under my skirt, pulling me closer. I tense, my body rebelling at the sensation of his hot hands on my bare skin. I clench my teeth and swallow, fighting the urge to knock him the fuck out for his presumptuousness.

"Did I ask you to touch me?" I grit out.

His smile falters, and he loosens his grip. I give him a meaningful look. Maybe he's remembering the reason for all this, too, because he drops his hands from my legs.

"Sorry," he mutters, sliding out of his chair and onto his knees in front of me.

I could sit and lift my foot for him, at least my toes, but I don't. I want him to bow all the way to the floor, to make it count. I don't owe him anything, not even making this easy.

SELENA

Duke's grin returns, and he hops into a pushup position. "Want me to drop and give you twenty?" he asks, lowering himself to quickly kiss my toe. He pops back up and claps his hands, showing his physical prowess. And damn, he does look good, his body all planes of muscle, his back defined through his dress shirt. But when his hands hit the floor and he starts to lower himself for another pushup, I move my foot, setting the pointed toe of my Louboutin on top of his fingers.

He's not taking this over, making it the Duke Dolce show. This isn't about him.

"One is enough," I say. "Now get up."

"Aw, you're no fun," he says, but he pushes up onto his knees again. There's a beat of silence, and then about half the café starts applauding. My gaze darts around as I try to figure out if they're clapping for me or Duke. That's when I see almost everyone clapping is female. I'm thrown off my concentration for a second, but Duke is used to applause, and he gives a big, sloppy grin and throws kisses to the audience. Then he turns to me and wiggles his brows. "Are you going to slap me in the face with your pussy? I mean, if we're reversing roles here. That's what I did to you."

"And I slapped you back."

He grins. "I'll slap your pussy any day, Cherry Pie."

The other guys snicker, but I silence them with a glare.

"Thank you for your service," I say, pointing to his chair.

"You sure you don't want me to lay you back on the table and show you how I really worship a queen?" he asks, giving me his wickedest grin. "I have a sweet tooth, and I haven't had dessert yet."

But under the showmanship, I know there's something real. He may clown around to hide it, but this boy is afraid of the power I wield. He knows as well as I do that the applause wasn't for him—it was for the girl who finally made him bend a knee for her.

I turn to Baron and cock a brow. "Your turn, psycho boy."

Baron stands, and even though he's not as big as Royal, his impressive build is still like a wall in front of me. The whispers in the room die as everyone holds their breath, waiting for the other Dolce boy to bow.

SELENA

He works his jaw back and forth, then gives his head a single shake. "No."

Our eyes meet, and he holds my gaze. For a long, breathless moment, no one speaks.

"I'm not sure you know the meaning of that word," I tell him, my heart pounding. If I play my cards wrong, this can still come crashing down around me. I thought I had this power, that I hadn't run out of what Royal gave me already. But maybe I don't have quite as much as I thought.

Baron lifts his chin, his eyes cool. "Dolces don't bow."

My mind races through the possibilities. I see it playing out how he thinks it will. Neither of us will give in, and we'll fight it out. If I knock him out, like I did in the pit, he won't let it slide. Not when it's in front of the school, when I'll make him lose face. He'll be out for revenge, and he'll come back even harder. I could rat him out about making drugs, but I have no proof beyond his word. And everyone knows who gets believed in that scenario. He'll win, and he'll come back to school and tell everyone I'm a rat who tried to take him down.

BROKEN DOLL

Then, they'll all hate me. It'll never end, just like their fight with the Darlings. Like Colt said, they're always just a little more crazy, a little more reckless, with a little less to lose. We all know who loses when it's comes down to the Dolces, no matter who the opposition is.

So, I do what I did in the pit—I pull back, conserving whatever power I have left. Royal didn't give me everything. He gave me a launch pad, a starting point. I have to take those lottery winnings and stretch them a little further, not retire and party them all away.

I nod to Baron and hold out a hand. "I can respect that," I say. "Truce?"

He takes my hand in a firm grip, his dark eyes intense behind his glasses. "What are your terms?" he asks quietly. "You want to be our number one girl?"

I can't help but laugh.

"No," I say flatly. "I don't want to be a Dolce girl. I know you boys are used to sitting on the throne by yourselves, but this year, I'll be up there with you. You can still be the kings. But make way for the fucking queen."

SELENA

thirty-five

Harper Apple

"Oh my god, what was that?" Dixie asks, catching up to me as I leave the café. "That was by far the coolest thing I've ever seen in my life! Duke Dolce just kissed your feet! When you said you had some tricks up your sleeve, I didn't expect *that*. How the hell did you get him to bow to you?"

I smile and shrug. "They're no better than me or anyone else."

"Can I quote that on the blog?"

"What? No," I say, drawing away. "Why would you even put that on the blog? Everyone saw it firsthand."

"People love to relive the excitement," she says. "The lunch drama blogs are my most popular."

"Fine," I say. "Here's a quote. If you can't beat 'em, join 'em."

"Okay, well, that was like the first time in the history of this school that the kings have done something like that," she said. "The Dolces rule with an iron fist and fear and intimidation. They've never even, like, nodded in deference to someone, let alone got on their knees. I can't believe that just happened. That was so badass."

"Maybe it's time they didn't have absolute power here."

"Yeah, but this school has been run by the elite since it was founded—or at least since the next generation, when the Midnight Swans were founded. The Darlings weren't nearly as crazy and scary as the Dolces, and even they would never have done something like that. Not even Devlin when he was in love with Crystal. Does Duke… *Like* you?"

"What?" I ask, then shake my head. "Of course not. It had nothing to do with feelings."

"Then what do you have on him?"

I just smile. "Enough."

Dixie heaves a worshipful sigh, like I'm suddenly her hero. "Wow."

We reach my locker, and I expect her to walk away, but she lingers. The hallways is crowded and ten times louder than usual, everyone buzzing with the charge of excitement from the lunchtime show. Dixie's right. They're already reliving every moment, talking over each other, as pumped as if they just left a football game.

When I close my locker, Dixie is still there.

"What's up?" I ask. "Need more for the blog?"

"No," she says. "It's just… Don't get me wrong, that was the best thing I've ever seen at this school, even before the blog. But I thought you weren't with them anymore. Last year, you would have walked away after making him kiss your feet, shown them you don't buy into their hierarchy."

"I'm not the same girl I was last year."

I can't explain it to her, but it's not that I choked, that I was afraid and backed down from Baron. It's just that I understand how the school works now. I don't need to be some solo badass who razes the Dolces and strolls off into the sunset. I can get more done from inside than I ever could from being their enemy. And I need other people to help. I'm not an island. I'm a survivor.

"I guess not," Dixie says, and I know she's disappointed, but this isn't her battle. "I guess I was hoping you'd rally the

Darlings after you asked about Magnolia, or at least help Colt. You told me to be ready."

"Oh, don't worry," I say. "I'm just getting started."

*

Royal is not waiting by my car when I leave school. When I pull up and park outside my house, his Range Rover is nowhere in sight. I close my eyes and tell myself to stop. I should be happy. He's gone, just like I wanted. He finally respected my wishes and left me alone, and I've established myself as someone not to be fucked with at school. I am a queen, worthy of their respect.

But all I feel like is the Queen of All Dumb Bitches, because some stupid, stupid part of my heart falls when he's not waiting, trying just one more time. I want to tell him what he did for me, and what I did today. I want to celebrate this win with him, this win that he should be taking credit for. I want his car to be outside, want him to tell me I'm worth trying just a little bit harder for.

I fucking hate myself for it, too.

SELENA

I know I'm worth it.

I shouldn't need him to say so. I shouldn't want him to beg and grovel for my love.

I know it's worth more than he can ever give.

I get out of the car, too disgusted with myself to bear my own company. God, I'm such a petty, pathetic little bitch.

Blue is sitting on her steps, staring off, her hair halfway covering her face. She doesn't even look at me, but I walk over anyway.

"Oh, hey," she says, sounding exhausted. She tips her head forward, and her hair swings over her cheek. "Want a cigarette?"

"Sure."

I take a seat beside her, watching her from the corner of my eye. I know that look, that stiff posture. The way she doesn't turn toward me when she carefully hands over my cigarette, keeping her face straight forward, is beyond familiar. I've been in her place enough times—first at my mother's hands, and then at the hands of better fighters at the Slaughterpen—to know what she's hiding.

BROKEN DOLL

We sit in the late September sun, the afternoon heat so thick and still that the smoke clogs the air around us. The silence between us hangs just as heavy, more awkward and dark than usual. I debate asking what happened to her face, but we don't have that kind of friendship. We allow for whatever comfort level the other wants, for the preservation of dignity. I might have told her what happened to me, but that doesn't mean she owes me the same.

Finally, I settle on the one thing that matters. "You okay?"

"That obvious, huh?" she asks, tapping her cigarette on the edge of the coffee can beside her foot.

"A little," I admit, taking a drag.

"I just…" She makes a force little laugh sound. "I tripped, y'know? I'm so clumsy."

"It happens."

She tripped and fell down the stairs at Faulkner a few years ago. Maybe she is clumsy. If that's what she wants me to believe, I won't question it.

"How's school?" she asks. "You went back, right?"

"Good," I say. "How's Olive?"

SELENA

"Fine. Did you see the football players?"

"Yeah," I say. "Turns out it was only three of them rotating the whole night. Not as bad as I thought."

She nods and drops her cigarette butt into the reeking can, then pulls the sleeves of her jean jacket down over her hands. It's way too fucking hot to be wearing a jacket, and I wonder not for the first time where she gets her bruises. I've never seen her at the Slaughterpen, but I'm not naïve enough to think that's where most girls get hit.

"These people are bad news, Blue," I say. "I know you asked if Preston has friends, but trust me, you don't want to get mixed up with them. They're a lot worse than the Crosses."

She nods. "Yeah, you're probably right. I'm not tough enough for that."

"It's not that," I say. "You're tough. Trust me. But hey, I have a car now. If you ever need me to take you somewhere, just come knock and we'll go. No questions asked."

"Thanks," she says, nodding and dropping her head forward to stare at her knees.

I finish my cigarette, thank her, and go back to my house. I feel guilty as I pull out my fancy school laptop. While I wait for it to connect to our slow-ass internet, I go to the fridge, now fully stocked with food Royal bought for us. For me.

I make a sandwich and sit down to work, but the food tastes like guilt and weights me down like a brick. After an hour, I open *OnlyWords* and type in the little black chat box.

BadApple: what r u doing Thurs
ThatsLo: nothing but nxt week I'll b getting ready 4 bye week, baby!
BadApple: that's next weekend?
ThatsLo: yeah girl where u been
BadApple: so u can do something this wk?
ThatsLo: it's a school nite
ThatsLo: but yeah maybe
ThatsLo: wyd?
BadApple: pick u up at 1130
ThatsLo: no way can't stay out that late on a weeknite! Esp since we have a game Friday
BadApple: it'll b worth ur while
ThatsLo: r u trying 2 seduce me?

BadApple: maybe if ur into that

ThatsLo: Still a d girl

ThatsLo: and by d, I mean dick, not dolce

BadApple: lol

ThatsLo: I'm still top girl, aka, head bitch. Cant risk losing my spot.

BadApple: is that in question this yr?

ThatsLo: idk maybe

ThatsLo: u coming after me nxt?

BadApple: ???

ThatsLo: if ur now head bitch in our circle, r u going 2 try to take my spot on the squad?

BadApple: lol

ThatsLo: srsly

BadApple: no

BadApple: I have no interest in cheer or dance or taking anyone's spot. I didn't mean to take ur spot in our circle, either. Is that what u think I'm doing?

ThatsLo: idk r u?

BadApple: no

BadApple: I like u, lo. Ur still my best friend. I may not have been a good friend 2 u last year, but I wud nvr stab u in the back

ThatsLo: except u did
BadApple: I kno.
BadApple: I want 2 make it up 2 u. I would never take ur spot on the squad. I don't know how 2 do any of that shit, and I'm not about embarrassing myself in front of the whole town
ThatsLo: u sure?
BadApple: k maybe I deserve that
BadApple: but unless ur DTF, u dont get WAP signs
ThatsLo: lol
BadApple: Not gonna force my way in & embarrass the squad 2 make u look bad if that's wut ur afraid of. No interest in cheer. Interested in hanging out bc ur cool AF.
ThatsLo: head bitch at school is always head cheerleader 2
BadApple: not anymore. Come thurs. Plz?
ThatsLo: I'll have 2 sneak out. Turn off headlights a block away & dont turn into driveway.
BadApple: kk

It strikes me how different our lives are. Maybe I wear the same name brands now, but I'm not like her. We drive nice cars and carry Gucci bags, but my mom doesn't give two

SELENA

shits if I leave the house on a school night or don't come home until dawn. In fact, she wouldn't even notice. Either she's out partying herself, or she's passed out drunk and wouldn't hear me. Since we moved into this house, I've had all the freedom I want and then some. No one's ever protected me from making my own bad choices and suffering the consequences. Even if it wasn't her intent, my mother has made me strong.

I walk into school the next day like I own the place, and no one stops me. I keep waiting for someone to step into my path and ask me who the fuck I think I am, parading around like I belong here when they all know I'm from the trailer park. But no one does. So, I keep being queen, despite the tension in the air, like everyone's waiting for a showdown, waiting to see how long it lasts.

Thursday night, I pull up outside Gloria's house at half past eleven, with the lights off as promised, even though the sky is pitch black with clouds and grumbling with thunder. I don't turn into the gravel drive, and I let the car roll to a stop so I don't make too much noise on the road. I send a text, and a minute later, a little figure drops out of the tree next to the house. Unlike the Dolce house, they have no upstairs balcony with stairs, but apparently that hasn't deterred her from sneaking out. As she races through the dewy grass on bare feet, her long blonde hair streaming behind her in the moonlight, I'm reminded just how damn pretty she is.

She hops into the car and pulls the door closed gently before turning to me with a huge grin on her face. "This better be good," she says, dropping her shoes on the floorboards.

"Oh, it'll be good," I promise.

"Not gonna tell us what it is?" Colt drawls from the back seat.

Gloria whips around. "Oh god," she groans, flopping back in the seat. "You brought the troll with you?"

"He's not a troll," I say, giving her a funny look. "In case you hadn't noticed, Colt's hot."

Colt chuckles. "Oh, she's noticed."

"Gross," Gloria says, crossing her arms and turning to the window. "If I'd known he'd be here, I wouldn't have agreed to come."

"I can make you come whether or not you agree to it," he says.

"Oh my god, make him stop," Gloria squeals. "He's like a slobbering dog."

"Colt, stop tormenting the drama queen," I say, glancing at him in the rearview. "Lo, chill. He's just messing with you because you give him the reaction he wants."

"It's true," Colt says. "You make it so easy. But don't worry, I'm just playing. I know you're all repressed and shit. You wouldn't know what to do with dick this good."

"I'm not repressed," Gloria says with a huff. "Just because a girl doesn't want your dick doesn't mean she's a prude."

"So you admit you're not getting good dick?"

"Shut up," she says. "That's not what I said. Rylan's dick is fine."

Colt snorts with laughter. I can't help but laugh, too, even when I try to hold it back.

"What?" Gloria snaps.

"Nothing," Colt says, still snickering.

"What?" she demands again, turning to me. "Why is that funny?"

"You know," I say, giving her a meaningful look. "Most guys probably don't want their dicks referred to as *fine*? Unless you're like, *damn, that boy's dick is so fine.*"

Colt's still laughing hysterically. "My dick's super-fine. Some might even say super mega fine."

"Okay, very funny," Gloria says. "I'm one hundred percent sure Rylan's dick is better."

"You never know until you try it," Colt says.

"That would be a hard no."

"You're right about the *hard* part."

Gloria cringes. "Eww, you're hard right now?"

"Wouldn't you like to know."

"I just threw up in my mouth a little."

"Did you just say that to let me know you're good at swallowing?"

She lets out a huff and crosses her arms, turning her nose up. "That's on a need-to-know basis, and you will never need to know."

SELENA

Colt just laughs. "I'll show you mine if you show me yours."

"Okay, troll. A girl doesn't care what your dick looks like. It's what you do with it."

Colt laughs. "So, your boyfriend does have a little dick."

I'm grateful for their bickering, which kept me from getting too nervous until we pull up to the school. Unlike the last time I came here at midnight on a Thursday, the parking lot is not deserted. A circle of cars is aimed inwards, their lights blazing into the center, where half a dozen guys have congregated under the ominous sky.

"Are you fucking serious?" Colt says. "No, Harper. What the fuck?"

"What is this?" Gloria asks.

"I figured you'd put it together a lot sooner," I say to Colt.

"I lost my memory, asshole," he says.

"Not that far back," I point out. "You should know what happens at midnight on a Thursday."

"Anyone mind filling me in?" Gloria asks, sounding annoyed.

"It's a Midnight Swans meeting," I say, parking and shutting off the engine. I turn to them both. "We can change things, y'all. This is our chance. Now that Royal's gone, things are shaken up. They haven't settled yet. We don't have to accept the status quo as it has been the last few years. But it's not going to change itself, and the longer we wait, the more it's going to settle back into the comfortable norm."

"Yeah," Gloria says slowly. "So tell me again why we're going to change something that's comfortable and benefits us? I mean, I'm not suffering."

"But Colt is," I say quietly.

"Fuck you," he says. "I'm not your charity case."

"I'm with him on this one," Lo says.

"Look," I say with a sigh. "I'm benefitting, too. I'm in the same crowd as you, Lo. I could sit on my ass and enjoy it, but what's the point in having this power if you're not using it to do something for someone else? I have no interest in being a status symbol. I want to help someone with my status."

"Oh, but Gloria doesn't want to help anyone," Colt says. "She just wants to shit on everyone under her."

SELENA

"Shut up, charity case," she snaps. "I can speak for myself."

"So?" I ask. "What do you say?"

"I don't know," she says. "I suffered plenty to get where I am."

I grab her hand and squeeze. "I know you, Lo. I know who you really are. You're a good person, and more than that, a strong as fuck person. We can do this. This right here, this is the heartbeat of the school. We can sit at their table every fucking day of our lives, can call ourselves queens, but the truth is, we'll never be their equals while their little boys club meets in secret and makes rules without us."

"That part's true," Colt says.

Gloria stares at me a minute before shaking her head and unbuckling her seatbelt. "So, what are we going to do?"

"Tonight?" I ask. "Tonight, we're going to join."

thirty-six

Harper Apple

We climb out of the car into the sultry night and close our doors. Thunder rumbles low in the distance, but summer's heat hasn't broken yet. The darkness feels close and thick around us with the thunderclouds so low overhead.

Gloria comes around the back of the car, grinning. "I'm kinda glad you talked me into this," she says. "Sorry I was being a bitch. I just... Can't stand that guy."

Speaking of that guy, Colt hasn't gotten out. I open his door. "You coming?"

"Nope," he says, crossing his arms.

"So you're going to sit here and let us take all the risk for you, while you're the only one who really benefits?" Gloria asks.

"Yup."

SELENA

"Colt," I say, putting a hand on his knee. "What's going on? You're really not coming?"

"Not even if you offered to sit on my face while Gloria rides my super fine dick."

"Ugh," Gloria bursts out. "He's disgusting, Harper. Leave him to stew in his filth."

"I have immunity right now," I say quietly, holding his gaze. "It might not last forever, but right now, they won't hurt you. Let me make up for what I did last year."

He tilts his head, giving me a funny look. "What'd you do last year?"

"I got you almost killed."

He scoffs at that. "You didn't do that. I did that. I knew what could happen. You had no idea."

We stare at each other for a long minute. "They'd threatened you," I say. "To me. They told me if I hung out with you, they'd hurt you."

"You think they didn't tell me the same thing?" he asks. "Harper, I never blamed you for that. Not even for a minute. Do you really think that's your fault?"

I shrug. "I mean... At least partly."

"Fuck no," he says. "I wanted to hang out with you because you were a badass new chick who didn't know I was off limits. But I also wanted to piss off the Dolces. That was on me."

"But... We were friends, and I still chose Royal after that."

"Yeah, well," he says. "That part's fucked up. But we weren't that good friends, were we? We'd only hung out a few times."

"I consider you a friend," I say. "And I need friends right now. Allies. Can you trust me just this once?"

He looks at Gloria, then back to me. "Fine," he says. "But this time, whatever happens is on you. Consider yourself a murderer if they kill me. And out of respect for our friendship, try not to fall on any of their dicks until my body's cold."

"Fuck you," I say, but I'm laughing. "I solemnly swear to avenge you if anything happens. Now come on."

We start across the parking lot toward the Midnight Swans, walking shoulder to shoulder. They saw my car drive up, and they stand in the spotlight of their headlights,

SELENA

watching us approach. The only sound is our feet on the pavement and the incessant summer song of the insects punctuated by another distant, uneasy roll of thunder.

"What are you doing here?" Baron asks when we step up beside their cars. At least, I think it's Baron. I remember his voice on the back of my neck, how I couldn't tell it apart from Duke's in the dark behind my blindfold. My throat tightens, but when I falter, Gloria pauses with me, keeping step like we're in one of her dance routines and she has to stay in perfect sync with me. She has my back. Colt's hand grips my elbow, giving it a little squeeze, reminding me that I have allies now. I'm not alone like I was that night.

That night, they destroyed me.

They did their worst.

And I survived it.

I'm still here.

Still standing.

I came back, rose like a fucking phoenix from the ashes of the decimated landscape of my soul. There's nothing they can do to me now. I step into the spotlight with them and reach into my pocket. Holding up my hand, I let the key dangle from my finger. "I'm the key master. Why are we meeting out here in the open? Let's go."

The other guys shift and look at each other, murmuring in surprise.

"What about them?" Duke asks, nodding to my companions. He's holding a beer and swaying slightly on his feet.

"I was a member of the society before any of you," Colt says smoothly. "Once a Swan, always a Swan."

I get a little jolt of shivers when he says the words that the Silver Swan said to me. Silver... Like the metal plate he had put in his head after the beating. I've never messaged Colt on *OnlyWords*. I don't even know his handle. But he could have easily gotten mine from Dixie.

"We changed that rule," Baron says. "That's why no one who graduated is here. Not even Royal."

"I didn't graduate," Colt drawls, sounding so unconcerned you'd never know I had to talk him out of the car. He may not openly defy the Dolces like Preston, but whatever he's done to appease them, he hasn't lost his dignity. If I had to guess, I'd bet he worked out some deal

SELENA

with them, made himself... If not untouchable, at least indispensable. He's cool under pressure and smart. He may not play the game the way Preston does, but he knows what he's doing.

He's a survivor, like me. Survivors do what has to be done just to keep breathing. We know that one day, we'll get out. Then we can do more than survive.

We can live.

"What about them?" Cotton asks, eyeing me and Gloria. "They're girls."

"We talked about letting a girl in last year," DeShaun says.

"I'm that girl," I say.

"But you're not a Swan," Duke says.

"I'm not?" I ask, planting a hand on one hip.

"How are you a Swan?" Gideon asks.

I swallow hard. I'm going to admit some seriously personal information, say it in front of the most powerful men at this school, men whose word is gospel if they decide to share my shameful acts with the rest of the school. Not to mention my own friends will know what I did to get here. I squeeze my hands into fists, pressing my nails into my palms. Here goes fucking nothing.

Not like anyone ever thought I was virtuous to begin with.

"I fought a Swan and won," I say, holding up my thumb. "Royal can tell you that. And if he doesn't count, Baron surely does. I faced my fear in the tunnel under the school. The twins witnessed that one." This time, I raise a finger, then another as I go on. "I betrayed a friend."

Baron holds up a hand to stop me. "You have to betray a friend *for* a Swan. Not betray another Swan."

I nod at Gloria. "The friend I betrayed."

Baron narrows his eyes. "But you didn't do it *for* Royal."

"Whether you like it or not, Preston is still a Swan," I say. "So, it still fits."

"There's still the gauntlet," Cotton says, smirking at me like he thinks it might be worth letting me in if he gets to fuck me.

Duke glances nervously at the others.

"I fucked three Swans," I say. "Technically five, if you must know."

475

SELENA

"What?" Duke asks. "Who's the fifth one?"

"Preston," Baron grits out, his eyes intense behind his glasses. "But unfortunately, you can't count shit that happened in the past. You have to state your intent to join and become a pledge. You have to fulfill the tasks for us, after you've put yourself forward as a candidate."

He looks so smug to have found a loophole. Hell, he probably figured out why I took the key and already came up with a plan to stop me.

Too bad it's not going to work.

"Actually, I did state my intention to join," I say. "I asked Royal. And he gave me the first challenge—to fight him and win. Everything I did after was part of my initiation, if you want to call it that. You and Duke even gave me the second challenge because you didn't think I'd ever complete the tasks. It's cute that you're going to try to stop me now that you forced me to endure the gauntlet."

DeShaun and Cotton exchange a questioning look.

"That's not what we were doing," Duke says.

"And yet, it holds," I say. "But if you want to get together with the elder Swans just to make sure, we can call them to join."

"I told you, we don't include them anymore," Baron says, sounding annoyed.

"Then I guess we'll have to be inducted by the current members."

"I put Harper Apple forward for induction as a fully vested member," Colt says, his voice strong and firm as it echoes over the parking lot. Lightning flickers overhead, and a chill rises on my arms. I can feel the charge in the air, the weight of Colt's words hanging there as everyone waits to see if they still carry the weight they once did.

For a moment, no one speaks. Then Duke raises a hand, his eyes wary as they meet mine. "I second the motion."

I want to fucking cheer, but I keep my cool and turn to Baron. He stares back at me, his jaw clenched.

From the corner of my eye, I see a flicker of movement.

"Third," says a voice I recognize as DeShaun's, though he's shifted so I can't make out anything but his silhouette in the blinding headlights.

Baron turns to him. "Seriously, man? Why?"

DeShaun's broad shoulders rise and fall in a shrug. "I joined the society thinking we'd be doing something that would look impressive on college applications, not tearing down everything the founders built all those years. I know the Midnight Swans itself looks good to schools who have alumni there, and you know Royal's my boy, but... I'm down for a change."

"You didn't like the way Royal ran things?" Baron asks.

"It was fun as hell," DeShaun admits.

"Hear, hear," Duke cheers, holding up his beer to let the headlights spill through the amber bottle.

"But we're seniors now," DeShaun says. "I'm ready to do something besides pulling pranks and making our forefathers look bad."

Gideon shifts on his feet. "Isn't the whole point of the Midnight Swans to make its members look good and give us a head start with the best schools?"

"Exactly," DeShaun says. "Don't get me wrong, it was fun, but how's the society going to make *us* look good if we're making the whole thing into a joke?"

"Maybe you should have thought of that before," Colt says. "You think the Swan on the admissions board at Berkely or Yale is going to look at y'all and think you're cool for kicking their sons out and using their organization like a high school frat? This town may have caved to the Dolces, but the Darling family name is strong with every living generation of the rest of y'all's families. The Swans have connections in every Ivy League school, and I guarantee they won't be happy about what you did to their organization."

"Facts," DeShaun says. "I wouldn't mind it being something different this year. We can still party after the games."

That leaves Baron, Cotton, and Gideon. I'm a little curious why Rylan isn't among the guys, since he rounds out the group at lunch, but now isn't the time to ask. I turn to the three holdouts.

"If she's completed all the challenges, I don't think we can block her just because she's a girl," Gideon says. "But I'm still a pledge, so... I'm not sure I get a vote."

"Half vote," Duke says.

SELENA

"Cool," I say. "That's three and a half for, two against. Guess we should head to the basement before it starts raining."

"What about her?" Cotton asks, nodding at Gloria.

"She's also completed the challenges," I say. "I'm a Swan. She fought me in the hall. She faced her fears by coming to school every day her sophomore year, when you heathens did God knows what to her. She betrayed Royal for me— Again, I'm a Swan. And I'm pretty sure she's passed the gauntlet."

"What's the gauntlet?" Gloria asks.

"You have to let us run a train on you," Cotton says, looking her up and down the way he did me. Guess he's down to fuck whoever. I shouldn't be surprised. You can't exactly be picky when your normal M.O. is taking advantage of whatever girl passes out first at the party.

"What? No way," Gloria says. "I have a boyfriend."

"It's fine," I mutter to her under my breath. "You've already done it."

"She never expressed interest, though," Baron says.

Gloria shakes her head and backs away. "He's right. I'm out. Sorry, girl."

I watch her walk away, torn between going after her and pressing forward with things. I don't want to lose whatever edge I got, and I don't want to give up the key. I'll never get it back if I hand it to Baron, and I'm sure he could persuade anyone else to hand it over to him. After all, he's the leader now that Royal's gone. I could give it to Colt and go after Lo, but I don't trust the guys not to jump him the second I'm not around—especially if he's holding the key they want.

Colt must be thinking the same, because he catches my little finger with his and gives it a squeeze. "Go," he says, ducking his head and speaking into my hair so the others can't hear him. "I'll check on Gloria."

"You're unspeakably awesome," I say, squeezing his finger before releasing him.

"You might even say super mega fine."

I toss my car keys to him and head inside with the Swans. Once again, a chill goes through me. I'm the only girl, alone with five guys. But even if they did the same thing all over again, I know I'll live. Instead of feeling despair that I don't matter, that my wants don't matter, I lean into it. It doesn't matter what they do, because I don't matter.

But it matters what I do. My actions can still matter, even if I don't. And if I can fix my mistakes, if I can make things right or at least make up for some of the selfish and hurtful things I did in my pursuit of destroying the Dolces, maybe I can matter again, too.

thirty-seven

Harper Apple

When we walk out of the basement into the stormy night an hour later, I am officially a Midnight Swan, the first and only female member. I was sworn in, and now I'm part of something, a member of a society that has each other's backs for life.

I'm not naïve enough to think they've suddenly started seeing me as their equal, but it's a step in the right direction. They'll get used to seeing me in the meetings, accept that I'm one of them, and eventually, they'll see my dedication to the group. Then, they'll have my back. Right now, if they did something for me, it would be out of begrudging obligation, the way they admitted me. But one day, they'll see I'm worthy. For now, having a place at the table, on the throne, and in their boys club is enough.

SELENA

I find Gloria sitting on the hood of my car, two empty Styrofoam cups beside her. The rain hasn't come, but the storm clouds have moved closer, and lightning flickers overhead. A breeze has blown up, but it's a hot one.

"Did y'all leave in my car?" I ask.

"We just ran down to get floats at Two Scoops of Love," she says.

"Where's Colt?"

"In the car," she says. "Probably jerking off in your back seat. He's such a freak."

"He's my friend."

She glances at something behind me and quickly shoves one of the cups into my hand. "I got you a shake," she says loudly. "To celebrate your induction. I'm not interested, but I'm still happy for my girl."

I give her a look, but before I can ask why she's gone full on fake, Cotton joins us. "Sweet ride," he says, looking it over. "This yours, Apple?"

"Yep," I say, leaning my elbow on the side and holding the empty cup Gloria handed me.

"Where's Colt?"

"How would I know?" Gloria asks, giving a fake laugh and running her fingers through her sleek hair. "I wouldn't hang out with that creep if you paid me. That's why I'm out here. So he wouldn't try talking to me."

Cotton shakes his head. "Rylan's going to find out, but it won't be from me."

"There's nothing to find out," Gloria says with a nervous little giggle.

Cotton shoves his hands in his pockets. "I just wanted to tell Colt to watch his back. He may still be a Swan by the official rules, but the Dolces will never accept his membership."

"Why are you telling us this?" I ask, narrowing my eyes at him. I've been around Cotton plenty, but like Dawson, I've barely ever spoken to the guy. All I know about him is his predilection for unconscious girls, so I've stayed away from him as much as possible.

"The Dolces are my boys, but that doesn't mean I've rewritten history," he says. "I grew up with the Darlings. Hell, Devlin Darling taught me to drive a stick, and Preston was my first fist fight. I've known Colt since we were stuck in the shallow end of the pool together. He's good people."

"And yet, you helped destroy his life," I say.

He rocks back on his heels and raises his brows at me. "You want to point fingers for that?"

"Nope," I admit. "Thanks for the heads up."

"Don't mention it." He gives Gloria a two-finger salute. "Later, neighbor."

When he walks off, Gloria sighs and takes the cup back from me. "Thanks for covering for me," she says. "You think he bought it?"

"What's going on?" I ask, climbing onto the hood with her so anyone driving out will see two girls talking and having a celebratory milkshake instead of… Whatever she's paranoid they'll see. I have to grab the empty cup again so it doesn't tumble away when the hot wind gusts across the lot, blowing our cover.

"Nothing," she says, sweeping her hair back as it whips across her face. "We just drank floats. I told you, I can't stand Colt. But I'll try to be nice, at least when I'm talking to you, because you're friends."

"Then what are you so worried about?"

"Rylan," she says. "He's... Really intense. Passionate."

"And he'd freak out if you had a Coke with another guy."

"It wasn't just a Coke," she says. "It was ice cream. That's date food."

"Okay, but it wasn't a date. Right?"

"Of course not," she says. "Look, you of all people should understand jealous guys. Remember how Royal was with you last year?"

"Yeah," I say. "He almost killed Colt when I hung out with him."

"Exactly," she says, slumping with relief. "So, you get it."

"I guess."

"That's why I bailed on the Swans thing. Look, I'll fight the good fight against toxic masculinity with you, but I can't have something like that get back to Rylan. Even if it's in the past. He has no idea about me and the Dolces, and believe me, that's by design. I'll take that secret to the grave with me."

"But you hang out with them," I say. "I hate to agree with Cotton Montgomery, but it's bound to get back to him."

SELENA

"Not if I have anything to do with it," she says. "I don't want to lose my spot, but it's been stressful as fuck trying to steer the conversation and make sure they don't spend too much time together when I'm not around. It's like I'm constantly waiting for a ticking bomb to go off. God, you have no idea what this year has been like for me."

"You're right," I say. We sit in silence for a minute, and I can't help hoping she'll trust me enough to talk about Dawson, but I'm not going to bring it up if she's not ready.

After a few minutes, when all the other cars are gone, a few fat drops of rain begin to fall, and Gloria slides off the hood. "Where'd you get this, anyway?" she asks, tapping her nails against the glimmering paint.

I shrug. "It was a gift."

Her mouth twists into a little smile. "From Royal?"

"No," I say, scowling at her.

"Hm, too bad," she says. "I hoped you'd work things out."

I give her a look. "Why? We were toxic as fuck together."

"And yet, I always got the feeling you were both exactly what the other needed."

"Maybe back then we were," I say, climbing up into the driver's seat. "But not anymore."

She climbs up in her side and snaps her seatbelt on. "If you say so."

"What's that supposed to mean?"

"I just think this is the kind of thing he'd do."

"Well, he didn't," I grit out. I'm pissed that I'm pretty sure she's right, though. Did Preston outright tell me he got me this car? I assumed as much because it's the same make as his truck, and I thought everything was coming from him. But if the food and couch came from Royal, could this have been his doing, too? It showed up right after he got all pissy about me driving Preston's truck. And then the admission board called me the next day. Was that him, too?

It pisses me off that I don't know, that he's still doing shit for me, that he's doing something that I'm supposed to be grateful for. And I am fucking grateful—so much that it pisses me off even more. This is the nicest thing anyone's ever done for me, and he didn't even ask for a thank you.

But I remind myself that this was something he did in the past, when he still believed there was a chance I'd forgive

SELENA

him. He knows better now. Since he made that confession and I told him it didn't excuse what he did, he hasn't shown his face, hasn't done a thing to try to prove himself to me. I finally made him understand that there's no coming back from what he did. And maybe that's what pisses me off most of all.

*

I drag myself into school the next day, groggy from lack of sleep and the weather. It stormed most of the night, and the morning is still cloudy with occasional sprinkles. As soon as I step inside Willow Heights, though, it's like the world outside doesn't exist. It's cool and sparkling with energy and excitement. Girls in tiny black and gold jerseys with different players' numbers gather in groups in the hall, fangirling over the football players when they walk by, giggling and planning for the post-game party.

At FHS, the team had to wear shirts and ties on Friday, but since that's the usual dress code here, they let the guys join us in casual Friday, the only day we can wear jeans. But

BROKEN DOLL

this year, the guys are all wearing their jerseys on game days, so it's easy to spot the football players and fawn over them.

Guys who aren't on the team are high-fiving and betting on the game, pumped up with adrenaline for tonight as well. I spot pretty little Magnolia and her friends in their usual spot across the hall from my locker, but I don't say anything. I've decided to keep an eye on her, but I'm not going to interfere in her life for now. Even though I don't believe what Baron said, somehow I feel like we're cousins, anyway, even if she doesn't know I exist. I feel some obligation to look out for her, as if we really are family.

I open my locker and start getting my books before a sense of *déjà vous* runs down my spine like a shiver. It takes me a second to realize it's the reaction around me, the simultaneous rise in excitement and quieting of voices.

"Hey."

I look up to see the Dolce twins standing behind me.

"Hey," I say, grabbing out my last few books.

Baron grabs the door of my locker when I start to close it. He holds it halfway open, creating a shield from prying eyes on one side.

SELENA

"Why aren't you wearing our jerseys?" Baron asks quietly, pulling his sucker out of his mouth to talk.

"Because I'm not a Dolce girl."

"Bullshit," he says, frowning. "You sit at our table. You're the head Dolce girl."

I shrug. "Sorry, but no."

"We can let you sit at our table every day, but if you don't play the part, no one will believe it. They won't respect you no matter what title you try to give yourself. They didn't give you the crown, Harper. You didn't earn it. You claimed it, and you sure as fuck better do what the top girl does if you want to keep it."

"And what exactly is that?" I ask, cocking a brow.

"Rule," Baron says simply. "Ask Gloria if you can't figure it out. She's fucking flawless. You're… A mess."

I try not to let his words sting. They're flat, not derisive, but that makes it worse. He's stating it like a fact, rampaging through the territory I've gained, dropping seeds of doubt as he goes. Because he's right. I have no fucking clue what I'm doing. I can wear all the right clothes, but I don't know how to be popular or rich, don't know how to be the queen bee. I'm not even sure how to be me anymore.

Maybe this is a terrible idea. I should have let Gloria have her spot as close to the top as a girl can get instead of trying to be their equal. She knows how to play the game. She's mean and bitchy to anyone who doesn't worship her, but she's kind and sweet and loyal to her friends. She's on scholarship, but no one would know it, and it's not just because she lives in the right neighborhood and drives a nice car. Like everything, she fakes it, though. She makes sure her car gleams, works after school to afford the clothes to fool everyone and the one party her station dictates she host each year.

"So, you want me to be fake?" I ask.

Baron sighs. "If you want to be a queen at this school, you have to *be* a queen. That doesn't mean making up rules and doing whatever the fuck you want. It's not an empty title. It's a job. There are expectations for you, just like there are for us. Show up at the parties. Show up at the games. And wear our jerseys."

SELENA

"You can wear Royal's," Duke offers. "From last year. If you don't have it, I'm sure Lo can give you hers."

I screw my lips to one side and shrug. "Again, no."

"You should wear *my* jersey," Baron growls, his intense eyes pinning me to the spot. "I'm the top guy. You're the top girl. People already think we're fucking."

"They do?" I ask, swallowing hard. I sway back against the lockers, gripping my books in front of me, trying not to show fear. I force down the rush of memory that slams into me—the way he felt inside me when he did fuck me, his brutality, how he made it hurt as much as he could, because the more it hurt me, the more it turned him on.

"Sure," he says, a little smirk tugging at his lips, his eyes alert and vicious. *He knows.* He saw something in my eyes or heard something in my voice, and he fucking knows. He's caught the scent of fear like a shark detects the faintest trace of blood in the water, and he's going in for the kill.

I can feel it coming.

"After all, we already fucked." He pushes his sucker slowly back into his mouth before reaching out and rubbing his knuckle gently along the top of my jeans. The heat of his touch claws through my shirt, and my skin crawls with sheer, primal revulsion. "Didn't we, Darling?"

"No," I say, forcing my voice to stay steady, my gaze to hold his. "We didn't fuck, Baron. You raped me."

"Oh, but you wanted it," he says, his finger becoming more assertive, hooking into my jeans and tugging me away from the locker where I'm backed into a corner with nowhere to go, no way out—

I squeeze my eyes closed.

"You asked for it," he croons, his voice low but edged with cruelty. "It's okay to admit you wanted us. Royal's not here anymore, Stalker Girl. He'll never know. But we both know the truth, don't we?"

His nickname brings back the night on the balcony when I watched him and Duke double-teaming some girl. It did turn me on. I got hot watching with Royal. Does Baron know about that?

"Royal always told you that when he was done, he'd pass you on to us," Baron says, moving into my space, so close I can feel him even though he's only laid one finger on me. I stiffen, but I don't open my eyes. I will endure this, and it will be over. I can feel myself moving away, as if it's that night, somewhere after the fifth or tenth guy, when I just hung there, and I knew I was beaten. I stopped fighting. I stopped living.

I don't fight it now. I sink into it, embrace it, pull it into myself. My brokenness is not my weakness. It's my strength, my shield. He cannot break me more. He cannot hurt me more. I am not in the hallway at Willow Heights, with my attacker breathing his cherry-sucker scent against my lips. I'm in an air-conditioned loft, where nothing can touch me, even when he does. I don't feel it. I don't feel anything in this cool void of weightlessness, a limbo of suspended animation.

"And you made sure he was done with you, didn't you?" Baron purrs into my ear. "You knew exactly what would happen then. You wanted it, just like she did. What was your favorite part? Was it at the end of the night, when we were both inside you at once? That's every girl's fantasy when she sees twins, right? I'll let you in on a little secret. That was my favorite part, too. Your pussy was loose after we'd fucked you all night, but your ass was still so tight."

I can't swallow. I can't breathe. I am frozen, caught in the teeth of the nightmare that gripped me all summer.

"We could do it again, you know," Baron says, moving his finger back and forth against the skin just inside my waistband. His lips brush my ear, warm and soft and inviting. "You can even pretend you don't want it if that's what gets you off. I won't put a gag on you this time. I'll let you scream."

His words are like ice water down my spine, and I suck in a loud, ugly breath. Before he steps back, I bring my knee up with all my strength, slamming it into his crotch. Baron's eyes go round, and his sucker drops to the floor when his mouth falls open. He can't even breathe, let alone speak. Before he can recover, I punch him right in the sternum with my rings. He reels back, and I slam my locker and turn to Duke.

He steps back, his gaze flying from me to Baron and back, looking like he's about to say fuck it and ditch this whole shit show.

"Maybe you should show up at my fights," I say. "Make a T-shirt with my name on it, and wear a necklace with an apple on it, just in case anyone forgets who your balls belong to."

I step around Baron and walk off, ignoring the chatter and stares. I sit in class, staring out the window at the dark sky that's still spitting rain. And I fucking fume.

I fume because Baron is psychotic and I can't change that, no matter how much I try to appease him and keep the peace, to see him as a human being and not just a monster. He still thinks he can talk to me like I'm scum. How many times will I have to crush his balls to make him stop? And what if he doesn't? I put myself in his path, and now our truce may be over before it really began. I know violence, so I used violence. I don't know what else to do. I've already tried compromise and understanding. What else is there?

I could go to the police. There's zero chance Preston disposed of any evidence. He has the blanket he wrapped me in that night, and it must be covered in their DNA. He has pictures. He has a doctor who came to examine me.

But he doesn't have power. He can't win against the Dolces.

I thought this shit was over, that I didn't have to fight them anymore. I already know I won't win. No one can beat the Dolces. No one has more power at this school than Baron, no matter how much I insist I'm his equal, how many places I insert myself. Baron is king.

But one person has more power than Baron.

Royal.

But no. I can't ask him for help now, can't bring him back into my life when I just got free of him. Besides, his status isn't the same at this school as it once was. It fades every day. He's an icon, a football god, but he's no longer involved in the day-to-day. Going behind Baron's back to rat him out to his brother won't help me. It will only make me look weak, prove that I can't do it on my own. Royal won't be there to fight my battles for me every time.

But other people can fight *with* me.

I don't have to do it on my own. That was my mistake last time. Those boys already proved that I can't do it alone.

Why should I have to, though?

Needing friends doesn't make me weak, exactly. It makes me fallible and a little bit vulnerable and human, all the things I need to be to connect with other humans. I'm not better. I'm not the queen who needs to lord her status over them. I'm one of them. I'm a basic bitch, no one special. I don't even have money.

Which makes it even more important to have friends.

thirty-eight

Harper Apple

At lunch, I grab Colt, since it's raining outside, and he can't go hide under the bleachers. "Come on," I say. "You're eating in the café today."

"I am?" he asks, giving me a skeptical look.

"Yep," I say, waving to Dixie. I join her and Quinn. "You ready?"

"For what?" she asks.

"We're taking the table."

"The… Dolce table?" she asks. "They'll never let me sit there. Or Colt."

"Someone has to stop them," I say. "It might as well be us."

"I'm good, really," Quinn says, holding up a hand and backing away. "I don't want to get on their bad side."

SELENA

"See?" I say. "They've created a fucking reign of terror. It needs to end."

Quinn scrunches her shoulders up to her ears. "I'm sorry?"

"I'm in," Dixie says. "We better get there before they do. Let me get Josie."

She grabs her friend from her locker, and we hurry to the café and sit down at the head table, taking up half the seats. We don't bother getting food and losing our chance.

A minute later, Duke and Baron arrive from the food line, their servants behind them.

"What are you doing?" Baron asks, looking at me like I'm insane.

"We're taking the best table," I say. "There are spots for you, too."

"This isn't going to work," he warns.

"Y'all going to run away like you did when I sat at your table last year?" I ask. The memory of that day, when I sat there and they all got up and moved, leaving me sitting alone with everyone staring, still makes my insides twist with humiliation. But this time, I won't be alone.

"You picked the wrong side, new girl," Duke says, shaking his head at Josie. She crosses her arms and stares back at him, looking bored.

Baron drops his used sucker stem in front of me, turns, and grabs the other table, the one pushed up against this one that usually holds the overflow. He pushes it away from ours. Everyone in the room turns at the sound of the legs scraping against the floor—those who weren't already watching the drama unfold. Duke grabs another table, shooing away the people already sitting there, and pulls it over so the group of two tables is back in place. Then he and Baron sit at their usual position while others begin to fill in the chairs around it.

"It's not working," Dixie says, looking nervous.

"It is working," I say, trying to ignore all the eyes turned our way. "We just have to show them we have supporters, too."

I wave at Gloria, motioning her and Rylan over. She gives me an apologetic little smile and shakes her head, turning to the Dolce table instead. I wince, my face warming at the very public rejection.

SELENA

I get it, though, and I don't hold it against her. Like I told Dixie, I don't want anyone to get hurt in this. The second Gloria betrays the Dolces, they'll tell her boyfriend they've both fucked her. She's in an impossible position. I'm her friend, and I want her to be happy and do what's best for her. So I smile at her, hoping she understands that I know she'd support me if she could.

"Even Lo won't join," Dixie moans.

Colt snorts. "You really expected the Homecoming Queen to defect?"

"She's nice," Dixie protests.

Colt rolls his eyes. "So everyone keeps telling me."

"We don't need the Homecoming Queen," I say. "We just need enough people to fill our table."

I spot Cotton coming out of the food line with his servant, and I meet his eyes and raise my brows. Not super keen on having a sexual predator on my side, but right now, we just need warm bodies.

He turns away and keeps walking like he didn't see me. He won't help dismantle a system that directly benefits him. Why would he?

"Just two more people," Dixie says, crossing her fingers on both hands. "Come on, come on. Someone's got to hate them as much as we do."

"I don't hate them," I say. "I just don't want to have to worship them."

I spot Magnolia Darling and her two freshman friends making their way toward a table, and I wave them over. Magnolia gives me a haughty look, like she doesn't know if she should deign to talk to me, but she says something to her friends, and they cautiously approach.

"Not her," Colt mutters when he sees his cousin heading our way, but it's too late. They're already at our table.

"Hey," I say. "Want to sit with us?"

"Are you making some kind of point?" Magnolia asks, pouting her glossy lips and toying with one of her pigtails.

"We're protesting the Dolce rule," I say.

She blinks her impossibly long, mascaraed lashes at me. "By sitting at your own table?"

I shrug. "It's a peaceful protest."

"Oh," she says, brightening. "Like Martin Luther King."

SELENA

"No," I say, shaking my head. "We just don't like the way they're treating everyone else. And since they did all that to your family…"

"Sitting here would be social suicide," says her curvy friend with the unfortunate eyeliner. She's not talking to me, though she's looking at me. She's muttering behind Magnolia's shoulder.

"Yeah," says the friend with skin issues. "They just got burned by the Dolces in front of the whole school. We can't sit here."

"We didn't get burned," I say. "We just chose to form our own pack."

"What's in it for us?" asks Magnolia, raising her chin and scrunching up her pouty, full lips.

"You'll inherit the school," I say. "We'll be gone by next year. But you'll still be here. If you stake your claim now, as a freshman, you can just slide into the top spot next year."

"We'll already do that," says the brunette.

"Okay," Magnolia says to me.

"What?" her two friends cry in unison. It's almost funny, how shocked they look.

Magnolia gives a sassy little toss of her bouncy pigtails, keeping her eyes locked on us as she carefully sits, not letting herself look around the room for reactions. She juts her chin out defiantly. "You know, I'm not as dumb as everyone thinks."

"I can see that," I say.

Colt snorts and shakes head. "You're fourteen."

Magnolia narrows her eyes at him and glares. "So?"

"We're out of here," says the eyeliner girl. "We can try next year, when all these scary senior boys are gone." She grabs the other girl, and they scurry away, leaving Magnolia with us. She visibly gulps, and for a second, I think she's going to change her mind and bolt.

But then she takes a breath and faces me. "Do you have a speech?"

"Why would I give a speech?"

She rolls her eyes. "Well, you can't just sit at a table and protest without telling people why. No one even knows what you're doing. I mean, no one remembers the people who sat at the lunch counters. They remember Martin Luther King. You know why? *He* had a speech."

SELENA

I wince. "Can you stop using that comparison?"

"Fine," she says, rolling her eyes like I'm her mom nagging her to do her chores. "But you don't even have signs. You're literally just sitting here on a hunger strike for no reason."

"It's not a hunger strike."

"The freshman has a point," Josie says. "Right now, we just look like scabs crossing the picket line."

"And no offense, but scabs are gross," Magnolia says, wrinkling her cute little nose. "So get on that chair and make a speech like MLK. Or… Katniss Everdeen, if you'd rather."

"What would I even say?" I ask.

They all just look at me, like I have the answers. Before I can come up with something to say to them, let alone the whole school, Gideon Delacroix starts in our direction. I tense, ready for a confrontation, ready to be told how I should be grateful the Dolces pay me any attention, and I should take the scraps they give me, just like he takes whatever girls they're done with.

He stops at our table and points to an empty chair. "Is this seat taken?"

I just stare at him, not sure what to say. "Don't you play football?" I ask at last, though it's obvious he does, since he's wearing his jersey.

He shuffles his feet and looks down, his cheeks going a little pink. "I know what you did."

"What did I do?" I ask carefully. My heart is beating so hard I can hear it thundering in my ears, and I think I'll miss his softspoken words if he answers. I don't want to hear them, anyway. I don't want to know if it's finally out, if Baron has started spreading the rumor that I took the team.

"Lindsey's my cousin," Gideon says, finally meeting my eyes. "Thank you."

"Well, what are you waiting for, an official invitation?" Josie asks. "Have a seat, little dude."

Gideon nods and quickly pulls out the chair and sits like he's afraid we might change our minds before he gets settled. He glances at us nervously, taking in the fact that he's the only one with food.

"Y'all want some of this?" he asks, pushing his plate toward the middle of the table. He's so adorably shy and earnest that I can only hope there are more like him coming up in the other grades. Once the Dolces graduate, maybe their perverted version of leadership will at least die down at little, even if it never goes away.

Magnolia gives him a shy smile and takes a sweet potato fry from his plate.

"Go on, Katniss," she says. "Make this worth skipping lunch."

"Okay," I say, pushing back from the table. Everyone's gone back to their food after the Dolce tables were taken, but there's an edge of excitement. They're all hoping there's more.

So, I need to deliver.

I climb up in my chair and clear my throat.

"Hey, y'all," I say, giving a little wave. A few people at nearby tables elbow each other and lean in to whisper before twisting around to watch. God, this is fucking torture. I have zero interest in being a leader or anyone's focus. I just wanted friends.

Or maybe that's not true.

Maybe I want more. I want freedom from the bullshit. And not just for me.

For everyone.

Not because I like attention, but because they need a leader—a real one, not a tyrant. And even if I don't want to be a leader, I have a voice, and for the first time in a long time, I want to use it. Because I know that there are more girls in this school who are afraid to use theirs, to speak up, to risk themselves. But the Dolces already took everything from me, so there's no risk left. I have nothing to lose.

If I'm going to be queen, this is how I can help others. I can be the voice for those who still have something left to lose, something they can't risk, so they can't speak up.

I can't do that by hiding in the shadows and avoiding attention, by being quiet and obedient, like the Dolces want me to be. I can't do it by pretending I'm Baron's girlfriend. I have to take a stand as my own person, one who represents something besides social status.

"Let's get you up here," Colt says. He stands and grabs my hips, lifting me onto the table.

I want to jump down and run because I feel like there's a spotlight on me, and more than that, a target. But I force myself to keep my head up. I plant my feet and begin. After a few words, Magnolia gives a huff. She climbs into her chair and then onto the table, her pink Doc Martens clomping loudly as she stamps her foot.

"Hey!" Her voice is surprisingly loud and bossy. "Listen up! We're not silent protesting over here for nothing. Shut up and hear what this girl has to say."

I give her an impressed smile, and she grins and hops down, flouncing into her seat, pigtails bouncing.

"Hey," I say again, forcing myself not to glance at the tables beside ours, where the Dolce crew sits. "Most of y'all know me as Royal's girlfriend, or plaything, or whatever."

No one says anything. A hundred blank faces stare up at me, and my hands get all clammy, and I wonder why I give a single fuck what happens to any of these people. They didn't give a fuck about me last year. They didn't help me. They didn't protect me. Most of them never even talked to me. They quenched their thirst for gossip with the columns about me in Dixie's blog.

But that's not fair.

They didn't know me. And I was so consumed by my ambition that I didn't bother getting to know them, either.

They don't owe me anything.

"A few of you might know that I'm a scholarship student—and yes, I know we're not supposed to talk about that—or that I can throw a punch."

A few people laugh quietly, and someone whistles. It's something.

"But a lot of you know me from Dixie's blog," I say, gesturing to the girl sitting behind me. "You know I fought against the hierarchy last year before I joined it. But I don't think you should have to join it."

There's an awkward beat of silence.

I force myself to keep talking. "If you want to join it, that's fine. I'm not about tearing everything down. I don't have a problem with football, or the Dolces, or anyone here. Gloria's one of the best people I know. Dixie here, she's on dance as well as running the blog. But I don't think we should have to conform to one thing in order to be allowed basic human decency at this school."

Duke cups his hands around his mouth and hollers, "Go home!"

SELENA

A bunch of people laugh. I wipe my hands on my jeans. "That's the thing," I say. "I have a right to be here. And so do all of y'all. You shouldn't have to look a certain way, or live in a certain neighborhood, or wear a certain thing on Fridays to be allowed to thrive here. You shouldn't have the threat of being thrown in a dumpster or dragged to the basement hanging over your head if you don't comply. You shouldn't have to worry that if a boy calls you, you have to go to his house whether or not you want to. Maybe that's the way things were, but that's not the way they should be. And it's not the way they have to be."

"Yeah, it is," Duke calls out. A bunch of guys laugh, but I see more than a handful of girls in the rest of the room averting their eyes, and that gives me strength. I'm not doing this for the twins. I'm doing it for everyone else, all the girls they've hurt. Maybe not the way they hurt me, maybe they just slept with them and didn't call them back, but it doesn't matter.

"So, that's what this protest is about," I say. "It's not against anyone. It's *for* someone though—for y'all. I have no beef with anyone, including the Dolce boys. I made a truce with Baron, and I stand by that. I'm not trying to take anyone's place. I just want to have a place, period. I want to have a voice, and more than that, I want everyone else who wants a voice to be able to use it."

"Boo," Duke yells. A handful of sweet potato fries bounce off me. I cringe, but I don't step down.

Two teachers come through the doors and head for our table. A buzz of excitement goes up around the room.

"And I want the teachers to have the same expectations of everyone and not treat some people different," I say, speaking over the voices.

"Miss Apple," says Mr. Harris, the science teacher who accused me of stealing his cockroaches last year. "Please get down from there."

"I want the administration to discipline everyone the same," I say, raising my voice until I'm almost shouting. "No matter if you pay tuition or have a scholarship."

The other teacher is speaking into a walkie talkie, and I know my time is up.

"We'll be here every day," I call over the roar of voices filling the room. "If you agree with our protest, you can sit

SELENA

with us, no matter who you are. We don't care what you look like, what you're into, or what car you drive. You can even eat lunch."

A few people laugh when they notice our empty table. Mr. Harris reaches for me, but Colt stands, stepping between us.

"Don't put your hands on her," he says, his voice low and filled with warning.

I remember him telling me he used to run this place. This teacher knows that. And judging by John Darling's estate, I'm guessing that family pays for more than my scholarship here.

Mr. Harris drops his hand, but I'm done. I give a little wave before stooping, bracing my hand on the edge of the table, and hopping down. I hold out my wrists. "Going to arrest me for daring to speak up?" I ask.

"Let's go," says the other teacher, looking annoyed. She holsters her walkie and waves me toward the office, a place I am all too familiar with by now.

thirty-nine

Harper Apple

MrD: So now you need me.

I straighten in the cushy chair outside the headmaster's office. I've been sitting here for thirty minutes while they decide what to do with me, since apparently they have no precedent for someone standing on a table and talking about making the admin accountable for doing their job.

BadApple: lol u kno it
MrD: Seems you caused quite the commotion.
BadApple: just telling it like it is
BadApple: So what r the charges? Disturbing the peace? Inciting a riot?
MrD: Was there a riot?

SELENA

BadApple: lol
MrD: Was there?
BadApple: u been 2 WHPA. Can u imagine anyone at this school rioting?
MrD: Did they?
BadApple: no

I get this creepy feeling, like I used to get when he'd text me and tell me he knew where I lived. Which is stupid, because it's just Preston. This man has literally ejaculated on my cervix. But it feels different somehow, when he's a faceless name on an app instead of the fastidious, elegant man who saved my life, cooked me dinner, and told me to find my sun. He feels like a stranger when he's behind a screen.

MrD: What if I could get you cleared of all charges?
BadApple: yes plz

I add a smiley face to make myself feel better. I wish he'd just texted, like he usually does. Or shown up. I haven't seen him in a while, not since we were told we're cousins. I'd like to talk to him about the incident in the garage, see if there's anything else he lied to me about. But mostly, I just miss him. I miss his safe, detached company, his clean apartment, the meals that started not when we took the first bite, but when our eyes took in the presentation on the plate.

And, as creepy as it is since I'm not one hundred percent sure we're not related, I miss the scent of him. That sense is visceral but deep, filled with memories I didn't know I was making. Just thinking about him, I can almost smell his shampoo in my hair, his skin when he held me pressed to his chest all night, his fancy sheets that held the scent our bodies made together.

MrD: How does teenage rebellion sound?
BadApple: familiar
MrD: As far as charges go, not too bad. Right?
BadApple: Thank uuuuu. Ur the best ever. C u soon?
MrD: We'll see
BadApple: ???
MrD: Now that I've dealt with your discipline situation…

SELENA

I close my eyes, dread building in my stomach. A door opens down the small hallway, and a girl I've never met steps out. She must be a freshman or transfer. I glance at the sign above the door. I've never been in that office—the school psychiatrist. I remember Royal telling me I needed help, and I shiver and pull my sleeves down over my hands.

"We'll be right here if you need us," says the school psychiatrist. "You don't need an appointment, Amber. Just come on down any time you want to—you have something to communicate."

The Amber chick stands stiffly outside her door. She catches me looking and stares back with a sullen expression.

"But that does require you to communicate something," the shrink says gently.

Amber's lips tighten, but she doesn't speak.

The shrink sighs. "See you next week, then."

As if she were just waiting for the gates to open, Amber charges down the hall and past me, past the front desk, and throws her shoulder into the door, bursting out into the school's fancy foyer. There's something familiar about her. At first I think she must be another transplant from FHS, and my mind immediately latches onto the text conversation I was just having. Maybe she's my replacement.

But that's stupid. Preston's not going to find some other girl to fill my shoes. He gave me my scholarship back. Then again, he controls all the money in the Darling estate. I'm sure they could write off more than one scholarship as a charitable donation. I watch the girl, telling myself it's just the poor kid in me sensing the poor kid in her. Poverty isn't something that disappears the moment a guy slides a pair of Louboutins on your feet. Hell, I could win the lottery for real, and I wouldn't be a rich girl overnight. I might have money, but I wouldn't be rich.

But that girl is wearing name brand jeans and new sneakers and a WHPA hoodie, and I can't tell for sure if she's poor. Maybe she's a fucked up rich girl. Poverty's an aura, something that takes months or maybe years to shed. Sure, a total makeover goes a long way toward erasing the stink of it. I'm a new person now, a rich girl with straight hair and dark eyes and a Gucci bag, but sometimes, in the rare moment that I remember who I am and feel like myself, I feel how fake it all is. The girl is gone before I can tell if she's a fake, if there was the right mix of desperation and defiance in her expression, the set of her chin, the challenge in her eyes when they met mine.

My phone buzzes in my hand, startling me. I look down at the screen.

MrD: …What are you going to do for me?
BadApple: r u serious? I told you, no more of that. U promised
MrD: I have no recollection of such a promise.

I want to scream and throw my phone. Didn't he promise? Or is this another instance where I said something, and he didn't respond, and I took it as an answer? I told him I wanted my scholarship back, but no more spying, no more bargains, no more games. Did he actually agree?

I can't remember.

BadApple: wtf, preston. Ur being a dick. I'm not doing this shit 4 u anymore. U kno that.
MrD: But we had so much fun last year, didn't we, darling?
BadApple: fuck off

BROKEN DOLL

MrD: I did you a favor. You owe me a favor in return. I will collect.

I uninstall the app and toss my phone under the chair. Fucking asshole. Is he pissed because I made a truce with Baron? Colt said he tracks their cars and spies on them. Does he have people at Willow Heights—maybe Colt himself? Or did someone around town see me with Royal and report back? Or fuck, what if he and Royal have some kind of deal now? After all, Royal gave me back to Preston when I was passed out. Despite Royal's denial, I can't help but wonder. What kind of bargain did they make that day? What did each one give, and what did they gain?

I'm so paranoid and fucked in the head I barely pay attention to the headmaster when he calls me in and gives me a long lecture about appropriate behavior and representing the school like an upstanding citizen. Apparently upstanding citizens don't actually stand up when they see something wrong. They accept it and obey. When he tells me to go to class, I almost ask for a punishment. No amount of detentions can be worse than owing Mr. D.

SELENA

It's my fault, though. I took too much. I took the car, the scholarship, the shoes and clothes, the bags, the jewelry. I told him I'd bring them back, and I didn't. And all I ever gave him was a hole to stick his dick in. It wasn't even good sex. I mostly just lay there and let him put his dick wherever he wanted it that day. The only time I even participated was when he wanted a blowjob. And not that I minded, but the dude's pretty vanilla considering all the shit he wanted to hear last year.

If I'd spent any time thinking about it, I'd have pictured him as having some kinkier fantasies. He wanted to hear all about my sex life with Royal, but when he had me for himself, the kinkiest thing he did was take little porn clips on his phone. He never even watched porn with me. He never pushed me up against all those windows and fucked me where the risk of someone seeing was close to zero but the thrill that they *could,* that it wasn't quite zero, would make it more risqué. Hell, we never even had sex on the roof.

The handful of times we weren't in bed, we did it on the couch. I literally let him do whatever he wanted, and all he wanted was regular sex, with an occasional BJ or anal thrown in for variety. He never suggested something even a little bit daring, like pegging or blindfolds.

Suddenly, Mom's words come back to me. She said men respect their wives, they don't want to choke them and pull their hair. And I told her Preston respected me because he never did any of that. Is that why? Or was it just pity? Did he not want to traumatize me, so he didn't enact his more perverse fantasies? After all, it's not like he could have tied me up. I would have gone apeshit, and he didn't want to deal with that mess. If there's one thing Preston likes, it's having everything in order.

But he had no problem making all kinds of nasty sexual comments to me last year. Asking me about watching the twins, and if it made me hot. Wanting detailed descriptions of everything from Royal's dick to what positions we tried, how good he was, how many times I came. Telling me the things he'd do to me if he could fuck me instead of living vicariously through my stories.

When he could fuck me, though, he was careful and perfunctory. Nothing like the texts he sent. Is Mr. D more than a screen name, but a persona? One he can use to be bold, something he can't be in real life, especially not to someone who's seen his face. He can fantasize when hidden behind a screen, but when he meets a girl, he's too self-conscious about his appearance to let go and do anything but the basics. He's not living vicariously through me, but through Mr. D.

It's always felt just a little off, like Mr. D was a different person than the man I met. And maybe he is. Maybe he's the old Preston Darling, the one who the Dolces destroyed. A man who will ask for what he wants, who hasn't been beaten down until there's nothing but helpless rage inside him while he watches the family that ruined his take over his town. A man who has fantasies he's too ashamed to ask for because he thinks he's already asking too much for just wanting someone to see him as a person and not a hideous monster. A man who only exists online.

Maybe that's a good thing. I remember Dixie saying Preston was the evil one. The man I spent the summer with may not have been perfect, may not be a hero, but he's sure as fuck not evil. He didn't always make the right choices, but I believe he tried. He was generous and gentle, considerate, broken, guilt-ridden, tortured, and nurturing. And even though I know he's filled with unfathomable rage, he never, ever took it out on me.

He knew I was Royal's. He knew what happened to his cousin because of me. In his eyes, I was Team Dolce. He could have fucking tortured me. Hell, that's what the Dolces did when they thought I was a Darling. Preston never hurt me in any way, physically or emotionally. He never said I smelled bad or that I was loose. He never called me trash or a bitch or a whore. Hell, when I called myself that, he fucking defended me—to myself. In six months of knowing him, he's never made me feel unsafe or belittled. He's never even raised his voice to me.

My heart breaks for him, but it also soars at the realization that I don't have to obey him. He might ask for things, but I don't have to give them. If I show up in person, he won't ask me to my face. The old Preston might be bold enough to ask, but the new one isn't. He won't punish my defiance. He has no control over me.

I feel strong as I walk into my math class. I don't even mind the stares and whispers. I usually sit with Gideon and

SELENA

Cotton, but I'm not sure I'll be welcome there or even what rift I might have caused between the sophomore and the senior players. The last thing I want to do is fuck things up for sweet little Gideon. But he looks up from his laptop and smiles, nodding to the empty seat at their table. It would be rude as hell to take the chair—the only empty seat—and drag it to another table. Especially because Josie's the only other person from the lunch protest, and I'm not sure she'll welcome me in her group.

So, I slide in at the boys' table. Gideon reaches over and gives my hand a quick squeeze. Cotton shakes his head and turns away. I squeeze Gideon's hand and pull away. I don't want Cotton or anyone else getting any ideas about that being a romantic gesture. The last thing I need to do is get this boy in more trouble than the stunt at lunch probably did.

Class is almost over when the dreaded little black box pops up on the corner of my laptop screen with the blinking green cursor.

GideonD17: I think ur brave

BadApple: how did u get my handle?
GideonD17: from dixie.
GideonD17: That ok?
BadApple: Thx 4 having my back at lunch. ur brave 2.
GideonD17: ofc.
GideonD17: more ppl should stand up 2 the bs that goes on around here.
BadApple: they will
GideonD17: bc u inspired them.
GideonD17: like u did me

I glance up from my screen and see that the poor boy is blushing. Shit. Not the direction I want to go with this. Gideon is two years younger than me, plus, he's so sweet I have to believe he's never had his heart broken, and there's no way I could be responsible for all that. He's too *good* for me.

Not better than me, but he's a good person, and I'm... Not.

BadApple: thx, G. ur a good guy.

SELENA

BadApple: a good friend.

GideonD17: u2

BadApple: don't lose ur other friends, ok? The team has ur back. Dont fuck that up.

GideonD17: if any of those guys were as good as u, they would stand up 2 it instead of joining in like cowards

BadApple: don't write stuff like that here. It's not as secure as u think. If u want 2 b part of this, I'm so happy. But not if it means u get hurt. We can't risk anyone, and u can't risk urself 4 the cause. K?

GideonD17: how much can u believe in it if u won't take a risk 4 it?

The bell chimes before I can argue, and I give him a tight smile and head for the door before he can try to talk to me and make this more awkward. This was not supposed to happen. My life is complicated and messy enough.

I have no attraction to Gideon—of course not. He's all wholesome and innocent.

I like dangerous guys with tattoos who can rock my world and wreck my soul.

I sit with Dixie in my next class, trying to focus and not think about Gideon. I don't want to lead him on, but I also don't want to lose him. His involvement in the protest today was huge. Just like it was huge of him to cast his vote for me with the Swans. That night, only the rulers of the school saw it, though. DeShaun had already broken rank, so they probably didn't think too much about a new guy saying which side he favored. They could keep it quiet, though. Only the Swans know there was dissention in the ranks.

Now, everyone knows. Everyone saw a football player say he didn't agree with how the football players treat other people. And yeah, it sucks that it's the man they'll remember, the only guy who joined the cause besides Colt, who is still a pariah as far as anyone else is concerned. Gideon isn't just a man, though. He's one with status, even though most people don't know he's pledging for the Swans. They know he usually sits with the Dolces. That he's one of the kings, or at least a prince. And more than that, he's a football player.

That comes with status baked right in.

I may be the one who started this, but I'm not suffering under the delusion that I'm the most important part of it. I never would have made that speech and told people what was going on if Magnolia hadn't convinced me to get up there and do it. And Gideon, he's the key to all of this.

I can't just upend everything the school has ever done, the social order of the whole town, of schools everywhere. Football matters in this town. Athletes have status in just about every school, and I'm not going to change that by putting up a fight about it. That's just the way it is. The best thing I can do is focus on the things I can change—the way they treat other people at this school. And I can't do it alone.

Without Gideon, we're just a bunch of disgruntled outcasts. Colt hasn't had status here in years. Everyone knows he's the friendless rebel under the bleachers. They saw me stirring the pot last year, so it's not exactly revolutionary for me to do it this year. Josie's radical. Dixie is popular, but she's also a goth chick and doesn't fit the standard norms for popularity. Magnolia does, but she's a freshman and everyone knows what the Dolces do to Darlings, so they probably expect her to refuse to join them.

Gideon is the wildcard, the unexpected one in the group, the one who has everything going for him and nothing to gain by joining us. Which means I have to find a way to make him realize he's misplaced his feelings without hurting them in the process.

"Are you going to the game tonight?" Dixie asks when class is about to end and everyone starts talking.

"This whole thing kinda started because Baron got in my face about being his Dolce girl, so… It kinda defeats the purpose if I go."

"You should go," she says. "Actually, you should be on the cheer squad if you really want to be queen bee."

"I don't."

"Then what's the point of all this?" she asks. "I mean, I put up a blog about lunch, and I'm going to put up another one this weekend about the idea behind it. But I thought you wanted to be up there at the top of the social ladder with the Dolces."

"I don't want to be up there as someone's cheerleader."

"You don't have to be someone else's cheerleader," she says. "I'm on the dance team, and Colt's not on the team. He doesn't even go to the games."

"True," I say, wondering if she knows where he is on Friday nights—running the fights at the Slaughterpen.

SELENA

"Be your own cheerleader," Dixie says. "It would be good for you to be there if you want a place on the social ladder. Hey, you could wear Gideon's jersey!"

The bell chimes, and I grab my stuff with relief. "I don't think that's a good idea."

She shrugs and gathers her books. "I don't really know him, since he was a freshman last year, but he seems like a good guy."

"Yeah," I say. "That's the problem."

"Maybe you could use a guy like that," she says. "I mean, I don't know what happened with you and Royal, but I know dating him couldn't have been easy."

"It wasn't," I say. "But I don't want this to be about who I'm dating. I don't want people to think Gideon's only joining our cause because we're together."

She gives me a sly grin. "I'm just saying. It wouldn't be such a bad thing."

forty

Harper Apple

I've never been so happy to see Colt. He falls in beside us in the hall, and Dixie drops the line of conversation about Gideon.

"Haven't seen you on a Friday night in a while," Colt drawls as we make our way to my locker. "Looks like you're back to your old shenanigans. Does that mean we'll see you tonight?"

"Got anything good for me?"

"Only the best," he says.

I groan. "Merciless? No way. Not for my first time back. I'm out of practice. She'll kill me."

He shrugs. "Maybe. It'll be good money, though."

"For you," I point out. "And for her. Not for me. I'll be in the hospital, and there goes my savings."

SELENA

Speaking of, I do need to get back out there, though. I can't rely on Preston, especially if he's back to being a demanding dick. And even if he wasn't, I already know what the DNA test will say. I can't expect him to support me forever. One day, I've got to have enough money to get out of this town, and for most girls like me, that would mean selling myself. Lucky for me, I have a skill. Fighting is my jam.

But overconfidence nearly got me killed by the Dolces, and I have zero interest in making that mistake in a fight. I'm not an even match for Merciless at my best, and I haven't fought in months.

"Actually, I thought I might go to the game," I say, arching a brow at Colt and opening my locker. "You in?"

He laughs, leaning against the locker beside mine, looking totally relaxed and sexy with his tattoos on display, since we can wear WHPA t-shirts on Fridays. "Nah, babe," he says. "But you go watch out for my girl here. Word on the street is that there will be Faulkner kids at the afterparty."

"And they're so much worse than Willow Heights kids," I say, rolling my eyes.

"She might meet some emo dude with a matching dog collar and fall head over heels."

"I would never," Dixie squeals.

"I don't think you have anything to worry about," I say. "But I'll intervene if I see her with any bad boys who smoke under the bleachers."

I give him a wink, but that little phrase I used to describe him must have disappeared with so many of his other memories. He doesn't smile or anything, just shrugs. "I'm more worried about the football players."

"I thought you had immunity because of the blog?" I say to Dixie.

"I do," she says, sliding her hand through Colt's arm and cuddling up to him. "They wouldn't risk it."

"I'm not worried they'll try to hurt you," he says, smiling down at her. "I'm worried they'll try to steal you."

"Aww, your jealous streak is so cute," she teases, leaning up to kiss him.

"God, get a room," Gloria snaps, appearing at my side. "Nobody wants to see bulldogs tongue wrestling in the hall. This is a good school."

SELENA

In response, Colt moans and wraps his arms around Dixie, and they start full-on making out.

"What's up?" I ask Lo, closing my locker.

"Are you going to the game?"

"I was thinking about it," I say, meeting her eye, lifting my chin in a challenge.

"Ugh, I can't even concentrate with these slobber goblins sucking the plaque off each other's teeth right beside us," she says. "Can we walk?"

"Sure," I say. I wave to the lovebirds, but they're too busy swapping spit to see me. I figure I'll text Dixie later if I decide to go.

"You really should come," Gloria when we're outside, where everything is soggy and waterlogged from the rain. The sky is still overcast, and an occasional drop splatters the wet pavement.

"Oh yeah?" I ask.

"I mean, I know about your little tiff with Baron this morning, but it's the Ridgedale game, the second biggest game after Faulkner. If you want to be in the middle of everything, then you can't skip the most important part."

"I figured you'd be here to convince me not to go," I say. "Since my status threatens yours."

"I'm sorry I didn't join you at lunch," she says. "You know I would if I could. But I have too much to lose, Harper. I've worked way too hard to get where I am. I can't just give it up."

"Because then you endured the Dolce hazing for nothing."

She shrugs apologetically. "That doesn't mean I don't agree with you. There should be room for a girl at the top, too. Not just one. And not just because she's Royal's girlfriend, or I guess Baron's girlfriend."

"Not a Dolce girl."

"Exactly," she says. "Someone there on their own merit."

"So you want to overthrow the monarchy for a meritocracy?"

"I mean… If anyone deserves that spot, it's you. You earned it."

"You have no idea," I mutter.

"Football is the real king in this town," she says, arriving at her car and peeling a few wet leaves from the door before opening it. "The Dolce boys were here almost a year before me, but from what I understand, they were more like thugs and bullies that year. They were outsiders who they came charging in and breaking shit, including the Darlings, who were very much the darlings of the town. A lot of people hated the Dolces. It wasn't until the next year, when they played football, that they became gods."

The sky begins to spit rain again, and Gloria ducks into her car. "Just think about it," she calls before closing the door and starting the engine.

I have another one of those startling moments, like when Josie wrote me off a rich bitch because of my clothes, where I miss being poor. Now I have this amazing car—which I'm so grateful for—but it's also isolating. Last year, I always rode with the Dolce boys. I was part of their crowd. Sometimes I rode with just Royal, if we were going to the river to fuck. If he had a late practice or something going on, or I wanted to hang out with Gloria, I rode with her. Now, this is where we part ways.

I wave as she drives away, then hurry to my fancy new Escalade. I climb inside, a little shiver of loneliness running through me. I have friends, but I miss the friendship that developed in the little moments in Lo's car—opening ketchup packets for her fries while she was driving; turning up some old *Just 5 Guys* song and singing along at the top of our lungs, then laughing because we both knew all the words; the random conversations about our dads and her old dog and our exes... Conversations that made us know each other better.

Colt and Dixie come running through the light rain toward my car, their hands linked, both of them laughing. My heart clenches in my chest. The Ridgeline beside me beeps as it unlocks, and they release each other's hands and scramble up inside.

I roll down my window, and Dixie sees me and opens the passenger side window of Colt's truck. "Of course Preston got me a spot next to you," I say to Colt.

Dixie looks back and forth between us, and I'm glad she doesn't know this gossip. Not sure even Royal's attachment to me could overcome rumors that I fucked my cousin.

SELENA

"Hey, you know who has an old jersey or two lying around?" Dixie asks. "I mean, if you're going to the game…"

"I am," I say.

Gloria's right. Even Baron's right. A guy couldn't come in and say he was king and then not go to the games. Football is the center of everything, and I can't expect to be in the middle of things and then not show up to the games. If I want to be queen, I can't just look the part. I have to play the part. I can't just show up when I feel like it, when it's comfortable for me. I have to show up for everyone, be their voice, their leader, even if I don't see myself that way.

"Not gonna wear Gideon Delacroix's jersey?" Colt asks, a shit-eating grin on his face as he rests his forearm on the wheel and leans forward to see me around Dixie.

"Fuck off," I say. "And please don't spread baseless rumors around school. There's nothing going on with me and Gideon."

"Ah, the poor guy just wants to lose his V-card," Colt says. "Throw him a bone." He winks at me before starting the engine. Dixie waves and rolls up the window, and I follow them out, done with my pity party.

I think about Colt's words. Apparently, everyone knows Gideon has a thing for me now, either because they think that must be the reason he joined us at lunch, or because he's that obvious, or because people just like gossip. They don't know where I fit, but if I'm with Gideon, it makes sense. I'm not a wildcard anymore. I have a place.

I don't want to endanger him, but I don't belong to Royal anymore. The thought sits funny inside me. I'm not the kind of girl who wants to be owned by anyone, and I fought Royal's claim tooth and nail last year. But once we were together, when it wasn't about being his property but about being his girl... Fuck yeah, I liked it.

I liked being claimed by him. It made me feel protected and important and powerful and cherished. Especially when we were fucking. I didn't want to be called *a* slut, but when he called me *his* slut... Nothing made me cum harder. I was a slut for him, and it was hot as hell.

But that was last year. I'm not that basic bitch anymore. I'm no longer Royal's plaything.

SELENA

Baron might point out the social advantage of us teaming up and pretending we're together, but he doesn't like me. He won't kick Gideon's ass for asking me out. Hell, he'd probably like it if I dated a football player. He'd think it got me under control. But I could do a lot from that position.

Maybe this girl—New Harper, Harper-Maybe-Darling, Miss A—could like a nice boy.

The thought is so ludicrous I almost laugh. After what I've been through, I can't date some sweet, idealistic, unsuspecting boy. I have way too much trauma and drama to unpack on any man, let alone a good, normal one. He would either run for the hills the minute I told him, or he'd stay, and I'd destroy him. And that's the last thing I want to do to a good man.

The only man I could risk would be someone as fucked up as me.

Like Royal, whispers a little voice in the back of my head.

I shake the thought away. I'm done with Royal. He's done with me. But yeah, maybe someday, I'll be ready to try again. Not with Royal, but someone like him.

BROKEN DOLL

Someone as fucked up as me, like one of the other Dolce boys, or even a Darling boy, once the DNA test comes back and proves we're not a match. Not that I want to be with one of the Dolce fuckboys who raped me, or even Preston. But there are other men out there as fucked up—convicts and gangsters and the men at the Saturday fights.

Maybe that's why my mother always chooses rough men, why it never works out with the nice ones even when she tries. Not because that's all she can get, but because that's the kind of man who can handle her damage.

At home, I open my closet and look at all the preppy designer clothes Preston bought me. I sift through them until I reach the back of my closet, where my own clothes hang—thrift store finds, hand-me-downs from people my mother has worked with, and an occasional splurge from after a good fight. At the very back, where I hoped my mom wouldn't find it, hangs a black leather jacket I've never worn.

I take it out and pull it on. It's too big for me, but just a little, so it still looks cool. Preston must have left it at his childhood home when he moved out because it was too small for him. I remember finding it in his closet, pulling it

SELENA

on, wondering why there were no mirrors in the room so I could see how it looked on me.

Now I know why. I know why he had paintings above his dresser instead of a mirror.

I sit on the edge of the bed and text him.

"Can we talk?"

A message comes back a minute later. *"Sure. Pick u up at 5?"*

"Can't tonight. I'm going to the game."

I wait a few minutes, but he doesn't answer. He must be pissed about my choices, thinking I'm going to cheer for the men who destroyed him. After all he's done for me, he has every right to be angry.

But I have every right to live my life the way I want, not the way he thinks I should.

I eat dinner, feeling more guilty with every bite I take. This is food Royal bought us. Yet another person who tried to buy my loyalty. It's never over with these two families. Even if the DNA test comes back and proves I'm not a Darling, I'm not sure I'll ever get out of the spot they've made for me, right between their warring families. I'm so fucking sick of it.

I'm not proud or stupid enough to throw away dinner just because Royal bought it, though. Girls like me don't waste food. We never know where the next meal is coming from.

That's not literally true—we have enough food for a few more weeks. But after that… It's anyone's guess. So, I won't waste something that will stretch this time of plenty for one more meal. Mom quit her job, and Royal quit me. If I piss off Preston, he's not going to pay for groceries, either. Looks like my time off from the Slaughterpen is about to come to an end. Which means I better get all the status I can out of the last few football games I'll get to attend.

I brush my teeth, throw on some makeup, and head to Ridgedale.

If you can't beat 'em, join 'em and all that shit.

Showing up at an away game means more than a home game, and this will prove my loyalty to football and therefore the entire school. It proves that I want to play the game, not just ruin things. People fear the unknown, so I have to be familiar, show them that I'm not going to make things worse. I'm not going to repeat what the Dolces did when they arrived.

Plus, I don't play football, so I can't be a star and convince everyone that replacing their kings is in their best interest.

I'm in line for snacks when someone taps on my shoulder. I turn around and see one of the last people on earth I want to see—Mr. Dolce. My heart shoots into overdrive, and I suddenly can't remember how to swallow. Does he know what his sons did to me?

"Harper?" he says, blinking at me a few times, like he didn't expect it to be me even though he's the one who got my attention. Maybe he knows what they did, but not that I lived through it.

"Hi, Mr. Dolce," I say stiffly.

He swallows, frowning down at me. "You changed your hairstyle."

Fuck. He's not surprised to see me alive. He thought I could be his daughter.

I imagine what that must be like for him, for all of them. How many times he's tapped on the shoulder of a short, curvy woman with long straight hair. How many times the impossible, intoxicating hope has risen in his chest for the split second before she turns around and shows him a face he doesn't know. How the pain can never really heal, can never really end, because they never found a body. Even though they had a funeral for an empty casket, there's still that one bead of cruel hope that remains suspended like a raindrop that never falls.

"I'm sorry," I say, my throat tight.

His eyes fixate on my chest, and I take a step back, my skin crawling. I know he's a perv, but eye-fucking the tits of a girl he just thought was his daughter is next level.

"Where'd you get that necklace?" he asks.

And then I feel like a colossal dick for thinking he was looking at my tits.

I hook my finger through the chain, pulling the charm away from my skin. I could tell him it's none of his fucking business, and to go creep on some girl who hasn't fucked his sons, but I feel bad for the guy, so I just lie instead. "I don't remember."

SELENA

"Can I see it?" he asks, stepping closer again. I can't back up without hitting the next person in line.

"Why?" I ask, my fist closing around the diamond ballerina charm.

"My daughter had a necklace exactly like that." His eyes meet mine, his gaze hard. In that moment, it's easy to see where the rumors about the mafia got started. He's scary as fuck, and I'm not immune. I don't do parents. I don't like cops or authority figures or other powerful adults. He's not just a man who lost his daughter. He's a man who made his son into a whore to benefit his business, manipulating him by threatening his younger siblings to gain his cooperation. He's a man whose own daughter sent a letter to the police saying that he orchestrated Royal's kidnapping, the event that probably made Royal the monster I know, the one who would go on to repeat the cycle against me.

"You think I stole from you?" I ask. "That while I was at your house, I went into your dead daughter's room and went through her jewelry box and stole this?"

Mr. Dolce cocks his head to one side. "Did you?"

There's something so repulsively familiar about him that it sends a chill down my spine.

Is it because he looks exactly like Baron, minus the glasses and plus twenty-odd years? Or because he looks exactly like Royal, minus six inches and plus those years? I didn't just fuck Royal. I loved him. And he's a product of this man every bit as much as I'm a product of my mother. I should never have fucked with this family, never have taken the scholarship in exchange for getting in with them, never have expected anything less than what happened to me when Royal found out my betrayal.

Suddenly, I feel dizzy and sick, and I wish I hadn't eaten that food. I keep repeating the words I said to Royal.

Monsters make monsters make monsters. It never ends.

"Fuck you," I say to Mr. Dolce, turning back to the concession stand, where it's finally my turn.

"That could be arranged," he says quietly.

I pretend not to hear as I order popcorn and a drink I no longer want. All I want is to turn and run away, to run back to my shelter, my savior, the other Mr. D. But I don't know if Preston would open the door if I came knocking.

SELENA

My hands are shaking when I take my food. I take a step away, but Mr. Dolce steps in front of me. "Did Royal give it to you?" he asks.

I stare up into his eyes, and I feel that monster inside me, the one Royal put there. The monster he made, that was made by his father before him.

The crowd shifts at the concession stand, and Mr. Dolce waves them to go on, skipping his place in line. A few people give us curious glances, and he steps further from the crowd, drawing me with him like some sick magnet. Why can't I walk away from this whole fucked up family and be done? Why are they still a part of me, even when I've exorcized Royal's demon?

The rest of them are still there, spiders watching me fight against their sticky web until I exhaust myself and become easy prey.

"You. Don't. Deserve. Him." I grit out the words one at a time, glaring my hatred back at Mr. Dolce, wishing I could hit him the way I hit Baron, knock him the fuck out right here in front of everyone. But I'd be arrested. He's a powerful man with connections to everyone from the governor right down to the boys who run my school. And I'm a girl like me.

"You think you're protecting him?" he asks, cocking his head again. "From me?"

"I think somebody needs to."

Mr. Dolce stares at me like he doesn't understand the meaning of my words. Maybe he doesn't. Maybe he doesn't know how much I know about his sons. Maybe he doesn't even know some of the things I know.

"After what he did to you," Mr. Dolce marvels aloud, shaking his head and staring at me with a mixture of disbelief and something way too fucking close to admiration.

So, they did tell him. Shame burns through me, silencing any smart retort on my tongue.

"And what you did to him," Mr. Dolce says. "How could someone who claims to love a man do such a thing?"

I stand there like a scolded child while he walks away. I reach for the anger I felt just minutes ago, but all I feel is a cold knot in my belly. I've never been so ashamed. He has every right to hate me, to do more than scold me, for what I did to his beautiful, broken son. Maybe Mr. Dolce is a

SELENA

monster, but that doesn't mean he can't love his children, despite what he's done to them. I'm the last person who should be passing judgment.

I'm the one who doesn't deserve Royal.

BROKEN DOLL

forty-one

Harper Apple

Dixie and Quinn call to me, rushing over all full of excitement. I barely hear their chatter as they convey me toward the stands. I feel as if I've lifted out of my body. They run onto the field, waving goodbye. I buy one of the cheap plastic ponchos someone is selling, and I sit in the bleachers with the other Willow Heights students. I cheer for their gods as they slide around on the field in the drizzling rain until they're all so covered in mud it's hard to tell what color their jerseys are. I'm here, I'm doing what I need to do, but it all feels fake and strange and just a bit off, as if I've detached from myself and can't quite snap back. I guess that's what being a fake is.

Last year, I was popular in a weird way. Everyone knew I was Royal's. He'd come over and talk to me at halftime. I

SELENA

wore his jersey like the other Dolce girls and sometimes his letter jacket to show I was his. The other girls admired and envied me, but not because of anything I did. They admired me because of Royal. I don't have Royal this year, so no one quite understands my place. I could move on to Baron like he said, and no one would dare call me a slut for jumping from one brother to another. Not if I was Baron's girl.

That's what Gloria would do.

But fuck that straight to hell. I don't want popularity nearly enough to let that sadistic psycho lay a hand on me ever again.

When the game is over, Gloria and her sisters drag me with them to the afterparty. We're early, so we get drinks and sit on the screened in porch on the back of the house. By the time we finish our drinks, I feel more normal.

"So, what's up with you and Gideon?" I ask Everleigh, who's on her second drink already.

"Ugh, there she goes again," Eleanor says, rolling her eyes. "Why are you always all up on our men?"

"Is he your man, though?" I ask.

"No," Eleanor says, scowling at me. "I'm with DeShaun. Are you going to try to steal him next?"

"He's a person, not a handbag," I say. "I can't steal him. If he dumps you, it's probably because he's realized he's too good for you."

"Ugh, I hate her," Eleanor says, turning to Gloria. "Why are we hanging with her again? She's such a slut."

"Pretty sure my body count is within the same range as yours," I say. "So you might want to find some other way to insult me."

Eleanor goes off in a huff, and Everleigh flops back on the patio sofa. "Me and Gideon are just talking," she says. "Are y'all talking, too?"

"No," I say. "I just heard you were maybe hanging out."

"Well, now that he's at the big boy table, I get to sit there, too," she says. "I never got to sit there last year."

"That's why you like him?" I ask. "Because he sits at the best table?"

"No," she says slowly. "Because *I* get to sit at the best table."

SELENA

I want to tell her how fucked up that is, but a big cheer goes up from inside.

The football players have arrived.

The Walton girls squeal and bounce to their feet. "Come on," Gloria says, grabbing my hand and pulling me up. "Time for the next game."

We head inside, where the kitchen is filled with football players clustered around three kegs, and fans fawning over them. I catch Duke's eye, and he holds up his red cup to me. I smile and mouth "good game," to him, tipping my cup back at him. Why not? He kissed my feet. He's tried to navigate the tension between me and his brother, and of course he's going to take Baron's side, but he also voted me into the Swans.

I get a beer and make my way over, and he high-fives me and pulls me in for a hug, lifting my feet off the ground. When he sets me down, someone else wants a high five, and he tucks me under his arm while he talks to the guy, and then a girl, and then another guy. I get this disconcerting sense of *déjà vous* as I stand beside him, letting him hold me against him the way Royal used to. It's a casual posture, almost like he's forgotten I'm there, but overtly possessive, too, and completely presumptuous. To anyone looking, we're a couple who's so comfortable together they'd never question it.

I ease out from under his arm, and he looks down at me. For a second, I think he'll pull me back, but he turns to some girl who's blonder and wearing less clothes. I duck out onto the screened porch, which is huge and now full of people. Leaning against the wall, I sip my drink and watch the crowd. I spot Dixie talking to some friends, and Gloria and Rylan in a corner arguing quietly. There are a lot of Willow Heights kids, but a lot of people I don't know, too. Colt said there would be Faulkner kids here. It strikes me that I've never met more than half the kids at Faulkner High, the two lower grades who've started since I changed schools.

They aren't my people anymore.

Suddenly, my gaze jerks back to the person I just scanned over as I was staring off. Royal Dolce is leaning against the railing inside the screen, watching me.

My heart flips, and for a second, forgets how to beat.

SELENA

I close my eyes, sure that when I open them, it'll be someone else, the way he must see his sister in a crowd now and again, only to realize it's a stranger.

But it's not a stranger. He's still there.

Our eyes meet, and I swallow so hard I nearly choke on my own tongue.

What is wrong with me? Why is my heart hammering, and not with fear?

God, I'm a fucking mess.

"Hey."

I tear my gaze away from Royal to find a safe boy standing a few steps away.

"Hey, Gideon," I say, trying to shake off the weirdness of seeing Royal here. He lives in my town. We run in the same crowd. Lots of the parties last year had a mix of high school kids and graduates, those who go to the local colleges, and those who get jobs right out of school. Which means I'm bound to run into him now and again, even if he's not doing it intentionally anymore. One day, maybe he'll be just some guy I pass in the grocery store and pretend not to know.

The idea aches in the pit of my stomach, cold and deep.

"You look… Really cool," Gideon says, glancing at my leather jacket.

"Thanks," I say, holding out my cup. "Congrats on the win."

He bumps his cup against mine before leaning on the wall beside me. I can feel Royal's eyes boring into us, but I don't look in his direction again.

"Are you having fun?" Gideon asks.

"Sure," I say, stepping away from the wall so I can turn my back on Royal, since he's being a total creeper and openly staring. "You?"

"It's my first time hosting, and my parents aren't really cool with this sort of thing, so I'm a little afraid of what the cleanup is going to be like," Gideon says. "But I hired a crew to come in tomorrow, so hopefully we can pull it off without them finding out."

"Ah, so this is a big night for you," I say. "A rite of passage."

"Yeah," he says, nodding. "Kind of."

I take a drink and fight the urge to turn around, to make sure Royal is still far away, where I need him to be.

SELENA

"What about you?" Gideon asks. "You're a senior. You must have hosted some of these. Tell me the aftermath isn't like in the movies."

My mind flashes to the shell of the Darling house we left last year, the house that belonged to his aunt and cousins. Then his words sink in. This guy was a freshman last year, and he sat at the adjoining table, so he was on the periphery of the group. He saw me on Royal's arm, and I'm sure we went to the same parties. But he must not know who I am—not really. At least, he doesn't know I'm poor. I wear the same thing as all the rich kids this year. I carry a fancy bag and drive a nice car. He thinks I'm some rich bitch.

I try to picture even a quarter of these people crammed into my smoky, derelict old house, and I have to fight back laughter.

"It's usually not too bad," I say, deciding I don't really need him to know I live on Mill Street or that these aren't my clothes.

"So, listen," Gideon says, shifting uncomfortably against the wall. "Homecoming's in a couple weeks, and I was wondering if…"

"Gideon," I say, holding up a hand. "I... No. I can't. But thank you. Really. You're, like, the best guy I've ever met, and you're insanely brave, like, you have no idea how brave you are to even ask me. But I can't."

"Why not?"

It's not Gideon who asks. I flinch, squeezing my eyes closed. When I open them, Gideon is staring over my head. I don't have to turn to know Royal is standing there. But I do, because I'm scared for my new friend. Royal doesn't look pissed, like he might put the sophomore through the wall, though. He towers over me, a slightly confrontational glint in his eye, but he doesn't make a move toward Gideon.

"How long have you been standing there?" I ask.

"Long enough."

Gideon's gaze moves back to me and then to Royal and then back to me. "I'm sorry," he stammers. "I—Gloria said you broke up. I had no idea."

"We did," I say firmly. "We're not together."

"That's right," Royal says, sipping from his drink. I know it's his first one, that over the next few hours, he'll nurse one or two more, nowhere near enough to affect a guy his size.

SELENA

Royal doesn't get drunk. He doesn't lose control. I hate that I still know him so well, that I know him at all.

"Look, I think you're great," I say to Gideon. "And I know a lot of other girls do, too. I hope this won't screw up our lunch thing, but if you don't want to be part of it, I totally understand."

Royal just stands over us, not saying a word. I glare at him, but he has no expression whatsoever on his face, and he makes no move to leave.

"It's okay," Gideon says. "You don't have to explain it. I knew it was a long shot."

"I'm... Just not ready to date anyone yet," I say. "Or even go to Homecoming. I'm sorry, Gideon." I lean in and give him a quick kiss on the cheek, and he turns beet red.

"It's okay," he says again, edging away from the wall. "I'll... See you Monday."

He ducks inside, and I feel like the biggest asshole on earth.

Royal chuckles. "That was fun. Want to do it again? There's another kid over there who was checking out your ass when you walked in."

I sigh and turn to him. "What are you doing?"

"Mingling."

I glare at him. "So, you're just going to follow me around chasing off any guys who ask me out?"

"Oh, you think I'm being protective of you?" he asks, drawing back. "No, Cherry Pie. I'm protecting the poor unsuspecting freshmen mice from being eaten alive by a Darling snake."

"He's a sophomore, and I think you know that."

"Sixteen," he says, sipping his drink and looking down at me with hooded eyes. "That's your family's favorite age, isn't it?"

"Guess we're back to hating each other."

"I never stopped hating you."

I gaze back into his eyes, but there's nothing there. He's not the hollow-eyed boy who almost killed me the first time we met, but he's completely closed off in a way I haven't seen in a long time, since before I really knew him. It's his cool, indifferent mask, as obscuring as the one Preston wears.

"Good," I say lightly. "I hate you, too."

SELENA

"Why are you here?" he asks. "Baron said you were done with the football crowd."

"You wouldn't have come if you knew I'd be here?" I ask, feeling unaccountably hurt.

Which is stupid. Of course he didn't want to see me.

"I do my best to avoid places where your kind are present."

I roll my eyes and don't bite on that one. But two can play this game. "I saw your dad tonight," I say, giving him a little smirk.

"Yup," he says, sounding zero percent surprised. "He never misses a game. Sacrifices every Friday night for the twins, and now every Saturday for my games. My perfect, doting dad."

I quirk a brow. "I thought you'd be upset that we talked."

He smirks down at me. "Why? You already know all my secrets."

The statement hangs in the air between us. What I would have given for his secrets last year. Now I know them, and he has no reason to want to keep me away from his dad. More than that, I mean nothing to him. He doesn't care if his dad hits on me, if I fuck his dad. After all, he's never going to want me again. Not after he let his brothers take turns with me, and they brought a friend to join. Royal's way too possessive to want to be with a girl who's been with his brothers. He hated that I'd been with a couple guys before we even met.

"I didn't tell Preston," I say quietly.

Royal fixes those unflinching, hooded eyes on me, tipping his chin up to look down his nose at me like the superior asshole he is. "Tell him what?"

I glance around to make sure no one can overhear. "What happened to you."

He holds my gaze a long minute, then lifts his beer to his lips and takes a sip.

"What?" I ask.

Royal takes a step forward, backing me against the wall where Gideon stood. He shucks me under the chin, bringing my gaze to his. For a second, we just stare at each other. Then he gives a little snort of breath. "And I didn't tell the twins what happened to you, Harper. And yet, somehow they seem to know. Funny how that works, isn't it?"

SELENA

He turns and pushes through the crowd on the porch and out the screen door, letting it slam behind him. I stand there reeling from his words.

He can't mean what I think he means. There's no way.

No.

Preston would never. He might be cold, but he isn't violent.

But was the old Preston?

I think of how different he is online, as Mr. D, and my stomach lurches like I might be sick.

I try to get a grip on myself. Yes, Preston is a dick online. He's bold and demanding, but he never asked me to hurt anyone. Being a voyeur who likes to hear about someone else's sexual exploits doesn't make him a rapist. It makes him sad and creepy. I understand what made him that way, though.

What Royal's saying he did...

No way.

Suddenly, Preston's words in that gazebo come back to me. He told me what he did to their sister, the thing he tried to do that the Dolce boys succeeded in doing to me. What was it he said?

I'd never have let anyone from the team touch her... I might have, though.

The beer in my stomach churns. I close my eyes and try to breathe, feeling the plastic cup crumple in my fingers, the cold liquid sliding over my skin.

I shove away from the wall, pushing through the people in front of me without seeing them, out the back door and down the steps. My feet slide on the wet grass, the soft earth. Drizzle splatters onto the shoulders of Preston's leather jacket. I stop and suck in a few breaths, bracing my hands on my knees, until the familiar scent of marijuana smoke reaches me. I straighten and move toward one of the huge oak trees in the backyard, hating myself for caring, for still being drawn to him. He's a magnet, and he filled me with shards of jagged metal so I can never, never stop going to him.

When I reach the tree, I see him sitting in a rope swing, watching me approach in the dark. Fat drops of water fall

SELENA

from the leaves onto us, but the drizzle is kept out by the thick leaf cover.

"Why'd you tell me that?" I demand. "Why do you have to keep making it worse?"

"Why do you keep talking to me when you know that's what will happen?" Royal asks, his voice quiet in the darkness.

"I can't help it," I admit, the words coming out strangled. "I can't get away from you even when you leave me alone. You're in my head, in my blood, in my nightmares."

"I know." Royal lights the joint, takes a drag, and hands it to me.

I take it with shaking fingers, relishing the dank smoke in my lungs, the way it stops the spiraling, careening thoughts. I lean against the thick, wet trunk of the tree and lay my head back, closing my eyes. Then I take another deep drag, not caring about etiquette right now, when I'm about to completely lose it if I don't find something to calm me down. It's either this, or I'm going to have to go find a razor and open my skin to release the pressure, and god knows what Gideon would do if he found me spilling the truth of my blood in one of his pristine bathrooms.

"You know the worst part about it?" I ask. "I can't move on. I can't just pretend it didn't happen and go about my life like I did before. Even if I wanted to, I couldn't date some nice, normal guy like Gideon. I don't know what normal is anymore. I don't know how to function around functional people."

"I know."

"How'd you do it?" I ask, handing the joint back at last.

"You think I'm going to give you advice on how to act normal when you fuck some other guy?"

"You know what, fuck you," I say, pushing off the tree. "Yes, I do want that, because you owe me that fucking much, Royal. Maybe the same thing happened to us both, but the difference is, I didn't even know you existed when that happened to you. You did this to me, Royal. *You* broke me."

"And I moved the fucking world for you trying to make it right. You threw it back in my face and told me to leave you alone. What did I do then? I respected your wishes. You're the one who followed me out here."

"You chased away a guy who was interested."

The flame of his lighter flickers on, and he tilts his face, lighting up and taking a long, deep drag. The firelight flickers over the angular features of his face, so beautiful it's not fucking fair.

"I'm not helping you hook up with someone else," he says through a mouthful of smoke. "I'm done granting your wishes. I'm not your fucking genie."

I remember Mr. D calling himself that in one of our first conversations. He asked my three wishes. Now I know the price of those three wishes. Nothing in life is free, after all.

"I didn't ask for a genie," I tell Royal. "I asked for advice, because as fucked up as it is, the person who did this to me is the only person I know who's been there. And now there's not a man on this earth who's going to want to deal with my baggage. I'm too damaged for anyone to ever want me."

"Good."

Some stupid little part of me is so pathetic that it wishes he'd contradict me, tell me I'm wrong, that someone still could. But of course he doesn't. He doesn't think I deserve anyone's desire. He's glad no one wants me, that everyone will see me as trash, the way he always did.

"Then tell me how to fake it," I growl. "Obviously you did it. Everyone still wants your dick."

"You don't."

"I did," I shoot back. "I didn't care about your damage until it ruined me, too."

Royal stands and tosses the roach into the mud. "You think it didn't ruin me, too? You think you're the only one who gets to regret that we ever met? That it's not torture for me to see you, too? At least I didn't give up. I fucking tried, Harper."

"Tried what? To make things right?"

"Yes," he says, his eyes full of misery. "You want to know when it'll be over? Get it through your head, Harper. It's never over. You said so yourself. You just keep going because you don't have a choice. Stop trying to move on. You can't."

He storms past me toward the house.

SELENA

I swallow hard, shaking my head. "No," I say, turning around.

He stops, the rain streaking his back, and lowers his head.

"You're wrong," I say, forcing the words past the ache in my throat. "It ends when someone forgives."

"And we both know that's impossible," he says quietly.

"No," I say. "It's possible if you make it possible."

He doesn't move for a minute. Rain drips through the leaves onto my face, running down my cheeks like tears.

"I can't," he says after a minute.

"I can," I say, my throat aching as I force the words out. "I forgive you."

My eyes sting, but I don't care. I'm doing this, even if it hurts. For him, and for me, and for this whole fucked up town.

"Why would you do that?" Royal asks at last, his voice empty, his back still turned.

"Because holding onto this isn't going to help anyone," I say. "It hurts you, and more than that, it hurts me. It isn't making me happy, and it never will. It doesn't matter if you deserve it or even if you apologize. I will never think what you did is okay. But I can forgive you because I don't want to carry this around anymore. I can let it go because it's the only way to let *you* go."

"You'd forgive me just to get away from me?"

"Yes," I say. "There's enough hatred in this town without me adding more. I've seen what it did to you. To your family. To the Darlings. I don't want to live like that. I don't want to be that kind of person. I don't want it to turn me into a monster like you."

He doesn't say anything.

I swallow past the ache in my throat. "And maybe because even though you did all those things for me, you never once asked me to forgive you."

"What do you want me to do?" he asks after a long pause, as if he thinks he has to keep going, keep trying to earn something I've already given. After all, in his world, the penance never ends, either. That's why he goes back.

"I want you to move on," I say. "I don't want to be another basement, another bridge for you to come back to. I don't want to be anyone's regret. Just go. Find some normal girl, and try to make her happy, and don't take this out on

SELENA

her. Stop repeating the cycle. That's how it ends. That's all I want."

"And you'll forgive me, just like that."

"Yes," I say, drawing a shaky breath. "At least, I'll start to. I think it'll be more of a process than a one-and-done kind of thing. But I'll let go of the idea that I can never forgive you, and I'll let the process begin. I'll work on it, work to make myself better instead of making you suffer. That's the best I can do right now."

Royal lifts his face to the rain and takes a deep breath. "Okay."

I sink onto the swing and watch him walk away, and I know I should feel relief because I let go of this burden and forgave, but all I feel is empty. I watch him walk up the steps and onto the porch. Gloria stumbles over to him, obviously drunk. He plucks the drink out of her hand, downs it, and then tosses the cup. She starts to protest, but he wraps his arms around her and kisses her.

I can't breathe.

I know that kiss. I know the way it consumes you, makes you feel like the only thing he'll ever need, like you're more than air, more than human, more than you've ever been before. It makes my toes curl in my damp boots and my breath catch. I don't blame her for raising her arms and sliding a small hand behind his neck after a minute, holding onto him while his big hands circle her little waist, making her feel small and protected. I don't blame her for what happens next.

My chest caves in slowly, but I hardly feel it. Tears blur my eyes, but I don't look away. Not even when he draws away, takes her hand, and pulls her toward the door, and they disappear inside the house together.

I tell myself what I've been telling myself all summer.

I can't break more than I'm already broken.

SELENA

forty-two

Harper Apple

I don't know how long I sit there. I don't hear the party inside, the voices, the chime when a few notifications go off on my phone, or the steady thrum of the rain. I don't see the big house with the manicured bushes along the back, below the screened porch. I don't smell the rain and the dirt, wet asphalt and leaves. And I don't feel anything.

The next thing I notice is someone walking across the grass toward me, his silhouette cast by the lights in the house behind him. He's big, but I know it's not Royal. I know the way Royal moves, the deliberate way he places his feet.

Even when he gets closer, I don't look at him. I don't care who it is. It doesn't matter.

He pulls a crumpled plastic poncho from his pocket and lays it at the base of the tree and sits. I see the light glint off his glasses, but I'm not scared.

"Rylan's gone apeshit because he can't find Gloria," Baron says, his voice totally devoid of concern, like he's just making conversation.

"You think he'll hurt Royal?" I ask.

"If I thought he'd hurt Royal, I wouldn't be out here."

I nod. We sit in silence for a minute, and the sounds fill in around us. I notice that my hair is soaked, that I can feel cold water running down my scalp and into the neck of my jacket.

"How'd you know I was out here?"

"I always know where you are," he says. "Call me Stalker Boy."

"I thought you were Evil Genius Boy, or Drug Chemist Boy, or Psycho Boy."

"I wear many hats."

A cheer goes up from in the house, and some guys start whooping and hollering. They're probably doing keg stands or taking body shots. I don't care.

"But *why* are you out here?" I ask Baron.

SELENA

"Don't worry, I'll sit with Royal and his regret when he's done fucking Gloria," he says. "Right now, you're more interesting."

"How do you know he'll regret it?"

"The same way I know you're sitting here regretting whatever just went down that sent him back to her," Baron says. He shifts against the tree to dig something out of his pocket, and in some detached way, I hope it's a joint. It's just one of his fucking suckers, though. He starts unwrapping it, the crinkling plastic noises adding to the dripping rain and the party sounds inside.

I push my toes against the soggy earth, making the swing move in tiny circles. I picture little boy Gideon out on this swing with the wooden seat that's soaked my ass and the long ropes rising to the branches high above, hidden in the dense foliage.

"I'm not sure regret it the right word," I say.

Baron pauses with his sucker halfway to his mouth and cocks his head to one side. In my mind, his face blurs with his father's. "Are you crying?"

I wipe my cheek, but my fingers were already wet. "I don't know. It's raining."

Baron puts his sucker in, leans his head back against the tree trunk, and looks up into the black cloud of leaves. "I wonder that, too, sometimes. Like, how do you know if you're really feeling the right thing, or if your brain has just told you that's the right thing to feel, so you think you're feeling it?"

I manage a small, empty laugh. "I don't think normal people have to ask."

"But we're not normal, are we?" He lifts his head, and we stare at each other for a minute.

My pulse speeds up, and I have to swallow the fear rising inside me, to remind myself what I do every day.

He cannot hurt me more.

My voice comes out in a whisper. "No."

That may be true, but I don't know the right thing to feel at all. I'm just drowning in all of it at once. I'm not wondering if I'm really feeling or just thinking. I'm feeling way too fucking much right now. Anger, hurt, fear, resentment, frustration, shame, love, jealousy, regret… They hit me like a spray of bullets, all of them mangling me until I don't know what I'm supposed to feel because they're all mixed up in there at once. I wish it was as simple as Baron makes it sound, that my brain would just pluck out the right one and tell me that's how I need to feel.

"A normal person wouldn't let her boyfriend go fuck some other girl right in front of her face," Baron says, but there's a question in his words, like he's guessing at them.

"Royal's not my boyfriend."

"Does it matter what you call it?" Baron asks, studying me from behind his glasses. "You love him. Even I can see that."

"What?" I ask, willing him to take the words back, as if that will somehow make them untrue.

"When we were in that basement, I really wanted you to give in," he says. "I saw what was happening even if my idiot brothers couldn't. I think that's where it turns into a good thing, not feeling the way other people do. They don't feel with their brains, and it's like, when they catch feelings, their brains shut off. It's like when guys say they can only think with one head at a time."

"What are you talking about?"

"When Royal locked us in the basement together," he says. "He may have wanted to test you, but I wanted it to work. Not because I wanted to fuck you, but because I saw how you were in his head, so he wasn't thinking straight anymore. I knew he was falling for you, and I knew you were bad news."

"But I didn't fuck you," I say. "Not willingly."

"Yeah," Baron says. "But even now, when you're supposed to be the ruined plaything he tossed in the trash, he can't stop pulling you out and playing with you."

My fingers tighten on the wet ropes of the swing. "You're the one who told him I wouldn't be at this party. You must have known he wouldn't come if I was here. And you knew I'd be here. I think you're the one fucking with both of us."

He shrugs. "Why keep you apart? It's too late. I failed. We all failed."

"Failed at what? Protecting him from me?"

"He's been sucked into your orbit," he says. "You were a passing sun whose gravitational pull was strong enough to pull him out of his solar system and into yours. Now you're stuck with him. He can't leave you alone. But I think you know that, Jailbird. I think you knew all along that men like Royal don't love twice."

I squeeze my eyes shut and shake my head, as if I can unhear his words. Somehow, maybe because he's right and we're more alike than I care to admit, he's the one who always gets under my skin.

No, that's not true. Baron doesn't get under my skin. He peels away my layers of protection like he's skinning me alive. And then he casually walks by, sprinkling words like acid on my raw, exposed insides.

"No," I say. "Royal hates me."

"Maybe," Baron says. "But it's the kind of hate that makes a man crazy, that makes him kill a man for hurting you, bail you out of jail at three in the morning even though he's the one who got you thrown in, haunt the streets at night looking for your ghost when you're dead."

"He did that?" I ask, my heart beating hard against my ribs.

"What?"

"Got me out of jail."

"Who'd you think it was?"

I don't answer. I remember that night, when I texted Mr. D a hundred times begging him to bail me out. He said he'd do it in the morning, and then suddenly, I was released in the middle of the night. I thanked him for that, offered my fucking body for it. And he accepted that thanks, just like he did for pulling me out of the truck. But it wasn't Preston at all. It was Royal.

Royal, who said he'd moved worlds for me. What else has he done that I don't even fucking know about?

"You'll keep orbiting each other, your own little solar system with only two planets, until you stop fighting it," Baron says. "The longer you resist it, the more damage you'll do. Both of you."

"Not planets," I say, sitting up straight on the swing. What was it Preston said? That on a cloudy day, when a sunflower can't see the sun, it still follows the path. "Suns."

Baron just looks at me blankly. He doesn't know everything.

SELENA

"I have to go." I stand, and for a second, neither of us move. "Thank you," I say, and then I cross the lawn, climb the steps, and enter the house. The party's in full swing now. There's a beer pong game going on in the kitchen. Dixie, Gideon, some girls from the dance team, and a bunch of people I don't know are dancing to some eighties music under a disco ball in the foyer. I pass them and climb the stairs.

I find them in the third bedroom.

They didn't even bother to lock the door.

When I swing it open, Royal looks at me as if I'm a perfect stranger. I don't think I've ever seen his eyes so completely void, as if he's blacked-out drunk. I'm not sure he's seeing me at all, that he can focus. He doesn't move or react to me opening the door on them. He's lying on his back on the bed, his head propped on his arm on the pillows, and Gloria's head is bobbing up and down on his dick.

I stand there holding the knob, feeling like I'm as far outside my body as he looks.

I step inside and pull the door closed and turn the lock. Then I cross the room and climb onto the bed. Gloria's head pops up, and she stares at me for a second with a bleary, unfocused gaze.

"Go on," I say. "Don't stop on account of me."

She looks confused, so I lean down, pulling my wet hair aside, and run my tongue up the side of Royal's glorious cock.

It's just a dick, I tell myself. It's not special. It's just a blowjob. I've given hundreds of them. It doesn't matter if it's Royal. He's checked out.

Gloria smiles. "You're nasty," she says, but she gets back to work, scooting down so she's propped on one elbow. Then she leans in and starts along the other side of his cock, running her tongue up the other side. I match my movements with hers, stroking along the outside of his cock, then the bottom, then turning our heads to work our way up with small strokes from base to tip. I wrap my fingers around his thick shaft, lifting his cock so we can both get the head at once.

Royal doesn't make a sound.

SELENA

His tip is salty, and my tongue strokes over the soft skin of his cock and swipes Gloria's tongue. For a second, we battle to get more of him, both trying to get the head of his cock into our mouth first. I pull back, because Royal doesn't deserve what I can do for him, but when I see her mouth slide down over his cock, a flash of anger whips through me. I grab a fistful of Lo's hair and shove her head down hard. Her shriek of protest is cut off by a retching sound as she gags on him. That's what she gets for letting me walk in on her.

I hold her head down while she struggles to breathe for a minute just to make sure she gets the message. Finally, she grabs my hand, her fake nails biting through the skin as her struggles grow frantic. I pull her head up by the hair.

"What the fuck?" she snaps, shoving her messy hair back, her eyes red and full of tears from choking on Royal's cock.

"Don't say I didn't warn you."

She blinks at me, and something about the mascara tracks of her tears makes me realize who I'm talking to, how fucking hot she is. No wonder Royal chose her to move on with. Before she can get back on it, I wrap my fingers around his shaft and lift his thick cock to my lips. She leans down, too, but her eyes are on me. After one lick, I drop Royal's cock from between us. Our mouths collide, sloppy and wet. I bury my hands in Gloria's hair, licking inside her mouth, tasting Royal on her tongue.

"That better not be the taste of your pussy on his dick," I say, my breath coming short. My wet lips slide across her soft ones, and she shivers, swaying against me.

I rise, pulling her with me, so we're kneeling on either side of Royal. Then I kiss her again. She gives a startled little sound into my mouth when I pull her in roughly, deepening the kiss. I can taste the salt of his precum on her tongue, and it makes me lose my mind. I angle my head, pushing my tongue as deep as I can, sucking him from her mouth with a mixture of desire and fury. We battle for the taste, sucking and moaning and biting. Her nails dig into my arms, and my grip in her blonde hair tightens until I feel her suck in a breath.

Still on my knees, I crawl over Royal and push Gloria back on the bed. She falls back, her head hitting the pillow with a whoosh. I climb on top of her, straddling her hips and leaning down, wrapping one hand gently around her throat. Her lips are shiny, her eyes wide. I grip her hair, pulling her head back and kissing her again, my tongue fucking her soft little mouth. She lets out a breathy moan, and I adjust my position on top of her, rocking my thigh between hers.

I feel the bed shift when Royal moves, but I don't open my eyes. Gloria digs her hands into my wet hair, gripping my head and kissing me harder, lifting her hips to grind against my thigh. She's so small, so soft and fragile compared to a man. I hold her more gently, cradling her small body against mine.

The door slams, and Gloria drops her head back on the pillow, a giggle escaping her. "I guess my job here is done."

"Not unless you want it to be," I say, sliding my hand from her neck and down her body, tugging up her skirt. "I've only been with one girl, but I think I can get the job done."

I slide my hand between her legs, brushing the soft skin of her inner thigh with my fingertips before touching her through her panties. They're wet, and it makes me wet. I press my knees together as I pull aside the fabric and slide a finger through the slippery lips of her shaved cunt.

Our eyes meet, and hers grow serious. "Harper?"

"Want to keep going?" I whisper against her lips, sinking a finger slowly into her. My pulse is fluttering like a trapped moth in my throat, and heat licks between my thighs. She's hot and so wet I wonder if Royal already came inside her.

She bites her lip, then shakes her head. I kiss her one more time, letting my lips linger in her soft, warm kiss before I draw away. I slide my finger from her and pull her skirt down. "Sorry."

She sits up and rubs her lips together, tossing her messy hair back and running her fingers through it to get it under control. "Well, I guess I can cross '*kissing a girl*' off my high school bucket list."

"I should have asked you first," I say. "I know you're not into girls. I didn't mean for that to happen. I got carried away."

"You meant for Royal to join us?" she asks with a grin.

"No," I say, gathering my wet hair and pulling it up into a bun. "That's not why I came in here."

"Then why did you?"

"I… don't remember," I admit. "It's possible I lost my head when I saw his dick in your mouth."

"I'm not mad about it," she says with a sly little grin, reaching out to grab the front of my wet leather jacket. She pulls me in and kisses me again, but I can tell she's not into it, that she's just playing around. After a minute, she pulls away and climbs off the bed. "This was fun, but I should go. Let you sort things out. I've got more than enough of my own shit to figure out."

When she's gone, I sit on the bed thinking about what Baron said. He's right. I will never be free, even after forgiving Royal. I keep trying to cut the ties, to cut him away, but he's still part of me. Not because of Royal himself, but because of me. Some terrible, twisted part of my heart still belongs to him. Our love may be infected with hate, poisoned and toxic, but it's still there. And even if I could somehow get rid of it, if I could shut myself off the way I did before, when I didn't feel anything, my mind wouldn't be free. Even if I never see his face again, I'll never stop going back to what happened, never stop reliving it and revisiting it the same way he goes to the bridge.

Some part of me never really left the swamp that night. Some part of me died there. Another part of me lives there still, caught in the nightmare of a night that never ended. And I don't know how to end it without ending everything.

SELENA

forty-three

Royal Dolce

I'm sitting at the top of the back staircase when I hear footsteps behind me. And because I'm so fucking turned around right now, I actually think for a second that it's Harper, even though I'm around the corner from the main hall, and she'd have to look to actually find me.

Of course Harper's not going to fucking seek me out. She's been running from me since I walked out of that swamp for the first time. Just because she walked in and stuck my dick in her mouth doesn't mean anything except that she's determined to finish driving me completely fucking insane, as if sending me videos of her fucking someone else didn't do the job. Just because she pulled Lo off my dick doesn't mean she wants to get on it. It means she's full of shit, and despite her big promises of forgiveness if I move on, she doesn't want me to move on with anyone else, not even someone comfortable and familiar and meaningless. She doesn't want me to have anyone. Hell, she'd fuck Lo just to keep me from doing it.

Gloria sinks onto the step beside me, like we're back at the Hockington and not in the house of a guy who just hit on the girl I once thought I could actually love. How fucking pathetic is that? Gideon's a good little dude, though. He'd be good for her, a fucking lot better than anyone in my family. If I had loved her, I'd have let her go out with him. But I didn't, so I don't. Not that I fucking know what love is.

"That was fast," I say. "She must be good."

"I figured you'd be balls deep in some other chick by now, drowning your pain in pussy," Gloria says. "That's the D-boy special, isn't it?"

"Because you know us so well."

"I think I know you pretty well," she says.

"Then you'd know that's not how I operate."

"True," she says. "That's more your brothers' M.O. But don't act like we're strangers just because you hate me. We've been friends for two years."

SELENA

"If that's what you want to call it."

"Hard as you make it," she mutters. "But yes, I do call us friends. We could have been more, if you weren't such an asshole."

"A real tragedy."

She shakes her head. "I'm sorry, Royal. I really am. If I'd known…"

"What?" I ask, twisting around to look at her. "That she'd tell the family that wants to destroy mine? Or that she was one of them, that she wanted to destroy us, too?"

"Both," she says, her big blue eyes filling with tears. "I never would have told her if she hadn't already basically figured it out herself."

"How?" I ask, my voice hard. I should be nice. She just lost her brother, and even if he was human garbage, he was still her brother. But after seeing Harper choose her over me, I'm feeling a little less than generous. It's way past time to hash this out, anyway.

"She… She came to the Hockington," Gloria whispers. "She followed you in one day, with one of your… Clients."

"They aren't clients," I snap. "They don't pay me."

"Okay," she says, wiping her hands along the top of her thighs and sitting up straight. "She followed you there and saw you with one of your *business associates*."

"And then she saw you," I say flatly.

"I wasn't going to tell her," Gloria says, swiping away a tear. "She would have figured it out, anyway. I thought I could explain it, make her see that you weren't cheating on her…"

"When was this?" I ask.

She shakes her head, lowering her face so I can't see her crying. She gets splotchy, and if there's one thing Lo can't tolerate, it's being ugly.

"When?" I grind out.

"I don't know," she says. "A while before you broke up."

"So she knew," I say, something inside me settling, heavy and cold in the pit of my stomach. "When we were together, she knew."

"She promised she wouldn't tell," Gloria insists. "And she didn't break up with you for it."

"But as soon as I broke up with her, that's the first thing she did," I say. "She must have been sitting on it, just waiting to destroy me after she'd gotten everything she could from me."

"It wasn't like that," Gloria says.

"Bullshit," I say. "It was exactly like that."

"I'm sorry."

"You know what?" I say. "Fuck you, Lo. You deserve each other."

"What?"

"I know why you told her," I say. "You wouldn't risk losing the advantage I gave you for nothing. Which means you told her so she wouldn't expose you as a fraud. I guess it worked out real fucking well for both of you. You got to keep your crown, even pretending to be my girlfriend after spring break so you could win prom. And Harper got the big secret she needed to bring down our family. You both fucking win."

"No," Gloria says, sniffling and wiping her face. "We both lost when we lost you, Royal. Don't you see, that's more important than anything we could have gotten."

"No," I say quietly. "I'm the only loser in the little game you played."

"That's not true," she wails. "I didn't know she'd do that, and look, even though she did, you're fine. Nothing ever happened because of it. No one exposed your family. It didn't break you and Harper up—you'd already dumped her when she told."

I almost laugh. Nothing happened because of it? She should go back in there and talk to Harper a little more if she thinks that's true, because she's missing a big piece of this puzzle.

"Stop making excuses," I say flatly. "You can't pretend it's okay just because you don't see the consequences."

"I'm sorry," Gloria says, clutching my arm. "I'm sorry I told her. I honestly was trying to help. Would you rather she'd thought you were cheating on her?"

"Yes," I say, pulling my arm away.

"I couldn't let her break up with you over that," she says, dropping her head again. "It would have killed you."

"You were only trying to help yourself."

She nods and takes a deep breath. "You're right. I was selfish, and I was protecting myself and my family, the same as you protect yours. I'd never have told her if I thought she'd tell anyone else."

"You know what's even more fucked up, Lo? You kept it from me. You could have fucking told me that she knew."

"I'm sorry," she says, swiping angrily at her tears.

"No," I say quietly. "You're just like her. You're only sorry I found out."

"That's not true," she insists. "I wish more than anything that I'd never told her."

"If you were really sorry, you would have told me right away. You would have let me make my own decisions about whether I wanted to keep either of you close."

"You're right," she says. "But I wasn't just using you, and neither was she. We both care about you. You know that, Royal."

"Do I?"

"I'm an idiot, okay?" she says, sniffling quietly. "I was just scared, and I didn't want you to break up because you're both my friends, and I didn't want to lose either of you. I should have told you."

"But you didn't."

She shakes her head, her blonde hair falling like a curtain between us. I'm glad I don't have to look at her face.

"You didn't care how much I had to lose," I say. "Just that you had too much to lose if anyone found out *your* secret."

"You didn't lose anything," she whispers.

I can't begin to tell her just how wrong she is.

"Here's a tip for the next time you pretend to give a fuck about someone other than yourself," I say. "When you care about someone, you don't fuck them over when they're at their most vulnerable. And if you do fuck up, you tell them the first chance you get, and then you do everything in your power to make it right."

"How can I make this right?" she whispers.

"By not being a selfish cunt," I say. "Why don't you start by telling your boyfriend you just hooked up with two people?"

"He broke up with me," she says with a sniffle. "That's why I'm drunk. And that's not what I meant. How can I make it right with you, Royal?"

SELENA

"You can't," I say. "It's too fucking late for that, Lo. You don't continue to use people until they find out you fucking betrayed them, and then try to apologize. You don't keep secrets because you're still getting something out of it, because you want to win prom queen. You're a social parasite, Gloria. Just like your mother."

"I'm not," she cries. "Royal, it's not like that! You're my friend, my best friend. Before her, and more than her. I loved you, Royal. I still love you, even if it's not the way she does."

"Bullshit," I say. "Neither of you know the meaning of that word, either."

"I do," she says quietly. "I know you won't believe me, that you don't think anyone can love you, but you're wrong. If you'd let someone know you, they could love you."

"I did let you know me," I say. "Both of you. And you played me like a pair of black widows, winding me into your web. I'm the fucking fly that just sat there and let you trap me. That's what I get for letting either of you close to me. I knew better. I don't need friends. I have my brothers."

"You have me," she whispers. "You'd have Harper, too, if you wanted her."

I have to laugh at that, but it's an empty, bitter sound. "You have no idea what you're talking about."

She shakes her head. "She didn't break up with you because of it. She'd take you back. Go talk to her."

"Don't you think I've fucking tried that?"

"Then try something else."

SELENA

forty-four

Harper Apple

After a while, a couple opens the door, so I get off the bed and give them the room. I hear voices further down the hall, but there's nothing for me here. I pull out my phone and see handful of texts from Preston. It's time to get this over with.

I'm almost to my car when I hear someone say my name. I don't turn. I'm too fucking tired of this drama to deal with more tonight. Hitting the button to unlock the Escalade, I hurry toward it, ducking my head against the rain.

"Harper."

I don't stop until his strong hand wraps around my upper arm, pulling me to a halt. I squeeze my eyes closed for a second, then turn back. Royal stands over me, silhouetted by the security light in front of the house and the rain slanting down in the glow. Then he steps closer. There's something different about him, an intensity shimmering off him, that has my pulse pounding. I squeeze my hand into a fist, comforted by the weight of the weapon on my knuckles.

"Why are you running from me?"

I don't answer. There is no answer. I know I'll never get away, but I can't stop trying.

He moves so fast, grabbing my shoulders and pulling me in. Before I know what's happening, his mouth crashes down on mine. I cry out against him. He thrusts his tongue into my mouth, a rough claiming with no warning. His big hands move up to cradle my head, and his lips crush mine so hard our teeth collide.

I respond instinctively, eagerly, as if I've been waiting for this all my life. I open for him, submitting to him with a trembling relief that fills me with each possessive stroke of his tongue. Everything in my body ignites, my toes curling, my body swaying toward his, and heat licking between my thighs. I grip his arms, never wanting to let go. I want him to throw me down and fuck every bit of damage out of me. I want to open my legs and get the relief that only opening my skin has given me. My eyes flutter closed, and for a minute,

SELENA

I'm washed away by the hunger in his kiss, his need, his desire. The cold rain sliding down our faces cools the feverish heat that rises to my skin at his touch.

And then my brain catches up to my body, and I remember the cost of letting Royal sweep me away. I fight his grip, twisting and writhing until I wrench myself free. I shove backwards and swing before the lust has even cleared from his eyes.

"How dare you?" I snarl at him.

My rings crunch into his nose, and I feel something give. His eyelids flutter as he blinks rapidly, stumbling back a step.

"How dare you think you have the right to touch me?"

I swing again, connecting with his mouth this time. The skin of his beautiful lips splits under my knuckles. I relish the sensation. I want him to hurt.

"How dare you think you can kiss me?"

This time, he ducks, grabbing my wrist. I go in with my left fist, sinking it into his ribs. He flinches, but he doesn't release my right hand. He pries it open, wrenching the weapon from my hand and hurling it to the ground. It skitters across the wet pavement and slides to a stop against the curb.

"How dare I *kiss* you?" he taunts. "You stuck my dick in your mouth not an hour ago."

"Don't you ever touch me again," I say, slamming my left fist into his cheek. "We are not on equal footing. You don't get to question me. You don't get to chase guys away from me and then go stick your dick in your fuck buddy. How fucking dare you think you can kiss me after that? That you can talk to me the way you talked to me in the hall at school? That you have any say whatsoever in what I do with my life?"

He just stands there holding my wrist, keeping me away as I writhe and kick at his shins.

"I can talk to you any fucking way I want," he snaps. "Because you're still mine, Harper."

"Fuck you," I scream, losing all control. "I'd rather you beat my face in like you did Colt's than ever kiss me again. So either do it, or let go of me and let me do it."

"Then do it," he says. "Get it over with, because I'm sure as hell going to kiss you again."

SELENA

His words lift me on a tide of pure, incinerating rage. He releases my hand, and I slam my fist into his face again. My knuckles slide against the blood, my blow muted by the swelling. I remember the way his blows sounded when he'd hit Colt so many times he wasn't striking bone anymore. I hit him again, and again, and again.

Finally, tears and rain blur my vision, and I stumble back, trying to catch my breath, to get control. I don't know how long I've been beating his face and neck and chest. His eyes are both blackening already, his eyebrow split and bleeding. Blood is pouring from his mouth and nose, down the front of his shirt, soaking it faster than the rain.

I stare at him in horror, wondering where the hell I just was, if I became a monster like Royal, out of my body, like someone else was acting in my place.

Before I can say anything, he grabs me by the shoulders again and smashes his bloody mouth to mine. I cry out in shock, even though he warned me. When I twist my face away, he pulls back and grabs my necklace in his fist.

"How dare *you* wear this fucking necklace and rub it in my face?" he growls, wrenching it from my neck. I stumble against him, but the clasp breaks, and he hurls the necklace across the road. "I know what that fucking means. It means you're spreading your legs for a Darling boy, just like my sister. It was bad enough seeing it around her neck, and now I have to pretend I don't see it around yours?"

"How dare you tell me who I can spread my legs for?" I scream at him. "You didn't give me that choice last spring, did you?"

"How dare you send me videos of you fucking the man you know I hate more than anyone in this world?" he snaps back. "And that's saying a lot, because the list is real fucking long. You want to see me lose my fucking mind, Harper? Send me one more picture of that motherfucker, and I swear, you won't like what happens next."

"Why do you even care who I fuck?" I snap. "An hour ago, you admitted that no one would ever want to touch me again. And *that* list includes you. So don't tell me I can't find whatever semblance of comfort I'm capable of with the only person you've destroyed more completely than me."

He stares at me, his eyes burning with rage. "Take off his jacket," he says, his voice low and deadly.

SELENA

"Fuck you," say, stomping to the car.

Royal steps in front of me just before I reach it, and I catch the look in his eyes. My heart stops. I dart to the other side, ducking past him, but he spins and catches me around the waist from behind. He turns and throws me backwards, and I land hard on the hood of the car. I roll up, but he hops onto the bumper and plows onto me, slamming me down on my back.

"I said, take off his fucking jacket," he growls.

I feel the metal dent under our weight, but I don't care about the fucking car. For a minute, we wrestle wordlessly as he drags the jacket over my arm. At last, I manage to roll over, but he uses the motion to peel the jacket off me and wrench it off my other arm. He throws it into the grass and flips me back onto my back, straddling my hips.

"I hate you," I rage at him, swinging a hand. My palm smacks across his cheek so hard it stings. "You're a sick, rotten bastard, and I can't believe I ever let you touch me."

"I hate you, too, you fucking bitch." He grabs my chin and squeezes, his fingers cutting into my cheeks until my mouth is forced open. He leans down over me, works his jaw, and spits a long stream of warm blood into my mouth.

I'm so shocked I swallow before I can help myself. Then I slap him again, my palm connecting with his crimson-streaked cheek and peppering my arms with flecks of his blood. I spit, trying to clear my mouth of his blood, and it sprays over his cheeks. He blinks it away and pins my hands, leaning down again. I think he's going to spit on me, but instead, he swipes his tongue up my face, leaving a wide, wet track of saliva up my cheek, replacing the blood and tears and rain.

"I'm not just going to kiss you, baby," he says. "I'm going to fuck you, and you're going to like it."

"Then you better fucking kill me first," I snarl at him. "Because that's the only way your dick is ever going inside me again."

"That can be arranged," he says, sitting back. He stares down at my stomach, where my shirt rode up when we were wrestling, and his eyes widen. He transfers my wrists to one hand, pulling them above my head, and toys with the little hoop through my bellybutton.

SELENA

"What is this?"

"It's a piercing," I say. "Preston gave it to me. He did it himself. And I fucking love it."

Royal's finger hooks through it, and he rips it out. A spike of pain drives straight from my navel through my body to the car. I can't even draw a breath to scream. I can feel hot blood pooling on my skin where he tore it. And it feels so fucking good. Each heartbeat is a throb of pain, and that's all I feel. The rage is gone, the hurt, the confusion.

He leans down, pressing his broken mouth to mine. I kiss him back hard, punishing his swollen lips with mine. I hear him unbuckling his belt, and I reach down, shoving his pants down, needing him in a way I don't understand, needing the pain to obliterate everything else that I don't want to feel right now. He lowers himself onto me, and I can feel the same desire in him. His cock is hot and stiff against my belly, throbbing against the torn flesh of my navel.

"You want to tell me again that no man can want you?" he says, his voice rough against my mouth, his cock sliding in my blood.

"What's the point in fucking me?" I snap. "You can't even finish when two girls are sucking your dick at once. You're not a closer, Royal. You choke."

"Oh, I'm going to fucking finish this time," he says, shoving my jeans down over my hips. "Trust me, baby. I'm going to cum so deep inside you that you can't remember anything but the way my cock owns every inch of you, inside and out. You're fucking mine, Harper. It never ends. You're right about that."

The rain beats down harder, hammering against the metal around us, drowning out a chance at a reply. He lifts his hand to his mouth, spitting a pool of blood and saliva into his palm, and then sinks it between my thighs. His slick fingers open me, skillfully stroking my center, sending a rush of longing through me.

"Then shut up and do it," I yell at him over the sound of the rain on the car, the sound of the hood denting under us, the thunder rumbling and the trees howling in the wind. "Or are you so fucked up you can't even cum for me anymore?"

He buries a finger deep inside me, and I gasp and arch up, trying to open my legs, which are bound by my wet jeans.

SELENA

"Shut that pretty mouth or I'll fuck it right this time," he growls back at me, leaning down to press his warm mouth against my ear. "You don't call the shots anymore."

He pulls back and watches me as his fingers slick into me quick and hard, his breath coming fast. Rain and his blood drips from his chin, and his eyes are alive and burning with lust. I'm shaking all over, my body hot and cold, thrilled and terrified, as if I've jumped from a plane with no parachute. This is how it ends. I need more, before it's over. I can feel it cresting, something inside me, some monster roaring to erupt.

A sheet of rain slams into his back, splattering over my face. He leans over me again, blood dripping from his mouth to mine. I yank his head down, lifting my face to his, sinking my teeth into his lower lip. His blood blooms across my tongue, thick and salty like cum.

He shifts onto me again, wetting his cock in the blood pooling on my stomach before moving lower, smearing the thick head of it through my wetness.

"Fuck me," I breathe, my voice shaking.

He thrusts up into me, and my blood turns to hot, shimmering electricity. A sound rises in me, climbing like the thunder rolling across the sky, a primal, animal scream that spirals up from my very soul. He pushes deeper, his thick, bloody cock stretching me and sending coils of pleasure spreading out through my body. When he fills my core, the raw, visceral sensation is too much.

I can't hold back, can't bear to feel this good again, can't contain it. It's too real. I open my mouth, and he presses his mouth down on mine, catching the sound that escapes, swallowing it. I can feel myself disappearing into him as I scream.

Something shifts inside me, and the urgency fades, the way it did when I cut myself. I can feel the hood denting and rising with each thrust at he pumps into me, his cock slick with my blood, and his blood, and his spit, and my own wetness. His muscles are tight, shaking, and his mouth is on my cheek. His body is hard and hot on mine, but I feel it in a different way, a detached way.

I know I made a mistake, that this is a mistake, but I can't find the words that stop it, that reverse time and undo this terrible thing we've done. This is Royal. The man who told his brothers they could have me, they could do whatever sick things they had wanted to do to me all along. He let them hurt me. He turned away when I begged for mercy. He made it known that his protection ended that day. I hate him. I want him dead.

But I told him to do this. I opened my legs and invited the monster in, even after it ate my soul the last time. What is wrong with me?

It's okay, though. It won't last forever. It'll be over soon.

It's okay.

I keep telling myself until it's true. I'm not being hurt. I can hardly feel him moving inside me anymore, into the deepest places. There's a vague pleasantness in it, like having a day off to do absolutely nothing. The heavy, wet air around us and the slick metal under my back fade away, replaced by luxurious, smooth sheets and a room with cold AC, the air dry and crisp and clean.

I'm safe. I'm safe because this is all he wants, and he can't take anything more. I know, because this has happened before. There's nothing else to give. This is the end of the line, the last thing, and I've given it all up. Now I can relax and know that I don't have to fight.

I submit, give over everything, like I did in the loft with Preston. And it's okay.

"Harper."

His voice is sharp, cutting through the haze of my thoughts, the veil of safety protecting me. His fingers cut into my cheeks again, the pain jerking me back. My eyes fly open. I try not to move, to let this be okay, to let this be part of the submission. If I can submit to everything he's done before, I can submit to pain.

"Harper." His voice is gentler now, but just as commanding. His grip on my chin loosens, but he doesn't release me. He slides two fingers into my mouth, the ones that were inside me. They taste like pussy and blood, mine and his. "Stay with me, baby," he says. "I'm right here. Look in my eyes. Don't go away."

He starts to move inside me again, holding my chin so I can't look away, his fingers on my tongue forcing my presence. I close my lips, taste our combined flavor, and heat pulses in my core. I can feel him inside me, so big, his cock straining against my walls, reclaiming the very depths of me, where it aches in my core. The dominating rhythm of his thrusts owns me, forces my response.

God, it feels good, too good, oh god, I can't—

I pull back from it, but I don't close my eyes. I'll let him see that I'm there, the way I used to with Mav, where it was something satisfying but I wasn't part of it. I'll let him have me here while he cums, but I can't join him. The last time—

He yanks his hand back, and his palm cracks across my cheek. The shocking sting of it shoots straight down my body to the center of my being. I'm suddenly thrust into my body with such brutal, physical presence that it hurts. My core clamps down so hard he sucks in an audible breath, his fingers gripping the top of the hood as he responds with a vicious thrust. He grabs my hip with his other hand, pinning me there with a bruising grip as he grinds into me.

He leans down, his eyes deep and commanding, blood darkening half his face. "Cum for me, my little slut."

He drives his cock so deep into me I almost choke.

I cry out, trying to slip away, to get away, but he slaps me again, this time on the other cheek. And he's inside me, taking me, delivering me, wrecking every inch of me. He pounds into me relentlessly, offering no respite, no escape. His cock is bare and thick and slick, and it hurts, and it feels so fucking good I can't bear it.

And I want it all.

I want him to consume me, to drown me, to possess me like the demon he is.

"Royal," I gasp, pushing at his shoulders, needing him off, I can't bear it.

"Cum," he growls again, his powerful hips thrusting his cock into the center of my core, hitting somewhere inside me that's so deep, so painful and raw that I can't hold back.

I cry out again, arching up, my body clamping down hard around him for a second time. This time, he's the one who makes a choking sound, his cock throbbing thick inside me. The sensation sends me over the edge, and I can't pull back in time. This thing that's been fighting to get out, this monster inside me, erupts. I feel it tearing free, raging like the storm around us, the rain slamming against us, the trees tossing like agony in the wind. As it takes me over, I cry out Royal's name, my nails biting into his skin, my body finally giving in, submitting to his dominance, his claim. I'm helpless to stop it.

I am his.

I cum. I'm crying and raging, I'm filled with hatred and helplessness and relief, and I'm still coming so hard I can't stop myself. I don't know what's happening, why it won't end. I think I'm saying something, but it's swallowed by the storm, and he's over me, watching me.

His hot cum floods into me, spreading inside me like a virus that's taken me over, racing through my bloodstream until he's part of every breath, every cell of my being. Because I'm not just his.

He is mine.

When I finally start to come down, I'm shaking uncontrollably. I want to take it all back. It's too much, and I can't deal with it. Because the thing that just broke free inside me, that's been howling and clawing and tearing me apart from within, fighting to escape, isn't a monster.

It's me.

Royal's hands are on my face, cradling it gently even as his cock remains painfully deep inside me, and his lips skim mine, still slick with blood. When my eyes meet his, I see everything in him, his rage and regret, his darkness and brokenness, his destructiveness and vulnerability. For a second, I can't breathe, can't move or speak, too crushed by the weight of the burden he carries by his very existence to react.

And then he speaks.

"Thank you," he whispers, his breath warm on my wet skin.

In that one breath, one heartbeat, the space between heartbeats where life is measured and decided, I'm weightless. I'm lost and I'm found, I'm destroyed and renewed, I'm insignificant and infinite. I am his, and I am free.

And then I suck in a breath, and I'm here, with his blood in my mouth and my blood slick between our bodies, the metal under my back, the rain on my skin. My cunt flutters around him, the helpless spasms of orgasm still racing through me, shivering along my limbs and up through my head, making me dizzy with power and bliss.

SELENA

Royal leans on his elbows, sinking his head down against my neck, his hot breath damp in the wet chill of the night. "Harper," he says, his voice barely more than a breath.

"Shhh."

We lie there for a long time, my body still clenched around him like a cramp. It takes a while for me to relax, for my heartbeat to return to normal. Headlights wash over us, but Royal just covers me with his body, hiding my face with his broad shoulders. The car honks and drives off, and that's when reality really comes back.

I push Royal up. He slides out of me, and a rush of his hot cum slides out with his cock. I wince as I sit up, revisiting the familiar but almost-forgotten soreness that comes from a Royal Dolce pounding. I slide off the hood and catch my balance on the side of the car, struggling to pull up my wet jeans. Tears stream down my face, and I'm grateful that the rain covers them.

I can feel his warm cum sliding down my cold thighs like tears of shame. I didn't think it was possible to hate myself any more than I already did, but somehow, Royal makes it possible.

forty-five

Harper Apple

I wrestle my jeans up, my head spinning, trying to come to terms with what just happened. My phone slips out of my back pocket, clattering to the wet asphalt. When I straighten, I toss my hair back, and Royal groans. He grabs me from behind, his thick arm wrapping around my middle and pulling me back against the car's grill. He nuzzles into my neck, and my throat tightens painfully.

"I have to go," I say, trying to ignore the insanity going on in my body when he touches me, growls against the back of my neck, nips at my skin.

"Who's texting you?" he asks.

"Preston," I say, twisting out of his arms.

SELENA

He looks like I just slapped him. He turns away to pull up his jeans and get himself situated before speaking. "Why is Preston texting you after midnight on a Friday?"

I sigh and slide my phone back in my pocket. "Does it matter?"

"Yes, it fucking matters." He holds my gaze, waiting. And I see it matters to him, even if it shouldn't. I want to be glad that I'm hurting him, but I'm not. It just makes me want to cry, and I've spent way too fucking much time crying the last few months.

"He got the DNA test back," I say, pulling my bloody shirt away from my belly. The rain stings the torn skin of my bellybutton. "To see if... What Baron said is true."

"And if it's not?"

"I don't know," I answer honestly.

"Are you going back to him?" Royal asks. "Is that what you want? That's what has you running out of here before my dick is even dry?"

"Royal..." I sink down on the bumper, and he climbs down to sit beside me. I watch him from the corner of my eye, this damaged, destructive boy who owns every part of me no matter how hard I fight it.

"You'd choose the Darlings, even if you aren't one." This time, he's not asking. His shoulders slump in defeat.

"I'm not choosing anyone," I say. "You're the one making the choice for me."

"What do you want me to do? Forgive them? Not everyone is like you, Harper."

"I would never ask you to forgive them," I say. "But I don't hate them. Preston's my friend. Colt's my friend. You can't hurt my friends and expect me to be okay with it."

"I'm coming with you," he says, standing abruptly.

"I don't think that's a good idea."

"I didn't ask what you think," he says, holding out a hand. "I don't trust Preston."

I can't help but laugh. "What exactly do you think he's going to do to me, Royal?"

"You fucked him," Royal says, glaring down at me.

"Yeah," I say. "I fucked him."

He flinches, but he keeps going, and I know it must be killing him because I know how much he hates to think of me with anyone else. But he's never been afraid of pain. "Without a condom."

I want to drop my gaze, to avoid seeing the way he's looking at me, but I don't. "Yes."

"You let him cum inside you."

"Yes."

His eyes narrow, his nostrils flaring. "Did you like it?"

I shrug. "I don't know. Sometimes, I guess."

"More than you like fucking me?"

"It wasn't the same," I say, shaking my head. "Can I go?"

"Did you cum?"

"How does that matter?" I stand to push past him, but he steps in front of me, blocking my way to the driver's door.

"Did you cum?" he asks again, gritting out each word.

"No," I say. "I never came. Happy now?"

"Asshole," he says.

"What about you?" I ask, crossing my arms and glaring up at him. "Who'd you fuck since we broke up?"

"No one."

We stare at each other a long moment while the trees toss in a gust of wind, rain battering our bodies and plastering our bloody clothes against us. "What about the women at the hotel?" I call over the noise.

"I told you, I'm done with that."

"Over spring break, when you'd just dumped me, and the Waltons were there for the taking," I say. "You didn't fuck anyone?"

He swallows. "Just Lo."

"Just Lo."

"No one since that night," he says. "Not even her."

"And how was she?" I ask, a taunting edge to my voice. "Did you cum?"

Royal scowls at me.

"Then I guess we're even," I say. "We both fucked one person since we broke up. Preston hasn't been with anyone since we met, so he's clean. And Lo hadn't been with anyone else since the last time you fucked her. I'm still on birth control, so we should be fine."

"Why are you acting like this isn't going to happen again?"

I swallow the anguish in my soul and force my words out. "We made a mistake. It doesn't change anything."

SELENA

He gives me that asshole smirk that gets me all hot and bothered, with hooded eyes and his chin tipped up so he can look down at me like the smug bastard he is. "Okay, Cherry Pie," he says, sounding zero percent convinced.

I clench my jaw and bare my teeth in my most ferocious smile. Then I repeat the words he once said to me. "Just because I made you cum, don't get attached."

"Give me the keys."

"It's my car."

He doesn't say anything, just holds out a hand.

I narrow my eyes at him. "Or is it your car, Royal? The custom color—is that black cherry?"

"You needed your own car."

His gaze is cool, like it means nothing. But it means everything to me. A vehicle is an escape, a way to run, security and freedom both rolled into one beautiful package. I have to give credit where credit's due, even if he never asked for it. Hell, he didn't even tell me he bought the car, let alone expect gratitude. He just wanted me to have it, even if I never knew where it came from. But because he knows me, he knew that I wouldn't accept a gift like this from him.

He let me believe his worst enemy gave it to me, even knowing I'd show my appreciation to someone else, and that breaks my fucking heart.

"Thank you," I say, my chest tight with emotion. "That's... Way too fucking generous."

"Shut up and let me drive."

"You don't make the rules anymore, Royal."

He stands there with his hand out until I sigh and smack the keys into his palm. I grab the knuckles and jacket from where he threw them and slide them back on before climbing in the passenger's side. I halfway expect him to rip the jacket off again, but he doesn't even look at it.

"Where are we going?" he asks.

"Grandpa Darling's estate."

He laughs. "Tell him to meet us at the river."

Ten minutes later, we pull up alongside the road like we have so many times before. Preston's truck is already there, parked on the far side, the lights illuminating the bridge and the steady rain falling between us.

SELENA

"I let you come with me," I say to Royal. "I let you drive. Now it's your turn to do what I ask. Either stay in the car or play nice."

His jaw clenches, and he stares back at me. "You want me to be nice to your little fuckboy cousin?"

"If you insist on following me around, you'd better get used to seeing him," I say. "If you don't like it, leave."

"You really are choosing the Darlings."

"I'm refusing to choose one side or the other. If you call that making a choice, that's your issue to deal with."

Royal just glares.

I sigh. "Look, you knew where I was going. You knew who I'd be seeing. I didn't ask you to be here right now. This was your choice. If you don't want to see him, stay in the car."

He keeps staring for a long minute. "Okay," he says at last. "Let's go."

We climb out of the car and start across the bridge. Preston is standing there with an umbrella. When I get closer, I see that he's holding a bottle of whiskey.

"Are you drunk?" I ask as we approach.

"What the fuck is he doing here?" Preston grits out. His question is directed at me, but his eye is focused above my head, where Royal's walking behind me.

"I'm watching her back," Royal says. "Apparently that means you'd better get used to seeing a lot more of me or a lot less of Harper."

"Where's your rope?" Preston asks. "Or did you bring a gun this time? Since you didn't bring the torture twins, I'm assuming you won't be lighting me on fire again."

"I don't need a weapon," Royal says. "I'll rip your dick off with my bare hands and shove it down your throat until you choke to death."

"Stop," I order. "Both of you. Royal, I told you to stay in the car if you can't play nice."

"Play nice?" Preston asks, a laugh escaping him that sends a chill down my spine. It's not the Preston I know, the quiet, mild man in the mask. It's a cold, heartless laugh with no humor. I'm reminded again that I only know one side of him, the side he chose to show me. With his mask glinting in the dark, he looks creepy and evil.

SELENA

"Both of you," I say, glaring at him. "You told me to find my sun. I guess I did."

"I meant a goal," Preston says. "A way out of this town."

"I found my sun," I say. "You don't get to decide what or who that is."

"Did he tell you about the last time he was here?" Preston asks. "You should have guessed it yourself, Miss A. I'm sure you heard about it at school, even if he already graduated."

"What are you talking about?" My stomach turns, and I glance back at Royal. But it's Baron's words that are racing through my mind. He said Royal's was the kind of hate that would make him kill a man for hurting me. I thought it was just an expression, but now I'm not so sure.

Royal just stands there, his face all broken and bloody, glaring at Preston and ignoring my question. He looks like he needs a hospital. His beat-in face makes my stomach turn for a different reason—his eyes are bruised, his nose swollen and crooked from the earlier blows, his lips split and bleeding. Fuck. The thought that I'm capable of that... I'm no better than any of them.

"Any time someone around the Dolce family dies, it's worth questioning," Preston says when it's clear Royal isn't going to answer me. "A suicide note's just a decoy."

"You don't know what you're talking about," Royal says flatly.

"Or maybe he really did it," Preston says. "Wouldn't be the first time someone jumped off this bridge to get away from you. At least he didn't waste a good car like your sister."

Royal charges forward, his feet thundering on the wood.

Preston drops his umbrella and backpedals, moving to the side and smashing the whiskey bottle against the railing. He swings it at Royal, but Royal ducks and slams him back against the rail. "Mention my sister again, and you'll be the next one over the edge," Royal growls, his hand around Preston's throat.

"Royal," I bark, shoving myself between him and Preston. I slam my palm against his chest, shoving him back. "Preston is part of my life. I'm not asking you to be friends with him. But you need to accept that *I am* if you want to be a part of it, too. That means you're not going to hurt him or threaten him. That goes for him, Colt, Magnolia, Gideon, Dixie and Gloria. These are my friends. They helped put back together what *you* broke. If I can forgive you, then you can do this for me. And if you can't, then you made the choice for me. So, leave. Right now."

He stares at me a long minute, rain dripping down his swollen face, his jaw clenched, his eyes filled with so much turmoil and hurt that it almost breaks me. But I can't break anymore. So I stand strong, and after the charged silence stretches until it becomes painful, he nods and steps back. "Okay," he says quietly.

I feel the weight of the moment settle heavy over me. It's something to be treasured, to be handled with utmost care. Because his word may be simple, but it carries the meaning of all that he feels for me. He knows this is the only way to stay in my life, and he's telling me I'm worth it, just like he did at the Slaughterpen when he gave me what I needed and showed that he thought I was worthy of him.

"You forgave him?" Preston asks, staring at me incredulously. "After what he did to you?"

"Yes," I say. "And the same goes for you. Royal's part of my life. I don't know what's going to happen, but I know that I'm tied to him now, just as I'm tied to you. So, if you want to be part of my life, you're going to have to put aside whatever came before me and accept that Royal's going to be part of it, too. He's not going anywhere."

"Yeah?" Preston says. "Well, I guess I am, then."

He pushes past me, but I grab his arm. "Preston…"

"Fuck you, Harper," he says, yanking free of my grip. "You have no idea what you're asking. What this psychopath has done to my family. Rape, murder, mutilation, dismemberment… Fucking name it, and he's done it. Don't stand there and defend him to me. If you're on his side, you're not on mine, and you never will be."

"I'm not on anyone's side," I say, throwing my hands up in frustration.

"Then you're part of the problem," he says. He turns and walks away.

"Guess you don't have to choose after all," Royal says quietly.

SELENA

I've never seen anyone move so fast. Preston spins around, and he's on Royal in the amount of time it should take someone to take one step, not five. He grabs Royal, and the two of them stumble and slide on the wet wood underfoot before crashing against the railing. Their bodies collide in a blur of taut muscle under wet fabric, both of them grunting and hitting each other with quick jabs, all they can manage while they're locked together, straining and breathing hard as they crush against the railing.

"Stop," I yell, leaping at them.

Royal's bigger, but Preston's got the end of the shattered whiskey bottle, and he shoves it against Royal's throat. I can see his muscles straining through his soaked dress shirt, the rage vibrating through every cell in his body. Royal's hand is locked around Preston's forearm, keeping the jagged glass from puncturing his throat.

"Preston," I say, my voice strong even though my heart is racing. I force the words out, firm and quick, afraid he'll kill him before I can stop it. "You don't want to do this. You're going to kill him. Do you want to spend the rest of your life in prison? You can't protect your sister from there. You can't help your family."

Royal drops his hand from Preston's arm, letting the smaller man press him back against the railing. "Do it," he says, his voice toneless. "Just fucking get it over with, Preston."

Preston's arm tenses, and he angles the bottle. Before he can slice through Royal's throat, I swing. The brass knuckles slam into his temple, and he reels sideways, the bottle clattering along the wooden planks and spinning over the edge, into the river below. His mask flies off, sliding along the wooden planks. Royal just stands there staring at me, blood running down his neck from where the bottle sliced his skin.

"What the fuck, Royal?" I snap. "If someone's trying to kill you, you don't fucking encourage them!"

Preston has dropped to one knee, his hand going to his temple, the other braced on the ground. "I gave you that weapon," he says, his words slow and measured. "I gave you everything."

SELENA

"I've fucking had it with both of you," I say, turning away and grabbing my hair with both hands, so frustrated I could scream. "This has to stop. This whole thing. Your families are going to kill each other and this whole town, and for what? You can kill every Darling on earth, Royal, and it won't bring your sister back. I'm sorry, but she's gone."

He doesn't flinch. He just touches the blood running down his neck. It's not a lot, just a few small cuts the bottle left.

I turn to Preston. "And you. I know you think they're alive, but you know what? It doesn't fucking matter. Colt was right. Devlin's not coming back to save you, to put your family together, to stop the Dolces. If he's alive, he's off living his best life, doing whatever the fuck he wants, and not coming back here. So stop waiting for him, and get out of your house, and fucking do something. You say I'm part of the problem because I don't want to kill Royal? You're just as much a part of the problem. They're your family, and you haven't done shit except for writing creepy messages and gathering information. You had everything you needed to ruin them, and you didn't do anything with it!"

"I saved your life," he says, sounding dismayed and defeated, like he can't believe I'm not throwing him a fucking parade.

"Don't be so self-righteous," I snap. "We all know you didn't do that out of the kindness of your heart. You're not some good Samaritan who happened by and saved me. If that's what you were doing, you would have taken me to a hospital and left me there. But no. You saw an opportunity to hurt Royal, and you took it."

"I wanted to help."

"Yeah, and you wanted to send Royal videos of you fucking me to drive him insane," I say. "Don't pretend you did it all for my own good. You saw how fucking out of it I was, and you wanted a little doll to dress up and play with, fuck with the Dolces by making me look like their sister."

"That's not what I was doing."

"Then what?" I ask. "You wanted to pretend she was your girlfriend? I'm not her, Preston. I'm me. And you weren't my boyfriend. You were my puppet master. Hell, I didn't even know your fucking name most of that time."

SELENA

"I never hurt you," he says, finally pushing up to standing, his eyes meeting mine, no mask over his face. A knot is already forming on the side of his head.

"True," I agree. "Not much, anyway. Not after the first few days. So congratulations. You aren't a sadistic fuck like Baron. But don't pretend you're a hero, either. You know, for a while I thought you were. I even gave you credit for how little I'm scared of sex, since you never let me freeze up about it. But now that I've been reminded what sex is supposed to be like…"

I try not to lose my train of thought. I made myself forget the ache of being filled by Royal Dolce, the way it hurt so fucking good I didn't know if I wanted to cry or cum. I made myself forget it could feel good at all, that anything could feel good. I just let Preston do whatever he wanted to me, like a good little doll, because I knew if I was good, he'd never hurt me.

"You fucked Royal?" he asks, staring at me like I'm a stranger, like it's a betrayal.

But I can't betray him because there was never anything to betray.

"You never once asked if I wanted to have sex," I say. "You just did it. You assumed I'd be fine with it, because I owed you my life."

"I never thought you owed me."

I shrug. "Then maybe you did it because I'm from Mill Street, so obviously I'm a slut who's down to fuck anyone at any time, even two days after I was fucking gang raped for eight hours."

"I never forced you to do anything."

"But you sure as fuck never cared if I wanted to, either."

"I made sure you were comfortable."

I can't help but laugh. "Comfortable? So, that's all a woman can expect during sex? You didn't care if I enjoyed it, if I got something out of it. As long as I wasn't physically in pain, that's all that mattered."

He glances at Royal's flawless face, then looks away like he can't bear to see what he no longer possesses. "I asked you once if you wanted me to make you cum. You said no. Don't act like what I did was as bad as what he did."

"Then don't act like you're a saint," I say. "You saved my life, but you didn't do it for me."

SELENA

We stand there staring at each other for a long minute, the rain streaking down our faces. Royal may look perfect, but it's Preston's face that draws my gaze. He's the only one of us who can take off his mask, whose face shows the truth—the beauty in one half and the tragic scarring on the other, the two halves of who he is.

Both these men have done terrible things to each other and to me, but we're all still standing. We're all victims of each other and the vengeance neither man can let go of. But I'm the only one who can see past the hurt and anger to see what it's done and what it will continue to do if they don't stop. I'm the only one who can let go of it and forgive, and in that moment, I know that forgiving them doesn't make me weak or foolish. It makes me the strongest one of us, the only one strong enough to stop this.

"Christ," Preston says after a long silence. "Is that how it was for you? I was trying to protect you, in case you ever left. That's not how I meant for you to take it. I'm sorry, Harper. I'm so fucking sorry."

He comes over and pulls me into his arms, squeezing me against him and pressing his lips to my forehead. "Fuck,

Harper. I didn't think about it from your perspective. I didn't mean to make you feel…"

"Used?"

"You're right," he says. "I was using you, even if I didn't see it that way. I was planning to, though."

"Planning to… What?"

"To use you," he says quietly. "To get back at them. I thought when you were strong again, you'd be the perfect weapon. That's why I made you look like her. But I couldn't go through with it after you tried to jump off the roof that day."

"You tried to what?" Royal demands behind me.

"I wasn't going to do it until you were better," Preston says quickly. "Until you were on board with it, and we could plan it together. But yeah. I'm shit. I'm so sorry I did that to you."

"It's okay," I say. "I'm not mad about it. I forgive you, too. I just want you to understand."

"I do," he says. "I didn't before, but now I do. And I—I really do care about you."

"I know," I say. "I care about you, too."

SELENA

"Really?" Royal demands, pushing away from the railing and giving us a disgusted look. "That's all it takes for you to forgive him?"

"You never apologized," I point out, pulling away from Preston. "And he's right—you can't compare what he did to what you did."

Royal doesn't answer. He knows better than to lie to me right now.

"Want to go open the DNA test?" Preston asks. "It's in my truck. I brought the whiskey so we could take a couple shots if we needed courage beforehand, or… Something else after. But I guess that's not an option anymore."

"Yeah," I say. "Let's get it over with."

Preston reaches out a hand, and I slip my fingers into his. He grips my hand tightly, and I realize he's nervous.

"What's going on there?" Royal asks, nodding at our linked hands.

"Shut up," I say, and I reach for his hand. He hesitates before taking it. I grip both their hands, and together we cross the bridge where it all began, to see if this is where it ends.

forty-six

Harper Apple

The three of us sit in Preston's truck, soaking wet and silent. Royal dragged me into the back seat and refused to let me sit up front with Preston, so Preston ended up climbing in the back. Now I'm sandwiched between them while the rain pounds down on the roof. The envelope rests in Preston's hands, still unopened.

"I want to open it," I say, reaching for it.

He hands it to me with a tight smile. "Do the honors."

I swallow hard, turning it over in my hands. "I wish you had some of that whiskey now."

"You could probably go lick some off the bridge," he says. "You might get some glass with it, though."

"Don't tempt me," I say.

SELENA

I wouldn't be the first person in my family to lick up spilled booze.

But I am not my mother.

I am me.

I hold the envelope, feeling the weight of it like something precious. It feels right to be the one opening it. Tonight, I took back my power. Not the kind Royal gave me, that has to do with my social standing and my position at school. That is still very much in question. I haven't resolved things with the twins, though Baron reached out to me in whatever capacity he's able. Duke's still avoiding me, and I don't know what to make of the mess with Gloria or Gideon.

But tonight's not about them. It's not about anyone else. It's not about social power, it's about personal power.

I claimed my own power, my agency. I had sex on my terms, the way it was meant to be, and it felt… Orgasmic. Not just in my body, but in my soul. Even if it was messy and unplanned, if it was with a boy I still hate as much as love, I wanted it. *Needed* it. I needed to remember how it was supposed to feel, not just lacking fear, but filled with recklessness and lust and passion. So I can't regret it, even if it was a mistake. Even when I regretted it right afterwards, I knew it was different from all the times with Preston. This time, it was my mistake to make.

My choice.

Royal was my choice.

But this time, it's not at the expense of everything else. Not at the expense of my friendships.

I forgave Royal for his part in it, not because he made some big gesture, but because I was ready.

And I confronted Preston about what he did to me. I let him know that *I know* how fucked up it is, that I'm not okay with being treated that way, even by a man who saved my life.

I'm here, too. I'm a human, a woman, and I'm not anyone's doll or plaything.

I'm my own person.

Finally.

At last, I feel like myself again. Even if I'm still broken and fucked up, if I'm never going to be the same, I know who this version of myself is. And maybe I was always

SELENA

broken. Maybe that's how I can sit between these two twisted, damaged men and understand them, even after all they've done to each other and to me. Maybe that's why I can forgive them regardless of whether they ask for it or deserve it.

"Open it," Royal says, his voice quiet and intense.

This is a big moment for him, too. All three of us have a lot to contend with based on the contents of this envelope. Either Preston and I have to face the fact that we were basically in an incestuous relationship for six months, or Royal has to face the fact that everything he did to me was based on a false assumption.

"Wait a minute," I say, setting the envelope on my knees and turning to him. "Baron told me that I'm a Darling. You think I am, too?"

He nods.

"Why?" I ask.

"We already got a DNA test," he admits.

"What?" I draw back, my heart racing.

He gives the tiniest shrug of one shoulder. "I wanted to make sure."

"Make sure what?" I ask, narrowing my eyes at him.

"We already knew you were. I just wanted to be sure. So, that night you slept over…" He shifts uncomfortably, but he doesn't drop my gaze.

I feel my face warm, thinking about him wiping my blood off his dick and asking me about it. I know it's stupid, but I feel weirdly violated by the thought that he was scheming on me that day. But I also understand why he did it. He had started to catch feelings, and he was looking for a way out. If I wasn't a Darling, he wouldn't have to destroy me.

Preston leans forward, resting his forearm on the seat in front of him and looking past me to Royal. "How did you already know?"

"Dad found her," Royal says before returning his attention to me. "Someone who works for him knew about your mom and their uncle. They were living together until right after you were born. They found some… Correspondences online between your mother and John Darling that proved you were a Darling."

I swallow. I know there's more to that story, that my mother was sleeping with two other guys during that time, but I keep that to myself. She was an underage, scared, and desperate poor girl who suddenly found herself homeless and took advantage of the only kindness shown to her. She deserves her privacy, her dignity. If she was lying, the DNA test will answer soon enough, and I'll confront her in private.

"How long had you known?" I ask Royal, because I want to know what led him to me in the first place.

"Since the beginning."

"The beginning of what?" I ask, my pulse thudding heavily, though I'm not sure why just yet.

"Since we found you at the tracks," he says. "With that teacher."

I sit back, thinking about it for a minute. They knew from the very start, before we even met. "You were looking for me," I realize aloud.

"Yeah," he says. "Baron was able to hack some account you had, and then track it on your phone."

"Well, that's fucking creepy."

He shrugs and gives Preston a withering look. "We'd settled the score with all the Darlings at Willow Heights, except for this asshole, and we couldn't get to him. So we were going to go after Lindsey next, but then we got word of you. And you made it too fucking easy, sucking a teacher off in public."

"That's why you decided to ruin my life?" I ask. "Because it was easy?"

"No," he says. "We didn't care about you. We thought we'd just release the video at your school and fuck with you a little, since you weren't even a real Darling. But then you showed up at Willow Heights and started fucking with us back…"

My stomach hollows out, and I can hardly breathe. I turn to Preston, my veins icy hot with rage. "Because of you," I say. "Was that your plan all along? To send me in there, knowing they'd target me, so they'd leave your sister alone?"

"I have no idea what you're talking about."

I just stare at him. "I don't even know what to say right now," I say, ripping open the envelope in quick, angry strokes. "Is that why you were so nice to me? Why you bought me all that shit, paid my bills, gave me scholarships? Was that some kind of penance on your part, when you realized I was an actual person and you started to feel bad that you'd sent them after me?"

"Again, no fucking idea what you're talking about," he says, sounding annoyed now.

I pull out the paper and unfold it, my eyes scanning it quickly.

"Not a match," I say, looking up. My eyes meet Preston's, and he smiles. The bottom half of his face is undamaged, still arrogant and beautiful, but when he smiles, it makes everything inside me ache.

He grabs my face between his hands and pulls me in, kissing me hard on the mouth.

"What the fuck?" Royal yanks me back. "If you want me to resist murdering your friends, then they need to keep their hands off you."

"Aww, are you jealous?" I ask, temporarily filled with elation at having this weight lifted. I didn't know how scared I was until my fears aren't realized. I lean in to kiss Royal, but he pushes me back and turns his face away.

"You better wash that mouth with bleach before it comes near me again."

I sit back, letting my head fall back on the seat, and I laugh. Fuck, it feels good to know I'm not a Darling. I got myself worked up enough to open the envelope without freaking out, but now I can let myself have this relief, this elation. My mother wasn't lying. And I didn't fuck my cousin.

Preston takes my hand and squeezes. He's still grinning, looking as relieved as I feel.

"Can I see that?" Royal asks, his voice low.

Right. He's the one who has to deal with the fall-out. He's the one who got the result he didn't want.

I hand it over, my laughter dying as I watch him read it, turn it over, then check both sides of the envelope. "Where'd you get this?" he asks at last.

"I sent away for it," Preston says. "You can do the kits yourself now."

"So, it's just some online quack doing the testing."

"No," Preston says slowly. "It's someone who has no stake in it. Not some local doctor your family bought off."

"That's right," I say. "If you already got a test, and it said I was a Darling…"

SELENA

"This has to be wrong," Royal mutters, frowning at the paper. There's no conviction in his voice, though.

"Why would your doctor fake a DNA test for me?" I ask. "I don't even know your family, and I definitely don't know any doctors."

"He wouldn't fake it for you," Royal says. "He'd fake it for my father."

"Why would your dad want you to ruin me? I'd never even met him, or any of you… Why would your dad want to target a poor nobody?"

Royal shakes his head. "It wasn't about you. It was never about you."

His voice sounds hollow and resigned, and his eyes are getting that hollow look about them, the one that used to be his regular look, when I met him. Now, I don't see it much.

"Then what's it about?" I ask, afraid to hear the answer.

"He found you," Royal says. "He thought you were a Darling. We were already invested before he got the test. It didn't say what he wanted, so he had the doctor forge one or did it himself, so he'd have something to show me."

"Why?"

"So we'd leave the real Darlings alone," he says. "He was working on the land deal last year. Preston's family owns all the property where the mall is located. Dad just wanted to keep us out of the way, and you were a distraction so we wouldn't fuck up his casino plans."

I gape at him in disbelief. "So this was all just… *Business?*"

He gives a bitter little chuckle. "It's Tony Dolce," he says. "It's always about business."

We sit in silence for a few minutes, all of us putting the pieces together and battling with our own thoughts and regrets. He's right. His dad would whore out his own children to close a deal. Why would he care about an innocent bystander?

At last, I turn to Preston.

"So that's why you never leaked what I told you. You had everything you needed to bring down the Dolces, but you were already in business with them."

"Fuck no," he says flatly, glaring at Royal over my head. "I would never do business with murderers and conmen. Dolce money is dirty money. It doesn't belong in this town, and neither does a fucking casino."

"But your family—"

"My mother's family," he says. "The Delacroixs. And they refused to sell."

"Then why didn't you try to bring them down? Just because you don't want to show your face?"

He swallows, his good eye searching mine. "I didn't want you to have to relive that. But I still have everything from that night, if you want it."

I realize he's not talking about the information I gave him. He's talking about the blanket he wrapped me in, the rope they tied me with, the hood they gagged me with. I shiver and close my eyes.

"But what about what I told you?" I whisper.

He lets out an exasperated sigh. "Yet again, I don't know what you're talking about."

"Preston," I say flatly. "Cut the crap. Royal knows you're Mr. D. I already told him."

He shrugs. "What about it?"

"Let's start at the beginning. How'd you find me?"

"I was tracking the twins' cars," he says. "When they parked on the road for half the night, I knew something must be going down. So I watched until they left, and then I went the way they'd come. And after a while, I found you."

"No, not that night," I say. "Before that."

"He didn't have a tracker on my car," Royal says, glaring past me. "I'd just gotten a new one after he blew up the old one."

"I didn't blow up your car," Preston says, sounding annoyed. "Though I wish I had. I would have done a better job, and you wouldn't be here right now."

"Then who did?" Royal demands.

"I don't know," Preston says with a shrug. "A lot of people want you dead. But you're right about me not having a tracker on it because you'd just gotten a new one."

Royal glowers at him.

"No," I say, trying to get back to Mr. D. "I mean last year. Online."

"Oh," Preston says. "Lindsey didn't know who pulled her out of the house, but she identified the person on the security camera from the front door. I had her show a picture around, and someone at Faulkner recognized you and said you'd transferred to Willow Heights. I showed it to

SELENA

Colt, and he knew you right away. I got your messenger handle from him."

"I never messaged Colt," I say, my skin prickling.

"He probably got it from Dixie," Royal says.

"Wait," I say, holding up a hand and shaking my head to try to settle the amount of information pouring in. "What are you talking about? I was talking about before that, at the beginning of the year. When you first messaged me on the Faulkner High computer. You knew who I was. And then you kept finding me after I made an account. If you didn't think I was a Darling, why were you stalking me?"

He sighs. "For the last time, I have no fucking clue what you're talking about, Harper. That was the first time I messaged you. I thanked you for saving Lindsey. That's it. I'd never even heard of you before."

"No," I say, shaking my head. "You're not the Silver Swan."

He glances at Royal and grumbles, "That's my screen name on that app."

"No," I say again. "You're Mr. D. I called you that all summer. It was on the jewelry tag."

"Yeah," he says slowly. "My dad is also Mr. D, and every other Darling, and all the Dolces, and anyone else whose name starts with D. Just like you're Miss A. What does that have to do with *OnlyWords?*"

"I asked the Silver Swan if he knew Mr. D, and if that's you, you said no."

He looks at me blankly. "I... Vaguely remember something like that, now that you mention it. It was part of a conversation, and you asked if I knew that person's messenger handle, and I didn't, and then we kept talking. I don't know who that is."

"Don't bullshit me," I growl. "You told me you were Mr. D."

"He's telling the truth," Royal says. "He's either the Silver Swan, or you were fucking some other asshole all summer and sending me videos of it."

I look back and forth between them, fighting the rising panic in my chest. "But... If you're not Mr. D, then who gave me the scholarship? You said you did."

"I went down there," Preston admits, dropping his gaze. "You told me to fight for you, that I owed you that much.

SELENA

But someone had already taken care of it when it got there. I can show you the records if you want. I have accounts of all the Darling estate money. I was going to make a second scholarship. Normally we donate one scholarship every year, but we'd already given it to someone else this year."

"Who?" I ask.

He glances at Royal, looking distinctly grumpy about his presence. "I don't know."

"Don't even fucking try me," I say. "You're the treasurer. You probably chose who to give it to."

Preston works his jaw back and forth before answering. "Gloria Walton."

"What?" Royal asks, straightening and glaring at Preston.

"Your family didn't renew her scholarship," Preston says. "I figured I owed it to her, even if she didn't know it."

"You told your father not to renew her scholarship?" I ask Royal.

He shrugs. "She's a conniving bitch."

I raise a brow. "You're being nice to my friends, remember?"

"Fine," he grumbles. "But yes, I told him not to renew her scholarship after I found out that she told you."

I press my fists to my temples, trying to figure out what I'm missing.

"Then who gave me a scholarship?" I ask.

"I did," Royal says quietly.

"So, instead of giving it to Gloria, you gave it to me."

"No," he says. "My father gave those scholarships out already. I told him not to give one to Lo, that's all. Everyone applying for a scholarship writes a letter, and the donors can choose from them or just let the school pick. I don't know who Dad gave scholarships to. I've never been involved in that, and I only cared this year because I didn't want her to get one from my family."

"So... You used your personal money to give me a scholarship?" Our eyes meet, and I'm suddenly sure I know where he got money for something he doesn't want his father involved in. I remember looking at his drawer full of cash and betting slips from the fights, wondering what he would do with all that money. Now I know.

SELENA

He gives the smallest nod. "I convinced the school to add an additional one for you, well after the deadline. I didn't use family money. I didn't want my father thinking you owed him anything."

"And you fucking let me thank you," I say, turning to Preston. "Just like when Royal pulled me out of your truck and gave me the Escalade. Yeah, I know about those things, too."

At least he has the decency to look guilty. "Sorry," he mutters.

"Why didn't you just tell me?"

He looks at me like I'm crazy. "I didn't want you to go back to him."

Royal strains forward, but I hold up a hand.

"That's not your decision to make, Preston."

"I know," he says. "But he doesn't deserve you, no matter how much shit he buys you."

"And you do?"

He scowls and turns to the window without an answer.

"What else did you let me think you did for me?" I ask.

Preston crosses his arms and sits back, a defensive posture. "I paid your bills starting last spring, when you told me they were coming after Lindsey. Half the time, I don't know what you're talking about, and I kept telling you that, but you insisted. After a while, I just stopped arguing."

"Fuck," I say, slamming my back against the seat in frustration. "Like when I kept asking for my scholarship back. You said you didn't know what I was talking about, and I thought you were being humble, but you honestly didn't, because you're not Mr. D."

"Why does it matter who he is?" Preston asks. "He's just some guy who gave you a scholarship last year? Write him a thank you letter and move on."

"It matters," Royal growls, glaring at Preston.

"I may have given him private, personal information about Royal," I admit, giving Royal a meaningful look. I told him I'd make sure Preston didn't tell anyone about the Hockington, and he told me not to talk to Preston about him, so I didn't. I want him to know that I never repeated the information, even when I thought Preston was Mr. D. I knew he wouldn't tell anyone if he hadn't already. But I had it all wrong. He wasn't hiding in his loft, hoarding information about the Dolces. He never had it to begin with.

So, who does?

"Okay," Preston says, taking a breath and uncrossing his arms. He looks at Royal for a second like he's deciding whether to go on. "If you want to know who gave a scholarship, it should be easy enough. Just follow the receipts."

"Spoken like an accountant," I say.

Royal tosses the DNA papers into the front seat. "Why don't we start with which sick pervert in your family would want to know everything about me, down to the size of my dick."

He glares at Preston like he might murder him if I wasn't between them.

Preston's brows lift. "If you're looking for someone that screwed up, it would have to be Sullivan," he says. "But he's indisposed right now, not to mention that he's a minor and doesn't have access to money."

"What do you mean indisposed?" I ask, narrowing my eyes at him. "Like, locked up?"

"Something like that," he says coolly.

"It's him," I say. "He said once that he wanted to hear about my sex life so he could live vicariously through me. I assumed your dad, since he's in prison."

"Again, Sully has no access to money," Preston says.

"Magnolia does, though," I say, thinking about the flouncy little brat who helped me at lunch and told me she wasn't as dumb as people think.

Preston shakes his head. "She's fourteen. She has a trust fund and her daddy's credit card. She doesn't have cash to do anything on her own, and neither does he."

"Royal has a trust fund," I say. "And he had money."

"I got that at the Slaughterpen," Royal says.

Preston chuckles. "You think Magnolia's an underground streetfighter? Next you'll be saying she was dealing Alice in the girls' bathroom in middle school."

"She could be Merciless," I say. "She's a masked fighter, so no one knows her identity."

"I can have Colt look into it," Preston says, shaking his head. "I'm sure he knows who even the masked fighters are.

But I guarantee it's not her. She's a typical little brat. She fights with petty rumors, not fists."

"Maybe we're looking at the wrong question," I say. "Y'all all have money. I'm sure anyone in your families could get some money if they wanted. The question is, who would want to take down the Dolces?"

Preston snorts. "Everyone."

"No," Royal says slowly. "Who would want to use me to do it? It has to be someone who went to Willow Heights, who knows that I was running things. They knew that taking me out would upset everything."

"Then it has to be Colt," I say.

We sit in silence for a minute.

He was incapacitated for months. Is that why he had to live vicariously through my sex stories? He's not in jail, but being in a hospital is still a way of being locked up. And since I've never messaged him, I don't know his handle.

"I don't think so," Preston says.

"Colt doesn't have the balls," Royal agrees. "He's beaten. That's why we let him stay. He bowed and groveled and did whatever we wanted. He doesn't cause problems, and he has connections for fights, so he gets to stay. That's the deal. He wouldn't risk fucking up again."

"What if…" I start, then stop, remembering something Dixie said. That's not the reason she told me they let him stay. "Could it be Mabel?"

"No," Preston says.

"How do you know?"

"Mabel wants nothing to do with this town or anyone in it," Preston says. "She never did. And she'd never intentionally get involved with the Dolces, knowing that would make her a target again."

"Who is it?" Royal asks, a muscle in his jaw jumping like he's about to reach across me and throttle Preston. "You know, don't you, you fucking cunt scab?"

"Based on what Harper just said and my own observations, I have a pretty good idea," Preston says, staring back at Royal with a cool gaze, though anyone else would be quaking in their seat at the look Royal's giving him—especially after they already lost an eye and had half their face burned off by him and his brothers.

SELENA

"Who?" Royal growls. "You better start talking, or I'll bulldoze your whole fucking family into the ground and be done with it. It doesn't matter who it is."

"Harper's right," Preston says. "You're looking at the wrong question. Everyone has money. Everyone hates you. And our family didn't think Harper was a Darling, so why would we even bother tracking her down?"

"Fuck," I whisper, turning to Royal. "He's right. It was *your* family."

We stare at each other for a long minute. I think of all the times I tried to get Mr. D to join me, to take down the Dolces. How he always had some coy response, some excuse. No wonder he never did anything with the information. He didn't want to bring down the Dolces at all.

How many times did he call me "darling girl"? The Dolce boys all called me that at one time or another. But now I realize they were calling me Darling girl, with a capital D, because they thought I was one of their enemies all along. I shiver in my wet clothes when I remember that sleazy Mr. Dolce called me that, too.

"Dad," Royal says, his voice hollow. "He has money for the scholarship, and he's always in our fucking business, trying to get information."

"That was my guess," Preston agrees.

I shiver again, shrinking down in the seat, a sick feeling gripping my stomach. Mr. Dolce's an older man with money who could give me a scholarship. At one point, I thought it might be Royal's older brother wanting information because Royal shut him out. But his dad could want information for the same reason. And he's gross enough to want that information, to want to hear all the details about his son's performance.

But something doesn't quite fit.

"Shit," I say slowly, my pulse thundering in my ears. "Your dad may be a creepy, nosy pervert, but he doesn't know how to hack into computers. He's not the one who likes to play sick games with people's minds."

"No," Royal says, shaking his head. "My brothers would never do that to me."

All I can think of is a conversation I had my very first week at Willow Heights, when the other girls were debating

SELENA

which Dolce was the scariest. I thought there was no way anyone could be worse than Royal, but maybe I was wrong.

I lay a hand on his knee. "I'm sorry. But it all tracks. The way he found me to begin with, and then y'all followed me to the tracks. The Swans were just a decoy. He found a Darling that your father wouldn't protect, so you could do the same things to me you did to Mabel."

"That's not what happened with her," Royal says, his eyes vacant, as if he's talking to himself.

I take his hand and squeeze. "Baron saw when things were getting too serious between us. When you didn't break up with me after we were locked in the basement, who knew to hack into my phone and show you the messages? He never told anyone because he wasn't trying to bring you down. In his own twisted way, maybe he was even trying to protect you. I was out to destroy your family, and he had all the ammunition ready to go the moment he decided it was time to pull the trigger."

I thought that Royal aimed the twins at me and fired, but I had it all backwards. He's the weapon. I'm the victim.

Baron was the shooter, the mastermind behind it all, just like Dixie said from the very beginning.

Royal just keeps shaking his head slowly back and forth, looking at me with a haunted, horrified expression. He knows what it means. He knows we both got played.

"No," he says quietly.

"I know you want to believe the best about your brother," I say, my throat tight. "I wish it was someone else. But it's definitely him. Baron is Mr. D."

SELENA

*

Ready for the explosive final book in Royal and Harper's series? Look for Blood Empire, releasing January 2!

Want to know how Royal became the man he is? I recommend reading the story of Royal's sister and the Darling boy she dared to love. Look for *WHPA: The Elite* complete trilogy, now available in ebook, paperback, and audio.

BROKEN DOLL

acknowledgements

Thank you so much to everyone who helped make this book possible! Special thanks to my patrons, who help keep me writing. Big shout-out and a thousand handfuls of heart-shaped confetti to the real life Midnight Swans: Jasmine, Annalisse, Jennifer S, Jennifer M, Heather, Kellie, Elizabeth, Nicole (extra sprinkles for finding my typos!), Renea, Doe Rae, Lena, Nikki, Nikki T, Megan, DesiRae, JG, Janice, Joyce, Yadira, Rebecca, Tasha, Michelle, Makayla, Yelahiah, Alyssa, Terra, April K, Alysia, Jessica, Tami, Jennifer C, Emma P, Melanie, Kajal, April H., Kat, Emma G, Shawna, Ashley S, Tatiana, Adriana, Iyesha, Shirley, Brooke, Kaelyn, Christina, Rowena, Lara, Mindy, Hilary, Cheryl, Carmen, Tina, Melissa, Trinity, Nicki B, Tessa, Jennifer S, Lucy, Marisa, Victoria, Audriana, Jaclyn, and Crystal.

I cannot thank y'all enough for your support!

Printed in Great Britain
by Amazon